STREETS OF WARSAW

A Novel of the Polish Resistance in World War II

Steven Lee Wiggins

Wiinggs Publishing Company

Streets of Warsaw: A Novel of the Polish Resistance in World War II. Published by Wiinggs Publishing Company, P.O. Box 2243, Ottawa, Illinois

ISBN 0-9745435-0-0
Library of Congress Control Number: 2003097111
First Printing, January 2004
Cover designed and text printed by Fast Print Inc., Ottawa, IL.

ATTENTION CORPORATIONS, COLLEGES, AND ORGANIZATIONS: Quantity discounts are available on bulk purchases of this book. Special books or book excerpts can also be created to fit specific needs. For information, please write to the publisher as follows: Wiinggs Publishing Company
P.O. Box 2243
Ottawa, IL 61350

This book is a dramatization inspired by a true story. Many of the characters are inspired by historical figures; others are entirely imaginary creations of the author. Some names, characters, places, and incidents are the product of the author's imagination, or are used fictitiously. All characterizations are the author's. Apart from the historical figures, any resemblance between these fictional characters and actual persons, living or dead, or business establishments, events, or locales is purely coincidental. Characters and scenes were created to advance the story.

Acknowledgments

I would like to thank Tadeusz Sokolowski, Theresa Sokolowski, January Nazorek, Witold Jastrzebski, Richard Zielonka, Christine Zielonka, and Andrew Hempel for their assistance in providing information for this book. They are proof that where there is hope, there is life.

I also want to thank The Polish Museum of America (Chicago, IL), Nicholas Boltuc, Katrin Krüger, Andrew Borosz, Bruce Markwalter, Mark Sokolowski, and Brother Mark Schlossburger at St. Bede Academy in Illinois for their help.

I also want to thank Christie Constantine for her help with the posters.

I especially want to thank Mrs. Dawn Wiggins, for displaying the patience of several saints.

A Note on the Posters and the Text

The posters included in this book are the author's translations of the originals. The originals had German text in the left-hand column, and Polish text in the right-hand column. Victims' names and dates of birth were printed in columns across the center. The formatting of the posters was irregular and crude. The posters have been reformatted to fit the page. Dates are in month-day-year format.

All spellings have been Latinized.

Major Characters

Bronislaw Pietraszewicz (code-named "Lot"), an Underground soldier. Also called Bronek and Benny.

Adam Przezdziecki (code-named "Nowak"), Bronek's commander.

Wiktor Kruczyk (code-named "Granit"), an Underground soldier.

Jerzy Kruczyk (code-named "Akrobat"), Wiktor's younger brother.

Anna Krzykowska (code-named "Golebica"), a student.

Marian Senger (code-named "Cichy"), an Underground soldier.

Zbigniew Gesicki (code-named "Juno"), an Underground soldier.

Kazimierz Sott (code-named "Sokol"), an Underground soldier.

"Poland can only be administered by utilizing the country through means of ruthless exploitation, deportation of all supplies, raw materials, machines, factory installations, etc., which are important to the German war economy, availability of all workers for work within Germany, reduction of the entire Polish economy to absolute minimum necessary for bare existence of the population, closing of all educational institutions, especially technical schools and colleges, in order to prevent the growth of a new Polish intelligentsia. Poland shall be treated as a colony; the Poles shall be the slaves of the Greater German World Empire."

– Hans Frank, Governor-General of Poland, 1939

"We have in this country one point from which all the evil emanates. It is Warsaw. If we did not have Warsaw in the General Government, we would not have four-fifths of the difficulties with which we have to struggle. Warsaw is and will remain the center of disorder, the point from which all disturbance in this country radiates."

– Hans Frank, in his diary, 1943

I

He was an eager young man, not shattered by his world. He knew he would be protected on this day.

It was a bright sunny September morning, as clear as a blue-sky day could be. People filled the wide sidewalks, hurrying to work or to the markets. German women in colorful dresses and felt hats led their clean German children off to their German schools. A tired, gaunt horse pulled a load of artillery shells in a wagon, its wooden wheels rocking over the streetcar rails.

This had been a proud neighborhood, once. Marshalkowska Street was a major north-south thoroughfare in the city. The paving stones rolled out unevenly, like an undulating brown carpet. Streetcars rumbled by regularly, powered by the electric wires strung overhead. Rows of carved stone buildings with intricate ornamentation rose on both sides, whispering of their greatness back in the eighteenth century. Here and there a wall was caved in, forming a pile of gray rubble – a reminder of 1939 that had never been cleared.

The young man stood strategically at the corner of Marszalkowska and Litewska Streets. His medium brown hair poked out from beneath his rumpled fedora hat, a well-worn gift from his father. With his smooth, soft features, he looked younger than his twenty years. This always helped him in his work. He wore a plain white shirt, gray wool pants, and a brown suit jacket; nothing matched, but it all helped to complete his costume. He had borrowed the jacket from his father, and it hung loosely on his lean frame; it easily hid the tools for his mission. His shoes were so old, he felt the sidewalk through the paper-thin soles.

The young man's forehead began to perspire. He slid his fedora off his head and pushed back his hair. As he did, his brown eyes darted around, glancing at everything in sight while his head remained steady. It was a skill he had mastered long ago. He spotted an academic-looking young man with round spectacles standing across the street; they glanced at each other but did not nod. The young man touched a silver locket that hung around his neck inside his shirt. The locket gave him luck. *I will be all right,* he told himself. *I will survive.*

In his hand the young man held a violin, brittle from age and lack of oiling. On the sidewalk beside him was a black violin case, heavily dented and scuffed, along with a dust-covered jelly jar. In this costume, he appeared to be a typical street beggar. He took a deep breath, to calm his nerves. At last he pushed his hat back on his head, tucked his violin under his chin, gripped his bow, and began to play.

The young violinist began Mozart's *"Eine Kleine Nachtmusik."* He could barely hear his playing above the general noise of the street. But it did not matter. In truth, he was a terrible violin player. He only knew a few snippets of Mozart, some Beethoven, "The Blue Danube," and some folk tunes. He also knew some Chopin, but he could not play that.

As he slaughtered the Mozart, he dipped his violin at the German ladies who walked by. Most of them ignored him, but every so often one would lean down and place some coins into his jar. He was sure to tip his hat in thanks, but he said nothing.

As he played, the violinist felt for the police. He could feel their presence. Across the street a local policeman, called a "Blue Policeman" for his blue uniform, walked by. He looked mildly foolish in his dented steel helmet with a Polish eagle painted on it. He seemed not to notice anything around him, and he rounded the corner without slowing. Otherwise, there were no *Schutzpolizei* (Protection Police, or Schupos), no *Geheime Staats Polizei* (Secret State Police, or Gestapos). He felt reassured.

Just then the metal wheels of a streetcar screeched hideously, and raised a cloud of brown dust. The young man squeezed his eyes shut. When the dust cleared, he opened his eyes and looked across Litewska Street. Seemingly from nowhere, a military patrol now stood across the street. There were three of them, SS men in gray uniforms and steel helmets. They formed an ominous gray presence. Their automatic guns, slung over their shoulders, pointed to the sky.

The violin player observed them from the corner of his eye. They probably stopped there because Litewska was barricaded, the start of the German neighborhood. They were not paying him attention. But these were SS men, not regular police. SS were the worst.

And then, a young German woman and her son chose this moment to stop and listen to his playing. The woman gave a Reichsmark to her young son, and pointed at the jar. The little boy walked up hesitantly, dropped the bill into the jar, and returned to his mother, standing bashfully behind her skirt. The violin player smiled and tipped his hat. Then the woman asked, *"Kennen Sie Vivaldi?"* (Do you know Vivaldi?)

The violin player pretended not to hear. He was concerned with the SS men.

"Please. Vivaldi? Vi-val-di?"

The young man stopped. He did not know any Vivaldi. He wiggled his fingers, but nothing happened.

"Nein, nein. Play a Vivaldi. *'Die Vier Jahreszeiter'* . . . um . . . 'Four Seasons.'"

He stared at her, desperately wishing that she would go away. This was bad; a complaint from a German woman could be disastrous. The young man with the round spectacles watched, but could not help him.

"Vi-val-di!" the woman repeated, loudly.

"*Nein. Kein Vivaldi,*" he answered hastily. He switched to "The Blue Danube." That was an easy one. He played "The Blue Danube" and danced around a bit, hoping that would somehow satisfy her request. All the time, he listened for the sound of boots marching. What would he do? He could run; no, he could never outrun them. He was trapped. Minutes – long, long minutes – passed.

At last the woman shook her head and led her boy away, muttering angrily in German. The violin player stopped dancing, and continued with his meager efforts at Mozart. The SS men did not move. But they certainly did now pay him attention.

Around the corner on Oleandry Street, a hulking figure appeared. He pushed a small wooden cart loaded with white sheets and paint cans. The man wore a tattered cap, a stained white shirt buttoned up entirely, and a vest from a blue suit that pinched at his waist. His large, dark mustache loomed formidably in front of his square, weathered face. He stopped across from the address known as 22 Polna Street. He laid a paint-stained sheet at a doorway, and opened a can of paint. Soon he was repainting the door frame a glossy white.

As the violin player pushed his bow across the strings, he checked his wristwatch. Just past nine-fifty a.m. The streetcar wires overhead now cast spidery shadows across the sidewalk. He swallowed, but his throat was suddenly very dry. Eight more minutes. The waiting was wearing on his nerves. But he could not let himself suffer an emotion – no fear, no hatred, no panic. His jacket bulged. It was the hand grenade in his inner pocket. When he strolled around the bulge was impossible to spot, so he decided to keep moving.

Another young woman, a Pole, dropped a zloty into his jar and dashed off. Still the SS soldiers hovered nearby. What were they doing? Why didn't they leave?

Then one of the soldiers called out to him. "Play a Wagner," he shouted in a cocky voice.

The young violin player hurried his playing, and he tried to smile. The other pedestrians circled around the soldiers, and diverted their eyes.

"Play a Wagner," the soldier called out again. He sounded angry.

The young man bit his lower lip. He hated, detested, Wagner. In all his years of studying, he had refused to learn any Wagner. He tried not to tremble. He switched to Beethoven's "Fifth Symphony" instead. It was easy, only four notes repeated at different spots on the strings. He dipped his violin down in supplication to the soldier.

It did not work. The soldier marched angrily across the street. His boots were deafening.

That quickly, the soldier was on the sidewalk. He was no older than the violin player, but his face was sharp, and arrogant. He bumped against the violin bow. "*Spiel 'Lohengrin'*! I said, play a Wagner!" His steel helmet pushed against the young man's wrinkled fedora. "Now!"

The street beggar swallowed, and blinked tensely. His fingers trembled on the strings. He glanced at the glistening rifle slung over the soldier's shoulder. It appeared to be an MP-40, a 9-millimeter automatic. The young man wanted to run, to flee. But he could not run. "*Entschuldigung*," he said politely, fighting the twitching in his cheeks, "*Ich weiss es nicht. Ich weiss es nicht.*" (I do not know it.) His hand grenade suddenly seemed horribly obvious. He fidgeted with his fedora and forced himself to smile. "*Strauss? Strauss, ja?*" He grinned as he began the strains of "The Blue Danube."

The soldier's face turned red. "No, no!" He reared his shiny black boot and kicked the dusty jar like a soccer ball. It bounced onto the street and shattered into a dozen pieces. Curving shards of glass rocked back and forth on the paving stones. Several Polish boys leapt into the street, grabbed at coins and bills, and dashed away at full speed.

The violin player watched the broken bits of glass. He had to mollify this soldier somehow. "*Entschuldigung.*

Entschuldigung. Mozart?" He tried a bit of Mozart's *"Eine Kleine Nachtmusik."* The notes suddenly left him; he had to stop and restart. He danced a silly jig as he slaughtered the tune.

The soldier watched the violinist's performance in disgust. Then he swung out his arm, and knocked the young man's hat onto the sidewalk. But he realized the young Pole would not quit his silly show. At last, the soldier returned to the other members of his patrol.

As the young Pole bent down to retrieve his hat, he listened closely. He did not know much German, but he heard the soldiers call him a "dog" and a "Polish pig." Relief coursed down into his fingers; they were not planning to arrest him. The young man brushed off his hat, and played some more. He wondered what they planned to do next. Arrest him? Shoot him? Request a polka? Some more SS soldiers and Blue Police, about 10 in all, appeared down the street, but they did not approach his position.

Just then, everything happened at once. The door at 22 Polna Street swung open. Peering between knots of pedestrians, the painter saw a figure emerge. Out came a young man with a beaky, misshapen nose, a grim mouth, and a hard, unfeeling stare. He was skinny and ugly, and his SS uniform hung from his shoulders. But he carried his authority around him like a cloak.

The painter noted the soldier's gray uniform, his rank, his square collar patches. Everything matched the pictures the painter had studied; here was SS *Oberscharführer* (Technical Sergeant) Franz Bürckl. The painter stoically nodded to the man in the owlish spectacles, code-named "Jeremi." Jeremi walked across Marszalkowska Street. This was the signal that the operation had begun.

But then the sergeant held the door open. A woman emerged, dressed in a pale green silk dress, a fox stole, and a frilly green hat. It had to be the sergeant's wife. And she was pushing a baby carriage. Together, the parents checked on the baby, pulled up the visor to protect him from the sun, and started up the street. The painter froze, his paintbrush dangling in the air. He struggled to hide his confusion. No one knew Bürckl was even married.

Over on Marszalkowska Street, a black Opel sedan quietly appeared and coasted south; the driver was disguised in a military cap and gray overcoat. A Polish teen with sloppy brown hair strolled over beside the car; his code name was "Dietrich." The SS soldiers were still standing several meters away, just behind a barricade. Jeremi watched the SS Technical Sergeant and his wife gingerly push the baby carriage toward him. In no time, they were at the corner of Oleandry and Marszalkowska. They did not notice Jeremi follow a couple meters behind them.

The young violinist played louder now, to reinforce the deception. He felt the hand grenade in his jacket pocket bump against his chest. He saw the SS Technical Sergeant, and the unattractive young woman pushing the black baby carriage. The wife was a terrible surprise. His mind raced; his orders did not include the wife and child.

The young couple crossed Marszalkowska Street, looking both ways for safety, and headed toward the barricades on Litewska Street. The mother rocked the carriage wheels across the streetcar tracks and continued toward the violinist. Now the black sedan coasted to barely a crawl. The painter held his paintbrush against the door frame and watched, motionless.

The woman tilted the baby carriage up onto the sidewalk. The couple walked right past the violinist, ignoring him. The young man jerked his bow across the strings. His mind raced through several options. He mouthed a soundless prayer and touched the locket through his shirt. *Blessed Mother, grant me strength. I will succeed.*

In an instant his mind cleared, his body became calm. And then he acted. As the sergeant and his wife approached Litewska, he strolled in a small circle back to his violin case. He crouched down and set his violin on the sidewalk. Leaning over so that his jacket drooped down, he unsnapped the case. Calmly, he opened the lid and pulled back the inner felt liner.

Hidden inside the case was a submachine gun called a *stenista*, meticulously polished and oiled. It had a wire stock, a breech clip, and a short barrel, to make it smaller.

He looked up at the ugly Technical Sergeant in the gray uniform and black boots. *"Herr Bürckl?"* he asked in a light, inquisitive tone. A peaceful feeling surrounded him. He gripped the gun calmly.

The Technical Sergeant glanced down with a dismissive expression. *"Ja?"* he asked casually.

They were barely a meter apart now. They could reach out and shake hands.

Now!

The violin player jumped up. Frantically he raised his gun and pointed. His words tumbled out: "In the name of the Polish Republic!"

The SS soldiers looked up, and wrinkled their brows in a kind of amazed disbelief. The wife raised her arms but then froze, unable to move. Bürckl's eyes flashed open. His mouth opened to speak; but the gun spoke first.

The violin player squeezed the trigger, hard. For a moment that felt like an eternity, he fired again and again. The shell casings arced through the air, bouncing on the sidewalk. Behind them, Jeremi reached into his coat and pulled out his Radom 9-millimeter handgun. Beside the disguised sedan, Dietrich produced his old Luger. They all started firing.

Bürckl ran two steps toward the safety of Litewski, but that was all. His body seemed to dance, suspended by the bullets ripping into it. His arms jerked about crazily. Bright red blood burst from his aorta, splashing out. Then the body dropped. Blood splashed onto Bürckl's wife, onto her elegant green dress and fox stole. She raised her hands, and she began to scream.

In two seconds, the *stenista* was empty. The young men stared at Bürckl's crumpled body. Then they heard a weak, amazed, *"Halt! Halt!"*

The black sedan lurched to a stop; the rear door swung open. They ran – fast. Jeremi jumped in first. Dietrich fired back at the soldiers, hitting two of them. The violinist caught up to the sedan and leapt in. "Go!"

Dietrich jumped in: "Go! Go!" The car sped past a streetcar and turned down a side street.

The driver, a Polish boy wearing the Nazi cap and overcoat, laughed. "Ha! Lot, we did it! We did it!"

The violin player, code-named "Lot," was stretched across the back seat. He heard bullets ricochet off the trunk lid. A bullet pierced the trunk and drilled into the front seat, on the passenger's side. Jeremi pulled on his *stenista.* "Lot! Let go, let go!"

Lot peered at his hands. Bright arterial blood was on his hands and arms, turning brown and stiff. He was still clutching the empty gun, his trigger finger frozen, still firing.

The SS soldiers fired several shots; but the car veered out of sight. The soldiers shouted back and forth desperately. The uninjured one dashed off to find the nearest car. Bürckl's wife bent over her husband. A pool of sticky red blood spread around her fine leather shoes, holding her in place like quicksand. She covered her face with her hands, and she screamed a shrill, desperate scream.

Pedestrians were still huddled together, crouching against the buildings. Slowly, they righted themselves and walked on, without speaking. A few smirked silently. One man whispered some words to Heaven and crossed himself before hurrying away. A streetcar rolled past the scene without slowing.

Over on Oleandry Street, Wiktor the painter (code-named "Granit") rolled up his drop cloth and returned it to his cart. It would be best to leave now, while the Germans were still chaotic. He checked his wristwatch. Two minutes after ten a.m., September 7, 1943. Wiktor nodded approvingly, being sure not to smile. It was a fine day for the Underground, a fine day for the new *Agat* unit. He turned his little cart around and wheeled it away from the blood-soaked body of SS *Oberscharführer* (Technical Sergeant) Franz Bürckl, deputy commandant of

Pawiak prison. Wiktor the painter turned the corner and disappeared from sight.

II

"Almost there," Bronislaw muttered.

Bronislaw Pietraszewicz was hunched over the coffee table, gingerly holding a little piece of metal with his fingertips. Below him was the ancient black typewriter he and his younger brother had disassembled in the parlor. Between his lips he clenched a tiny brass screw. "Almost," he repeated as he maneuvered the metal typewriter bars.

"Bronek! Eugene!" Their father called out from the kitchen. "It's time to eat."

Startled, Bronislaw looked up. As he did, the screw fell back into his mouth. Suddenly he gagged as the screw scratched his throat.

"Bronek!" his brother exclaimed. "Careful!" Eugene reached across the table and slapped Bronek on the back.

Bronek gagged again. The screw flew from his mouth, like a watermelon seed. It rolled around on the coffee table, behind a small framed photo of their hero, Pope Pius XII.

"Where is it?" Eugene asked.

Bronek's eyes were watering. "I don't – I don't know –" he said with a croak. He took several deep breaths.

Eugene reached behind the photo of the pope. "Here it is," Eugene proclaimed. "Successful mission."

"Give me that." Bronek took the screw and wiped the saliva off of it.

"Bronislaw! Eugeniusz!"

"We better eat, Bronek," Eugene said, matter-of-factly. "He's using our full names." Their father always used their full names when he wanted their attention. "We're coming, Papa."

Bronek groaned. The typewriter was the old kind, with the keys suspended from metal bars that struck down onto the roller. The keys were forever sticking, and he and Eugene had it apart again. They huddled over the machine as if it were a small fire on a cold night. "Hand me the smallest screwdriver," he said quietly to Eugene.

"He'll be mad if he sees this in here again," Eugene said.

"Then hand me the screwdriver right now."

Eugene sighed and held up the screwdriver. He was eighteen, two years younger than Bronek, with a paler, more boyish face. Everyone babied him.

Bronek screwed the letter "z" back on. "There!" He pressed the "z" key; it struck the roller with a click and a thud. "That key likes to fall off, doesn't it, Eugene."

"But it's no good at all without the 'z'!" Eugene said exasperatedly.

"Eugeniusz! Bronislaw! Come in here and eat, right now!"

"Let's go, Bronek. We need to eat." Eugene pushed himself onto his knees. Using his well-practiced technique he stood up from the coffee table, supporting his body against his black painted cane. Bronek watched him struggle, but he knew to never offer to help.

"Let's hide this thing," Bronek advised, "So Papa won't know." Owning a typewriter, of course, was forbidden, punishable by death. They could not leave it out during dinner.

As Bronek lifted the heavy contraption, he noticed something missing. "Say, Eugene," he asked, "Where is the ribbon for this thing? Are you hiding it?"

Eugene sighed. "No, I don't have a ribbon. Typewriter ribbon is a – casualty of war."

Eugene had a way with turning a phrase. "What do you use, then?"

"Well, I have a rag, and some black ink. I make do."

"That's no good." Bronek thought about his little brother, dangling a rag in front of the keys. The image depressed him.

"Eugeniusz! Bronislaw!"

The typewriter and remaining parts safely hidden away, the two brothers went out to the kitchen. The kitchen was small, and cramped, and the center of their home. The floor of black-and-white tiles had several tiles missing. On the pink counter were several candles, a carbide lamp, a loaf of black bread. The table and mismatched chairs cluttered the room, and blocked people's way. And on one end was a big black stove. The smoke from the wood fire often leaked out, but it was still a terrific old beast. And standing there, stirring the stew, was their father, Karol Pietraszewicz. "Sit down, sit down, boys, dinner is ready."

Eugene leaned his cane against the kitchen counter and lowered himself onto his chair. Bronek, however, checked his wristwatch. "Papa, can I just take something and go?" He still had a job to do, and curfew was approaching. He had to be back inside before curfew.

"Sit Bronek," his father said encouragingly. "We see you so rarely. Besides, it's stew. You can't take it along with you."

Bronek frowned. He should not have visited at all; he seldom slept here. He was supposed to limit his contacts. But he was a part of this family. He could not abandon his father and – especially – his brother. He felt the warmth from the fire fill the cramped little kitchen.

"Sit, son. Stew is ready."

He sighed. "Yes, sir." He slid onto his chair, and slouched against the table.

"Elbows off the table, Bronek."

"Oh." The kitchen table was an ungainly collection of parts of junk furniture; all four table legs were different. But the tabletop was inlaid with an intricate abstract pattern of thin brass strips. Their father had cut and inlaid the brass design from scrap parts he had collected. Karol was a repairman. He worked at the rail yard, fixing the streetcars. He had been a skilled craftsman once, forging curved brass rails, steps, and handholds. Now he just did heavy lifting beneath the hard scrutiny of the police. But he was a fine metalworker.

"And sit straight."

"Yes, sir."

Karol set the bubbling pot on a towel on the table. He pulled off his apron, hung it on a wall hook, and sat at the chair nearest the stove. Bronek looked up at his father. Karol had pale skin, light blue eyes, a narrow nose, and the pronounced, square Slavic jawline. His blond hair was receding from his forehead, making his forehead even higher and revealing most of his smooth scalp. With his thin frame and gentle demeanor, he no longer frightened Bronek, and Bronek now realized that. But he still had the authority of being the head of the household.

They held hands in a circle, and bowed their heads. "Heavenly Father," Karol began, "By the Blessed Virgin, we give thanks for this meal, for our health, and our lives. We pray for General Anders, and the Air Force in Britain, and for Roosevelt and Churchill, and for General Patton." Karol had a near-mystical regard for Patton. "And we humbly ask for our liberation. In the name of the Father, the Son, and the Holy Spirit, amen." They all three crossed themselves and prepared for the Pietraszewicz family meal.

The stew was a kind of barley meal. It was grainy and bitter. Slices of potato floated on top, like lily pads on a brown pond.

"I bought a piece of pork at the market today," their father offered. "Keep looking for it."

Bronek poked at a piece of pork. He turned it over and studied it. "It's a snout."

"Say, Bronek," Eugene said, "I'll trade you a knuckle for your snout."

"Shut up," Bronek retorted with a smile, "I'll stuff this

down your snout!"

"Stop that, boys! You show respect at the table."

Bronek and Eugene could not stop themselves. There was just something about the situation. They had received one-third of a snout. What else could they do when the stew consisted of the waste pieces of a pig? "Yes, sir."

"Oh – I forgot the bread. You boys stay still, now." He got up and shuffled across the worn tile floor.

Bronek waited until their father was hunched over the counter, slicing the loaf of bread into equal sections. *As if bread can fix this meal,* he thought glumly. He reached into his pants pocket.

Bronek spun the cap off a steel hip flask. Suspecting another inedible meal, he had grabbed the flask while putting away the typewriter. Keeping one eye on their father's back, he poured a shot of vodka into his water. Eugene watched in wide-eyed surprise as Bronek poured the clear liquor into Eugene's glass. He hid the flask at his side just as his father turned around.

"Here we are," Karol said. He set a thick slice of black bread before each bowl, and sat down. "Everyone gets one slice."

Eugene tore off a chunk of his bread. "Wind bread!" he blurted jokingly, with his mouth full of food.

"It's just wind bread for you," Bronek scolded mockingly.

"Well, we don't discuss that at the table," their father said.

"It *is* wind bread," Eugene repeated. It was true. The official bread in Warsaw was so doughy that it produced certain foul effects on the digestive system. Everyone knew.

Bronek bit off a large piece of bread. He said nothing. He bit into his bread again. Then he stared at it incredulously. Inside the crust, the bread was just a black, doughy, inedible mass. The dough stuck to his teeth, like grainy wet clay. All three men chewed and chewed, trying to swallow the black substance.

"Did you boys hear any more about what happened yesterday?" Karol asked.

Eugene laughed out loud. "They got old Bürckl. Serves him right!"

Bronek drank some more vodka. He did not have time for chatting. He had a job to finish.

"Just imagine," Karol replied. "Did you hear how it happened?"

"It was the Underground." Eugene bit into his bread, and he chewed. "They killed him with a tommy gun," he said. He craned his neck forward and swallowed hard, as if he were swallowing a sparrow. He coughed. "The story I heard was, an Underground soldier hid his gun in a violin case. He even played Bürckl a tune, just to taunt him. Then – just like that – he pulled out his tommy gun and shot him dead. Just like in a gangster movie!" he added in admiration.

Bronek wanted to correct Eugene's story, but he stopped himself. *Say nothing, say nothing.* He ground his teeth together.

"Here, boys, soak your bread in the stew. That will make it softer." Karol took a long gulp of water. "Well," he began, forcing down a glob of bread, "I understand he was at Pawiak prison."

"He was," Bronek said. He suppressed the urge to shout out the truth to his father and brother. No one could know. Instead, he bit down hard on his bread dough. "Bürckl was an interrogator. He shot Stefania Olszowska – a 70-year-old woman. Two Soviet pilots. Stanislaw Kryk, a Polish Army lieutenant. He even hunted Jews in the Ghetto!"

"– All right, Bronek, that's all."

"He was the worst one there, Papa."

"Well, I'm sure it was justified," Karol offered.

"It was," Bronek replied. "Now all the others have to try to not be the worst."

"Tat-tat-tat-tat-tat!" Eugene pointed his finger at Bronek mockingly. "I got you!"

"Stop that at the table," his father said.

"I'm glad. I hate them all."

"Eugeniusz!" Their father glared at his son. When he needed, he could use his piercing stare to great effect. "We do not hate. Ever. Do you understand me?"

"Yes, sir."

Bronek understood his father's feeling. Bronek never hated Bürckl. The man was another SS brute. There were dozens more. Killing the one was a calculation, an example for the others. Their father was right. Hatred was a dangerous emotion. "You shut up, Eugene."

Without warning, Eugene flipped his spoon. A glob of wet barley meal flew across the table. It stuck to Bronek's bare arm.

Bronek grabbed his own spoon. "Here, Eugene. Have some more," he said. He flung a spoonful back at Eugene. Bronek was a better shot; it stuck to his younger brother's cheek. Eugene giggled, and dipped his spoon for another shot.

"Bronislaw! Eugeniusz! You two stop, right now!"

The two sons grudgingly held their spoons.

"You eat what is served. Or I'll take your food away from you!"

Eugene coughed slightly. "Yes, sir," he said. They both wiped themselves clean.

"We'll eat," Bronek said meekly. He really felt ashamed.

Bronek stared into his glass for a while. Then he eyed his younger brother. Eugene had a boyish face, sandy hair like their father, delicate white fingers for a boy, and a mole on his cheek. When he smiled, he looked like the cherubs that were painted on the church ceiling. But whenever Bronek looked at him, he thought of bombs, and explosions, and fires. The vodka only strengthened that association in his mind. Bronek downed another swallow of vodka. He was feeling depressed.

Eugene sensed it. He always could tell when Bronek felt downcast. "To the Polish Republic!" Eugene said to Bronek, with a little giggle.

"To the Polish Republic!" Bronek repeated. The two sons clicked their glasses together, and laughed heartily.

"Bronek – elbows off the table."

"Yes, sir."

* * *

Later that evening, while Eugene and his father were out talking to their neighbors, Bronek slipped back into the kitchen. He reached hastily into the cupboard, and took down an old tin can. He rifled through the bills inside. He pulled out ten zlotys, replaced the tin can, and delicately tip-toed out the door. No one would know he was gone.

Bronek bounded down the stairs and out of 37 Mianowskie Street, in the Ochota neighborhood southwest of the city center. At that moment he hated – yes – he hated many things: the Nazis, Hans Frank, Pawiak prison. But mostly he hated not being able to help Eugene, who was trying to do his part. Well, today Bronek would help him.

Instinctively, Bronek looked both ways down the street. The evening sunlight was slanting across the roofs, and the street was lost in shadow, as in a canyon. Warsaw had many wide, beautiful boulevards; this was not one of them. It was a cramped neighborhood of narrow apartments, not heavily patrolled by the Nazi police. Nonetheless, Bronek felt himself assume his defensive posture. By habit, his movements slowed, his ears tuned to every random sound, the muscles in his neck tightened. He walked down the street and turned the corner.

Raszynska Street was still busy, despite the approaching curfew. Polish women in their babushkas and threadbare skirts flowed in different directions. There were no red flags, no swastikas, no posters of Adolf Hitler; they were torn down years ago by boys like him. A black car carrying three *Schutzpolizei* (Schupo) men bounced over the streetcar tracks. Bronek tried to sense their purpose without looking at them – he could feel the speed of the jeep, and the ranks of the men inside. But tonight the vodka made his head feel a bit distant, and fuzzy. He shook his head, trying to clear his mind; he had to stay alert. *I will survive,* he told himself.

Bronek ducked around the corner. The first shop was the old

general store. The big square window, where merchandise was once proudly displayed, was virtually empty. A couple plates still sat in the display case, but even they carried the disclaimer sign, "For Display Only – Not in Stock." The store was closed, but Bronek knew the door would not be locked. He went inside, pulling the heavy door shut behind him.

Immediately, a pungent smell assaulted his nose. Everything in the old store had a layer of dust. Once, the shelves had been filled with the thousands of little things people needed: soap, thread, screws, radio tubes, irons, magazines, hard candy. Bronek had come here often, to buy gum, candy, and soda. This store was a part of his life. But now it smelled like an abandoned basement. The shelves held nothing but dust. It was the same dust that hung over all Warsaw. No one ever cleaned it.

Bronek went straight to the large counter, with its intricate carved wood moldings. "Mister Znaniecki?"

Mr. Znaniecki was leaning back in his chair, hunched over to balance himself against the wall. He was nearly bald, except for a narrow band of silver hair above his ears. The dust appeared to have settled over him, as well. He almost vanished against the wall. He did not like to get up, even to lock the door. He looked towards Bronek without moving his head. "Hah?"

"Hello, Mister Znaniecki. It's Bronek. Bronek Pietraszewicz."

The old man did not move. "Ah – Bronek." Finally he tilted his chair forward and stood, wearily. His shoulders, however, remained hunched over as before. The old man was tall and gaunt, but he had a brittle, sharp voice. He was still a bit intimidating. "Are you here to shop?"

"Yes. Do you have anything?"

"Do I? Do I?" He turned to the rows and rows and rows of shelves, from the floor to the ceiling behind him. "Look at all I have!" He waved his arm before the shelves.

Bronek looked up. There was almost nothing there: spools of string made from paper, some old German magazines, some spoons.

"This is all," Mr. Znaniecki continued. "This is all – those bastards let me sell. What do you want? A spoon?"

Bronek nodded. Mr. Znaniecki never used the words "Nazi," or "SS." Just "bastards." Hans Frank, Ludwig Fischer, Himmler, the local policeman: they all carried the same title. "I need – something special," Bronek said. It was the common code. He wanted something from the black market.

"Ah," Mr. Znaniecki said, nodding with his entire upper body, "I see. What do you need?"

"Well, I need –"

"Wait!" The old shopkeeper raised his bony hand. "Are any of those bastards around?"

Bronek hurried to the window, looked both ways, and then returned. "No. We're fine."

"All right, then. What do you need?"

Bronek lowered his voice to barely a whisper. "Do you have a . . . typewriter ribbon?"

Mr. Znaniecki did not move.

"It's not for me. It's for – someone else." This was an extra precaution; if the police came and asked questions, Mr. Znaniecki could honestly deny knowing who had the typewriter ribbon.

Mr. Znaniecki still did not move. Bronek began to feel nervous. Was something wrong with him? Was it time to flee?

At last, the shopkeeper spoke. "I believe," he said, "You may be in luck." He pushed open a curtain, and went into a back room. As Bronek waited at the counter, he thought of his brother, pathetically holding an ink rag over his paper. *Eugene will be thrilled*, he thought. After a while, Bronek began to tap the counter nervously. This was nerve-wracking, buying black-market goods; he was glad his father bought their food. He heard some jostling noises from the back. Still no Mr. Znaniecki. Bronek tapped a bit faster.

After what seemed like ten minutes, Mr. Znaniecki appeared. "Ah-ah – you are in luck."

Bronek looked down at the shopkeeper's frail, wrinkled hands. In his hand were two metal spools, a black ribbon wound between them.

Bronek's eyes grew wide. "You have it!" Bronek knew that the ribbon was well-used, but that did not matter. He had found it. "How much is it?"

"Eh, well, prices are going crazy, Bronek. How much do you have?"

Bronek thought of his brother, probably typing some important Underground document, as the ribbon rolled smoothly from spool to spool. "I'm afraid I don't have much." He reached into his pocket, and showed Mr. Znaniecki his money.

The old man inspected the offering carefully, as if he were examining a relic. "Ten zlotys?" he finally said. "Eh, well . . . that will just do it."

Bronek sighed, relieved. "Thank goodness. He'll be so happy." He set the money on the counter. "Now I need to sneak it home." He tucked his prize into his back pocket, and he swung his backside around, so Mr. Znaniecki could inspect him. "Can you see anything?"

"Eh – nothing those bastards would notice."

"Thank you, Mr. Znaniecki." Bronek left the old man in his dusty store.

Now he had to hurry. It was 7:40 p.m. Curfew time was drawing near. Bronek walked, as quickly as he could without being noticeable. He went over to Kaliska Street. It was a small side street, and served his purpose well. It was about halfway between his family's home and his fictitious address. Curfew was close. Still he felt for police. He could feel them in his skin.

At Kaliska he walked behind a portion of a brick wall. It had been the outside of a house, but it had been bombed during the invasion of 1939 and never repaired. Most of the house was a pile of rubble. The inside could not be seen from the street, but no interior rooms were intact. If any police followed him here, there were no rooms to search. He could simply pretend he had ducked behind the wall for a sip from his hip flask.

Behind the fragment of wall, Bronek walked down a hallway. Much of it was open to the sky. Small trees were actually sprouting up, atop the bricks and plaster chunks. Bronek went to a brick in a corner. It dislodged easily. Bronek pulled that brick out of the wall. Inside, it had been hollowed. A slip of paper lay inside; his messenger girl had done her work. Bronek pulled out the paper and slid it into his underwear. He would decode it later. He returned the brick, poured some vodka on himself to complete the charade, and left the bombed-out house.

With a new bounce in his step, Bronek walked back home. Two successful missions. The streets were clearing out now, getting that lonely, empty feeling. He checked his watch: eight minutes until 8:00 p.m. He would make it home just before curfew. He hurried his pace, without running. As he headed home, he softly, so that no one else could hear, whistled Chopin's "Polonaise."

III

"Well, gentlemen, you made it. Thank the Blessed Virgin."

The three men sat in a cafe on Marszalkowska Street, near Saint Savior's Square in the city center. The sign outside read "M. Jablonski, Butcher;" but because of the ugly stuffed boar's head in the dining room, everyone called it "Under the Snout." It was a cheap place, with worn wooden tables and dirt on the floor, but it was popular because old Mister Jablonski often slipped pork chops and cutlets to his hungry friends. Germans never went there, and that also made it popular. This afternoon the place was crowded, and noisy. A hazy cloud of cigarette smoke hung in the middle of the room.

Three men sat at a table near a side door. Little glasses of *bimber* (illicit vodka) were on the table, waiting to work their magic. Adam Przezdziecki (code-named "Nowak"), the older man, threw back the jigger and swallowed. "Granit, Lot, please drink. You earned it."

"Sounds good," Bronek said. Bronek looked forward to his Underground meetings. He had great admiration for these men. He seemed to enter a different world when he was with them. And how many twenty-year-olds were given such vital missions?

"You know why I need to speak with you," Adam asked

routinely. Adam had salt-and-pepper hair that dropped down in wiry bangs that always looked uncombed. His plain shirts and well-worn pants always looked rumpled and aged. He had soft features and a fatherly smile, but his skin was rough and craggy, as if he had too much skin for his face. Bronek knew nothing about this man, even though he trusted him with his life. He just knew that his commander's name was certainly not Nowak. Hundreds of men used Nowak as their code name. "I need to verify what happened."

Bronek smiled. "The Allies landed in Italy," he whispered excitedly.

"Yes, that is good news." Adam spoke in a perfectly controlled hush, so that even the people at the next table could not hear.

"On Italy itself." Bronek drank his liquor. This was cheap *bimber*, it burned as it went down his throat, and it kept on burning in his stomach. He thought about the change. The Allies were no longer just in North Africa. They were on the continent. It was an encouraging feeling. "They're moving north," he said hoarsely.

"Nowak," Wiktor said abruptly, "You will never believe what I heard today." Wiktor Kruczyk (code-named "Granit") rolled his glass in his thick fingers, to warm the vodka. He had on his white shirt and blue suit vest and pants, seemingly his only clothes. Wiktor had dark hair and a large, swarthy face. His wide, dark mustache hung menacingly over and past his lip. When he wanted someone's attention, he got it. "Even I cannot believe it."

"What, Granit, what?"

"I cannot believe it." The vodka apparently being warm enough, Wiktor downed it all in one swallow. Quickly he made a face, and spat onto the floor. "There's a piece of something or other in this."

"What did you hear, what?"

"I heard a rumor that Mussolini escaped from jail."

"Escaped? How can that be?"

"Apparently the Nazis sent a platoon of soldiers in a glider, to evade the radar. They attacked the jail, shot the guards, and freed Il Duce."

"That can't happen," Bronek said, incredulously. "How did they escape, with a glider?"

"The Nazis landed a plane on the mountain top. They flew Mussolini right off the mountain."

"Where is he now?" Adam asked.

"That, I do not know."

"What a story," Bronek retorted.

"It's crazy. It must be a lie," Wiktor said. "But, we're in crazy times." Wiktor pulled out a cigarette, one of the wrinkled hand-rolled things he regularly smoked. He licked the end and lit it. Soon a dense gray cloud hovered just above his head.

"True," Adam said, touching his square jaw. "We must believe it's possible. We will have to check our other sources, and find out if it's true."

The waitress, a tired-looking woman who was probably younger than she appeared, came by the table. "Another round please, Wanda," Adam said with a polite grin. Bronek observed that Adam knew her name. He must trust this place. Not just the owner, but everyone who worked there.

Then Adam changed the subject. "Well, Lot, Granit, you surely know what everyone is talking about."

Wiktor and Bronek nodded, but did not speak.

"Everyone in Warsaw knows by now. I've heard six different versions of the story myself. In one story, Bürckl was stabbed with the violin bow."

Bronek smiled.

Wiktor craned his neck around. "Where's that silly waitress?"

"Lot, you did a wonderful job. Very brave work."

Bronek felt his cheeks turn red. This was strong praise from his commanding officer, who was usually cool and calm. "Well, Mother was with me."

"Where's that waitress?" Wiktor asked again.

"It's a busy day in here," Adam offered.

"At this rate we'll be liberated first."

Adam looked at Bronek. "Why don't you go up and get us our drinks?" He handed him some zlotys. "Here you go."

"Sure." Bronek obediently sprung from the bench and headed for the bar.

The restaurant was crowded, and he had to twist and nudge his way between the tables. When he finally reached the bar, Bronek caught the bartender's attention. He ordered three *bimbers* and leaned on the bar. He glanced up at the strange boar's head, and smiled. As he was waiting, Bronek noticed a woman sitting at the table next to him. The table was pushed into the corner beside the bar, and people walked past constantly.

He glanced at the young woman. "Hello," he said. The woman had soft blond hair. Something was tied into it on one side. Bronek noticed that it was a piece of blue yarn.

"Hello," the woman said.

A woman did not usually sit alone in public. "How did you get put into the corner?" he asked.

And then Bronek saw her. She had dark blue eyes, as blue as sapphires. She had a true Slavic jawline, wide and strong. Her cheekbones were high, her nose precise and distinguished. She was not beautiful like Sonja Henie or Greta Garbo, although she was closer to Sonja Henie. But Bronek could not take his eyes off her. "Wow," he whispered.

She giggled slightly. "Are you here to drink?" she asked.

Her hair, parted on one side like a boy, stopped at her shoulders. But it was wavy and full; as it got longer, it lightened to a yellowish blonde. Her hair framed her face like a golden halo. "Oh, um, no. I'm not here to drink."

"You're not?"

"No." Just then the bartender set three shot glasses before him. Bronek looked at them, then at her.

"Oh. I see." She giggled again. Her cheeks rose up and her blue eyes squinted when she laughed.

The young woman paused. Bronek stared. She was wearing

a blue short-sleeved blouse, faded from far too many washings. Her shoulders were somewhat wide; her arms were smooth and white, her fingers elegant. Her traits did not fit into any unified impression. For all her strong features, she still looked petite and girlish. She was fascinating, a mix of strength and fragility that made his heart race. "Wow!" Bronek's eyes moved farther down, but that was all he could see.

"You must be thirsty," she said.

"Oh – these are not for me," he responded abruptly. "They're for – well, they're for – other people." He carefully counted out his money, and handed it to the bartender. "Well – I need to get back –" For what seemed like an eternity he stood before her, confused. "You're not leaving right now, are you?"

"No."

He sighed. "Thank goodness. I need to –" Bronek arranged the three shot glasses. "I need to get back. . . ." Awkwardly, he left.

When he returned, three glasses were already on the table. "What are those?"

Wiktor glared at Bronek. "Wanda already came back."

Bronek sat down. "I'm sorry, I – I didn't see her."

"We don't care to be here all day, Lot." Wiktor dropped the tiny cigarette butt onto the floor, and twisted his shoe on it.

"I know, I know," Bronek replied meekly.

"Pay attention, Lot," Adam said. "Now – tell me exactly what happened."

"I, um. . . ." He leaned forward, and tried to peer over the other tables. She was still alone. Occasionally she sipped from her cup of coffee. Her smile was gone.

Bronek suddenly realized he did not know her name. What if she left, and he did not have her name? Bronek looked desperately at Adam; a passionate urgency rose up in his throat. "I need to get up," he said quickly.

"Why?"

"I just – do."

"Lot, you sit still –" Adam said, but Bronek was already

walking across the room. He maneuvered around the tables and returned to the bar, beside her table.

She had watched him cross the room. "Do you need more already?" she asked teasingly.

"No. Are you leaving?" Bronek pushed his hair back off his forehead. He had combed his hair into a pompadour today, and it was not staying up.

"No. Not yet."

"Well . . . can you tell me your name?"

"Yes . . . I suppose."

"What is it?"

"Anna."

"Anna." She was smiling. Bronek guessed that that was a good sign.

"What's your name?"

He opened his mouth to say, "Lot." But then he froze. "Um –" He swallowed; he could not use his code name with her. "Bronislaw."

"Bronislaw?"

"My family call me Bronek. What are you doing here?"

"I'm waiting for my sister," she said. "She's in the kitchen. She deals with Mister Jablonski for food."

"Oh. Really."

"We're trying to buy some pork. But the prices are so high." "I know." He pointed up at the boar's head on the wall. "I hope you don't get the snout. They don't taste so good. I've tried them." Bronek laughed good-naturedly. Anna did not laugh; she emitted a slight sigh. Bronek stopped laughing.

"What are you and your friends doing?" She pointed toward the two unkempt-looking men in dirty shirts. One had silver hair and messy bangs. The other was darker, with brown hair and a wide mustache. They were quite unimpressive-looking.

Bronek opened his mouth to speak. "We're just. . . ." But then his voice trailed off. He struggled for the words to say. "I – I mean, we –" He thought and thought for a cover story, but he could think of nothing. "Will you wait here?"

"I'll wait here," she said, her head perfectly still. She still smiled.

"Thank you," he said with a sigh. "Anna," he said. Then he left.

When Bronek returned and sat at the table, Adam and Wiktor stared at him. Wiktor spoke, simply. "Lot . . . sit . . . still."

Adam's stare was businesslike, not fearsome. Wiktor's stare, however, was quite fearsome. Bronek looked down at the table. "I'll stay," he mumbled.

Adam continued. "Did you get his papers, his identification?"

"A patrol was right there," Bronek explained. "And the mission was to be sure of his identity. Not to retrieve his papers."

"True. We need to verify, though. Granit?"

"I only saw him from –" Abruptly, Wiktor stopped.

Wanda approached them. "Your glasses?" she asked hastily. She leaned over the table and collected up the empty shot glasses. As she did, Wanda whispered: "Gestapo."

The three men looked at her. Suddenly they were listening very intently.

"By the door. Gestapo," she repeated. She picked up the empty glasses, and she left.

Bronek turned to see the front door. There, just inside the entrance, stood two tall young men in plain black suits. They scanned the entire room, turning their heads in slow arcs, as if they were zeroing in on a radio transmission.

Adam looked at Wiktor. "There."

Bronek nodded. The Gestapo men were obvious. Every Pole wore patched clothes, and was covered in a layer of dust. These men's suits were clean and pressed, their shoes polished. But what really set them apart was the cold arrogance in their eyes.

"Let's go," Adam said quietly.

"We can't leave together," Wiktor said. "I'll leave first."

"Should we go home from here?" Bronek asked.

"We still must meet. We have time before curfew. Room two is close by."

"Let me try first," Bronek suddenly said.

"No, Lot, wait!" Adam whispered.

But Bronek was already up. He slowly shuffled toward the bar.

The Gestapo men did not seem to pay him any attention. Wiktor and Adam watched him, tensely.

He leaned against the bar, and casually moved his head down near Anna's. "Where is your sister?" he asked.

"She's still in back."

Bronek sighed heavily. "Gestapo," he whispered under his breath.

Anna saw. She froze in place. No one said anything. The cafe grew embarrassingly quiet; then a low, rumbling kind of talk began. People tried to say things, and still watch the Gestapo men. Everyone waited.

The two agents strolled, slowly, through the room. They looked like department store mannequins displaying black suits. Bronek lowered his eyes. *Never look them in the eye. Never look them in the eye.*

"They have someone in mind," Bronek whispered. But it was impossible to discern the focus of their attention. They walked along the dirty floor, until they were near Anna.

Suddenly Anna reached up and grabbed Bronek's arm. She gripped tightly, and suddenly he was sideways, nearly off balance. She grasped his arm with all her strength. Bronek spun around and crouched down beside her. He had to hide her fear. He forced a smile to his face. Gently, but firmly, he rested his hand atop hers.

The Gestapo agents strolled past them. No one watched the Nazis directly, but everyone followed their path. From a corner booth, two young Polish women stood up and casually walked to the entrance. The Gestapo agents ignored them. They were looking for men.

Two Polish men sat at another table near the bar. They

touched their forks to their plates, but failed to secure any food. The Gestapo agents circled around that table. Suddenly they pounced. "*Hände hoch!* Hands up! Your papers! Your papers!" They grabbed the two men, and yanked them up.

People instinctively cowered in their seats. From one corner, a Polish man leapt from his bench and bolted out the door. The Gestapos did not even notice him. They pushed the two men's hands to the table. They pressed their Walther P-38 pistols against the Polish men's heads, and groped for their identification papers.

Bronek looked back at his team. Adam and Wiktor were gone, out the side door.

Anna was still clutching Bronek's arm. "Dear God, help us," she whispered.

"Anna," Bronek warned desperately, "Don't look." Anna was watching the Gestapos, staring with wide child-like eyes. "Don't look!"

Her fingers were trembling. Bronek rubbed the back of her hand, trying to help her relax. He leaned over until his head was next to hers. "Just breathe. Don't look. Don't look," he whispered. She was panicking; every muscle in her arm was tense and rigid. He had to calm her. He stared into her wide, terrified eyes. "You know, when you smile you look like an angel."

"Bronek . . . go. Go now."

"No. I'll never leave you," he whispered into her ear.

"Go. While you still can."

"When can I see you?"

"Please, go!"

Over his shoulder, Bronek heard the spectacle unfolding. The Polish men were shouting the usual excuses about being poor, ignorant workers. The Gestapo men told them to shut up. They opened the identification papers they had found. "When?" he whispered.

"Tomorrow."

"Same time?" Bronek asked.

"Yes, yes."

"God be with you." He stroked her hand, until Anna let go.
Bronek looked at her, at the piece of blue yarn knotted in her
hair. At that moment, he realized that it matched her eyes. "I'll
be here," he said. The Gestapo agents studied the seals on the
identification papers while the Underground assassin escaped.

* * *

Bronek walked down the dusty hallway to Apartment two,
not far from Under the Snout. He was sure that no one had followed him. Then he knocked twice, paused, and knocked once
more. After an exchange of passwords indicating the all-clear,
the heavy mahogany door swung open and Bronek slipped
inside.

Apartment two was a bare room. The furnishings consisted
of some wooden chairs, a large table, a few old suitcases, and
several discarded sheets and blankets. Heaps of broken plaster
lay on the bare wooden floor, beneath gaping black holes in the
high ceiling. However, the place was perfect for their purpose.
Most of the stately old home was destroyed from the invasion
of 1939, and only a couple of its rooms were still intact. It stood
abandoned and forgotten. Now only a huge fireplace and intri-
cately carved moldings everywhere hinted at the beauty that
once had been.

Adam and Wiktor were already inside. "How did you both
get here?" Bronek asked.

Wiktor was sitting in the deep windowsill. "I know a short-
cut," Wiktor said dryly.

"You're a fast runner," Bronek commented, impressed.

For a time no one spoke. Adam paced in a circle around the
room. He seemed to need time to recover from the close escape.

"Damned Gestapo," Wiktor muttered. The window behind
him was blocked by heavy shades, so the police could not see
inside. The room was dark and shadowy. Every sound echoed
off the bare plaster walls.

Bronek turned a chair backwards, and leaned forward
against the backrest. He said nothing, waiting for his com-

mander to recover.

Finally, Wiktor rested his hands against his knees. "Is there any *bimber* in here?"

"I don't think so," Adam said.

"Damn." Wiktor twisted the end on another hand-rolled cigarette, and lit it.

Adam stopped pacing. He leaned against the farthest wall. "Well," he began, "We should not press our luck. Let's finish our business. We had a mission. What exactly happened, Granit?"

"I was at Oleandry and Polna," Wiktor began. "Directly across from Bürckl's residence. Lot was on Marszalkowska Street, imitating a beggar. In a perfect location. There was an SS patrol, but they did not search him. Quite fortunate."

"What do you mean?" Adam asked.

"Any experienced police would have searched him just on suspicion. These boys were new in town. They did not understand how Warsaw works."

"I see. What happened then? Lot? . . . Lot?"

"Oh." Bronek's eyes snapped back to Adam. "I saw an SS *Oberscharführer*. Followed by Jeremi."

"Of course, Lot, of course. Did you see the man you shot?"

"Mm," Bronek said.

"Lot?"

"Mm," Bronek said blankly.

"Granit?"

"I saw his face," Wiktor answered. "The man I saw matched the photographs. And, I believe Lot made further confirmation."

"What was that?"

"He answered when Lot called his name."

"Lot, I thought you had a hand grenade. Your mission was to use a hand grenade."

"Oh, yes – hand grenade. Something . . . happened," Bronek said blankly. He rested his chin on his hand.

Adam continued. "What happened?"

"Bürckl left home with his family," Wiktor explained. "His wife was pushing a baby carriage. "The hand grenade would have killed all of them. Certainly the baby."

"Hm," Adam said. "Our reconnaissance never showed that he was married." Many others were involved in the attack, including intelligence gatherers, drivers, and cover agents. They were all led by a man known as "Dyrektor." But Lot never met any of them. Only Adam had contact with the other members of *Agat*. They had to trust that the others had done the best job they could. "What a surprise. Still, it's a dangerous move, grabbing for the gun."

"My orders weren't to kill children," Bronek interrupted. "They were to kill Franz Bürckl."

"So you had your *stenista* gun with you. Well! Superb work, Lot. You're an excellent soldier for a young man. You kept a cool head. Was anyone else hit? Any civilians?"

"I stayed at the scene," Wiktor said. "The SS men were hit. No civilians were hit."

"Where is the gun now?"

"Hidden away."

"And the car?"

"Also hidden. At a junkyard in Praga."

"All right. I think I can make my report," Adam said. "It was a great feat for our *Agat* unit. A great feat! This shows them how little they are in command."

"Except for at Under the Snout," Wiktor commented dryly.

"Well, perhaps we should leave now. Let's not press our luck. Lot?"

Bronek had not moved. "Hm? What?"

"Do you want to leave first?"

"Oh – I guess I wasn't paying attention."

"I am aware of that."

"Well . . . there was a girl. At Under the Snout."

"Hah!" Wiktor chuckled with a loud snort. "Perhaps our young soldier is not always so cool under fire."

"Did you see her? Did you see her?" Bronek asked.

"There were quite a few girls there," Adam observed.

"Lot needs to get his mind off of girls, and back onto his job."

"What do you know about it, Granit?" Bronek wrinkled his brow angrily.

"Granit, perhaps you should leave first."

Wiktor stood up from the windowsill. "Well, good luck, gentlemen." Wiktor headed for the door.

Bronek lifted his face to the ceiling. "Dear God, I hope she got out of there." He whispered a few words, and crossed himself.

* * *

At 7:30 p.m., Bronek slipped into his apartment and, as quietly as he could, tiptoed across the kitchen. The room was dark. Bronek was encouraged; perhaps no one had noticed his late arrival.

His hope was soon dashed. "There you are," he heard a voice say.

Bronek recognized the voice. "Oh. Hello, Papa." He knew he was in trouble.

Bronek's father switched on a little lamp on the kitchen counter. Bronek was surprised; the electricity only worked three or four hours each day. Even the electric light unsettled him. Slowly, Karol sat down at the kitchen table, the tin can looming in front of him. "Why don't you sit down?" he asked quietly.

Bronek fervently did not want to sit down. But he sat in the chair opposite his father. As he did, he scooted his chair away a bit. He wanted to sit in the shadows.

"Bronek, do you know why ten zlotys are missing?"

Bronek thought about an answer. Should he invent a story, or tell the truth?

"Tell the truth, Bronek."

"Oh. I – took it."

"I see. For what purpose?"

"It was for Eugene. It wasn't for me."

"What – exactly – did you buy?"

"A typewriter ribbon."

Karol rubbed his chin, and sighed. "Bronislaw, Bronislaw." He stared at Bronek with a strange look of deflation on his face. "Bronek, a typewriter ribbon does not cost so much. I could have bought it much more cheaply."

"I know . . . I was mad. I – just went out and bought it."

"Besides, shopping on the black market is dangerous. Why were you out doing that?"

Bronek fidgeted on his seat. Why did his father ask such hard questions?

"We decided that I do the shopping for this family." Karol leaned forward, and Bronek suddenly felt surprised. "Ah, Bronek – you are my hope for the future, and yet you cause me such anguish," he moaned, to no one in particular. "If they arrest me, I can accept that. But not you. You are my hope. You are the hope for all of us. Do you understand that?"

"I . . . I know."

"You missed dinner again tonight."

Bronek did not know what he was supposed to say. "Is that a question?"

"Bronek, I know you are frequently away. I know you live half your life somewhere else. But still, it worries me when you do not tell me where you are."

"I'm out. I can't say more."

"You cannot say," Karol observed, nodding his head sadly somehow. "You are a smart young man. But no one can be lucky forever. I lie awake nights, worrying about you."

"I'll survive," Bronek said determinedly. "They'll never catch me."

"Well, we'll hope to God. But this family's money is for all of us. And I decide how to spend it. Do you understand that?"

"All right."

"And please, be very – very – careful."

"Yes, sir."

* * *

At 8:00 p.m., a cold darkness fell over Warsaw. The autumn wind blew through dark, empty, chilly streets. The lights were dark, the streetcars and autos gone. All electricity, having functioned for three hours, ceased. People closed their curtains and stayed inside. The hour of curfew had come. Now the night belonged to the police. They marched in twos and threes through the city, their rifles loaded. After curfew, any Pole could be shot on sight. After curfew, it was a cold, lonely city.

At the Krzykowski home, the card games had been played, the prayers all said. Now it was time for bed. Anna Krzykowska lay in bed and stared at the ceiling. Her bed was a mattress and blanket on the floor in the parlor. She was already in her pajamas, one of her father's white shirts that came down to her knees. One little candle offered the only light in the room. She watched the flickering light on the ceiling, and she listened to the noises of her sister and brother shuffling about. In the hushed quiet of curfew, their little noises echoed through the apartment.

"Krystyna, are you coming to bed?" Anna asked, still staring at the ceiling.

Her older sister came in from the kitchen. Krystyna was tall and broad-shouldered, with straighter, darker hair, almost brown. She wore an old sleeping gown from before the war. "Shh," Krystyna whispered. "Mama and Papa are in bed." She was their mother's second-in-command of the household. "Don't wake them."

"I'm already in bed. You just like bossing me around," Anna muttered beneath her breath.

Krystyna blew out the candle and lay on the sofa, which was her bed. "We were lucky today," she whispered. "We got some real pork. Mr. Jablonski had two entire pigs smuggled in."

Anna did not say anything. She pulled her scratchy blanket up to her chin. She watched the ceiling until her eyes grew accustomed to the dim shapes in the room. "Is Aleksy in bed?"

As if in answer, a loud screech came in from the kitchen. Anna winced.

"I guess not," Krystyna replied. "Aleksy, be careful!"

"Sorry!" their younger brother called out from the kitchen.

Krystyna sighed. "We need to tell him everything three times."

"He'll learn," Anna said. "He's only thirteen."

"He knows not to slide the table across the floor. We've told him over and over." Aleksy slept on the kitchen floor. Usually, he dragged the table to one side. But as often as not, he just set out his mattress between the legs, and slept beneath the table.

"Sorry," Aleksy said. "Good-night."

"Sorry Mother," Krystyna said. "Good-night."

"Good-night," their mother Izabela said quietly.

"Good-night, Papa," Krystyna said.

"Good night," Anna and Aleksy said. At last there was silence in the home. With the curfew, Warsaw was devoid of sound.

Anna listened to the huge silence. Several minutes passed. Then, abruptly, Anna sat up on her mattress. She curled into a ball, wrapping her arms around her knees. "Krystyna," she whispered.

No sound. "Krystyna!" she repeated.

"Yes?"

"Are you asleep?"

Anna heard a frustrated sigh. "Not now. What is it, Anna?"

"Can I tell you a secret?"

"You have a secret?"

"Yes."

"Is this why you were acting so crazy all night?"

"I guess. I didn't know I was doing anything."

"You kept jumping around. You never sat still, all through dinner. Well, tell me," Krystyna asked, her voice reflecting more interest now, "What's your secret?"

"You can't tell anyone else."

"All right, all right. I promise. What is it?"

Anna paused. "Oh, Krystyna! I met the most wonderful boy." And then her words tumbled out in a giggling, giddy, gush. "He's handsome, and so sweet, and his hair was combed back, but it was a little messy. And the Gestapo came in and walked right by us, and he held my hand to keep me calm, and he wouldn't leave without me. But I told him he must leave to protect himself, and he looked into my eyes as if he could look right through me, and he told me I smile like an angel, and he has deep-set eyes and a dimple in his chin, but it's not quite in the middle, it's a little off to one side. Right here," she added impishly, pointing to her own chin.

"The Gestapo? At Mr. Jablonski's?"

"They came when you were in the back."

"Oh, my Lord. I didn't know that. What happened?"

"They walked all around us. They arrested two men. Right behind us."

"Oh, dear Mary . . . have mercy on them."

"But he stayed with me. He said he would never leave me."

"Really?"

"Really. Krystyna, I can never tell you who he is, or anything. Just in case."

"Will you see him again?"

Anna stared out the front window. The sky was black as coal, and the stars twinkled brightly. She hugged her knees. "If he asks me to marry him, I'll say yes."

"Can I tell Mother?"

"No, no. You have to promise."

"But Anna –"

"You can't tell anyone! Promise!"

"Oh . . . all right, I promise."

"Thank you. Good-night." Anna lay on her mattress, and pulled her blanket over her.

For a minute the home was silent. Then Krystyna sighed. "Now I can't sleep. Thank you, Anna."

"Good-night, sister."

IV

Bronek awoke with no feeling of relief. He rolled onto his
back in the pre-dawn dimness, and he watched the dust float in
the air above him. The parlor was plain, with beige window
shades, an old sofa, a dusty dresser, and a dingy, lint-covered
rug. The only soft touches were the little framed photos on the
coffee table of their heroes: Roosevelt, Churchill, Pope Pius
XII, an old family photo. Already, through his mental fog,
Bronek's mind began to plan the day, determining his actions,
setting his routes. And today he had an extra mission. He was
surprised to feel excited about this day.

He rolled off the blankets that served as his bed. He put on
his plain white shirt and wool pants from the day before. Then
he stopped: *Should I wear something nice today?* He poked
through his dresser drawer, and was distressed by his options.
He had not bought any new clothes in over two years. There
were no new clothes in Warsaw; and even if there were, he
could not afford any anyway. He looked in the dresser at his
three shirts and two pants; everything was patched, and worn
through in places. At last he decided on dark cotton pants, and
a work shirt; his cover identity was different for today, and he
had to look the part. And at least these clothes did not have
obvious patches.

He got dressed and put on his flimsy leather shoes (shoe soles were also unheard of in Warsaw). Then he felt the wide mopboard along the far wall. It was still snug; no one had moved it. Behind the mopboard was his pistol, a Walther PPK. It used the smaller 7.65 millimeter bullets, but its snub nose made it compact. No one, not even his father, knew about it. Bronek often took it with him on missions. But he decided he would not need it today. He left it behind the wall.

He went out and down the hall to the bathroom. The neighbors had built a cupboard there, to store supplies. Bronek pulled out the straight razor, and he thoroughly scraped it across the canvas strop. He struggled to shave himself, but it was not easy. He cut himself only a couple times.

Bronek returned and went into the kitchen. His father and brother were already sitting at the table. "Bronek is finally up," Eugene said with a smile. "It's a headline."

Bronek sat at the table across from Eugene. "I don't think I slept well," he said.

Karol was at the black iron stove. "I have breakfast just about ready for you, son."

"Oh, boy," Bronek groaned under his breath, "More."

"Well, I heated the bread in the stove. At least it's thoroughly cooked."

Bronek smelled hot coffee. "Can I have some coffee, please?" Bronek used to detest it. All they drank was a foul *ersatz* coffee, made from he knew not what. But now that he was a grown up, he drank coffee. He liked something bitter to wake him in the mornings.

His father took the coffee pot off the stove and filled a cup. "Here you are, Bronek. I'm afraid that's the last we have."

"Thank you, sir." Bronek tasted it. It was weak, but it was hot. He looked at Eugene, who was pulling apart a piece of black bread. "How's the bread, Eugene?"

"I think it counts as a war crime," Eugene said. "Dip it in the coffee. That helps some."

Bronek was too tired to laugh, but he chuckled. "I can get

by on coffee, Papa. Give Eugene my share."

"Nonsense," Karol said. "You must eat at every meal." This was one of the iron-clad family rules: everyone ate equal portions, no matter how skimpy or distasteful. "Here is your breakfast." Karol placed a plate of black bread before him, and some marmalade on a teaspoon.

"Thank you, sir." Bronek tapped the black bread. It did seem stiffer, at least. Bronek glanced at his brother. "How are you doing, Eugene? Are you working today?" A German civil bureaucrat had given Eugene a job filing papers at his office. The office was nearby, so Eugene could walk to it. Eugene's job did not give the Pietraszewicz household much extra income. But it freed Bronek from having to find one.

"Of, course I am, Bronek. It's Friday."

"It is?" Bronek thought for a moment. "Oh – it is." His life was so unpredictable that he sometimes forgot what day of the week it was. "Friday, Friday," he reminded himself. He bit into his bread, and he rethought his plans. Various factors would change, because of what day it was: the police presence, the streetcars, the marketplaces.

Karol set out his own breakfast, with exactly the same portions of bread and marmalade as his sons. He sat down at the head of the table. "Well, Bronek? Can you fill us in on what you're doing today?"

Bronek paused. His family knew that he had no job. He was gone most days, and many nights. "Well. . . ." He could not tell anyone, not even his family. "I'll be out today."

"Well, will you be safe? Do you know where you'll be?"

Bronek hated this routine – always being asked questions. His father tried to be discreet, but there was no way to tell him. It was for his own protection. If he were arrested, he could honestly say he did not know anything. Bronek wanted to tell his father more. But he said nothing.

Karol waited through several seconds of silence. Then he turned to his other son. "How about you, Eugene?" their father asked. "What are you doing today?"

"Well, you know. I'm . . . going out to work."
Bronek looked at his brother inquisitively. Eugene was hiding something, too.

Bronek remembered one more thing he needed. "Can I borrow your suit jacket again, Papa?"

"Can you tell me why about that, at least?"

"Well . . . I'm . . . I'm seeing someone today. A . . . girl."

"Oh, you are? That's wonderful! Did you hear that, Eugene? Bronek is seeing a girl today."

"Does she look like Greta Garbo?" Eugene adored Greta Garbo.

"No, she doesn't look like Greta Garbo."

His father leaned forward, resting his elbows on the table. "Who is this girl, Bronek? Is she from a good family?"

"What? I don't know." His father was breaking his own rule, putting his elbows on the table. Bronek got an unpleasant feeling in his stomach, and it was not from the bread. "She's a girl I met. That's all."

"Let's begin with basics, then. What is her name?"

"I don't know. I just met her. Honest." Bronek began to squirm in his seat.

"You don't know?" That answer seemed to unsettle Karol, and he leaned back. "Well, when can we meet her?"

"You can't. I mean – I don't know."

"I would like to meet her, of course."

"Let me talk to her first, please?"

"Bronek, don't raise your voice. I'm just asking –"

"Bronek is in love! Bronek is in love!" Eugene called out mockingly.

"Shut up, Eugene!" Bronek groaned. He was beginning to feel sorry he had ever mentioned her. "I'll wear my work jacket." He had a short-waisted cloth jacket with oil stains on it, like factory workers wore. It looked poor, but it fit his cover identity. "I'll just look terrible when I meet her, that's all. Isn't that wonderful. I think I need to go now."

* * *

Later that afternoon, Karol returned from work at the street-car yard. His joints were stiff and creaky from the labor, but he entered quietly. He was relieved to find that his sons were still out.

He went back to his bedroom. It was a small, neat room, carefully arranged to make his things fit. His bed was made, his shelves dusted. On the dresser were a couple black-and-white photos of his wife and sons from a trip to Krakow and the Tatry Mountains. Beside them was a brass paperweight he had once made, hammered into the shape of a mermaid holding a sword over her head. He had worked in fine details, such as the scales on her tail. He had meant for it to be a family heirloom; but his boys did not seem to care about heirlooms.

Karol opened the third drawer of his old dresser. He had to pull carefully, because he could no longer oil the wood, and it squeaked terribly. He pulled out the false drawer bottom. Here were all his heirlooms, the treasures that remained from his life. Everything was sorted: the old pocket watches and wristwatches, some stocks in Prudential Insurance Company (his stocks in Polish stocks all rendered worthless), a micrometer, photos from the peaceful days, and three rings.

At the bottom was a slip of paper. It was from a report Eugene had obtained from the Underground, showing the food rations for adult Poles in 1941. Karol had kept it. Perhaps he would show it to his grandchildren some day.

Paper-clipped together were his food ration cards. Karol thumbed through his remaining green ration cards (Germans received red cards). He did not have many left. And the official food rations were not available anyway. Meat, sugar, and eggs never came any more. Karol was struggling to get food for himself and his sons to amount to 600 calories per day. Like most in Warsaw, he was turning to other means.

And that was why the next item was so important to him. It was his *Ausweis* (identity card) clearing him to inspect and repair streetcar wires. It was a forgery, made by friends at work.

	Jan.	Apr.	May	June	July	Aug.	Sep.	Oct.	Nov.	Dec.
Rye Bread (pounds)	13.2	8.9	9.2	14.8	10.8	10.0	9.5	13.1	13.3	15.3
Wheat Bread	—	1.5	—	—	—	—	—	—	—	—
Wheat Flour	.9	—	.9	.9	—	—	—	—	—	1.8
Oat Flour	—	—	—	—	.4	.9	.9	—	—	—
Macaroni	—	—	—	—	—	—	—	—	—	—
Buckwheat	—	—	—	—	—	—	—	—	—	—
Sugar	.9	2.2	.9	1.1	4.0	1.76	—	—	1.8	1.1
Meat	.7	.9	.7	1.3	.8	1.1	.3	.9	2.2	1.1
Ersatz Coffee	—	.4	.1	—	—	—	.2	.1	—	.4
Potatoes	—	11	—	—	—	—	—	66	66	—
Marmalade	—	—	—	.9	—	.9	.9	.9	.9	.5
Melted Butter	—	—	—	.2	.4	.2	.2	.2	—	.2
Candy	—	—	—	.1	.1	.2	.2	.2	.3	.3
Eggs (each)	2	3	3	1	4	1	3	2	—	7

But with it he could roam the city; if stopped, he had a reason to be out. He slipped the paper into his pocket and closed the dresser drawer.

Karol opened the squeaky armoire, and with dry fingers pulled down his big, loose overcoat. His bones creaked a bit as he pulled it on; he remembered that he had not been so stiff even the month before. When he was dressed, Karol went to the closet door in the back of the bedroom. He unlocked it with his key, and he went inside. This was a tiny room, really a closet. He negotiated past the carefully stacked rubbish of his life, and pulled down a green tarp. He was glad his boys did not have to witness this unpleasantness.

Behind the tarp was the entire operation. In one corner was a pile of dirty, dusty potatoes and a packet of black-market yeast. In a cabinet were the iron boiler, the cooling column, the glass condenser, the filter tube, a bag of ground charcoal, a thermometer. And in the other corner, Karol opened a cedar floor chest that had once held his wife's sweaters. He reached in and, one by one, pulled out the glass bottles of vodka.

He checked each bottle for sediment. This was fine vodka,

not acidic *bimber*, it was redistilled twice, to achieve clarity. The clarity meant he could sell it at a good price, saving his family from starvation. His supervisor at work was sympathetic to the Polish plight, and gave him a few hours a week to work the black market. Still, it was an embarrassing thing.

He slipped the bottles into secret pockets sewn inside his coat, until he was carrying twelve bottles of clear vodka. Then he replaced the tarp and locked the door. In the parlor he whispered a few hopeful words before the little figurine of the Virgin Mary. Now he was ready to do his shopping.

Outside, Karol squinted in the slanting sun. He spotted his neighbor, Misses Rogala. He impulsively ran his fingers through his thinning blond hair.

"Good afternoon, Misses Rogala," he said pleasantly.

"Oh – good afternoon, Mister Pietraszewicz." She smiled a brittle smile at Karol. Halina Rogala lived in their building and had short dark hair and brown eyes. Her thin lips gave her a weak smile, but she was always wonderful to the Pietraszewicz family, giving Karol recipes and sometimes potatoes. She was wearing a long coat and a huge, billowy skirt that could have held three women. "Have you been shopping yet?"

Karol knew what her clothes were for. "No, no, I'm just going. What do you know?"

"Oh, nothing. I bought some fresh potatoes yesterday."

"Fresh? That is news. They're not rotten and soft, like all the other potatoes?"

"They're good. Look for a tall woman with red hair. She shouts quite a bit."

"At Hale Mirowski?"

"At Hale Mirowski. You can't miss her."

"Will she take what I am selling?"

Misses Rogala eyed his bulging coat, and nodded. "Yes, I believe so."

"Wonderful. If I can't find her, can I buy some from you? I'll pay, Misses Rogala, you know that."

"Yes, yes, Mister Pietraszewicz. I know you will."

"It's so difficult, with two boys. Sometimes I can barely feed them."

"I know, I know."

"Thank you so much, Misses Rogala. You're a terrific help."

"Someday I will need something from you. I know you will help me."

"Whatever you ask. God bless." He turned and headed north, to shop.

* * *

Later that afternoon, Anna entered the old brick warehouse, by the railroad tracks on the western edge of downtown Warsaw. She walked slowly, and felt for any unusual motions around her. She hated this part most of all. She always felt that she was being followed. Her guilt must show on her face. *Anyone who looks can surely tell*, she thought.

Anna entered through a creaky side door, and went into the warehouse offices. She went to the second door and knocked twice, then twice more.

A big-faced old woman opened the peephole. Anna thought she looked mean. "Yes?" the woman asked sternly.

"I think my brother Karl is here," Anna answered nervously. This was how she indicated she was not followed.

"I believe Karl just left," the woman replied. This was her code answer that there were no police. "Do you need him?"

"We need him at home," Anna answered, thereby confirming the same to her. "He just got a message."

The woman nodded. She unlocked the door and let Anna inside.

Anna slipped into the musty-smelling office. Four other students, another girl and three young men, were sitting at rickety old tables. In front was their teacher. "Hello, *Ryzy*" (Red), she said quietly.

"Hello, *Golebica*" (Dove), Ryzy said. Ryzy had a low, grumbly voice that was often difficult to hear. His thinning hair was white now, but it was probably red at some earlier time, leading to his code name. He was tiny, hunched over, and poorly dressed; his suit could have been twenty years old. His tired expression suggested that he had no energy left inside him. "You're exactly on time."

"I should have been early." Anna (whose code name was "Golebica," or Dove) nodded politely. She felt terribly sorry for him. Ryzy was a brave man, risking his life to help his students.

Anna sat at the table and nodded to the other students. With the table to protect her modesty, she reached up inside her skirt, into a large pocket sewn inside, and pulled out her mathematics book – actually a facsimile from a prewar textbook. She hurriedly straightened her plain wool skirt as Ryzy addressed them.

"Before we begin," Ryzy began, "Has anyone heard a statement from our authorities? Anything about the brave men who killed SS Bürckl?"

The students shook their heads.

Ryzy sighed weakly. Age and defeat seemed to weigh down on his shoulders. "No statement from the Governor General, Hans Frank. Nothing from District Governor Ludwig Fischer. I must admit, I am troubled."

They sat in silence for a few moments, pondering what the lack of official statement might mean.

"Well," Ryzy said, "We can also express our freedom. Let us learn some mathematics."

* * *

It was another sunny afternoon in the neighborhood of Wola, west of the city center. A large Nazi flag flew above the neighborhood police station, one of the few buildings protected enough to display one. Before the entrance a police guard stood at attention, a Gewehr rifle slung over his shoulder. The sun warmed his dark gray helmet, and heat rose from the sidewalk. Soon a trickle of perspiration rolled down his smooth, disciplined cheek. The guard did not move.

Just then the guard heard a scuffle of shoes to his right. He heard a shrill, boyish voice. *"Heil Schicklgruber!"*

The guard glanced up the sidewalk. Two Polish boys had darted out from the alley. *"Heil Schicklgruber!"* They held their index fingers beneath their noses, and made a comical Nazi salute. *"Heil Schicklgruber!"*

This had been the born name of the *Führer's* father before he had renamed himself Hitler. These Polish boys were mocking the *Führer.* The guard dropped his shoulders to chase them. Instantly, the boys darted into the alley and out of sight. Just that quickly, the boys were gone. There was only the fading echo of boyish laughing. The guard bit his lip angrily. Taking the opportunity, he wiped the perspiration from his cheek. Then he returned to attention.

Around the other corner, two young men were assessing the street. Bronek glanced this way and that.

"How does the street look?" Jerzy asked eagerly. Jerzy's code name was "Akrobat."

"Wait. Let me see." Bronek carefully peered around the corner. "There are some people at the end of the street. One guard at the police station. Some kids are harassing him." He and Jerzy rested their backs against the wall. They were on a narrow, winding side street. "He's not going anywhere."

"Are we ready?" Jerzy asked. He was younger and shorter than Bronek. He looked barely fifteen, although he bragged about being older. He had dark, heavy-looking hair.

"Of course we are." Bronek reached inside his jacket. "Here's the brush." He handed a ratty paint brush to Jerzy. "Are you ready?"

"You bet." Jerzy opened his coat. Inside his coat was a tin can, smashed so that it was nearly flat, like a whiskey flask. It fit inside his coat with no bulge.

"Good. Let's wait one more minute." Bronek's head dropped back against the stone wall with a mild thud.

"Careful, Lot. You'll knock yourself out."

"Oh. I'm – thinking."

"About what?"

"Well . . . there was this girl yesterday. I met her at Under the Snout –"

"A girl?" Jerzy leaned forward eagerly. "Really?"

"Yes, really."

"That's why you've been so strange today! Who is she? What's her name?"

"Anna."

"Is she beautiful? Is she?"

"Well, I think so."

"Blond or brunette?"

"Sort of both. Mostly blond, around her face."

"What color eyes?"

"Blue. The bluest eyes in the world. Amazing."

"Oh, boy. Is she tall, or short?"

"A bit short. Akrobat, you're as bad as my brother."

"I just want to know."

"Well, she doesn't look like Greta Garbo."

"When are you seeing her again?"

Bronek's mind instinctively snapped shut. "That's none of your business. Come on, we have work to do." He peered around the corner. "I don't see anyone. . . . No one." Bronek waited a few more seconds. He waited for that feeling, an inner signal that now was the time. "Okay. Pray for success." He and Jerzy whispered a hasty prayer, and crossed themselves. "Ready?"

"Ready."

"Now."

Bronek and Jerzy strolled from the alley onto the street. There was no streetcar line here, and few pedestrians. They were at a wrought-iron fence enclosing a vacant lot. Attached to the fence was a wide wooden board, where the Nazis posted decrees and propaganda. There was a bend in the street, so that the police station was just out of sight; but if he left his post, the guard would probably see them. The two young agents in baggy jackets stopped at the board. Jerzy let his coat drop open. He dipped the paint brush into the tin can. It was filled with black paint.

Bronek stood directly in front of Jerzy, facing the street. The heels of their shoes touched. If there was a problem, the slightest movement would be a signal to run.

Jerzy began painting quickly, but accurately, with strong brushstrokes. Drops of black paint dripped onto the sidewalk. Bronek stood stiffly, his eyes darting back and forth. *I will survive, I will survive,* he repeated to himself. He spotted a woman in the window across the street. The woman looked at him, nodded, and disappeared. "Hurry, hurry," Bronek sighed.

"I'm going, I'm going . . . done." Jerzy stood up. Bronek glanced back at the board. Smeared across the German propaganda were the vivid black words, "*Pawiak pomscimy!*" (Pawiak will be avenged!)

"Perfect," Bronek said with satisfaction. His mind raced ahead to better thoughts; in his mind he was already sitting at a little booth. Anna was smiling at him.

Just then he heard a shout, in Polish. "Stop! Stop!"

Bronek glanced up. At the end of the block were two uniformed policemen. "Blue Police!"

Suddenly everything changed. Jerzy's paintbrush dropped to the sidewalk. Bronek and Jerzy bolted away like two horses from a starting gate. They ran at breakneck speed back down the alley. Bronek's heart was racing, his temples pounding. At the end of the alley they abruptly stopped and stepped out onto Wolska Street.

"Good luck, Akrobat," Bronek muttered.

"God be with you, Lot."

They walked in opposite directions on Wolska. This was their escape plan. Wolska was main east-west street through the heart of Wola, with a streetcar line and regular streams of traffic. Bronek walked east, knowing the police were still in pursuit. Now he had to blend into the street, disappear, and move to another street as quickly as possible. He crossed Wolska, hastily shuffling his feet across the paving stones, being sure not to run or to turn his head.

There were no automobiles on the street. The traffic was streetcars, horse-drawn wagons, bicycles, pedestrians. Bronek spotted something across the street. He got onto the sidewalk and ducked behind a large brown horse and wooden wagon going slowly his direction. Two men in civilian clothes were sitting atop the wagon; Bronek guessed they were hauling non-essential supplies. He paced himself so that he remained beside the wagon but just behind the wagonmasters. Luckily, they did not pay him any attention.

It occurred to him that the Blue Police would be looking for a man wearing a work jacket; so Bronek wiped his forehead, pretending to be warm in the bright sunshine, and he pulled off his jacket. He nonchalantly wrapped his jacket into a ball and carried it under his arm. Now he was just wearing a work shirt and dark pants. Still he heard nothing behind him. No gunfire, no shouts. Were they still after him? Had they given up? Did they go after Jerzy?

At the next intersection Bronek turned south, onto Karolkowa. Inside, he angrily cursed himself. Those police had caught him completely by surprise. He was the lookout; but he had let his mind wander. He could never have let that happen. That was stupid – stupid, stupid, stupid. They might be arresting Jerzy at that moment. It would be his own fault. *If I'm surprised, I'm dead,* he angrily reminded himself.

As his mind fretted, he suddenly realized that his jacket resembled a package in his hands. So he unrolled his jacket and pulled it back on. He checked his wristwatch, and gasped. He had to get to Under the Snout. Anna – Anna – was already there, waiting for him. Bronek worried over his options. Should he run? Find a streetcar? Had she left, never to return? Was the Gestapo there again? He felt a cold sweat break over his face. This was worse than carrying out a mission. He cursed himself as he headed for the cafe, thoughts and fears spinning in his head.

V

Bronek rushed into Under the Snout out of breath, his
mouth dry. He scanned all four corners of the room. He feared
seeing a roomful of strangers. At first his fears were confirmed.
The room was crowded. No one looked familiar.

Then he spotted her, sitting at a little table out in the middle
of the room. Somehow, studying the booths, he had not seen
her. Slowly his fingers relaxed, and he felt himself breathe
again. Then he realized that he was panting. Bronek tried exhal-
ing heavily; but that just made him sound ridiculous. He sounded like a tired dog.

From across the room, Anna's eyes met his. Feeling a
twinge of panic, he hurried over to her table. For a second he
stood over her, unsure what to say. "Anna," he at last got out.
"Bronek. There you are."

"Thank you for waiting." Bronek reached out for her hand.
He held her delicate white fingers and, following the Polish
custom, kissed the back of her hand. "I told you I'd never leave
you." For a long moment, Bronek felt her warm hand near his
lips.

Finally she pulled her hand away. "Were you delayed?" she
asked nonchalantly.

"I'm – sorry I'm late." Bronek sat at the chair beside her. He felt some relief when he saw a smile spread across her face. "I hope you weren't waiting long." A young lady should not be left alone in a cafe.

"The old rules don't seem to matter any more," she said, anticipating his concern. "Besides, I feel safe here. Where were you?"

"I – I can't. I wish I could –" The waitress appeared, and Bronek stopped trying to make an excuse. "Please, have something."

Anna looked up at the waitress. "I'll have a small coffee in a large cup."

"Yes. A small coffee in a large cup." That was a common order. If the owner was generous, he might fill the large cup, and only charge for a small coffee.

As soon as the waitress left, Bronek's eyes drifted over her again. She was wearing a short-sleeved white blouse with a flowery design on it, and no makeup. She looked unglamorous, but yet perfectly wonderful. He wanted to just look at her for a while.

"Were you running?" she asked.

"Why?"

"Well, you're still panting –"

"I'm sorry."

"—and your hair is all over."

"Oh, no." Bronek had forgotten to work his hair up into a pompadour. "I bet my hair is a mess," he admitted unhappily. "I ran almost the whole way."

"From where?"

"Well, from Wola." He could say that much. Bronek cursed himself. His hair must be a thorough mess. He ran his fingers across his head in a futile effort to tidy himself. "Is that better?"

"Of course it is," Anna replied.

"No, it isn't. You're just being polite."

"How can you tell?"

"Because you're smiling." Bronek stopped fussing with his hair, and just gave up.

"I wonder if I look funny."

"Why?" Bronek asked.

"Because you're watching me."

"No, you don't look funny. I'm just watching you smile. When you smile, you start slowly, then it builds and builds. It's like watching the sun rise."

Anna's cheeks turned a rosy pink. "Oh." She returned to their conversation. "Is that where you live? Wola?"

"No, I live in Ochota."

"Really? Who do you live with?"

The waitress came, and served them hot coffee in large white cups. Bronek raised his cup. "Yes, Mister Jablonski must like you," he observed, "They're full."

"Mister Jablonski is so wonderful to us. We've known him for years." Anna sipped her coffee. Then she winced.

Bronek tried his coffee. "It's pretty bad, isn't it."

"It's – something, at least."

"This German *ersatz* coffee. It tastes like battery acid, somehow."

"Let's don't even talk about Germans. . . . So, who do you live with?"

"Well, my father, and my brother, Eugene."

Anna nodded. "Is your brother older or younger than you?"

"He's just eighteen. He's a pest, really."

"I bet he's not a pest."

Bronek chuckled.

"Am I asking too much?"

"No. It's – cute, really. Nobody ever asks me about my brother." She had a way of asking questions; she sounded wholeheartedly fascinated. He continued talking. "He's a clerk in an office."

"Yes?"

"My father works at the streetcar yard."

"And you?"

"I . . . I keep busy."

"I see." She sipped some more coffee.

Bronek watched her every movement. When she looked down, lowering her big blue eyes, the light in the room seemed to dim momentarily. He wanted to sit there all day, just watching her and carrying on with her. He put his hand on the table, and rested his fingertips on her bare arm. "I wish I could give you some real coffee. The kind that tastes good."

"I know. I wish for so many things."

"I live on Mianowskie Street," Bronek suddenly announced.

"You do?"

"We had to move. Our home was – bombed."

She watched him sympathetically, not blinking. "I know how that hurts." She rubbed his hand on the table for a second. "I understand. Things are so difficult these days."

Everything he said Anna listened to, almost excitedly. "I've told you about me. Where do you live?"

"I live in Wola. Between Wola and the city center, really." Bronek nodded. "My father was an insurance executive, before the – he was a manager."

Bronek felt a twinge of regret in Anna's voice. "Before" meant before the invasion. "Is that where you lived before?"

"No, we lived up north, in Zoliborz." Her face took on a sweet, faraway expression. "In a beautiful red stone house. It had old wood floors, and rugs all over. We loved that old place. That's where we grew up."

"What happened to it?"

"They took it from us." Just that quickly, the smile on her face vanished. "It was requisitioned by . . . their civil servants."

"I understand. And who do you live with?"

"My father and mother, and my sister Krystyna, and my brother Jan. We're all together, thanks be to God."

Bronek nodded. "Your coffee is getting cold," he said.

"So is yours. We should finish it."

"Let's go somewhere."

"Now? I'm not done."

"I don't like staying in any one place."

"Where do you have in mind?"

"I have nowhere in mind." Bronek leaned forward and whispered. "Just out of here."

Anna grinned. "I need to thank Mister Jablonski for the coffee."

They finished their coffee, and Anna went back to the kitchen. Bronek paid the waitress with money borrowed from his father. "Let's go," he told her, and they walked outside.

The sky was still bright, although a few clouds now appeared to the west. Shafts of yellow sunlight soared across the city. They walked north on Marszalkowska Street. "Do you like to walk?"

"Of course! Oh, but these shoes. . . ."

Bronek looked at her shoes. They were practically worn through in front. "Oh, I see."

"Don't look at them."

"Well, how about walking over to Lesserow Palace?"

"I'll try," Anna said eagerly.

Now that they were outside, Bronek snuck glances at Anna. She was wearing a gray wool skirt that showed her slim waist. Her legs were bare, but they looked smooth. Her shoes were indeed worn through in front. "My shoes are just as worn as yours," he commented encouragingly.

"That's the first thing I'll buy when we're liberated. New shoes. I can do without makeup that one extra day, but not shoes."

Bronek smiled. He thought he detected a flutter in her voice. Was she nervous? "You still look fine to me."

"There are no stockings, no jewelry, no makeup. It's impossible to look pretty."

Bronek paused. Her eyes were a deep blue, her lips pink without lipstick. Her drab clothes meant nothing. "You don't look pretty. You look beautiful."

She began to smile again, that slow smile with a little pink rising in her cheeks. "The sun has blinded your eyes."

Bronek hesitated. Then, gingerly, he took her hand. "I'll

help you." The panic he had felt in her the day before was gone now, or at least much reduced. They walked casually toward the palaces on Nowy Swiat, Bronek walking slowly to accommodate Anna's tender steps. There were no Nazi flags, they having been torn down long ago. Except for a few jeeps, some bombed-out buildings, and the Nazi police on patrol, he could almost imagine there were no Germans, that he was just enjoying a walk with the most enchanting woman in Warsaw.

They reached Nowy Swiat, the north-south street through the city center. It was a wide boulevard, with trees lining the median, where the old palaces and ministry buildings were. Ahead of them a streetcar pulled away, lumbering north. VW jeeps bounced on the paving-stone street. And everywhere, there were hundreds of pedestrians: police, wealthy German civilians (walking in groups for protection), SS and Schupos, and Poles, countless Poles, in ragged clothes or scraps fashioned into clothes. For being an occupied city, Warsaw was a busy, noisy place.

Out of habit, Bronek and Anna kept away from the police, losing themselves in the swarms of dirt-covered Poles. There were women in babushkas, beggars selling pencils, fortunetellers sitting cross-legged on the sidewalk. "Discover the future!" an elderly woman shouted hoarsely.

Bronek looked down at her. "Tell me, how will you do that?"

"With my dice!" she shouted, waving her wrinkled fist. "I sense great changes coming. Changes are coming!"

"You are correct about that."

"I am?"

"Yes," Bronek said. "I'm leaving."

They left the old woman and walked farther north. "That's sad," Anna said into Bronek's ear as they walked. "People are that desperate."

"That's just foolishness. If people believed in God, they wouldn't listen to fortunetellers."

Anna wrapped her fingers around his arm, and they walked

together for a while, Anna leaning against him as they pressed between people. Up ahead, a Polish boy was shouting: "*Nowy Kurier Warszawski! Nowy Kurier Warszawski!*" (*New Warsaw Courier!*) In his hand he waved several copies of the daily newspaper.

Bronek approached the newsboy, who could not have been older than fourteen. Bronek noticed that his shirt was a potato sack, with holes cut out for his neck and arms. "Look, what is this?" Bronek asked the boy. "Who wants to buy this?"

"The *Nowy Kurier Warszawski,* sir!" the boy shouted. "The day's news!"

"Look, who wants to buy this rubbish? It's all German propaganda. There is no news in here."

"Oh, but you'll want to see today's paper, sir. It has special news in it today."

"What?" Bronek leaned near the boy's head. "There's special news in this one?" he asked quietly.

The boy nodded, with a serious expression on his childlike face.

"I see," Bronek said. "Then I want one of those." Bronek reached into his pocket for a coin.

Other people heard what the boy had said. Suddenly a small knot of Polish people huddled around the boy. They were all reaching for newspapers. Bronek bought a paper, and pulled himself away. "Let's go," he said to Anna.

"Where are we going –?" Anna asked, but Bronek did not stop to answer.

Bronek led her down a narrow, twisting alley. There was barely a meter between the brick buildings. Over their heads, steel staircases clung to the walls. The sunshine could not penetrate the alley, and it felt cold and dank, like a cave. About twenty meters from the street, the buildings angled. Bronek stopped and leaned against the brick wall.

"What is it? What is it?" Anna asked excitedly. Back here, no one from the street could see them.

"What trash," Bronek said disgustedly. The *Nowy Kurier*

Warszawski was the official German newspaper in Polish, and it was full of lies: lies about the Jews, lies about the Nazis, lies about the war, lies about the occupation, and pleas to turn in Underground agents. He opened the front page. "Here it is," he whispered.

There, tucked inside the official Nazi newspaper, was a copy of *Biuletyn Informacyjny*, the newspaper of the Polish Underground. It was just a flier, a smeary copy on white paper. But Bronek touched it reverently. "Look at it, Anna."

Anna leaned her head down beside his. "What does it say? What does it say?"

"Look at this headline," Bronek said, sliding his fingertips down the page. "'The German Army began evacuation of Sardinia on September 10. They are expected to evacuate to Corsica. The evacuation has been hampered by US naval bombardment.'"

"Anything about us?"

"Hmm . . . I don't see anything. 'The Soviet Army has liberated the city of Mariupol. The Soviets also landed at Novorossisk. Fighting continues.'"

"Is it liberated?"

"It doesn't say. The news is unclear, sometimes. A city gets attacked, but then no news comes out until after it's liberated."

"It's good news though, correct?" Anna asked.

"It's falling apart. Don't you see, Anna? It's all falling apart." Bronek returned to the Underground paper. "Look, here's an essay." He read hurriedly, excitement building in his voice. 'Once again, the Nazis are burying one of their own. SS *Oberscharführer* Franz Bürckl was found by the Underground court to be an interrogator guilty of excessive cruelty and brutality, and a sentence of death was passed. On September 7, the sentence was carried out. Too late, Bürckl learned that working at Pawiak prison is the most dangerous job in Warsaw. Governor-General Hans Frank can do nothing about it. District Governor Ludwig Fischer can do nothing about it. Brutality has been met with justice. Trust in God that the Underground has acted justly, and will do so again. We will continue to act when we are treated in this way. The Underground acts on behalf of the people, and with the support of the people. We will continue to resist the illegal German occupiers until we are liberated.' Signed, 'Z.'" Bronek raised his face to Anna's, and he gripped her bare arm. "Don't you see?" Their faces were nearly touching in the shadows of the alley. "Anna, it's falling apart. Just keep faith. It will happen."

Anna's face was beaming, as if from an inner joy. "Thanks to God. But when?"

Just then Bronek heard a sound. His jaw dropped. "What's that?"

"What?"

Bronek heard footsteps. "Police!"

Anna's eyes grew wide, wide with terror. "Oh, no!"

"Stand straight!" Bronek said in a loud whisper. The footsteps approached, and two men appeared in the alley. They were Blue Police. The clutched their rifles as they ran forward. "*Heil Hitler! Hände hoch! Hände hoch!*" (Hands up!)

Bronek whispered from the side of his mouth, "You don't know my name!"

"Hands up!" the taller one shouted gruffly. They raised their rifles to their shoulders, in firing position.

Bronek and Anna raised their hands dutifully. "What's going on here?" Bronek asked with a relaxed chuckle, trying to ignore the rifles. "We are doing nothing."

The taller policeman motioned to the wall. He was overweight and, with his receding hair, looked more Polish than German. The shorter one had a face like a weasel. "*Hände hoch!*" the taller one repeated. The Blue Policemen wore regular dark topcoats. But their old helmets were rusting steel covers from the First World War. The helmets had a Polish eagle painted on the front, meant to show that these were still good Poles. Something was ridiculous about giving guns to these men.

Bronek and Anna turned around and pressed their hands

against the cold brick wall. "Say," Bronek said, "I can explain everything to you, but it will be easier in Polish. Speak Polish?"

"*Kennkarten, bitte!*" Keeping their rifles raised, the two policemen groped in Bronek's and Anna's pockets. Soon they pulled out two identity cards.

"This is simple to explain," Bronek said. He took the calculated risk of turning around. "Look, our papers are in order."

The taller policeman inspected Bronek's gray identity papers, studying the seals, the stamps, and the photograph. "That is me," Bronek said.

The short policeman held up Anna's identity papers. "Is this all right?" he asked blankly. His helmet dropped down on his forehead, nearly blocking his eyes.

Admitting confusion before prisoners was a foolish mistake, and Bronek seized on it. "Say, are you both *Volksdeutsche?*" *Volksdeutsche* were Poles of partial German blood. If they registered on the German National List, they received extra food rations and access to bureaucratic jobs. *Volksdeutsche* were all filthy traitors; Bronek felt utter contempt toward them. "Anna, these gentlemen are *Volksdeutsche,*" he said with a grin. "How about that."

"Your *Ausweis, bitte!*" the taller policeman said.

"Certainly, certainly. If you can ask me in Polish."

The officer eyed him suspiciously.

"In Polish?"

The policeman at last relented. "Yes, yes. Your work papers."

Bronek smiled. "That's better." He reached into his jacket and pulled out a work permit. "Here you go." He handed over his work papers.

At last the policemen lowered their rifles to their sides. They both looked over the work permit curiously, as if they had never seen one before. "Who are you?"

Bronek began to feel a bit of relief. "My name is . . . Stanislaw Kwiatkowski. It says so, right there. My address is 78 Platynowa, number 4."

"What is your job?"

"I work for the power company. I inspect meters for sabotage, and find broken pipes. I fix things."

They eyed him curiously, the young man in cotton pants, stained jacket, and work shirt. They were not what a power company worker obviously would wear. But his clothes were old, and the threads were barely holding. In the new Warsaw, workers often wore second-hand clothes. Bronek felt immeasurably safer wearing the clothes he had chosen that morning.

"Then . . . why are you back here?"

Bronek chuckled. "Well, fellows, you see, I was down on Nowy Swiat, repairing a pipe, and on my way back I decided to see my girlfriend here."

The shorter policeman checked the identity card. "Anna. . . Krzykowska?" He seemed to have difficulty reading her name. "Yes . . . Anna. She lives with her parents, so, you know, we snuck back here. I'm very embarrassed."

The two policemen eyed him, disdainfully. Bronek was not sure what they were thinking, so he went on. "Just look at her. Isn't she pretty? Wouldn't you do the same! Of course we snuck back here! Right, darling?"

Anna nodded nervously "Yes . . . yes, darling," she replied with a dry voice.

The taller policeman inspected the identity papers in his thick, stubby fingers. He glanced at Bronek and smirked.

"Look, we have no contraband, no secret documents. You checked us."

The officer nodded resignedly. Then he pointed behind them. "What is that?" he asked.

"That? I have no idea. It was here."

"That is a newspaper. Karlik, get it." The shorter officer picked up the newspaper and handed it over.

"That's just a *Nowy Kurier Warszawski*. It was already here." Bronek shrugged his shoulders.

The policeman flipped through the pages. Bronek glanced at Anna. Her lips were trembling, her skin pale and colorless.

Bronek sensed her arm trembling. He wanted to hold her hand, to calm her nerves. *I will get us through this*, he told himself.

They waited and waited. Bronek sighed, as if he were bored. At last the fat policeman let the paper slip from his hand. "You will report for work!" He leered at Anna with a hungry gleam in his eye. Then the two policemen handed back the identification cards. They turned their backs and marched away.

Bronek waited. Finally he breathed a deep, relieved sigh. "They're gone."

Anna reached out for him, nearly stumbling. "Bronek!" she gasped. He held out his arms, and she fell against him, trembling. For a long time, he simply held her, as she shuddered quietly against his shoulder.

After a while she looked up at him. Her eyes were misty. "Bronek – I was so frightened."

"I know you're frightened. I can feel it."

"Where – where did you hide that Underground newspaper?"

"I took care of it," Bronek replied. "That's all that matters. I know how to deal with men like them. Polish police are a bit more understanding. And easy to bribe, if you have to."

"Bronek," Anna said weakly, "Those men frighten me so much. I – I can't bear it." She slid her ghostly white fingers up around his shoulders, holding on to him. "Someday they will come for me, and they'll take me to Pawiak prison. I have nightmares imagining it."

Bronek squeezed his arms around her slender waist. "Tell yourself it won't happen. You will survive. Believe it, every second of every day."

She held her arms around his neck. She looked into his steady eyes. "You're never frightened?"

"I keep my mind on my mission."

At last she took a deep breath, and her lips relaxed. Her arms slid down to her side. "I'm all right now."

"Have you recovered?"

"Yes. I'm fine."

They inched back to Nowy Swiat. Bronek peered out, to make sure the police were gone. "They were just *Volksdeutsche* anyway," Bronek said. "Traitors. Lower than rats." They left the alley to find the nearest streetcar stop.

* * *

Anna rested her hand in his as they walked home. The sun was down past the buildings now. Anna was wearing his jacket over her shoulders. Neither said much, as Anna pondered many questions of her own. She was content, but troubled all at once. She could not quiet the turmoil she felt in her heart.

They turned the corner onto Twarda Street, just west of the city center. "This is it," Anna said, motioning toward the drab-looking brick apartment building. She squeezed his hand, not wanting to let go. "I have to leave now. My parents will be worried about me."

"I know."

"And you! You must get home before curfew! Can you make it?"

Bronek checked his wristwatch. "Of course. I can make it in time."

Anna felt the determined confidence in his voice. His answer was as direct as could be, as right as stone.

She took a deep, difficult breath. Her smile vanished from her face, and she looked up at him. "And now you must tell me something."

"What is it?"

"It must be honest."

"Yes."

She did not want to ask; it embarrassed her to ask; but yet she had to ask. "Who are you? What is your real name?" She studied his soft eyes, searching them for where the truth lay. "Not your code name. Your true name."

"Oh. Yes." Delicately he held her hands in his, sending nervous shivers up her arms. "My name is Bronislaw Pietraszewicz. I swear it to you."

"And is that the truth?"

"My identity card and work permits are forgeries. Stanislaw Kwiatkowski did live at that address. But he left Warsaw to join partisans in the north. He is lost to the world now. I took over his identity."

"But what if he returns? What if he is captured?"

"Anna, I knew Stanislaw before the war. They will never take him alive."

"But, Bronek –"

"Do you see? I did not lie to you, Anna."

"Well, I'm glad for that. But there's still so much I don't know about you."

Without warning, the loudspeakers crackled jarringly. Loudspeakers were strung all around the city, hanging from streetcar poles and streetlights. Through annoying static a recording of a Strauss waltz pierced the air, to bolster the morale of the Germans.

"I have secrets, Anna. Secrets I must keep to myself."

"I know. But you must be honest with me. That is what I must have. Never, never lie to me. Promise me that."

"I promise you. You must believe me, Anna."

"My parents want to meet you. It's expected."

"My father wants to meet you, too. He wants to know if you're from a good family." Bronek chuckled. "I cannot meet your family. It's for their safety. I'm sorry."

"I – I understand."

"And never tell them who I am. I'm trusting you, too. With my closest secret."

She held on to his fingers and looked into his eyes, searching them for any hint of deception. His face was full of understanding and sympathy. His eyes were dark and intense, but also youthful. His hair was a perpetual mess, gracing him with a boyish charm. "All right. I trust you, Bronek. And my name is Anna Maria Krzykowska. I live in that building over there, and I'm nineteen years old, and my favorite color is royal blue, and I have two parents and a bossy sister and a brother, and I never go to German movies. And I have secrets, too."

"I'll never leave you, Anna Maria."

"This is yours," she suddenly remembered. Anna took off his jacket and laid it across his arm. "Thank you." She found herself close to him. She felt his body warmth as the cold wind chilled her cheeks.

"I'll come see you again, Anna. Very soon."

"I insist." Her fingers lingered in his hands.

She felt his arms wrap around her waist. She was pulled close to him, and she did not struggle. His shoulders inside his shirt were strong, and she felt herself warming to his bravery, his inner confidence. "I can't kiss a boy on the first date," she warned him.

"Can't? Or shouldn't?"

She took one step away from his grasp. She let him go, even while she detected something like regret in her fingers. Her heart raced at the possibility. Hurriedly, she rose up on her toes and kissed his cheek.

When she stepped away Bronek was grinning, like a boy who had been surprised with candy. *How can such a brave man be such a giddy boy?* she wondered. "Can you get home?"

"I'll make it home. They'll never catch me."

"Oh, of course. You're so certain," she said, smiling. "Good night." Again she pulled her hands away from his, and she hurried into her apartment.

Her mother, Krystyna, and Jan were in the kitchen. Anna smelled potatoes cooking. "Anna! Thanks to God, she's back!" her mother exclaimed. "You fool, getting home just before curfew!" Her mother wrapped her arms around Anna, hugging her as if she had been gone for a year. "Where have you been all this time?"

"Hello, Mother. I'm fine."

Then it was Krystyna's turn. "Were you with him?" Her eyes were wide with wonder. "Come with me." Krystyna took Anna's hand and led her into the parlor.

Her mother turned to Jan. "Was she with a boy?"

Krystyna took Anna to the sofa, and they sat facing each other. "Anna, you have to tell me everything! What happened?"

"Oh, I can't, Krystyna. It's a secret."

"Tell me, Anna."

Anna waited just long enough to catch her breath. "Well, all right." Then out came the entire story, every last detail and her analysis of every detail. She told how he had rushed in late, and how he had kissed her hand, which showed that he knew polite customs, and they had chatted over coffee, and he had told her all about himself and his family, and then they had walked around the city center, and he had held her hand, and he had complimented her in a very sweet way, and they had read a *Biuletyn Informacyjny* together in an alley, and then the police came, and she was terrified they would be arrested, but he talked them out of it, and he had hidden the paper somehow. And how he had walked her home, and he had lent her his jacket, and he had said he would see her again soon, but she did not know how, but she knew it would happen because he could do anything, and somehow he was very mature and a silly boy at the same time. She told Krystyna everything but his name, because it was a secret. That and the kiss, because that was none of her business.

* * *

The September sky was just darkening to night. The indigo evening carried chilly winds from the Baltic Sea. At 8:00 p.m., the police squads were dispatched. It was curfew. For the next nine hours, and only then, the police would rule the streets.

South of the city center was a short, angled street called Szucha Avenue, but renamed *Strasse der Polizei* by the Germans. On Szucha Avenue was what had been the Polish Ministry of Religion and Public Education. Now it was Gestapo headquarters, one of the most heavily defended buildings in the city. On the sidewalk were two machine-gun nests, with sandbags and stacked cement blocks. At Gestapo headquarters, the Nazis were able to keep a red Nazi flag flying in the sky. The flag proclaimed their fiction that they were in charge, that they ruled Warsaw without fear of assassination or sabotage.

On this September evening, a long black Mercedes-Benz staff car pulled up to Gestapo headquarters. An aide opened the rear door and made the Nazi salute. Out stepped an SS officer. He was a young man of thirty, with fine, somewhat bland features. He wore a plain black overcoat, black gloves, black boots. He had no insignia of his Brigadier General's rank. He seemed to disappear into the black night.

The General stepped from the car, refusing to return the salute. Two bodyguards leapt out and huddled directly behind him, blocking the General from any Underground snipers. The General did not stop to speak or to scan the street. The aide shut the car door, and the Mercedes sped off. Staying close together, the trio strode purposefully into Gestapo headquarters. That quickly, the new police chief was gone from sight. SS *Brigadeführer* (Brigadier General) Franz Kutschera had arrived. The Underground had had its way long enough. Now things in Warsaw would be different.

Decree

For the Prevention of Attacks against the German Work of Reconstruction in the General Government.

October 2, 1943

Under Section 5, Paragraph 1 of the Decree of the Führer of October 12, 1939 (Reichslaw I S. 2077), I order until further notice:

§ 1

(1) Non-Germans who, with the intent to hinder or disrupt the German work of reconstruction, infringe against laws, decrees, or official orders and decrees of the authorities, are to be punished with death.

(2) Paragraph 1 does not apply to the relatives of those connected with the greater German Reich or those in the war effort.

§ 2

The instigator and the assistant will be punished as the perpetrator, and the attempted action will be punished as the completed action.

§ 3

(1) Jurisdiction for sentences is with the Summary Security Police Courts.

(2) The Summary Security Police Courts can take the matter from the German prosecutor's office for exceptional reasons.

§ 4

The Summary Security Police Courts shall consist of an SS Führer of the district of the commanding officer of the Security Police and the security service as well as from two related districts.

§ 5

(1) Permanently closed are
1. Name of the judge.
2. Name of the condemned.
3. Evidence by which the conviction was obtained.
4. The offense.
5. Date of the conviction.
6. Date of the execution.

(2) In the remaining particulars the proceedings of the Summary Security Police Courts may be within their official estimation.

§ 6

The sentences of the Summary Security Police Courts are to be carried out immediately.

§ 7

So far as an offense under Sections 1 and 2 of this decree at the same time come under another summary proceeding, the regulations of this decree take precedence.

§ 8

This decree takes effect on October 10, 1943.

Krakow, October 2, 1943

Governor General Hans Frank

VI

The autumn sky spread pink stripes over Warsaw, and the wind blew cold. Fall showers came, turning the layer of dust into mud that left brown streaks on the beautiful baroque buildings. The people of Warsaw went on, fearful, hopeful, unyielding. They whispered rumors to each other, and went to church, and shopped for food on the black markets. Slowly they began to accept that the prayed-for breakthrough would not happen this year. The Allies would not sweep through Italy; the Red Army would remain at Kiev, nearly 500 miles away. Things happened, and nothing happened, and the people went on.

Bronek worried about Anna. It was an ordeal to even communicate with her. There were no telephones in his apartment building, and he did not use the German telephones that were in some cafes. He bypassed the mail completely. He knew of people who were arrested after the police intercepted their mail. Instead he wrote notes and delivered them himself, sliding them under her door. He met her in cafes for coffee and conversation, but these were tense episodes. They fidgeted with their coffee, and asked about each other's families, and nodded. Their coffees went cold before they finished them.

Saint Casimir Catholic Church was packed every Sunday. In Warsaw there were no lapsed Catholics. Mass was held three times every Sunday, and at special times on holy days. Attending Mass was a trying, uncomfortable experience. The old limestone church had a gaping hole in one side where a bomb had slammed into it, and most of the stained glass was shattered. The voids were covered with a patchwork of boards. Then the rain had come in, turning the carpet into a smelly, mildewy bed. Of course, all the statues, and all the chalices, and all the fine woodwork, had been stolen by the Nazis long ago.

Saint Casimir was filled again this Sunday. Parishioners jostled each other in the pews, their shoulders pressing together. Bronek squeezed between his father and brother on the hard wooden pew, and listened to the chants from Father Marian. With classic Polish features, Father Marian was a timid speaker, perhaps too timid for these times. But he had a beautiful voice, high and tender. From him the phrases formed a kind of divine rhythm.

Normally, Bronek loved the chants and hymns. He adored "Ave Maria." But this afternoon, the phrases flowed past him. This was his third holy Mass of the day, and he could not concentrate. Instead, he worried over endless questions. How could he meet her again? Was she safe? What about this new police chief? Were the rumors true? Bronek itched to find out more. But just attending church was an act of defiance. So he sat and listened as the cadences flowed slowly past.

After Mass was finished, and people were still milling near the confessional booths, Bronek went outside. The sky was a little warmer than usual, and sunny. A police patrol marched by, but lately they had been leaving the Poles alone during church. The neighbors had already collected into clusters. Bronek's father was standing with the older people in one cluster. Eugene was farther down the steps, leaning on his cane, talking and laughing with a group of teen-agers. Bronek was a man now, so he edged over near the group of adults.

"I heard something: Naples was liberated," Mister Stachowiak proclaimed eagerly. Mister Stachowiak lived alone in Bronek's building. He was a head taller than everyone else, and his proud bald scalp sported only faint hairs by his ears. He smiled a big, natural smile beneath his narrow, trimmed mustache. "They are free, down there."

"Yes, Naples," Karol reiterated. "Thank God for them." Bronek felt a curious flatness, a solemnity, in his father's voice. There was no rejoicing today. Bronek stood by his father and folded his arms sternly.

"I do not care about Naples!" Their neighbor, Mister Zukowski, was waving his arms. "I want to know about this new decree. What does it mean? What does it mean?" He had a deep, frequently loud, voice. Mister Zukowski had lost his wife to influenza the winter before. He had a grown son, who was missing.

Misses Rogala spoke up. "Oh, you know nothing so far," she answered forcefully. "Let's wait and see. That's all we can do, wait and see." Halina Rogala's husband had been taken to a forced labor camp in Germany in 1941, and her daughter was believed to be at Ravensbrück, so she was all alone.

"Have you read this new decree? It's not good, I tell you." Tadeusz Zukowski shook his head mournfully. "It is not good."

Bronek's father continued the debate. "What do you know about it, Tadeusz?" he asked. "We have seen a thousand decrees. Owning a radio, owning a typewriter, buying food, helping a Jew. We can't walk home from church today without committing some capital crime."

Mister Stachowiak, a tall, bald presence in any group, spoke. "That poster looked rather vague to me," he commented. "We've seen worse than this one." The other adults murmured their assent.

Mister Zukowski lowered his voice, and his heavy eyebrows darkened his eyes menacingly. "I've heard stories."

"Well, so what?" Karol asked. "I've heard stories, too. Let's not make up our minds until we know more."

"Bad things are coming. Very bad things." Mister Zukowski let his prediction settle over the group. The other grownups listened intently. "They're going to come after us. We are next."

"Oh," Misses Rogala commented, "You don't know anything yet."

"We don't know yet," Bronek's father said. "We don't know. We'll have to wait and see." But Bronek knew by the tone in his voice that his father was unsettled. The conversation trailed off, awkwardly. Mister Zukowski had raised the unspoken fear that hung over Warsaw. *They started with the Jews. We are next.*

For a few seconds, they stood and said nothing. Then the adults nervously dispersed to collect their children.

Bronek knew that there was more to this new decree. He had heard rumors about the new police chief. He believed them. Mister Zukowski had won this argument, he decided.

As he was heading down the worn church steps, Bronek felt a tug on his shirt sleeve. "Bronek! Wait, wait."

Bronek turned around. "Mister Skonieczny? Hello." The Skoniecznys lived upstairs in Bronek's building. No one knew much about them, but they seemed to be unusually well-fed. Every so often, gossip spread that Mister Skonieczny was collaborating with the Germans. "How are you?"

The stumpy man shook his brown head mournfully. "Ah, Bronek, something is wrong, very wrong." Mister Skonieczny's head was bald, but it was not smooth; instead, it had widely spaced straight hairs, like a field of weedy reeds. His hairs waved annoyingly as he shook his head. "It's my son."

"Leszek?" Bronek glanced down the sidewalk, where Leszek was standing with his usual friends. Leszek told some joke; then he laughed louder than anyone else. "What about him?"

"It's not good, Bronek. It's not good." Mister Skonieczny leaned forward. He was one step above Bronek, which allowed him to look directly into Bronek's eyes. "Leszek, he's a good boy. He really is. But he - he has some friends."

Bronek shifted his weight from one foot to the other. When would he see Anna again? How could he get a message to her?

"You see, Leszek, he – I think he's done some bad things.

He may be – going to German movies."

Bronek blinked, surprised. "Oh? Leszek goes to German movies?"

"Not so loud, Bronek, not so loud! I don't know anything for certain. But I asked him, and he – well, he did not answer either way."

Bronek wrinkled his brow. Movies shown in Warsaw were made by Germans, and had names likes "Drink, Drink, Drink," and "Four Men, One Woman." The Underground had forbidden Poles from attending movies. Leszek knew that. The last movie Bronek had seen was in 1939. It was a Sonja Henie picture.

"Bronek, he respects you. All the young boys respect you. Perhaps you could, you know, speak to him. Quietly. Let him know how important this is. Could you do that?"

Bronek pondered several of his own questions, all in a row. Then he nodded, very slightly. "Certainly, Mister Skonieczny. I'll let him know."

"And you won't – tell this to anyone else?"

"No, Mister Skonieczny. I won't get him into trouble."

"Good, good. I knew I could count on you. I told my wife this morning. Bronek is an honest young man. We can trust him with this."

"I'll take care of it, Mister Skonieczny."

"Thank you, thank you. God be with you, Bronek Pietraszewicz." Mister Skonieczny patted Bronek on the shoulder. Then he left to fetch his wife from the cluster of women farther up the church steps, as the last of the confessors left the church.

* * *

It began on Wednesday of that week, October 13, in the Old Town first. The Old Town square was crowded beneath a gray, cloudy sky. Shoppers were going about their business, smuggling food inside their clothes, haggling over their cigarettes and cabbages. At one end of the large square, a little boy waved his arm and shouted with youthful vigor, "Bread for sale! Fresh bread!"

From the south, four black Opel trucks turned into the square. They were followed by three Volkswagen jeeps, filled with SS officers who stared into the distance with determined expressions. The vehicles sped through the square, rumbling over the paving stones without slowing for pedestrians. They traversed the hundred meters of open space in a few seconds as people leapt out of the way. Then the trucks lurched to a stop.

The backs of the trucks opened, and dozens of soldiers jumped out, SS and Schupos and *Wehrmacht* and *Luftwaffe* and even some Hitler Youth youngsters, holding their rifles in front of them. The soldiers dashed into the alleys, pointing their rifles as if they were surrounding a foxhole of American soldiers. Shouts of *"Hände hoch! Hände hoch!"* filled the gray air. They expertly surrounded a crowd of civilians who were loaded down with smuggled food.

Other soldiers went into the homes. They pounded and pounded and pounded on the doors with their rifle butts until the doors swung open. Then they dashed inside, conquering each home and pushing their prisoners outside with the others. The citizens looked back with expressions of shocked surprise, then glum acceptance.

The soldiers formed a circle and then inched forward, their rifles pointed into the crowd. They shouted *"Hände hoch!"* until the civilians surrendered, dropping their bags and lifting their hands to the sky. The soldiers advanced until they were shoulder to shoulder. They jabbed their rifles at anyone who made a sudden movement.

After the civilians were subdued, the SS officers entered the circle to do their work. Before each prisoner they commanded sharply, *"Kennkarte, bitte!"* Then they studied the prisoner's gray identification card. If the card identified that person as a German citizen or a Polish *Volksdeutsche*, the officer returned the card and commanded, *"Gehen Sie!"* Labor cards, except for those working for the German war industry, were not honored. In this precise, orderly manner, the SS officers weeded the prisoners down to 120 Polish civilians. They included women, children, and the elderly.

After the Germans were released, an officer climbed onto a truck. Standing on the running board, he addressed the terrified crowd. "You are under arrest for violations of the Decree of October second! You are now prisoners of the SS! You will come with us for transport!"

The gray ring opened on one end, and the soldiers in back surged forward. The prisoners, frightened and confused, climbed into the trucks. One man, a haggard-looking older gentleman, objected. "This is not fair! Why are we being arrested? Tell us why!" But an SS soldier swung his rifle butt across the man's jaw, silencing him. The old man held his jaw and groaned, and he leaned against the truck's tailgate. The soldier, shouting angry oaths in German, pushed him inside.

When all the prisoners were loaded into the trucks, the soldiers climbed inside and swung the doors shut. The SS officers climbed into the jeeps and looked ahead triumphantly, eager for more victories. The prisoners were subdued; the trucks were full. Their mission was an efficient, disciplined success. As the vehicles swung around and drove back across the market square, pedestrians hastily averted their eyes. Then they all rushed to the bags left on the sidewalk.

* * *

Bronek was headed north for his Underground meeting. The cold wind blew around his work jacket, sending a chill into his neck. Bronek puffed into his fist and jammed his fingers into his pockets. He kept walking, as quickly as he could while still avoiding detection.

He was at the southern entrance to Old Town. Before him stood the Column of King Zygmunt III. In 1596 Zygmunt had moved the capital from Krakow to Warsaw. In a time when the Protestant tide was washing across Europe, he had secured Roman Catholicism as the national faith. Now he stood atop a 15-meter column, Catholic cross in his hand, over a people defeated once again.

Beyond the column stood the Royal Castle. It resembled not a castle but a massive palace, with five sides surrounding a courtyard within. Dozens of uniform windows punctured its long, flat walls. It used to have a tall clock tower and onion-shaped dome that had soared above the roof, capped with an ornate spire. Bronek could not remember when the castle was built – it was sometime in the 1570's. Once again, the Germans were fools for letting this building stand. Seeing the Royal Castle, and King Zygmunt before it, emboldened everyone. The Royal Castle was the very heart of the city. The onion dome was smashed, the sloping roof was burned, the artworks were looted. But the castle still stood.

Bronek felt something. Police. A patrol of Schupos – gray police uniforms, green eagle-and-oak-leaf patches on the left sleeve. Bronek walked mechanically. *Never look at a policeman. Never meet his eyes.* The Schupos walked around the corner and disappeared. The tension in Bronek's neck eased a bit.

Then he spotted the girl. She was always bundled up, in an oversized winter coat and worn-out boots. Bronek struggled to keep himself from grinning.

The girl was approaching him, walking as nonchalantly as himself. "Didn't you go to school with me?" he asked her. This was today's signal that he was not followed.

"Do you mean Warsaw Technical Institute?" This was her message that she felt safe. By naming different schools, she gave Bronek different signals.

Bronek nodded. "Yes. Professor Mierszczyski."

The girl smiled widely – too much, Bronek thought. He wished she would be less demonstrative. "Yes, that's him. Tell me how he is." They walked together in front of the Royal Castle.

"Exactly on time, Zebra," Bronek said under his breath. "I can set my watch by you." Bronek, like his mentor Adam, changed his meeting routine: sometimes in abondoned buildings, and sometimes in public.

"Hello, Lot," the girl said. "How are you today?"

Bronek squinted, surprised. It always seemed strange, the way she exchanged polite pleasantries as if they were at some tea party. Wiktor and Adam never asked him how he was. "I'm here," he replied. "That's enough."

"Oh, Lot," Zebra said, amused, "You try to be so cold and heartless. But I know better."

"Hm." None of this was about the mission. Zebra was fifteen or sixteen, not really glamorous or beautiful. Her drab brown hair was in two tight braids above her ears, and light freckles speckled her face. She was always so heavily bundled that Bronek could not even recall whether she had a good figure. But he admired her, as he admired all messenger girls. He knew that she faced greater risks than he. Her actions naturally aroused attention, she had to be available to Adam at all times, and she carried incriminating documents in public. If she were arrested, the SS would not be gentler to her. On the contrary, they would be doubly savage to her Slavic body. "Thank you, Zebra."

At that moment, Bronek eyed a Blue Policeman approaching them. "I haven't seen you in so long," he said loudly, "Tell me what you've done since the university." Bronek clenched his jaw. He was ready to run. But the policeman passed by them without slowing.

"Lot," Zebra asked quietly, "What's wrong today?"

"What? Nothing. Why?"

"Something is wrong. I can tell."

"I'm just thinking about someone – I mean, something."

"Someone? A girl?"

"No."

"Yes. You're thinking about a girl."

"Zebra. . . ." Bronek's voice trailed away. "You're a good guesser."

"I can tell." She smiled again, in a way that let Bronek know he mattered to her.

"Zebra, it's just – it's tough to do this. We can't go to

movies, I can't afford the restaurants, I can't do anything that I want to do for her."

Zebra giggled. "I knew it," she said sweetly, "You *are* romantic."

Somehow, Bronek felt himself squirm as he walked. "Pretty soon you'll guess where I live."

"Lot, you are funny sometimes."

They walked until they reached a small cluster of people standing just off the Castle Square. "This is my streetcar stop," Zebra said.

"I'll wait with you until you board," Bronek said. Their short time together was over.

Zebra turned around and stood still. Bronek waited a minute, until he saw a streetcar roll up to this stop. Hunching his shoulders forward, Bronek slipped his finger inside the belt on Zebra's coat. There, attached inside the belt, was a slip of paper. Bronek watched everyone else; no one noticed what he was doing. Pretending to be cold, Bronek wrapped his arms around himself. As he did, the slip of paper came up, inside his jacket. He slipped the message into a pocket in his jacket sleeve. Just that smoothly, it was done. He said nothing to Zebra as she boarded the streetcar. As it rolled away, Bronek headed home.

* * *

"Why did you want to see me, Nowak?" Bronek was sitting across from Adam in the Nectar, a small café on St. Cross Street.

"Please, please," Adam commented reassuringly, "Drink your coffee, Lot."

Bronek wondered what Adam wanted. They had never met in the Nectar before, and Bronek felt slightly on edge. But that was Adam: his only habit was that he had no habits. Bronek sipped the coffee Adam had bought him. It was *ersatz* coffee, of course, but it still warmed him inside. "I received my orders from Zebra."

"Yes. We haven't set the date for the operation yet."

"I like it. Attack the lottery. Destroy the lottery tickets. It will hurt their finances."

"And," Adam added, "It will be public. We will remind people not to play the lottery."

"They shouldn't," Bronek said. "It's against the Rules of Civil Resistance."

"True. But," Adam said with a sigh, "People become depressed, and they forget the rules."

"Well, they shouldn't," Bronek said quickly.

"Granit is still watching the lottery building. When he reports back to me, I'll want to see you again."

"Sounds good."

There was a strange pause between them. Adam fidgeted with his coffee cup. "Well, how are you doing, Lot?"

"What?" Bronek recoiled at this idle question. Adam was acting as strangely as Zebra today. "I don't know," he said. "I've heard some bad news."

"Ah. Yes," Adam commented sadly. "I'm sure it cannot be good. What have you heard?"

"There was another arrest this morning. About 120 people."

"Where?" Adam asked.

"On Leszno Street. No shots fired."

"Hm."

"Is this all because of the new police chief?"

"I believe so."

"Who is he? What do you know about this man?"

Adam sighed ruefully. "He is Franz Kutschera. SS man, Brigadier General. He is very close to Himmler himself, I am not sure how. He has been all over: Belgium, Norway, Holland, Czechoslovakia. His specialty is – persecuting resistance movements."

Bronek tried to listen, but his attention faded. Instead, images of Anna swirled in his mind: her deep blue eyes, her delicate hands, her quirky smile. Everything else in Bronek's world was base, and miserable. He had gotten used to that. But

Anna was above it all. Her touch was always tender, her voice always reassuring. He did not even know when he could see her again.

"What do you think, Lot?"

"What?" He did not even hear what Adam had said.

"Don't be embarrassed, Lot." From behind his craggy face, Adam smiled knowingly. "Are you thinking of someone?"

Bronek nodded, embarrassed.

"That's what Zebra told me. Bronek, what affects you affects this entire unit. We nearly had a disaster with Akrobat. He barely escaped."

"I can't tell you her name."

"I realize that, Lot."

"But she's that girl from Under the Snout."

Adam nodded. "As I suspected. Have you seen her since then?"

"Yes, a few times. But it's difficult."

"Are you worried about her?" Adam asked.

Bronek nodded.

"Well, Lot," Adam responded, "I remember how it feels. Perhaps I can help." Adam paused. Then he spoke quietly. "Look between the slats. Beside you."

Trying to appear casual, Bronek looked down. He noticed something between the wooden slats of his seat, something shiny. "Nowak, is that –?"

"Yes, it is. I hope it serves your purpose."

"Nowak, thank you!"

"Quiet. Sit still." Adam smiled a weathered, weary, but gratified sort of smile. "I'll call this my contribution to the resistance effort. Good luck, Lot. And stay in touch with Zebra." Adam motioned very slightly, and Bronek noticed that their waitress nodded. "Wait five minutes before you leave." With that, Adam quietly rose and left the café, leaving Bronek to conceal the key.

* * *

It was Friday, October 15. Bronek paced back and forth in apartment two, where he, Wiktor, and Adam had met previously. He worked the details over and over in his mind. It was the single detail that led to trouble. He had followed his plan, he had slid the invitation beneath her door, but still . . . anything might happen. He anxiously fidgeted with his red pattern tie, his last one. It did not match his father's borrowed jacket, but this was as nice as he could look. A torn overcoat, which even his father never wore, lay bunched up in a heap on the floor, beside his fedora hat. Bronek ran his fingers through his hair. His hair was in a pompadour, he hoped.

Bronek approached the high, deep window. He slipped his finger behind the heavy shade and eyed the street. The darkening sky was an endless gray, and now a cold, misty drizzle was falling. This was bad. Perhaps she could not get around in this weather. Or perhaps she never got his message. Or perhaps – something worse?

Just then he heard a knock at the door. Bronek turned, startled. There was one knock, then two more knocks. Then silence. Tensely, Bronek touched his silver locket for luck. Then he remembered his hat. He dashed back, put on his fedora, and hurried back to the door. Bronek took a deep breath, to slow his racing heart. Then he turned the lock, and opened the door a crack.

VII

Bronek peered around the door, his hand gripping the door-knob nervously. For a moment he froze.

"May I come in?" Anna slipped inside. She was wearing a long trenchcoat, so long that it touched the ground behind her, and a colorful babushka on her head.

Bronek immediately locked the door behind her. For a second he searched for something to say.

"You made it?"

"Yes," she observed.

"Oh – your coat!" He nearly lunged at her, his arms outstretched.

Anna slid off her wet coat and her babushka. "Thank you," she said politely as he took her things. "It's much too big for me. It's my father's, actually. I don't have one."

Bronek folded her coat and set it on the floor, on top of his own. He turned around. He just stood and looked.

She blinked her eyes. "It's very dark in here."

"Maybe the electricity is on. Let me try it for you." Bronek hurried over to a small lamp that sat on the floor, and turned the knob. It came to life, sending a cone of light up to the ceiling. "There!" He turned around, nervously. "It's . . . on."

"Is something wrong?"

"No. I just want to see you." She was wearing the same pale blue blouse as the first time he met her, a black skirt, and black shoes without heels. She had tied a blue ribbon in her hair. Without speaking, he walked toward her. He lifted her hand and gently kissed it, following the Polish custom. "Thank you for coming." He kept her hand up near his lips, and he stared into her rich blue eyes.

"I bet my hair is a frightful mess," she said meekly.

"It's just a little damp on top," he said reassuringly. Her hair hung around her face in a wet blond tangle.

"It's not a mess?"

Bronek did not answer her. "You're beautiful."

Bronek loosened her hand. He still felt hesitant, unsure how to act. "No one lives here. This is a safe room. Do you know what that means? A safe room –"

"I know," she interrupted. Her voice echoed off the bare walls. "This must have been a beautiful place, once."

"It sure was. I think maybe aristocrats lived here once. Look up there." He pointed eagerly to the ceiling; a wide, shallow dome was scooped out of it. "A big chandelier was there, once. It was probably stolen."

"Why the heavy shades? It's not dark yet."

"They think this building is abandoned. The rest of the house is bombed out. So it's a perfect safe room." Bronek playfully kicked away a chunk of plaster that had fallen from the ceiling. It skidded across the wood floor like a hockey puck.

"Oh."

Her response sounded uninterested. She did not care about the house. Bronek cursed himself. He was trying, but it was not working well.

She stepped across the room, her shoes making a disconcerting echo. "What's back here?"

"Wait!" Bronek shouted. He jumped in front of her. "That's your surprise."

Anna stopped, surprised. "What do you mean?" Then she began to smile, her slow, inevitable smile. "Oh, Bronek –"

"Are you ready?"

"But you shouldn't have done anything!"

He slowly doffed his fedora, and bowed deeply. "Dinner is served."

Bronek threw aside his hat and went ahead. The room was almost totally dark, until he struck a match. In the center of the room, on a walnut table with elaborately carved legs, was a tall candle. Beneath the candle were two china plates filled with food, and fine crystal glasses with water.

Bronek watched Anna guardedly, studying her for her reaction. When she raised her hands and gasped, "Oh, my!" he at last smiled.

Bronek stood at one of the six high-backed chairs at the table and waved his arm, like a waiter in a fine restaurant. She sat down, and he pushed her heavy chair forward. He sat adjacent to her, to enjoy a fine dinner in the bare, chilly, abandoned room.

Dinner was a tiny piece of kielbasa – a rare treat – a potato, beets, and some black bread. "Where did you find all this?"

"The dishes and silverware were already here," Bronek said. "In that butler's pantry, back there. The kitchen is gone, but there's a small sink back there."

Anna peered into the darkened corner.

"This must have been the dining room – the Germans left the table and chairs." Bronek looked over everything on the table. "Is it all right?" he asked.

"Bronek, you – you –"

"It might be a little cold," he commented apologetically. "I can't light a fire here. Smoke from the chimney."

"This is – this is –" she stared at her plate.

"Yes?"

"This is wonderful."

"It was the best I could do."

"Thank you, darling."

"Well, go ahead." He tasted his kielbasa.

"Wait!"

Bronek stopped his fork in mid-air. "Hm?"

"Put that down."

Bronek set down his fork, and Anna held his hand. She cast down her eyes. "Heavenly Father," she said, "We thank You for the food we are about to receive, and we ask Your grace in liberating us. In the name of the Father, and the Son, and the Holy Ghost." They crossed themselves. "Now we can eat."

"Bronek, how did you manage all this?"

"My father helped me cook everything. And then he thought of putting everything in tin cans, for carrying from home. We flattened the cans a little bit, so they would fit in my coat."

"He's a smart man. I'd like to meet him."

"I wish you could." They began the slow process of eating. In Warsaw, people cut their food into tiny pieces and ate very slowly, to make it seem to last longer. They tasted their food together in silence, letting it rest in their mouths.

Bronek glanced hopefully at Anna. She was smiling, holding up her knife and fork. Then he noticed: she was dragging her elbows against the table edge. "Oh," he muttered, ashamedly. He pulled his elbows off the table, and he cursed himself once again. He was relieved she did not say anything; that would be even more embarrassing.

"There was a big bombing raid yesterday," Bronek suddenly volunteered.

"Really? Where was –?"

"I heard, Schweinfurt," he continued, too excited to let her finish. "At the ball bearing factories. One of the biggest of the whole war."

"Ball bearings?" Anna asked, quizzically.

"Sure. You need precision machines to make ball bearings. If you knock out the ball bearings, you knock out the trucks, the airplanes, all those things."

"Let's hope it worked." Anna thought about the information. "Were Polish fliers involved?"

"I heard they were. As air support. Through the RAF."

"I wish they could reach us here."

"I know," he said. "Imagine seeing American bombers over us. That would be a marvelous sight."

So they continued, slowly eating their dinner on fancy china plates, chatting about news and gossip. Bronek remembered that Anna did not like discussing Nazis, so he only told positive stories. But somehow just being with her, without keeping up a conversation, was fine too.

"What are you looking at?" she asked innocently.

"Your face. It shows everything. I can see every emotion, every thought."

"Oh." The candle was burning down, and the light fading to a flicker. "Thank you, darling."

"For what?"

"I was frightened to come here. Because of – out there."

"Out there doesn't matter. We're here, together. That is all that matters." Then he asked her, "Are you done?"

"Well, almost."

"Are you ready, then?"

"Ready for what?"

Bronek suddenly jumped up and ran out of the candlelight. He fumbled through his overcoat. In an instant he returned, holding a bottle. "Here we are." Bronek hastily unscrewed the cap and filled their glasses with a clear liquid. Bronek raised his glass. "A toast!" he said ceremoniously. "To our victory."

Anna eyed her drink. The surface bubbled ominously. But she raised her glass. "To our victory," she repeated. They clinked their glasses together. Bronek swallowed his entire drink, and smiled. Anna took a swallow. She froze. Then suddenly she coughed uncontrollably.

Bronek patted her back. "Anna! Are you all right?"

Anna gagged. She leaned forward, and coughed and coughed. "Stop!" The liquid dribbled down her lip and off her chin. "Oh –!"

Bronek waited tensely, as she bent over the table. Finally she leaned back, and wiped her chin with her fingers. "I'm sorry." She coughed a few more times. "What was that?" she asked hoarsely.

"It's just champagne," Bronek replied defensively.

"Champagne?"

"Well, homemade champagne. Vodka and seltzer water." He looked at the bottle, searching for some way to blame the bottle, and not himself.

Anna sighed deeply. "Thank you. That's enough." She wiped tears from her reddened eyes.

"Oh." He said nothing. He looked down at the floor morosely.

Quickly, she changed the subject. "Your note mentioned something about music."

"Yes!" Bronek leapt up from the table. "Leave the dishes. Come with me." He blew out the candle, grabbed her hand, and pulled her into the living room. The huge room was dark and cavernous; just the light shined upward from behind the beige lampshade.

Bronek went through his overcoat, bunched in a heap on the floor. "I promised you music," he said impatiently, digging into his coat pocket.

"That's fine if you can't," Anna offered.

"Here it is!" Bronek turned to her. He held his hand to his mouth, and a tinny sound came out. He walked forward, sliding some spit along the worn brass parts. "This is my B-flat. Just listen." He tooted once, then started again. "I have to play quietly." He began a slow version of an American jazz song. As he played, he watched her for her reaction. She smiled, so he played some more, swaying slightly to keep the beat.

"What's that called?" Anna asked.

"It's an American song. 'Moonlight Serenade.' It sounds good on harmonica." He played some more, slowly and softly. He played expertly, adding bass notes beneath the melody.

"That's such a pretty song. Can I sit down?"

"Sure," Bronek said. They both sat on the hard wood floor, Anna spreading her skirt around her. Bronek watched her face, barely lit in the dim light. He played "Moonlight Serenade," and Anna closed her eyes and thought.

"Do you like American jazz?"

"I've never heard much," she admitted, smiling bashfully.

"I like it quite a lot. Glenn Miller, Benny Goodman. It's wonderful."

"Benny Goodman?" Anna asked. "Is that an American name?"

"Yes, why?"

"Benny. That's cute. I should call you Benny."

"Oh? Anna, are you teasing me?"

"No. Keep playing." She waited until he was about ready to play, and then she added, "Benny." She giggled.

Bronek felt his face turn red. He decided to change the subject. "I used to play piano," Bronek explained. "But we had to sell it for food. Now this is all I have." He tooted softly across the reeds. "Let's see if you know this one." From his lips came a soft nocturne.

Anna watched him with a look of amazement on her face. "Chopin!" she whispered. "But – Chopin is illegal."

"I don't care," Bronek said matter-of-factly, and restarted the song. The composition did not translate perfectly well to harmonica, but Bronek played it proudly.

"Beautiful!"

"This is a harder one," Bronek told her. "Try to guess what this is." He started again. His lips slid up and down the harmonica, as he tried to include little flourishes.

Anna listened intently. Then she suddenly clapped her hands. "The Polonaise!" she exclaimed.

"Right! It's hard to play on harmonica." He did not need to mention that it was also by Chopin.

Just then, the loudspeakers outside crackled to life. Bronek tensed: "Not Wagner," he whispered. Fortunately, a German dance tune came forth.

"Tell me something," Bronek said. "What do you dream about?"

"Why?"

"In Warsaw, everyone dreams. You know my dream. To play music, Chopin, jazz, everywhere. What do you dream about?"

"Nothing so important."

"Tell me."

"Just about – not being afraid. In my dream I'm not afraid any more. And I have four children, and I tell them all about what I've done, and how we survived, and they're never afraid of anything." She paused for a second. "I guess that's not so much."

"Yes, it is. I like that dream, Anna."

Bronek played a few more notes, but then stopped playing again. "What are you thinking about?" he asked her. He hoped she was thinking something nice, and not that she was bored.

Anna was staring into the dark corner, her mind far away. "I'm just remembering – how things were before."

"Be careful, Anna. It hurts, thinking about before."

"Warsaw was so beautiful, once. It was full of life, and music, and gaiety. Now it's – fear, and police, and the Ghetto."

"Don't, Anna. It's dangerous to think about it."

"I know. My family is still together, thanks to God," she said before mumbling something and crossing herself. "It's so difficult. It's worst for my father."

"Why? Was he injured?"

"He is a victim of the occupation, too." She spoke with a hurried, forced formality.

"I understand, Anna."

"Just hearing that beautiful Chopin reminds me . . . it reminds me."

Bronek knew he should cheer her spirits. "Anna, listen to this –"

Abruptly, the dance music outside ceased. A voice declared, "Attention! Attention!"

"Oh, goodness!" Anna lifted herself off the floor and hurried over to the windowsill. Bronek went over beside her, and he rested his hand reassuringly on her shoulder. They listened intently to every word, every crackle.

The voice reported that the *Luftwaffe* had successfully defended Schweinfurt against a vicious and unprovoked Allied air attack, aimed at the women and children of Germany.

Anna kept her ear by the window shade. "Is that true?" she asked quietly.

"No, the opposite is true. You can tell, by the way he says it."

The voice was forceful, determined. It filled the air with a feeling of doom. Anna reached out to the window shade.

"Anna, no!" Bronek held her wrist tightly. "Don't open the shade!"

"The Security Police Summary Court," the voice continued, "Has convicted the following persons as reprisal for attacks against Germans. They have been sentenced to death, and executed."

Anna grabbed Bronek's arm fiercely, just as she had when the Gestapo was near.

"Be calm! You must stay calm!" He held her, and pressed her head to his shoulder. Had they looked, they would have seen groups of shabbily dressed people clustered beneath the loudspeakers, listening intently for familiar names.

Together they listened to the names of the dead. The faceless voice listed seven names in all.

The voice continued. "The Security Police Summary Court has furthermore sentenced to death the following persons convicted of violations of Section One or Section Two of the Decree of October 2, 1943."

The voice droned on and on, listing more than 100 names, including several women.

"Dear God . . ." Anna whispered, unable to finish.

Finally, the voice concluded. "In the event of any further attacks, the condemned will be executed at a rate of ten Poles for every German who is assaulted. These executions will be carried out on the same day and in the same place as the attack. The condemned will be chosen from among communists or so-called 'nationalists,' depending on who is responsible for the assault. The condemned are subject to reprieve. The public is urged to cooperate in the apprehension of the culprits, in return for which some of the condemned may be reprieved. By order of the SS and Police Leader for the Warsaw District." As abruptly as it had started, the voice stopped. Silence filled the night.

For a few seconds Anna leaned against Bronek in the dark. She shuddered, a deep tremble that went though her entire body. "What does it mean, Bronek?"

"This must be Kutschera's strategy," Bronek replied, bitterly. "The SS has arrested more than a thousand people. There haven't been any trials. He's offering to release people if their relatives betray the Underground."

"Is that his name, Kutschera?"

"We believe so. He's very secretive. The Germans we have bribed won't reveal his name, or where he lives. A secretary sympathetic to us found his name on one memo. We don't even know what he looks like."

"Bronek, darling, I – I can't." She wrapped her arms desperately around his waist, as tightly as a terrified child, as she whimpered quietly. "I don't know how to bear any more. I'm not brave, or heroic. I'm just a small girl. For four years I've been afraid. I can't always be afraid. I just can't."

Bronek held her close, and he knew that she was crying. "You are brave, Anna. You're very brave."

"Is the rumor true? Is it true? Are we next?"

"I don't know their plan," Bronek said.

Through a mist of tears, she looked into his eyes. "Will it work? Will people inform on the Underground?"

"Never. He'll never break us."

"And you're – you're sure?"

"You bet I'm sure." He felt the tension that still gripped Anna. He looked into her large blue eyes, wanting to reassure her but not knowing how. "Do you want to hear another song?"

"No. But thank you. For helping."

"Oh." Bronek did not know what to say.

She was staring at him and smiling, a forced, fragile, but sweet sort of smile. His eyes were fixed on her radiant face. She was not tiny, but her beauty was fragile, easily broken. Tenderly, he reached out his hand and touched her porcelain cheek. When she delicately kissed his fingertips, he was no longer uncertain. He stood over her, and softly tilted her face up. She did not speak; her tenseness just softened, and Bronek finally understood what that expression meant.

Just then the light bulb blinked off, came back on for a second or two, and then went off completely. "Oh, my!" Anna exclaimed. They were now in complete darkness.

"It must be eight," Bronek said. "The electricity is off for the night."

"Then that means . . . curfew has begun?"

"Curfew has begun," Bronek repeated.

Anna fell silent. He rubbed her bare arm. "You have goose bumps. Are you cold?"

"Well, a little bit, I guess."

"I wish you had told me." Bronek slid off his jacket. "Where are you?"

"Over here."

Bronek held out his jacket. He missed. Eventually he wrapped it around her shoulders.

"Thank you," she said.

"You wear that jacket more than I do," Bronek said.

"If you could see me, I suppose I would look pretty silly."

Bronek could distinguish the faint outline of her body, but he could not see any features. "I don't need to see you. I know exactly how you look."

"How can you?"

"You're wearing a light blue blouse. You have a little ribbon in your hair."

"Oh, that," Anna said. "I tie a ribbon in, just to add some color."

"I know. It matches your eyes."

"The only colors I ever see are gray, and black."

"You have the bluest eyes I have ever seen."

"Oh."

In the darkness, Bronek felt a bashful grin. "And your hair is a little darker near your face; then it gets lighter."

"It used to be all blond. I guess without enough food, my hair has gotten drab."

"It looks like a halo around your face."

"I used to wear it down on my shoulders," Anna commented. "But when I combed it, it fell out. So my mother cut it shorter."

These details were utterly trivial, but they fascinated Bronek all the same. "See? I know exactly how you look."

"Oh? Then, what side is my hair parted on?"

"Hm." Bronek pondered. "Your . . . left side."

"Right! Well, I know how you look, too."

"I don't look any certain way. I'm just normal."

"Oh, no, Bronek. You have dark eyes and they're deep-set, and you have a very soft face and soft lips, and a high forehead, and tonight your hair is combed, but usually it's sort of messy. And you have a little dimple in your chin. Only, it's a little bit off center, over there." She put her finger exactly on his dimple.

"Oh." Bronek felt embarrassed.

"I'm not criticizing you."

"You're not? I thought there was a problem."

"You silly boy."

He heard a smile in her voice.

"Where is your shoulder?" Anna asked softly.

"Here."

Anna leaned over by Bronek, and rested her head against his shoulder. Bronek rested in the deep windowsill, and he held her snugly, and they formed a single dark outline in the night.

"I have one more thing," Anna said. "I have to tell you something. But you must never betray me to the SS. Please."

"Of course not."

"Even if they threaten to kill someone you love? Like that

voice said?"

"Never."

"Bronek, I am – I am in a school. An Underground school."

Bronek said nothing.

"I'm hoping to be a teacher. After we're liberated. With the colleges and high schools closed, we will have to start teaching our children again."

"I know. Children are falling behind."

"It's very important work. But it's so difficult. So many of us get arrested."

"You will survive. You will. Always tell yourself that – no matter how dangerous it is. You have to be certain, inside your soul."

"I'm always afraid. I wish I could be more like you."

Bronek nodded. "I have something to tell you, Anna."

"What's that?"

"Well . . . About what I do."

Anna giggled. "Oh, you silly boy. I know that already."

"You do?"

"Of course I do. I figured it out when you showed the police your false papers."

"Oh." He held her for a long time, and neither one said anything. She knew the most private and dangerous secret about him. And he knew hers. It had happened in a heartbeat.

"Bronek, I'll never tell. No matter what they do to me."

"And I'll protect you, just the same."

Her head turned. Bronek felt her warm breath on his chin. He bent down his head and kissed her, their lips blending in the dark. It was a light, tender, reassuring kiss, a kiss that seemed to never end. Bronek felt something, a vital bond, now connect them. He felt a new kind of risk. His life was in this person's hands. He had to trust this person wholly and completely.

At last she stopped. "I feel stronger now."

"We can't go home," he reminded her. "It's curfew."

"No. I warned my parents."

"That's a good idea. I forgot to warn my father."

"Won't he worry about you?"

"Well, he knows me. I'm gone quite often."

"We'll sleep here, then?"

"We can't start a fire. But we have some blankets."

"And?"

"You can sleep in the other room. I'll sleep in here."

"Thank you, darling."

They unfolded several scratchy wool blankets that were in the dining room. The butler's pantry had a sink that trickled ice-cold water, and Anna patted her face. "You can keep my jacket," Bronek said.

He watched as she slipped off her shoes and pulled a blanket over her. She wriggled for a second. Suddenly she was holding her skirt outside the blanket.

"Can you hang that over a chair?" she asked. Surprised, Bronek lay her skirt over one of the big chairs. "Get all the wrinkles out, please."

Bronek tried to smooth it.

"Thank you."

He dropped to his knees, and leaned over her. He could not even see her in the darkness. "Well . . . good night, *Aniosia*" (Angel). He lightly kissed her cheek.

"Good night – Benny."

"You're not teasing me, are you?"

"Of course not."

"All right. Tonight, dream of not being afraid."

"Can I have four children?"

"Sure."

"And – darling?"

"Yes?"

"You can take off your tie to go to bed."

"Oh. Sure." He got up, tip-toed to the other room, took off his shoes and tie, and crawled beneath his blankets. And at some time during the night, Bronek felt a person slip beside

him. He felt her shiver against him, and he held her until she relaxed and fell asleep.

VIII

Bronek felt a chill across his legs. He rolled over on his blankets, dazed, until he realized that these were not his usual blankets. Then the fuzzy realization struck him that he was in a cold, foreign room. It was Saturday, October 16.

He was still wearing his shirt, pants, socks, and locket. For a while he lay on his back and watched the dust float in the air, and he let his thoughts float down onto him. He remembered images, feelings, sweet memories. Then he remembered: another person was present. He sat up and looked down at the figure beside him.

Anna was lying there, an olive-drab blanket wrapped around her. She had wrapped herself so tightly that the only parts still visible were her nose, cheeks, and mouth. As Bronek watched, her lower lip trembled. Cautiously, he rested his hand against her cheek.

Anna stirred. She emitted a kittenish moan, and stretched inside the blanket. Bronek quickly withdrew his hand, just as her eyes opened lazily.

"What's happening?" she asked dimly.

Bronek recoiled. "I was trying to warm your cheek," he admitted. "I guess my hand was too cold. I'm sorry."

Anna pulled his hand back to her cheek, and kept it there.

"Thank you."

Bronek watched her as she rested. Her cheek felt as soft and smooth as a satin pillow.

Presently Anna glanced up at the sunlight streaming in past the window shade. "It's time to get up, I'm sure." She closed her eyes again for several seconds. "Okay – I'm ready." She sat up, clutching her blanket in front of her, and motioned into the other room. "Bronek – please?"

"What?" Bronek looked behind him. Still lying neatly over the dining room chair was her skirt. He crawled over, scraping his palms against the wood floor, and retrieved it for her.

"All right – I need to put this on now."
Bronek shook his head slowly. "I'm not leaving," he said with a sly grin.

"Bronek," Anna said, embarrassment rising in her voice, "Give me that."

The gray light in the room cast fascinating shadows across her face. Her hair was a mess, but it looked adorable in its way. Seeing her unkempt – unprepared, really – made him smile. "Anna, I'm not moving."

"Ohh!" Anna sighed. "Boys!"

"It's not so embarrassing. Don't you have one of those – those – things?"

"A slip?"

"That's it. A slip."

"No, I haven't had a slip in years. The General Government does not produce women's underwear."

"Oh. That's true."

"It's quite true. Mother has shopped for them on the black market, but they're terribly expensive."

"True. Well. . . ."

"Do you –?"

"– I'll just –"

"– Promise not to touch?"

"If I have to."

"Promise!"

"Yes, yes, I promise."

Anna studied Bronek's face, knitting her brow skeptically. "Give me that," she said. She took her skirt from his hand. The blanket slid from her fingers.

Bronek was motionless on the floor as he gazed at her. Anna turned away from him, and looked the other direction. She rose until she was standing. She was wearing her blue blouse and patched white underwear: no necklace, no makeup – nothing about her was adorned or prepared.

She glanced back over her shoulder, and Bronek believed he saw a grin on her face. "I'll need to tuck this in," she said as she flirted with the bottom of her blouse. She turned to the side, but still looked away.

Bronek was dazzled; he felt he was peeking in on some terrific secret. Her neck was delicate porcelain, her torso small, her legs smooth and well-curved. She was thin, of course; but all Warsaw women were too thin. He watched wondrously as she held up her skirt and stepped into it. Her figure moved elegantly, enchantingly. It was unlike the way he pulled on his pants. The room was still cold, and she shivered slightly. Finally, she tucked in her blouse and buttoned her skirt. Just that suddenly, her legs were hidden behind a triangle of black wool.

She turned around and grinned at him. "Bronek, you are silly," she remarked. "You can blink now." She sat on the floor beside him, and tucked her legs beneath her.

"Oh," he said bashfully He touched her fingers, lightly. "You lost your ribbon."

"It must be in the blanket. I know my hair is awful."

"No, not at all."

"Is it that interesting? Watching me?"

"Yes," he answered defensively. "Everything is different when you do it. All I ever see is men doing things."

Anna nodded, considering what he had said.

"I think we have to go now, Anna."

"I know. I have to tell my family I'm safe."

"I sleep away from home quite a lot. My father knows I

might be gone."

They put on their shoes. Bronek slipped her trenchcoat around her and walked with her to the front door. "You leave first. I'll leave in ten minutes. Don't look behind you."

"I know all that, Bronek."

Bronek unbolted the door.

Anna stopped, and she turned around. She reached up and rested her frigid hands around his neck, sending a chill down his spine. Bronek wrapped his arms around her waist. "Watch after yourself, *Aniosia*" (Angel), he whispered.

But Anna did not lean up on her toes. Her face was somehow blank. "That is all, then?"

"Yes," Bronek said, politely.

"When will I see you again?"

"What? I don't know. I can't think so far ahead."

For a long time, she stood immobile. "So," Anna asked, "I'll see you when you decide it's best? When I get your next note, Bronislaw?" There was a matter-of-fact tone in the way she said his name.

"Maybe in a few days. Next week some time. How is that?"

Anna said nothing.

Bronek was confused. He studied her face, hoping to somehow divine the answer she wanted. "I don't know what else I can do. I'm sorry, Anna."

She did not move. Bronek felt something changing in her. Somehow she shrank in his embrace. "All right," she said quietly. She reached up and kissed his cheek, fondly, softly. Bronek did not know it was possible for a kiss to be sad. She opened the door and slipped out.

Something was not right. Bronek wanted to dash down the hallway after her, to stop her. But he could not leave yet. Dejectedly, he closed and bolted the door.

* * *

Bronek knocked twice, then twice more, on the apartment door. He was more nervous than usual this afternoon.

Adam answered. "How can I help you?" he asked. This was today's code exchange, as Zebra had related.

"Your neighbor reported a gas smell," Bronek said, rushing his code words. "Do you know about it?" His cover identity let Bronek roam the city, checking gas pipes and meters.

"You can check if you like," Adam said. He let Bronek slip inside.

Adam and Wiktor were standing in a dingy apartment. A layer of dust covered everything in it. Most likely, no one lived here. Still, the place felt ominous, disconcerting. Or perhaps it was just the excited tension in the air.

"What do you know?" Bronek asked. The fact that the meeting was in a private room was troubling. Like most conspirators, Bronek was nervous about new places.

"It is not good," Adam admitted. "Not good."

"More arrests," Wiktor said glumly. "It's all I hear. More arrests." As usual, Wiktor was smoking a hand-rolled cigarette.

"I don't know," Adam said. "I really don't know."

"I heard there was another big arrest," Bronek added. "In Ochota."

"Sixty people," Wiktor said. "I heard."

"It's the threat that bothers me," Adam commented thoughtfully. "They have arrested people before. Nothing unusual. But there's something new in this. The announcements. All those names."

"I've kept track of what I've heard," Wiktor said. He held on to his little hand-rolled cigarette. "Fifteen hundred arrested. I'm pretty certain."

Adam shook his head. "What is happening at Pawiak?"

"No trials, I know that much. The prisoners are being held as hostages."

"Are they going to put all those people through show trials?" Bronek asked.

"I'm sure they won't." Adam walked in a nervous circle. "It's those announcements that I dislike. Over and over. They're almost – begging people to betray the Underground." He was about to say more, but he stopped.

Wiktor grumbled something inaudible, and puffed on his cigarette.

"Well," Adam said abruptly, "We must move on."

"Nowak," Wiktor asked in a cool voice, "What is the news from command?"

Adam glanced around, even though no one else was there. "We have our next order," he said in a flat monotone.

"Yes," Wiktor observed, "The lottery."

"How is the surveillance, Granit? What do you know of the place?"

"The building is in the city center. It is not well-guarded. There are usually just a couple police there. The money must go to a different building."

"Well, we don't care about the money. We care about the tickets."

"Not the money?" Bronek asked. "We're just stealing the tickets?"

"Exactly. The casino and the lottery are important operations for them. The Underground has forbidden Poles to gamble, but, well – some people are tempted."

"A straight sabotage?" Bronek asked.

"That is all. Disrupt their operations. But it will do more. It will send a message."

"Hm." Bronek nodded admiringly. He liked sending a message.

No one said anything until Wiktor remarked, "Is this the best time?"

"Yes. Why not?"

"I think General Kutschera might become upset, when we break into his building and sabotage his lottery."

Bronek glared at Wiktor. If Adam said the lottery was their target, then that was that. Wiktor always questioned everything. "You heard the order, Granit," Bronek told him.

Wiktor glanced at the younger Bronek. He did not respond.

"So," Adam continued, "We know our next step."

"I'm doing surveillance," Wiktor said. "It's taking longer than usual. Police patrols are everywhere."

"What should I do?" Bronek asked.

"Work with Wiktor for now. We must know the Germans' habits – the guards, the employees, everything." Adam kept pacing. "Perhaps now is the right time. This might be just what people need to see. To remind them."

Bronek felt a rising excitement inside him. It was the most dangerous thing in the world, attacking the General Government. But he never panicked. He thought only about the mission. He would do so again, even though Bronek, the man inside Lot, worried for the lovely blonde girl with the quirky smile. "When do we attack?"

"The twenty-eighth," Adam said. "Does that give us enough time, Granit?"

"It's a nice number," Wiktor replied.

"The twenty-eighth it is, then."

They discussed a few more details of the surveillance. Finally, Wiktor dropped his cigarette butt on the floor, and ground it with his shoe. "Gentlemen, good luck," he offered, and he left.

Bronek waited for his turn to leave. Without warning, Adam leaned over toward Bronek. "So, Lot," he suddenly began, "Did you use the room?"

Bronek was surprised by the question. "Yes, yes. The room was – beautiful." He did not know what else to say.

Adam nodded graciously. "Well, what kind of a girl is she?"

"Oh. She's fine."

"Well, is she a sensible girl?"

"Uh – yes?"

"Good, good."

"She's delicate, really. She needs someone to protect her."

"Hm. You'll see her again, then?"

"See her? Of course I will. I love her." Bronek suddenly felt his cheeks blush, surprised by what he had said. He had not meant to say that.

"That's good – because that room is yours now."

"What?"

"It's compromised. We can't use it."

"It's mine?" Bronek thought about the key, hidden behind the mopboard in his home. He had an apartment now. "Thank you, Nowak – thank you."

"Of course, I cannot vouch for that building. I don't know who else uses it."

"Other people use it?"

"Most likely. There may be many keys out there."

"Oh." He thought of Anna, dressed indecently, while a complete stranger walked in.

"Lot, it's very important. To me, to all of us. You are our future. Please fall in love."

"I – I will?"

"And that's an order, Lot."

* * *

Anna was heading to her Underground class that afternoon of Saturday, October sixteenth. The sky was still gloomy and gray; the wind had shifted to the west. The air was warmer, ominous. Anna shivered inside her father's trenchcoat. She felt the school book tucked against her private area, in the secret pocket in her skirt. It was a mimeograph of a pre-war English book. She treasured that book; it seemed even more revolutionary than math. She battled the sense of foreboding that tormented her mind; she had a class to attend. She turned onto Madalinski Street, southwest of the city center, and she tried to focus on Bronek's certainty, his reassuring voice, his strong confident hands.

Anna kept her eyes down. The city was busy this Saturday afternoon, and she walked slowly. There were police patrols out, and many black trucks. She tried to think about her Bronek. He surely carried out many brave, dangerous missions, and yet he never showed any fear. She would go back to Under the Snout, and retrace their steps. If he was safe, she would certainly spot him, eventually. She repeated his words: *I will survive. They will not catch me. They will not catch me.*

She walked down an alley behind a deserted gas station, another reminder of how the city once was. She went inside the back door, and walked through the musty smell to the last door. She knocked once, then four more times. Something in the air felt wrong. She would be glad to be finished with this class.

Nothing happened; no one answered. No sound at all.

This was not right. She knocked her code knock again. Nothing. Anna's arms dropped to her sides. They were gone.

Where were they? She swallowed, and tried to think. *Think one thing at a time*, she told herself. They might have been arrested. If they were at Pawiak, being tortured, they might tell them. The Gestapo.

She had to leave – fast. She turned and shuffled outside. She crossed back onto Madalinski. No one paid her any attention; but now she was vulnerable. If the Gestapo were there, watching her, watching anyone who went in that door. . . . She hid her eyes from the police walking by, and she repeated to herself, *I will survive. I will survive. I will survive. Mother Mary, protect me!* She felt her mouth go dry.

She hurried. She could not run – that was too dangerous. She wanted to be home, inside, safe. She tried to hide inside her father's large coat. Not daring to look around, Anna turned the corner from Madalinski Street onto Niepodleglosci (Independence) Avenue.

And there, beneath the gray sky and the restless wind, Anna beheld a scene unreal. Her fear dried up inside her, replaced by a horrific dread. There before her, facing a brick apartment building, was a crowd of Polish civilians, their worn coats fluttering in the wind. But what was most unnatural about them was their expression, a sort of absolute shock coupled with disbelief. These people stared ahead, unblinking, as if they had been blinded by a meteoric light. Old women in brown babushkas folded their hands, moaning sad prayers, their rosary beads swaying beneath bony fingers. And on the sidewalk were puddles and puddles of blood, already darkening into a brownish red.

Anna stared and stared, not knowing what to make of it. She drew closer. The only sound was the feeble wailing of the old women. Little children stood by timidly, wanting to explore but not willing to come forward. The wall was sprayed with bullet holes. A girl, about twelve, dashed forward and inserted a red flower into a crack in the mortar. A few other people came up to insert flowers into the wall. Soon more came, and suddenly the sidewalk was littered with little flowers and big flowers and new flowers and old faded flowers.

She drew closer, and saw that the wall was splattered with droplets of blood, the same dark color as the brick. People dashed across the street, dropping flowers onto the sidewalk, praying to the gray sky, and then running away. The old women, however, did not move.

She drew closer. The odors of dried flowers and unwashed clothes wafted up to her. She found a young man near her, a bit younger than herself. "What – what happened?" she asked. Her own voice sounded unnatural to her.

The young man stared at the wall, as if transfixed. He did not answer her. He stood behind the praying women, and he stared.

She tried again. "Who was shot here? How many?"

The young man shook his head slowly, unbelievingly. "They were –" His voice sounded as if he were relating the most fantastical story. "They were – just –"

"Oh, dear God." She looked at the wall, whispered a prayer to the sky, and crossed herself. "How?" she asked. "How did it happen?"

The young man never turned away from the wall. "They were lined up. Right there. SS men – were over there. Machine pistols."

Two little boys overcame their hesitation. They approached the wall and whispered to each other.

"Was there – a battle?"

At last the young man turned, slowly. "There was no battle," he said, to no one. "Their hands were tied. They wore prison clothes. There were . . . twenty."

She felt her mouth open, her eyes grow wide, her ears unready for the news.

"It was no battle. It was – an execution."

The two young boys turned to face her. They raised up their hands, as if to display what their bravery had accomplished. Their fingertips were red.

The young man staggered off, his balance unsteady, and the empty wind blew over them all.

Announcement!

<u>For the protection of lives and property of the population against infringements of criminal elements</u>, the Governor General has enacted a decree for the fighting of attacks against the German work of reconstruction, which came into effect on October 10, 1943.

According to this decree, offenses against the laws, decrees, or official orders, with the intent of hindering or disrupting the German reconstruction work in the General Government, will be punished by death.

Co-conspirators and assistants will be punished as the perpetrator, and an attempted deed will be punished as the completed deed.

Offenses against this decree will be tried by the Security Police Summary Court. The sentences of this court will be carried out immediately.

The decrees are directed exclusively against criminals and saboteurs of the work of reconstruction, and are aimed to allow the working population to carry out their work in safety and security.

The High SS and Police Leader
In the General Government,
State Secretary for Essential Security

IX

Everyone listened. As soon as the loudspeaker crackled, all activity in Warsaw ceased. People collected together, and they listened. Each execution was followed by a bland, bureaucratic announcement over the loudspeakers. On the sixteenth, the voice announced that 20 hostages had been killed in retaliation for the killing of two German soldiers. On the eighteenth, it announced that 20 people had been executed at Pius XI Street. On the nineteenth, it reported the execution of 20 more hostages, including several women. On the twenty-first it listed 20 hostages executed the day before near the Gdansk train station. After the names were announced, the loudspeaker returned to playing soothing German classical music.

The city was aflame with rumors. Stories spread quickly, and a rumor begun in Zoliborz at noon could reach Mokotow in an hour. Hostages taken in Praga: more hostages taken on Marszalkowska Street: hostages again taken in Praga: two thousand hostages in all. Killings in Radom and in Lwow. Posters appeared on walls and kiosks, listing the dead in long, tightly spaced columns. Every evening, the loudspeaker crackled to life. The air was bitter, and the cold wind howled.

The frightful cold attacked his cheeks as Bronek peered over the brick wall. "Nothing," he muttered.

Wiktor lay on his belly beside him. He blinked his eyes and squinted.

"Why are you squinting?" Bronek asked. "We're not far away."

"I'm focusing my eyes. You'll understand when you're older."

They rolled over onto their backs. They were lying on a rooftop in the city center. Across the street was the lottery building. The autumn sun shined down, warming them on this chilly Friday afternoon. The black roofing paper felt warm against Bronek's back. He was wearing his darkest clothes, to camouflage himself against the black roof. Wiktor, however, wore his same cap, white shirt, and blue vest and pants. "Are we safe up here?"

"We're safe," Wiktor replied, not opening his eyes. "I know the landlord. He'll tip us off if there's any trouble."

"Of course." Bronek shook his head. "Do we really need to be up here again?"

"Yes."

"But we've already watched this place. All week."

"Listen to me, Lot. I'm in charge of surveillance. Akrobat is down on the street, and we are up here. We need to know all about the lottery building. When employees come and go, the guard schedule, everything."

"But isn't our plan to break in at night?"

"Yes."

"Then why are we here in the daytime?"

Wiktor groaned. "Listen. Lot, you're a smart young man. Here's your assignment. Watch the street. Tell me when you see any police, from either direction."

"Yes, sir." Bronek rolled over onto his stomach and gazed over the brick wall.

"Not all the time. Someone might see you."

"Yes, sir." Bronek pulled his head behind the edge of the wall. "I'm just nervous, I guess."

"Hm," Wiktor sighed in a way that suggested he did not

want to hear any more.

"I'm thinking about – that girl."

"Oh? Have you seen her again?"

"No, not this week."

"Does she even know you're alive?"

"Well, I wrote her a letter. I slid it under her door."

"Do you plan to marry her?"

"What kind of question is that? I don't know. I guess. Well . . . maybe."

"I see."

"Granit, how can I marry her? How?"

"How do you imagine? You drop by and see your priest."

"But things are too dangerous. For now, at least."

"Later?"

"I don't know. I haven't thought about later."

"Well, that's an answer, anyway." Wiktor still did not look up at Bronek. He looked as if he were leaning back in an easy chair, listening to a radio show. "Well, Lot, I think you should see her."

"But it's dangerous to arrange a date."

"It's dangerous to sabotage the lottery, too. Lot, you are a member of *Agat*. What are you talking about?"

"The police are everywhere. I haven't even been home in three days. You know what I mean."

"I certainly do know. And you're being a fool."

"I'm not!"

"Trust me, Lot. You are. Find a way to see her. Even if it's for five minutes in a café. Even if you just pass each other on the street. See her."

"Hmm." Bronek heard a motor from the street below. He leaned against the wall and peered over the edge. "A truck. Not marked. . . . It's going past."

"Lot, she wants to see you, to know you're safe."

"I suppose so." Bronek thought about what Wiktor had said. Wiktor was always a surprise. If they needed a car, he found one. If they needed guns, he obtained them. And he even knew how to deal with women.

Bronek lay back on the roofing paper, and he thought some more. "Well, that makes sense," he decided. "I'll try to see her. Even if it's just for a minute."

Wiktor, after his burst of advice, went silent. Bronek checked the street again. "Granit – a jeep."

Wiktor rolled over onto his stomach. "Yes, I see it." The black four-seat *Volkswagen* rolled to a stop at the guard house across the street. A silver-haired SS man got out.

"Who's that?" Bronek asked.

"I don't know. A *Sturmbannführer.*"

The SS major spoke with someone at the guard house. Then they both disappeared inside.

"Why SS?"

"I don't know."

"We're not planning on any SS."

"Come on," Wiktor said, crawling toward the attic door. "Let's check with Akrobat."

* * *

Anna was in an upstairs apartment in the Old Town. The only light was what filtered through the heavy shades. There were two other boys and one other girl, sitting at two folding tables in the living room. But Anna felt on edge. She had never been here before. She had no idea who lived here, if anyone. And one student was missing.

Ryzy, their instructor, came in from the other room. He seemed even more stooped than before, more weighed down. Anna immediately felt terribly for him. The aged man's fingers trembled as he spoke. "Thank the Blessed Virgin, you are here."

Anna nodded, even as uncertainty rose inside her.

"As you know," Ryzy explained weakly, "We had to cancel several of our classes. Now you understand why. It was one of our students, *Wielblad"* (Camel). Ryzy seemed to have to force the words from his tired lungs. "He was arrested."

The students looked at each anxiously. Anna's heart raced

with worry, her mind beset by questions. Had Wielblad been followed? Were they all at risk? Why were they meeting here? But she made a different inquiry. "Is he – alive?"

"We are still making investigations. God willing, he will be sent to forced labor in Germany."

"Are we in danger?" one of the boys asked.

"I believe that we are not compromised," Ryzy responded. He seemed to need a moment to regain his strength. "Now," he continued, "Let us study our English." They repeated their English drills for a tense hour until they left, one by one.

Outside, Anna stood at the edge of the Old Town square. The house fronts crowded together, nearly sealing off the square from the rest of Warsaw. Anna liked being here; the old buildings were painted pastel yellow and blue and lavender, colors she nearly never saw any more. Her English text safely hidden inside her dress, Anna buttoned her father's smelly, stained trenchcoat and made her way toward home.

She had no money for a streetcar; but the sky was sunny, and perhaps walking would calm her troubled heart. A cold northern wind blew in her face, scattering her hair in every direction. She spotted a patrol of Blue Police marching toward her, so she cautiously crossed the street.

"Carrots! Carrots!"

Anna turned. At the corner she spotted a young boy, gripping a burlap bag in front of him. The bag was so heavy that it seemed to pull him down.

Anna hurried over to the little boy. "Shh! Quiet!" she warned. "Police!" She pointed behind him.

The boy stared dutifully at the police. His expression did not change.

"Do you see those policemen? In the blue uniforms? Always stay away from them."

The little boy watched the police turn the corner, out of sight. Then he stared at her forlornly. "They came, and took my father," the boy said meekly.

The little boy barely came up to Anna's chest. He had no

jacket for the cold weather, and his burlap sack was nearly as big as he was. "Your father is gone?"

The lad nodded. "He's at a factory. Mama said it's in Germany." He looked down at his sack of carrots.

"I am so sorry." Anna rested her hand on his shoulder. "Well, how much for a carrot?"

He held up his sack for Anna. "Four zlotys," he said.

"Four zlotys apiece? Well, let's see." She knew that was too high a price, but she made a show of checking for money, just to entertain him. She held out her hands, and she made a big frowning face. "Oh, look. I don't have any money."

The boy studied Anna's palms. "Mama said, I can't give you a carrot until you give me the zlotys first." He sounded very determined when he said "first."

"Well, that's right. Your mother is right." Anna imagined this child's mother, sending her son to one corner to sell carrots while she shopped at another. "I see," Anna said politely. "Well, I'll bring some money with me tomorrow, all right? And then I'll buy a carrot from you. Will you be here?"

The boy nodded.

Anna smiled warmly. "Good! I'll look for you tomorrow. Remember – stay away from the blue uniforms. Never let them catch you!" Anna squeezed the boy's hand, and she noticed that his hands were almost as weak and bony as Ryzy's. The lad nodded. "God be with you!" Anna turned to leave, her cheeks somehow red with shame.

At last Anna made it inside her home. She locked the front door with a reassuring click, and hung her father's coat on the coat stand. Pushing her hair from her face, she went into the kitchen. Their home, cramped and old as it was, felt quiet, almost normal.

Her father, Jan Krzykowski, was sitting in the kitchen. A hand-rolled cigarette dangled from his lips. He looked up at his daughter. "Anna, you're home, you're home!"

"Hello, Papa. Don't get up." Anna kissed her father on the forehead. "I'm safe." Her father was 48. Before the war he had

been an actuary at an insurance company. But during the occupation, he had grown progressively weaker. He had worked on
the assembly line at the Kammler factory, but he became slow
and careless, a crime for which he could have been arrested. But
the manager had assigned him general cleanup duties, at less
pay, and the family survived on that. "Papa, you are not home
too early, are you?"

"No, no," Jan declared loudly. "I am home, just like you.
Mother is out shopping for us."

Anna inspected the procedure her father had set up. He was
hunched over a wooden box. On the counter was a small pile of
potatoes. "What are you doing, Papa?"

Her father pointed with the paring knife in his hand. "I have
to peel these," he said, with a nervous flutter in his voice. "I
have to peel them all."

"You're putting the peelings back into that?"

"That's the potato bin."

"I know that. I don't think the peelings go back in the bin.
Don't we have a pan for the peelings?"

"Mother said I need to peel the potatoes. We have to save
the peelings."

"Yes, we do, Papa." Something was just missing in her
father's mind. Anna knew to expect odd thoughts from him. But
he still unnerved her. Once he had been a father, and now he
was nearly helpless. Anna watched her father peel potatoes, the
peelings falling into the wooden potato bin. "Papa?"

"Yes?"

"What does Mama think of you smoking over the potatoes?"

Her father stared at her inquisitively. He took several
breaths, as if he were preparing a long-winded defense. "Well!
Well!" he began.

Anna interrupted his effort. "Forget it, Papa. It's fine. We'll
wash them."

Anna walked into the parlor. Krystyna and Aleksy were sitting on the floor, playing a game of rummy at the coffee table.

"Anna, you're safe," her sister exclaimed, relieved.

"Yes, I'm safe. Hello, you two," Anna said.

"Did you learn more English?" Aleksy asked eagerly.

"I know a lot of English, Aleksy." She watched them play rummy, feeling alien, lonely.

"What can you teach me?" Anna was teaching Aleksy some English as she learned it.

"How about spelling the numbers? One: o-n-e. Two: t-w-o. Three: t-h-r-e-e." For some reason, Aleksy liked the crazy rules of English spelling.

"One," Aleksy repeated. "Two. So, *one* has a *w* sound, and *two* has a *w* letter."

"That's right, Aleksy." Anna noticed something strange about her younger brother. "Aleksy, are you all right?" She bent over him. "You look sick. What's wrong with you?"

"I'm fine. It's just dark in here."

"Krystyna, look at him. Look how pale he is. His eyes are sunken. Is he sick?"

Krystyna looked up from her cards. "I know, I noticed that too."

"Aleksy," Anna asked, lifting his chin with her hand, "Are you eating?"

"Yes, I eat everything –"

"And his legs are soft," Krystyna remarked.

"Soft! What's wrong with him?"

"Mama says it's just no calcium. But I bet it's rickets."

"Rickets! Aleksy, are you getting outside?" Boys, even as young as Aleksy at 14, tended to stay inside if possible. They were more vulnerable during forced labor roundups.

"Yes!" Aleksy finally responded, in an irritated voice. "I mean, I try to. I don't know."

"You have to get sunshine. Krystyna, we ought to take care of him. He doesn't look well."

"We haven't had any powdered milk all week. Mama is out trying to get some cheese. We'll see about that," Krystyna concluded in her dismissive tone of voice. "I've got something for you, Anna."

"You do? What? What?"

Krystyna set her cards on the coffee table, and got to her feet.

"Wait!" Aleksy exclaimed. "You can't quit. I'm winning!"

"You play solitaire," Krystyna said. "We have to discuss something."

"Solitaire is boring. I want to play cards!"

"Solitaire is cards."

Krystyna led Anna into the bedroom, and shut the door behind them.

Anna blinked her eyes; this was her parents' bedroom, and she seldom entered it. The shades were pulled, and she had to adjust to the dimmer light.

"Sit down, Anna."

"Should we?"

"Sit down. Mama lets me in here, to work on our book-keeping."

As Anna sat on the bed, she smoothed her dress; it was her last wearable dress, and she could not let it get wrinkled. She ran her hand across the pink floral bedspread; it was so much softer than her scratchy blankets.

Krystyna went to the dresser, lifted the massive jewelry box, and slid out an envelope. "I found this beneath the front door," she said. "It's for you."

Anna jumped, her heart suddenly pounding. "For me!" The envelope was addressed, "For Anna," with no return address. But she knew the handwriting. "When did he come?"

"I don't know, I found it this morning. Is it from – that boy?"

"I can't say. I promised." She clutched the letter as if it were a precious gem. "He writes such beautiful things." And then she whispered, "Why now, why is this happening now?"

Krystyna sat on the bed across from her. "What is happening, Anna?"

Anna was glad they were alone. She often complained about her bossy sister, but she found it easier to talk to her than anyone else. "Krystyna, can I tell you something?"

"What is it?"

Anna swallowed, surprised at how difficult it was to force out the words. "I don't want to go to school. Not any more."

Krystyna reached out, and held Anna's hand. "Anna, what are you saying?"

"I can't, Krystyna. I just can't. With Papa's problems, and Aleksy looking like that – we have to do more."

"We do. I help mother with shopping."

"And I do nothing. Nothing."

"Anna, we agreed. All of us. You are going to school. To be a teacher."

"Krystyna, today I saw a little boy. He was selling carrots, trying to raise money for his family. He was so young. But he was helping."

"Anna, you are helping this family. You're going to school for all of us. That's important, too."

Anna thought about what her sister had said. "Do you think so?"

"Yes, Anna. We know the risks you take. It's for our future."

For a long time Anna said nothing. "I never thought of it that way."

"Mama may be getting me a job. That will help our food situation."

"Well, all right. For now. But if things get any worse –"

"Now, show me what's in that letter."

"Never! That's for me. But maybe I'll tell you about it. Later."

"Anna!"

* * *

"Where's my *bimber?*" Wiktor Kruczyk asked impatiently.

Magdalena Kruczyk did not budge from her seat at the kitchen table. "You know where it is. You can get it just as easily as I can."

"Eh!" Wiktor grumbled something unintelligible. "All I do

is work around here." He pushed himself up onto his creaky knees, went to the cupboard, and pulled down a large clear bottle.

Jerzy tapped the empty glass in front of him. "Don't forget me, Wiktor."

Wiktor filled their glasses, and sat down beside Jerzy. The kitchen was nearly dark. One electric light on the counter provided all their light. "Magdalena! Where's Zbig?"

"He's in the other room. He's just playing."

"Zbig! Come in here."

"Daddy!" Zbigniew squealed happily. He ran into the kitchen and leapt at his father, his little arms outstretched.

"Zbigniew!" Wiktor shouted with exaggerated emotion, a wide smile carved into his rough face. "Come in here with the grownups!" Wiktor grabbed his son and pushed him overhead like a little bag of cement. Zbigniew laughed heartily.

Wiktor rested his son on his knee. "Magdalena! Why is our son barefoot?"

"Zbig, where are your shoes?"

"I took them off. They're too small," Zbig complained.

"Oh, Zbig, I know they are," his mother conceded. "We'll go shopping for you next week. I might not find him any shoes," she added, speaking to her husband.

"I'll find him shoes," Wiktor stated flatly. "Get him his milk."

Magdalena got up and handed their son the glass of powdered milk left over from dinner. Then she wiped her hands on her faded brown house dress, and sat down again. She was a solid woman with a big Slavic face, and gray was appearing in her dark hair. But she still managed to look attractive, and her friendly smile brightened their home.

The three adults raised their glasses of *bimber*. Zbigniew dutifully held out his glass, using both hands. "To General Anders!" Wiktor announced. His gruff, forceful voice echoed through the room. They all drank a swallow of *bimber*. Zbigniew lifted his glass and drank his powdered milk.

"Do you understand, Zbig?" Wiktor said. "Who is fighting for us?" Wiktor bounced his son up and down on his knee.

Zbig, his head bobbing, watched his father, then his mother, and then his father again. "Anders?"

"That's right! Another toast! To the President, Roosevelt." They all, including Zbigniew, had another toast.

Without warning, the lamp shut off. Suddenly they were cast into darkness. Only faint moonlight filtered through the front window.

"All dark!" Zbigniew observed.

"Is it curfew yet?" Jerzy asked.

Magdalena checked the windup clock on the wall. "No, fifteen more minutes. The electricity ended early tonight."

"It's almost your bedtime, eh, Zbig?" Wiktor said, more as a statement than a question.

"No!" Zbigniew protested.

"Now, Zbig. I'll come in and read to you after your mother puts you to bed." Wiktor put his son onto the cold tile floor. "Give your father a hug." Zbigniew squeezed him around his neck. "And give your Uncle Jerzy a hug, too."

"Good-night, Uncle Jerzy," Zbigniew said. They hugged, and Magdalena led their son off to bed.

"And put some socks on!"

Jerzy watched Zbigniew walk into the bathroom. "He seems to be healthy."

"Yes, thanks to God." Wiktor poured himself another large shot of *bimber.* "He's at that nice age. He still thinks I'm the center of the world." He let the fiery liquor rest on his tongue before it slid down his throat. "He still thinks I can change things."

"Hm. What have you heard about Kutschera?"

"Shh!" Wiktor waved his hand angrily. "Don't let Zbig hear us." Wiktor pulled one of his wrinkled cigarettes from his pocket. It had become damp in his pocket, and he had to work to light it. The small red point was the only light in the room, illuminating his wide mustache.

From the bedroom, Wiktor heard his wife say, "No, Zbig, you can't wear your boots to bed. Put on your pajamas!"

Wiktor chuckled. "Magdalena likes the lamp at night," he told Jerzy. "Light the carbide lamp."

Jerzy got up and worked the carbide lamp. Soon a sharp light pierced the darkness. "What do you know about Kutschera?" Jerzy whispered.

"What number do you want to hear?"

"How many?"

"Ten on Friday, twenty more on Saturday. I don't know what's true or not any more."

"We knew this would happen. After they burned the Ghetto, last spring. They'll start on us next. You predicted it."

"Yes, yes," Wiktor said with a weary sigh. "Magda was able to obtain a newspaper today." He reached behind the stove and pulled out the copy of *Biuletyn Informacyjny* his wife had obtained that day.

"What does it say?" Jerzy asked anxiously.

"This essay is excellent." Wiktor squinted in order to read. "'The government policy is now exposed for the world to see. Only the height of Prussian arrogance could believe that the policy will succeed. The occupiers will be defeated. The entire Allied effort centers on Poland. The Atlantic Charter assures this. Our suffering inspires the world and motivates the Allies to victory. Poland will again be the deliverer of freedom.' It's signed, 'Z.'"

"True, true. Every word."

"This is a bad time, Jerzy. We are all outlaws. Sitting in my own home, reading this newspaper, makes me a criminal. Who could have predicted? The worst thing is what's going on with our children."

"They're surviving. Zbig is safe."

"No, Jerzy. They are not safe." Wiktor smoothed his oily hair. "When you try to raise children – then you'll understand."

Jerzy poured them some more *bimber*. Suddenly he jerked up his head. "Police!" he whispered.

Wiktor listened. He heard the sound, growing outside his door. It was the sound of boots marching on stones. The two Kruczyks were silent as the patrol passed outside. Then the sound faded down the street.

Wiktor breathed a sigh of relief. "Your hearing is better than mine," he admitted.

"Wiktor, why don't we go to Nowak? We must do something."

Wiktor stared into the darkness. "You and I, we're soldiers, Jerzy. Soldiers of the Underground. We follow orders."

"Come on, Wiktor –"

"I said, no." His voice carried a tone so determined, few people challenged it. "We cannot go to Nowak. He cannot know that you and I are brothers."

"I know, I know. I'll never tell him."

"Brothers should not be in the same unit. Nowak would never allow it."

"I know. I insisted on joining."

"And I only agreed because I trust you. You may be just a boy –"

"I'm grown up! Twenty-one is grown up."

"Well –" Wiktor began.

"We only have fourteen years between us, remember."

"Well, yes." Their age difference had once seemed huge. Now, perhaps, it no longer was so great. "– But, anyway, you are dedicated."

"I just wish there were something I could do, Wiktor."

"There is something, Jerzy. There is a job that does not involve guns."

"What, then?"

"Record all the killings."

"Record them?"

"Dates, names, locations. We need evidence. So that no one can deny them. In the future, everyone must know what happened. When. Where."

"All right. All right, I can do that."

"You're not in school, so you have all day. Keep your ears open. Follow SS trucks. Track them down. Be a witness, with your own eyes. That will be important, believe me. So children and grandchildren – like Zbig – can understand."

"I can do it, Wiktor."

"Excellent. Now, it's reading time. Zbig won't go to sleep until I read to him." Wiktor raised himself up onto his sore knees, his balance showing some effect of the liquor. "You'll need to stay here tonight. It's curfew."

X

"Bronek! Wake up!"

Bronislaw rolled over on his blankets and squinted his eyes. It was Eugene. "Hm?" he mumbled blankly.

"Come out here! You have to see this!"

Bronek thought. Then he remembered he had come home to eat dinner, and had stayed past curfew. He was home this morning. It was Monday, he guessed. "That's right." He pulled himself up to put on some clothes.

Outside, a small crowd of people had already gathered on the sidewalk. Bronek and Eugene hurried down the steps. Neighbors and passersby looked up, squinting their eyes in the morning sunlight.

"Bronek! You!"

It was Mister Skonieczny. "Good morning, Mister Skonieczny," Bronek said, his eyes still sleepy.

"Don't 'good morning' me. I want an answer!" His scant hairs waved annoyingly atop his bald head.

"I don't know anything," Bronek offered in his ignorant voice.

"I don't believe you! What about that?" He pointed with his stubby finger back at their apartment building.

Bronek looked up. There, across the Skonieczny apartment

on the second floor, was a slogan painted in thick black paint. The message was stark:

"THE PIG WHO LIVES HERE ATTENDS GERMAN MOVIES."

"Wow!" Eugene said admiringly. "What a job!"

"Look at it! Look at it!" Mister Skonieczny's face was now red with rage.

Bronek merely shrugged his shoulders innocently. Behind him a pedestrian, an older man, muttered "Traitor!" and went on.

"Isn't it interesting," Mister Skonieczny remarked, "That this happens just after I discuss my son with you? About a matter I asked you to keep secret?"

"I didn't get him into trouble," Bronek said dryly. "Just as I'd promised." Bronek truly felt blameless. The matter had gone to the Directorate of Civil Resistance. An agent had followed Leszek, and had seen him going to a German movie house. So, there it was. Leszek had gotten himself into trouble.

"Look! Look at that! How do you explain that! Oh," Mister Skonieczny said, moaning loudly, "This is terrible. I have never been so humiliated. Never!"

Bronek looked around. Beside the front stoop was Leszek Skonieczny, pouting, looking wounded. His mother stood over him, holding his hand and patting his arm. She seemed to be consoling him.

"Bronek, this affects more than just my son, you know. Look at his mother! She did nothing, and she must suffer, too." He held Bronek's arm, and leaned forward so that their noses nearly touched. "Is that fair? Is it?"

"Well," Bronek replied, "Then it shouldn't happen again. Excuse me, Mister Skonieczny." Bronek tugged his arm from Skonieczny's grip. He had missions today. First he had to check his dropoff site for any messages from Zebra. Then he had to visit the railroad yard, and search for pieces of coal that might have fallen off the trains. Even this simple job might take hours.

Hiding a secret smile, he slid back inside, leaving Mister Skonieczny with his embarrassment.

* * *

Karol Pietraszewicz was at Hale Mirowski, the black market, that afternoon. He was finished at the streetcar shop for the day, and he was now wearing his big overcoat, with the pockets sewn inside to hold his bottles. He calculated that he had 90 minutes to shop before he had to be home to prepare dinner; perhaps he could arrange some quick deals.

This was the new Hale Mirowski. It had once been one of Warsaw's busiest shopping districts. Everyone came here, to purchase all sorts of things for their families. But now the store windows were empty, and nearly all the selling was done on the street, in the illegal trade. Despite the ban, despite the police roundups, people wandered this way and that, buying and selling. A churning hunger drove them. Risking arrest was simply part of the new way.

Already the shopping square was crowded. The sky was mostly cloudy, and the air was bitingly cold. The street was cluttered with wooden stands, where vendors sold legal goods. But the legal goods, when they appeared, were far too expensive for Poles to afford. More important were the people standing like monumental Greek columns, their overcoats bulging. Karol wandered around for a while, just to listen to the vendors. On one corner, an emaciated little boy shouted, *"Nowy Kurier Warszawski!" (New Warsaw Courier!)* On the next corner, an old woman in a babushka, ignoring all pretense of secrecy, shouted feebly: "Kielbasa! Pork kielbasa!"

Karol was immediately interested; his sons often went months without pork. "How much for kielbasa?" he asked in a loud whisper.

The old woman was hunched over in a permanent crouch. "Eh – prices are bad today. I smuggled this from Czestochowa."

"Oh, all the way from Czestochowa, really?" Karol remarked with a chuckle. "Well, perhaps it is blessed. How much for this wonderful kielbasa?"

"Prices are bad, very bad . . . fifty zlotys apiece."

"Fifty? For one normal kielbasa? That's ridiculous."

"Twenty. Twenty zlotys."

"That's still ridiculous."

"Twenty zlotys. I cannot ask for less."

"I'm sure I can do better." Karol turned to leave.

"But this is the finest kielbasa! From Czestochowa!"

Karol left the old woman waving her arms after him. He decided to mingle in with the throng, to learn what he could. Over here, children were selling apples and newspapers. Over there, an aristocratic woman was hawking her diamonds; a German woman stopped, and the two huddled together to finish the purchase.

Unfortunately, the old woman was right. Karol discovered that prices for meat had doubled from the week before. All he could find were some exorbitantly expensive chicken gizzards, some headcheese that had a foul smell, and some pork that was mostly fat. Karol listened some more to the street hubbub. A tinge of desperation built up inside of him; shopping was not going well today. "Vodka, vodka, vodka," he whispered hoarsely, hoping to be both heard and not heard. "Highest quality. Vodka, vodka."

After several minutes, some people approached him, and he began the arduous task of bartering. There was no set price for his product; he talked, he cajoled, he flattered. He raised his price for old men who said they were in chronic pain; he lowered his price for people who offered valuables, such as jewelry. The whole process was degrading to Karol Pietraszewicz. He was a metalworker, not a street hawker.

After about an hour, he possessed a gold ring without any stone in the setting, half a head of cabbage, a bag of wet sugar, a few zlotys, and none of his bottles. This was good work. With some goods to trade with, he meekly went back to the old woman whom he had previously shunned. He found her in the same spot.

"Hello again," he said.

The old woman laughed a cackling kind of laugh. "Eh – back again. You discovered I was right!"

Karol tried to be polite. He had to get meat for his boys. "I suppose you are," he replied. "Do you still have your kielbasa?"

The old woman began to think. "Yes, yes. Prices are going up again, you know."

"I have a beautiful ring. How much kielbasa can it buy me?"

"Eh, well, let me see it."

Karol held on to his ring (his prize catch) and glanced around, looking for police. He opened his hands so she could see it.

Suddenly Halina Rogala, his neighbor, hurried past him. "Karol Pietraszewicz! Have you heard?"

"Halina! Heard what?"

She slowed but did not stop. "There's a shipment of turtles. From Greece!"

"What?" Karol asked incredulously. "What in the world –?"

"Gourmet turtles! Come with me!"

"Good-bye, ma'am," Karol hurriedly said. He clutched the ring and dashed off with Misses Rogala to chase after turtles.

"Wait, wait!" the old woman called out after him. "I'll take the ring!"

* * *

Bronek's first two missions were done; Zebra had delivered a message from Adam, and a small pile of coal sat beside the stove at home. Now he was sitting at a booth in the Sim cafe. The Sim was run by famous actors from before the war, and it was possible to spot famous people there. It was a small room with white plaster walls and dark ceiling beams overhead, and small windows that blocked the street noise. The tables were solid old wood, darkened over the decades. With two baby grand pianos in the corner, the Sim was known for piano music – so long as it was not Chopin. The Sim still had the feel of old

Warsaw about it; Bronek could imagine that Warsaw, if he ignored the Germans.

Bronek rubbed his fingers on the varnished table top and glanced around. The place was not crowded yet – a few workers sat at the small tables, a couple more at the stand-up bar. They were laughing and drinking vodka. The Sim had high-quality vodka. He decided to wait at the bar, to make sure he would see her. He got up and walked over to the bar, avoiding eye contact with the others.

Bronek smoothed back his hair. That was another concern. His hair was combed into a decent pompadour, and he had decided not to wear his fedora. Now he wished he had. He should have his hat. Bronek felt the muscles in his neck tighten as he tapped the table.

At last he spotted Anna entering the café. She was still shivering from the cold when she came to his table. "Hello," he said. "You're here." Bronek hastily kissed her hand.

Anna was wearing her father's well-worn trenchcoat, and her faded beige dress; but she still looked wonderful to him. There was something not lively about her eyes, however. "My mother showed me a note," she said hurriedly, "It told me to be here in an hour –"

"Yes, yes." He took a deep breath, trying to calm his nerves. "I decided I wanted to see you. Even if it's just for a little bit. So . . . how are you?"

"How am I? What in the world do you mean?"

"I just want to ask. That's all."

"Bronislaw, you brought me all the way down here just to chat?"

"Well, I – I –"

"I'm terrified to be here. I had to talk my mother into letting me go."

"We'll be all right." He squeezed her hand. "I just want to visit with you. Mister Maszynski, the waiter, he'll watch after us."

"What are you thinking, Bronislaw? Warsaw is dangerous."

"I know that. I just –" he stammered bashfully. "Let's sit down."

Bronek felt a cold hand on his shoulder; he instantly stiffened. It was the man beside him. "Calm down, my friend. Have a drink with me."

He was a short, squat man, with a red face and a button nose. His bald, egg-shaped head was broken by a constant smile, which never changed. "Join us all in a drink!" He was a German. Probably some civil servant.

"No thank you."

"Nonsense, it is a fine day for a drink." He motioned for a drink. The bartender promptly served Bronek and Anna drinks in shot glasses, but his expression made it clear that he did not enjoy this job. Bronek eyed his drink. The liquid in the glass was a filmy gray color. Bad *bimber*. Usually the Sim had quality drinks.

Now Bronek understood why people had gravitated to the bar. The Sim was not in the boycott, and Germans were allowed to frequent the place. Usually this no longer happened; Germans traveled in groups, because of the risk involved. Seeing a German amongst them, speaking passable Polish, was an unheard of occurrence. And he was even alone. His liquor gave him the courage to come in here. Another German, looking for friends.

The German gripped his glass of *bimber* tightly in his stubby fingers. "Drink my friend, drink!" He spoke Polish pretty well, with a southern accent. Not quite Bavarian, perhaps from Stuttgart. For some unknown reason, he focused on Bronek. Perhaps he was done lecturing the others. "Now, I want to ask you something," he started, leaning toward Bronek. "You look like an honest young man. So I know you will answer me directly. We are not all that bad, are we?"

The foul stench of liquor hung on the German's breath, and his egg-shaped head wobbled on his neck. Bronek felt Anna's hand clutch his arm. Through his father's suit jacket, he felt her tremble. She was terrified.

The German continued intently. "Now, I have nothing against the Poles. I have been here for two years, and I like Warsaw. I like Warsaw!"

Behind him, Bronek felt other people shift uncomfortably and touch their drinks, as if they had already heard this part.

"It is this Underground that is the problem. All this, here –" (he waved his hand in the air to symbolize "all this") "– Is the fault of the Underground. Can't you go to these leaders, and convince them to stop?" His thin crack of a smile never wavered.

"I don't know of them," Bronek said quickly. He fidgeted with his drink, afraid to lift it from the bar.

No one else offered a word, so the German continued. "When I first arrived, this was a nice place. Once we cleared out the Jews, with their typhus. I have seen your Old Town, the Adolf Hitlerplatz, the Royal Castle –"

"– Pilsudski Square," Bronek said, quietly but firmly.

The other drinkers seemed to collectively catch their breaths, all at once. Anna froze; she gripped so tightly that she hurt his arm.

The German nodded graciously. "Yes, it is Hitlerplatz now. But it was a nice city. Now, thanks to this Underground, we cannot go outside without fear."

Bronek felt the others hunch their shoulders. But he did not flinch. "Yes. Things are . . . frightening now."

The German leaned forward, until he was near Bronek's face. He seemed wholeheartedly determined to convince Bronek, or at least to make Bronek like him. "I know that is true. For you as well as for me. We must – create order here. That is all the police are trying to do. Bring order to Warsaw. Then it can be a safe city again!"

Bronek stared nervously at him. "Safe enough to play Chopin again." Bronek said hopefully.

The German did not respond at first. His beady eyes were shiny from the liquor, like the glass eyes inside a toy bear. His wide smile gave way a bit. Then he waved to the bartender.

"Here, finish your drink," he said. Then he shouted, "Give the young man another one!"

The German was regaining his smile. Bronek did not smile. He did not raise his voice. "You may have my drink. I have work to do." He left the German leaning against the bar. As he was leaving, a middle-aged man whispered, "Thank you."

Outside, the clouds nearly touched the roofs of the century-old buildings, and a cold, gray drizzle hung like a mist in the air. "Can you spare some time?" Bronek asked.

Anna shivered inside her coat. For a long she did not move. But she said, "Yes. Yes. I suppose so." She tied a colorful babushka over her head.

"Good. Let's walk together." He led her north from the city center. The street was still crowded with knots of people. Above everyone the sleek, art deco Prudential Building towered over the city. It was built in the 1920s, for the insurance company, and was the tallest building in Warsaw. It, too, was cruelly out of place in the Nazi empire.

They waited as a patrol of Blue Police marched by, and then they crossed the street. Anna tried to huddle against him as they walked. "Benny, will we be out long? I'm so frightened."

"I know." He shook his head angrily. "On Saturday, there was another execution: twenty more people. Two of them were women."

Something seemed to happen to Anna. Her eyes blinked, uncontrollably. She looked down. "Last week – I saw a little boy. I promised I would buy a carrot from him. But he's missing. I've looked for him every day since. I don't know what happened to him."

"I understand, Anna."

"One little boy should not matter to me. But – I can't make him not matter."

Bronek kept them moving. He had something he needed to show her. He reached Leszno Street, and he turned west.

Bronek took a nervous, hesitant breath, to brace himself. He knew the sight well, but every time it unnerved him. There, along the entire north side of the street, was a long brick wall, dark and foreboding. Shards of broken glass protruded menacingly along the top; they shined brilliantly when the sunlight struck them just so. The wall looped in a vast, misshapen ring around the northwestern part of the city. Inside was the deserted Jewish Ghetto. On this side were policemen, and posters, and crowded streetcars. Inside were burned buildings, a black emptiness. And high in the window of a burned-out building sat a human skeleton. It was propped against a window frame, its bones nibbled by rats to a ghoulish white. It was missing an arm and a foot, but otherwise was intact. From its window perch, the skeleton smiled freakishly over the city.

Bronek crossed to the wall. For him the wall was like the wrong end of a magnet; the closer he forced himself, the more it repelled him. He stopped and stared. With cold, trembling fingers, he touched the brick barrier. He yearned to get behind that wall, to something that had existed many years before. But all he could do was whisper, and hope that he was heard. He touched his locket and whispered a greeting that only he among the living could hear.

"I don't like being here," Anna warned him. "We should go."

"We will tear down this wall," he said at last in a dry voice, "We will tear it down. But the wall will never go away."

"Bronek," Anna asked cautiously, "Why are we here?" He did not answer. "Is there something you want to show me?"

"Inside. In there."

"What is, darling? What is it?"

He looked down at her with sad, anguished eyes. "Me."

"How is that? I don't understand."

"Me. I lived in there."

Anna was so startled, she staggered backward. "You – you lived in the Ghetto?" Shock and concern were etched into her childlike face.

Just then, something happened. "SS! Street hunt!"
Bronek saw nothing; but he heard the whispered warning. And

then he felt it. "Quick!" he commanded, "This way!"

"Why? What are you doing –?" Then she felt it, too.

Ahead of them, pedestrians began backing up, pushing to go the wrong way. A black truck appeared before the throng of people, attacking them all. "Run! Now!"

The black apparition lurched to a stop. Bronek heard the soldiers leap out, their boots rumbling on the paving stones. They were fanning out, trapping their quarry against the Ghetto wall. People pushed against each other to get away.

"Go!" He shoved Anna into an alley.

Anna shrieked, and stumbled onto the cold stones. He jumped into the alley, hitting his knees on the stones, and slid on his stomach until he was beside her.

Behind him, Bronek heard voices. *"Halt! Halt! Hände hoch! Hände hoch!"* He grabbed Anna by the waist and dragged her behind a small pile of paving stones and debris. She hit her shoulder against the wall and shrieked. He pushed her head down and crouched down beside her. "Shh!" Drops of rain fell silently from his hair.

From the street, Bronek heard the noises. Protests of "We did nothing wrong!" Authoritative shouts in German. Instructions from an SS officer: "You are under arrest for violations of the Decree of October Second! You are now prisoners of the SS! You will come with us for transport!" Then he heard another brief discussion, in German. He pulled Anna close to him. He touched his locket, hanging inside his shirt. It was still there.

Anna placed her lips by his ear. Ever so softly, she whispered, *"Die Gassen* means the alleys."

Bronek jumped. "This way!" He grabbed her hand and they dashed down the alley. He heard her panting, her shoes scuffling. Then he heard the command: *"Halt!"*

Bronek reached the next street and turned. Abruptly, he stopped. *Don't run*, he told himself. *Never run.* A rifle shot pierced his ears. "Oh, God!" he exclaimed. He felt Anna grab his arm through his coat. "Anna! Are you hit?"

She did not answer.

Bronek looked at her, half-expecting to see blood. "You're not hit?"

She shook her head.

"Thank God. Don't run. Walk as fast as you can." Bronek led her westward, tugging on her arm. He listened intently for any sound behind them.

They walked through another dank alley. Bronek felt her grip his arm with both hands. He knew she was holding on with all her strength.

They reached the far end of that alley, and emerged onto another street. They zigzagged through another alley, then another. Finally they emerged onto a quiet street, he did not even know which one. There were few people here. The lack of commotion was palpable. These people must not have heard the rifle shot; they had no hint of the street arrest that was underway. Slowly, Bronek felt himself breathe again. "Anna – are you all right?"

For a long time she said nothing, but Bronek heard her panting. He glanced down at her; she still stared straight ahead.

"I – I just –" She mumbled some unintelligible thoughts.

"Anna?"

"I ran from the SS. I nearly was arrested. To – chat in a café."

"We just have to be careful. Next time we'll make a different plan."

"Next time?" Anna shook her head, hesitantly at first, but then forcefully. "Benny, you are so sweet. Can't you see? This is not the time!"

"It's not?"

"We can't meet just to make conversation. It's wrong!" Worry was etched into her face. "You are – so sweet and so brave. If I were able to – I would pray that we could be in love."

"Anna – what are you saying?"

"But not now. The world is too cruel. We can't – we can't."

"Yes we can. We can try meeting in safe rooms. We just

must be careful –"

"No. No more!"

To Bronek she looked as frightened as a wounded bird. He wanted to hold her, to protect her. He raised his arms to wrap himself around her; but she pushed him away.

"Benny, precious – good-bye!" She turned and dashed down the street, leaving Bronek standing alone on the sidewalk.

At first he darted after her. "Anna, wait!" He crossed the street after her, but his voice only made her run faster. His confusion got the better of him, and she was gone. He stopped at the corner, dismayed, as she vanished from his sight.

* * *

That evening, everyone talked about turtles. Even before he got inside, Bronek heard the news from his neighbors. He also heard it from his brother. But mostly he heard it from his father, all during dinner.

"Isn't this wonderful, boys? Real turtle soup."

His father made a grand production of setting out their antique china serving bowl. It was brimming with a pale brown broth. "Here it is!"

"They're not snapping turtles, are they?" Eugene said jokingly. "I hope they don't bite."

Karol ladled equal amounts into the three soup bowls. "I don't want to hear any jokes about snouts and knuckles. I used the whole turtle, and that's that."

Karol sat down and said their prayers. But immediately, he started again. "Well, Bronek, don't you want to hear how we came to have turtle soup tonight?"

Bronek's hair was dry, but he had not made the effort to comb it. Now he stared at his bowl. "Sure. I guess."

"I was shopping at Hale Mirowski today. Not having a good day at all, to be honest. Anyway, I was bartering for some kielbasa, when suddenly Misses Rogala rushed by me, as if she were being chased by a lion. So I followed her to some smugglers she knew. Do you boys want to know where they came from?"

"The smugglers?" Eugene asked.

"No, the turtles," Karol said. And then he added, "Oh. You are making a joke. Well, I will tell you. Greece! All the way from Greece!"

"Oh."

"It so happens that an entire boxcar load of gourmet turtles was heading to Berlin. But the train was derailed outside Warsaw. Well, some smugglers heard about it, and bribed the railroad workers for the entire boxcar. They smuggled thousands of these turtles into the city. How about that? Eat, boys, eat. Don't let it get cold."

Bronek dipped his spoon into the soup. It was turtle soup, all right, with chunks of stringy turtle meat and potato slices for filler. It felt – soft. But for some reason, he could not even taste it.

"Well," their father asked, "Did anyone hear any news?"

"The British," Bronek said sluggishly, "Moved toward Rome. I heard they crossed the Trigno River."

"Well, that is good news," Karol remarked.

"Kassel was bombed, too," Eugene added.

"That was on Friday," Bronek said. "The British bombed it."

"Any news about General Patton?" Karol asked. Their father had a near-mystical regard for Patton.

Bronek and Eugene shook their heads.

"They'll have to hurry to get here before winter. If only they could release Patton. He could move his army to Russia, and attack from the East. Then this war would be over quickly."

"I don't think the Skoniecznys should get any turtle," Eugene commented. "They're traitors."

"Don't insult them, Eugene. They still need to eat."

"But –"

"Eugeniusz!"

"Yes, sir."

"We should be thankful when things like this happen. The

Lord is blessing us. And we have more." Their father paused, to let the suspense build. "I bought – nine turtles. I hid them inside my coat."

They ate together silently for a little while. Bronek continued to poke his spoon into his soup. "Papa?" he finally said.

"What is it, Bronek?"

"Why do things have to be so complicated?" Bronek mumbled.

"What was that?"

Bronek stirred his soup, tasting nothing. "Good soup," he finally said.

XI

On Thursday evening Bronek waited. He waited until night, until his father and brother were asleep. In the dark, he slipped out of his blankets, and he put on his darkest clothes. Then he tiptoed into the kitchen and fumbled for his jacket.

"Bronek?" Eugene whispered from the parlor. "Are you up?"

Bronek grimaced unhappily. "Eugene, go back to sleep," he whispered.

"What are you doing?"

"Nothing."

"Where are you going?"

"Nowhere." He pulled on his short worker's jacket. He touched his locket, for luck, and he whispered some hopeful words. Then Bronek snuck out of his home.

Warsaw after curfew was black; not a streetlight or window was lit. And it was silent. The stately stone buildings seemed frozen, as in a grainy photograph. But Bronek did not need daylight to get around. He could navigate Warsaw's streets blindfolded. Keeping to the shadows, avoiding the numerous police patrols, Bronek made it to the alley behind the lottery building.

The alley was deep and narrow. He felt as if he were in a canyon. Even his own breathing seemed too loud. Now he began to worry. Only the last message from Zebra, delivered that day, had told him the time and location of the rendezvous. Were they here? Had something happened?

He heard a catlike meow. He stopped.

"Lot."

"Granit." Squinting, Bronek just made out two outlines against a brick wall.

"No time to waste," Wiktor whispered. "Let's go."

"Where's Akrobat?" Bronek asked. "Is he in place?"

"He's on the street, keeping guard," Adam said. "Let's get to work."

Wiktor and Bronek crouched before the rear door of the lottery office, while Adam stood behind them. The door had a large deadbolt lock. Coolly, Wiktor slipped a key into the lock. It worked; Wiktor knew, and bribed, some employee inside for a key. Gingerly, he swung open the door.

"How did you know the key fit this lock?" Bronek whispered.

"I'm sure of it. I've already been inside."

And on the morning of October 29, Varsovians found their streets littered with lottery tickets, thousands of lottery tickets, as if they had held a ticker-tape parade without informing the Germans. People grabbed for the scraps, expecting some announcement. The tickets all had "Boycott the Lottery" stamped across them.

German investigators later determined that, in a well-coordinated action, six lottery offices had been entered at once. All the records inside had been destroyed, and thousands of lottery tickets stolen. Then the Underground conspirators had driven through the city, tossing tickets everywhere. Many fundamentals remained unknown. The Germans never learned that the attack was coordinated by "Dash," an Underground branch of the Labor Party. Dash organizers never knew Bronek. Bronek never knew them. But it was an excellent boost for Polish morale. For an entire day, people watched the German patrols sweep the gutters. For a day, they remembered that they were not powerless.

Far from powerless, the Underground attacked and attacked Warsaw's targets. On October 22 Underground soldiers strafed several police cars with machine-gun fire, killing and wounding several German policemen. On October 23 agents of the Youth Union of Struggle threw a bomb into the Podlaski Bar, which was open to the SS and police only. The next morning, outside Warsaw, Home Army soldiers derailed the Warsaw-Berlin express train and two other supply trains, injuring train employees and damaging boxcars and rolling stock.

The police struck back. SS and other police forces carried out extensive street sweeps, arresting hundreds at a time. So efficient were the police efforts that Poles were set to be executed without real conspirators ever being apprehended. SS *Oberführer* (Senior Colonel) Bierkamp, the Security Police and SD Chief, recommended that prisoners be brought before a police summary court, so the government could declare that persons were convicted but subject to reprieve. This tactic fit Kutschera's plan perfectly. On October 22 the General Government executed 10 prisoners at Mlynarska Street. The next day police executed some 300 victims at Pawiak prison, and 20 more at Miedzeszyn Embankment. On October 25, 20 victims were shot at Pawiak prison. On the 26th, about 30 more on Leszno Street. Terror was the order of the day.

After each execution, the loudspeakers blared across the city. The speaker dryly announced the latest execution, and listed the names of the most recent hostages convicted of violating the Decree of October 2. These announcements always ended with soothing German music. The loudspeaker reports caused great alarm and confusion in the population, for listeners could not keep track of all the names as they were being read. So on October 30 a poster, ominous red to attract attention, listed 37 persons scheduled for execution. The poster ended with a plea to end all Underground actions. It was the first poster to list the names of victims. They would soon earn the nick-name "raspberry posters."

But Warsaw burned with a heat that would not cool. On the contrary. November 2nd and 3rd saw attacks on German soldiers and police officials, who were seriously wounded. And on November 5, a German civil servant was walking home from his job. There was nothing evil or even noteworthy about him. However, he commanded a rail yard, and its efficient operation depended on him. As the German turned the corner onto Krzyzanowski Street, two Polish teenagers leapt from an alley. The boys raised their Radom 9mm pistols and fired. In seconds, it was finished. The Polish boys dashed away without uttering a word, as the German sank to the sidewalk.

Whispers and rumors were rampant. But all questions were soon answered by a terse announcement. The posters of November 10 were tacked to walls and kiosks everywhere. Immediately, people collected together in clusters. They inspected the posters as they would religious documents, touching the parchments as if they held talismanic qualities. For indeed, the posters had an awesome power. Lives were transformed.

At the Pietraszewicz home, Karol's questions filled the kitchen during dinner. "You checked the poster?" their father asked.

"Yes," Eugene answered.

"Which poster was it? What was the date on it?"

"Today. The tenth."

"And it had no names we knew? None at all?"

"No. I didn't recognize any names."

"Praise God for that." They said their prayer. To the prayer Karol added, "For the liberation of Kiev this week, we give thanks. And for having Bronek with us here today, we humbly give thanks." Bronek sat silently, but he squirmed nervously. He now spent most evenings away, at his cover address at 78 Platynowa. But occasionally he returned home, to see his father and brother. Yes, there was risk involved. But he could not just leave them.

Karol still wanted to know about the posters. "Did you learn any other information?" he asked.

Bronek stirred his soup blandly. The turtle stew was gone. This concoction consisted of barley and some chunks of potato, thickened with flour. The barley husks stuck to his tongue, and he had to grind them with his back teeth. The soup had no taste at all.

"There were fifty new names," Eugene replied. "Of people sentenced."

The strain showed on their father's proud face. "Terrible. How can they expect to get away with this? How?"

Bronek had nothing to say. A knot had formed in his stomach, and not from the food. Bronek was straining to maintain relations with Anna. He had written her several notes, and slid them under her door. But he had only seen her once in nearly two weeks. They met at the Fregata café. But she was tense, and did not talk. Bronek let her leave after a few minutes.

"Any news of these summary courts?"

"Papa, don't even believe anything about the courts," Eugene objected. "They're nothing."

Bronek turned his problems over and over in his mind, but he uncovered no answers. It was impossible to court a girl. Not in these times. There was just no good way.

"But the posters mention a summary court. What is this court?"

"I can show you," Eugene exclaimed. "I have a copy of *Biuletyn Informacyjny!*"

Bronek suddenly paid attention. Their father was taken aback. "Eugeniusz! Be careful!" Possessing a copy of the Underground paper was yet another capital offense.

Eugene reached for his cane, and left the kitchen. In a second he returned with a small newspaper. "Here is the truth," he declared.

Bronek peered admiringly at the newspaper with its emblem, a sword across a page displaying a Polish eagle. He no longer risked buying newspapers himself.

"Here it is, Papa. From November 4." Eugene looked down

the page and read. "'We all hear what is broadcast over the loudspeakers. And we know the statements to be lies. The Germans are trying to dress up their terror in legal form and place the blame for the murder of their innocent victims onto the Polish community. But they have lied and defrauded us too often for anyone to take their promises seriously. The very substance of the announcements is an insult to us: executions take place without the actual culprit being captured. They are attempting to convict us all. We are all guilty of resisting them. And this is how it must be. Warsaw will resist. We will never surrender.'" Little Eugene actually spoke forcefully, his voice full of conviction.

Their father listened silently. His furrowed face softened. "I see."

"It's signed by 'Z'." A proud smile brightened Eugene's cherubic face, as if he had written the entire paper himself.

"Thank you, Eugene," Karol said, nodding appreciatively. They finished their soup quietly.

After the dishes were put into the sink, Bronek checked his wristwatch. "It's time, Papa," he said. The Pietraszewics' pulled on their coats and went downstairs.

Behind their brick apartment building was a small empty lot, surrounded by a rusty chain fence. Only a few hardy weeds poked through the hard-trampled earth, and they shriveled in the cold air. All the neighbors, Mister Stachowiak and Misses Rogala and even the Skoniecznys, met in the back lot, bumping shoulders as they nestled into the square space.

When they were collected together, Mister Stachowiak spoke. "Let us pray." All the neighbors held hands; parents helped their children to find someone's hand to hold. Then they spoke together in the fading sunlight, with voices low and eyes closed. "Our Father, who art in Heaven, hallowed be thy name . . . ."

* * *

Jerzy Kruczyk wandered purposefully among the crowds at Hale Mirowski. His long coat fluttered loosely behind him, for he did not bother to button it. His light brown hair sat atop his head in a playful mess as he listened here and there, to every conversation he could.

Jerzy was 21. Before the war, he had been a Boy Scout. He was not a great student, but he studied diligently and earned respectable grades. He considered entering a seminary, when he was old enough. These were impressive achievements, for his father had not valued education highly. A factory foreman and a socialist, his heart had simply stopped early in the occupation; Mother had followed him, peacefully, soon after. He and Wiktor agreed that they were whole-hearted Poles, and could not have survived seeing the new Poland. Jerzy's memories of them drove him to be make them proud.

But then the General Government closed all the universities and high schools for Poles, and Jerzy was forced to delay his plans. He did not even have his high-school diploma. But he was eager, and he had pleaded with his older brother for something to do. He took the code name "Akrobat;" he liked how that sounded. At first Wiktor gave him propaganda tasks, such as painting slogans on walls and throwing smoke bombs into German theaters. But Jerzy learned to curb his enthusiasm, which all good conspirators must do. At last Wiktor let him into his confidence. The attack on the lottery was his first sabotage operation, and he had performed well. Now he burned to show his older brother again. He was a grown-up.

He was at Hale Mirowski because the shopping areas were places where people still collected. It was November 12, the day after Independence Day, and the market was crowded. People seemed nervous. Jerzy watched as several people dashed into stores, remained only a minute or so, and then rushed away. For some reason he thought of a film he had seen in school. The film showed wildebeests in Africa as they collected at watering holes. The holes were surrounded by lions. But the wildebeests had to drink, so they crept forward, lapped up some water, and then darted off into the trees. At the time, he thought the film was very amusing.

Soon enough, he heard something. He heard it in several whispers: "Nowy Swiat!" Protected by his false identification papers and work permit, Jerzy headed across the shopping square, walking as quickly as could without drawing attention. He had to find out what was happening.

Nowy Swiat was the main north-south street in the city center. Jerzy walked down the wide boulevard, beneath the shadow of the Prudential Building. Then he reached 49 Nowy Swiat, across the street from the fancy Savoy Hotel. He looked this way and that. And then he saw the commotion. Old women were crouching on the cold sidewalk, swearing and crossing themselves. The sidewalk was wet, as was the burnt-out brick wall before them.

Jerzy approached an older man. "What happened here?" His voice sounded eager; that was no good. He cleared his throat, and tried to calm down.

The man, taller and thinner than Jerzy, did not move.

"Did you see what happened?" Jerzy asked again. He had to hurry. The Germans always returned. To scatter the mourners.

"Right in front of us." The man turned away. "Right here. On Nowy Swiat."

Jerzy noticed that the man had balding blond hair, sunken eyes, and several missing teeth. He only appeared old. "What happened?"

"No. You're a boy."

Jerzy knew this might happen. "I'm a reporter," he said. "Tell me everything. Quickly."

The man stared at the wall and shook his head.

"The government in London will be told. They will know."

The man jammed his hands into his pockets. And then he began. "I saw it," he said. His voice dropped, until it was barely a whisper. "The police came first. There must have been a dozen of them. They cleared the whole street, and blocked the traffic. The street was empty, except for them, with their rifles drawn. They even shot at a woman who looked out from her window. But I hid in an alley, I could still see. Then a truck pulled up. The prisoners – the men – were taken out. They were blindfolded, and tied together in groups of six. They were gagged. No one spoke, it was all – silent. The police walked the first group over to that wall. There. Then the firing squad lined up, with their rifles. That was when the order came: *'Schiessen!'* And they went down. But they didn't die, not all of them. Some of them . . . moved. So another policeman went up, and put his pistol against their necks. I saw them, they were trying not to move, but they cried out in agony, they couldn't stop . . . . Then the second group went up against the wall. And then the third group."

"*Schutzpolizei*? SS?"

"Schupos." The man's eyes did not focus on anything. "Right here on Nowy Swiat."

"How many prisoners were there?"

The tall man's body shuddered. "I did not see," he uttered at last. "I hid in the alley. Groups of six."

"All men?"

The young man nodded. "Two of them. I saw them. Were just teen-aged boys. No older than fifteen."

Jerzy could not look suspicious by writing. He tried hard to remember. "Who washed the wall?"

The young man shook his head grimly. "The trucks left. People appeared. With flowers. Setting flowers on the ground. And crosses. Then the police came back. They chased everyone away again. Civilians came, with buckets. They – scrubbed the wall, and the sidewalk. They scrubbed the whole thing away. Look – look! Water! That's all there is. A bit of water on the pavement."

Jerzy knit his brow, trying to remember the date, the location, the details.

"You will report this?"

"I will," Jerzy replied. "I promise." He had to leave now, to avoid the Germans.

"Promise me one more thing." For the first time, the taller man glared at Jerzy. "Never forget. Never wash this from your mind. Do that for me."

* * *

Anna sat on the overstuffed sofa by her front window. She was trying to study mathematics, but the mimeographed lessons lay on her black skirt, ignored. Her mind all too easily drifted away. Anna stared out at Twarda Street, her street. It seemed lifeless to her now. What a change from that summer, when children played soccer and people gossiped about war news and food deals. Now, no one would guess that it was a Saturday. No children played. People kept their heads low, and hurried inside as quickly as they could. Occasionally a patrol of Blue Policemen marched through. They gave the street its only activity.

As she looked around her, she remembered longingly the night in September, when she stared at the stars through this same window, and talked so admiringly about Bronek. Her heart still raced when her sister handed her his latest note. He wrote such simple, direct letters, filled with his emotions and his confidence in the future; she saved every one. But now, seeing him was frightening, and nerve-wracking. The last time at the Fregata, she was so frightened she could barely speak.

Was he a Jew? Was that what he tried to tell her? Had he escaped from the Ghetto? She shuddered at the very prospect. But she was puzzled. She had, after all, seen him cross himself. Then again, he might do anything to blend in. Or perhaps he had a Jewish grandparent; such a heritage did occur in Warsaw. She had wanted to ask him at the Fregata. But harboring a Jew was punishable by death. Even mentioning the word aloud was risking arrest. She detested worrying about such cruel, brutal concerns. She pushed the thought from her mind.

Anna glanced down at her math lesson. She tried to force herself to study; but her petite arms hung limply at her sides, like sticks. A dozen worries weighed her down, tearing at her heart. She still went to her classes, after her instructor determined they were not compromised; but she fretted she was not keeping up. Her father and her brother, in the kitchen peeling potatoes, were both in bad condition. And Anna remembered the little boy selling carrots. After several visits, she had never seen him since that first day. Was he arrested? Worse? Why did she anguish over a boy she had met just once? Everything she saw affected her somehow.

For an instant, she remembered when she was much younger. She had felt awestruck upon seeing the saints in the stained glass windows at her church. There was a window that depicted Saint Stephen, being stoned as a martyr. His face in the colored glass looked so tormented, so twisted, that she had felt the pain too. The window image had overwhelmed her. She had stared at the glass every Sunday, her heart aching, pitying poor Saint Stephen with the twisted face. She did not comprehend why a message from God, like a stained glass window, should make her feel so anguished. She had hoped to return the following Sunday, and see him happy. But he never was.

She could no longer absorb so much fear. Nothing made sense any more. Well, she had to find some sense. With a sudden flash of insight, she realized what she had to do. She forced her limp arms to sort through her smeary pages. And then Anna brushed a tear from her cheek.

Anna was so lost in her own thoughts that she did not even hear someone knock at the door, or her older sister answer it. "Misia," Krystyna said with relief, "You made it."

"Krystyna!" Misia said brightly. "Of course I had to come."

Michalina Myzwinska entered the kitchen. She was a tall, attractive young woman of Krystyna's age. Her shiny blonde hair tumbled down to her shoulders, longer than the current fashion. Although clearly malnourished, her classic Slavic features and tender smile brightened the dingy kitchen. Her looks, wisdom, and politeness all revealed her connection to the Polish aristocracy.

"I received your note," Misia said. "Of course I had to come over. How is everyone?"

"Good, thank you." The two families had lived near each

other, in the neighborhood of Zoliborz, before the war. But poverty had forced both families into smaller rooms.

"Well, here are the boys. Mister Krzykowski and Aleksy, God bless!"

"They're not the problem," Krystyna said abruptly, leading Misia to the parlor.

Cautiously, they entered the parlor. The only light came in from the wide front window. There sat Anna, a mere dark shape on the sofa, nearly lifeless.

"Is she in a bad way?" Misia asked in a whisper.

"She just sits, like a bag of onions," Krystyna whispered in response, an angry tone in her voice. "She won't talk to me, of course. But she won't even talk to Mama."

"This is troubling."

"But I remembered she always seemed to be able to tell you things. That's why I hoped you could come over."

"Well," Misia said, "Let's see what we can learn." They delicately approached the sofa. "Anna?"

Upon hearing her name, Anna instinctively pushed her math lesson beneath a cushion.

"Anna? Do you remember me?"

At last Anna's eyes seemed to focus, and she saw the two women standing before her. "Misia. Misia," she said weakly.

"Misia came by to help," Krystyna said.

Misia pulled a small paper sack from her overcoat. "Look, Anna. I brought some radishes. I remembered you liked them. Don't you?"

Anna managed to nod, ever so slightly. "Yes, yes. Thank you."

"Is your mother out shopping still?"

Anna nodded again.

"Yes? So is mine. I need to hurry back home, in fact. But I was wondering about you. I haven't seen you in so long. How long has it been, Krystyna?"

"July, I think."

"Yes, four or five months. Remember, Anna, how we used

to hike, out in the Kampinos forest? You had to nearly run, just to keep up."

"She never gave up, though," Krystyna recalled. "She was stubborn."

"Well, Anna, we all care about you. We want to know how you are. Can you tell us?"

Anna rested her hands on her knee. For seconds, she did not move. "Yes," she said at last, limply, "Yes."

"Anna," Krystyna said, "Tell Misia what's wrong with you."

"Krystyna," Misia retorted, "Let me try." Misia smiled again. "Anna? Are you receiving letters?"

"No."

"No?"

Anna said nothing.

"Anna," Misia said firmly, "Never give up on your own life. Never abandon those you love. Keep them. That is how we will triumph."

"One person," Anna said softly, "One person's happiness seems so meaningless now. It all means nothing."

Anna spoke so softly that Krystyna and Misia had to concentrate to hear her. "Have you received letters, Anna? You can tell us. What is that about?"

For a second there was silence in the darkness. "No. No more."

"What's that?" Krystyna said. "Why no more?"

"I can never see him." Anna stared at no one, for she was speaking only to herself. "Never. Never again." She drifted far away, leaving Krystyna and Misia to stare at her in puzzlement.

Announcement

By order of the Security Police Summary Court the following persons, convicted for offenses under Section 1 or 2 of the Decree of October 2, 1943, have been sentenced to death:

1. Slon, Mieczyslaw   b. 7/22/1920
2. Debica, Wladyslaw   b. 5/5/1922
3. Wyszomirski, Jozef   b. 10/6/1904
4. Tuszynski, Stanislaw   b. 9/25/1921
5. Porada, Roman   b. 8/9/1900
6. Somschor, Witold   b. 5/3/1920
7. Glowczewski, Jozef Zygmunt
                             b. 10/12/1917
8. Wisniewski, Eugeniusz b. 7/16/1908
9. Pluzanski, Wlodzimierz b. 1/9/1900
10. Schönfeld, Kazimierz Stanislaw
                             b. 6/26/1918
11. Jedrzejewicz, Juliusz Czeslaw
                             b. 10/10/1916
12. Nowicki, Waclaw   b. 4/9/1923
13. Schiele, Jerzy Antoni b. 5/10/1924
14. Kowalski, Czeslaw   b. 4/7/1911
15. Kazanka, Stefan   b. 8/1/1903
16. Laworski, Marian   b. 8/31/1924
17. Kozlowski, Ryszard   b. 3/27/1925
18. Kowalczyk, Jan   b. 5/13/1923

19. Donner, Edward Karol b. 8/8/1911
20. Kowalczyk, Mieczyslaw Marian
                             b. 3/23/1919
21. Gaska, Jozef   b. 1/16/1902
22. Pieskun, Aleksy   b. 5/11/1910
23. Kacperski, Jan   b. 5/4/1907
24. Wasilewski, Waclaw   b. 2/4/1908
25. Kwiatkowski, Franciszek
                             b. 10/3/1901
26. Roguski, Stefan   b. 11/14/1905
27. Polkowski, Boleslaw b. 5/5/1919
28. Pindych, Boleslaw   b. 9/26/1913
29. Gibala, Stanislaw   b. 1/5/1913
30. Rosner, Benno   b. 11/5/1919
31. Ciuk, Jan   b. 2/6/1902
32. Dobrzynski, Aleksander b. 3/7/1901
33. Pasamonski, Wincenty b. 1/22/1890
34. Pasamonski, Jerzy   b. 10/12/1921
35. Pasamonski, Wieslaw b. 1/6/1923
36. Skruza, Marian   b. 9/7/1921
37. Baranowski, Stanislaw b. 3/14/1895

Of these the following:

1. Kowalski, Czeslaw   b. 4/7/1911
2. Rosner, Benno   b. 11/5/1919

have already been executed. The remaining persons are eligible for clemency. Should there be in the next three months any attacks on Germans, citizens of states allied with the Greater German Reich, or non-Germans engaged in the work of reconstruction in the General Government, for every attack at least ten of the above-named persons will be publicly executed: namely, for offenses by communist elements, members of communist organizations, and for offenses by other resistance groups, persons belonging to these circles. It lies in the hands of every Pole, through the immediate arrest of the perpetrators, or by influencing deceived elements, or by reporting suspicious persons, to save the above-named who have already forfeited their lives through their sentences but by the Government's mercy will be spared.

Warsaw, October 30, 1943

**SS and Police Leader
for Warsaw District**

XII

Jerzy Kruczyk hurried westward, out of the city center. He had been at the Fregata café that afternoon when he had heard some big news, and he had to go out to investigate it. It had just stopped raining, but the sky was still a gloomy gray, and his worn shoes slipped on the wet sidewalks.

When he reached Kopinska Street, just before the tangled tracks of Western Station, he stopped to regain his breath. Droplets of rain dripped off his coat as he surveyed the scene. The train tracks going into Western Station were raised above the street, and a grassy embankment led up to the tracks. There in the misty drizzle were several old women, their babushkas plastered to their scalps, kneeling before the embankment, praying fervently. Their rosary beads swung wildly beneath their flailing arms.

Jerzy approached the embankment. He noticed that blood stains were washing down the embankment, blending into the rain on the sidewalk. He tried asking the old women some questions, but they ignored him as they wailed their prayers. Impatiently, Jerzy stepped away.

Beside him stood a woman not so old, about thirty. She stood quietly, whispering a few words to herself. He had already learned that women were better to interview than men.

They could never estimate times and distances, but they usually could talk through their emotions better than men. "Hello?" Jerzy asked.

"I have seen one," the woman said. "Now . . . I have seen one."

"When did it happen?"

"It just happened. And yet – it's still before me, isn't it." She had a dazed expression, as if she were profoundly confused.

"How many were there?"

The woman had a grim, tight face, with thin lips. She struggled to maintain her composure.

"I'm reporting this. So the world will know." Jerzy waited for her to calm down before asking more questions. "Did you see what happened?"

"I saw it all. I'm seeing it still."

"How many were there?"

"I could have run away. Everyone else ran. But I hid. I watched. I watched it all." Droplets of cold rain hung from her drab babushka, and fell onto her cheeks.

"How many were there?"

"Ten. Twice."

Jerzy repeated *twenty* to himself. Kopinska Street at Western Station, November 17, twenty victims.

The woman, Jerzy noticed, forced back her tears. "They seemed – uncertain, somehow. Tired."

"Tired?"

"The people. They – staggered as they walked. They were sleepwalking."

"Staggering? Were there rags in their mouths?"

"I don't – I don't – remember. They wore prison clothes."

She was struggling with the information. Jerzy tried not to interrogate her, but he had to learn the details. "What about their mouths? Did they have rags in their mouths?"

The woman nodded.

"They probably soaked the rags in morphine," he explained. "Were they all men?"

"Three of them . . . were women."

"I understand."

"I saw them. They were women."

"Yes. What next?"

"They dumped them . . . back into the trucks. The trucks simply drove off. They were gone." With each breath, a little puff of frost collected before her face.

Jerzy nodded. "You did help."

A little girl dashed across the street. When she reached the embankment, she carefully set down a handful of delicate flowers. Other children appeared, setting out little crosses, and laying down bunches of flowers. The woman leapt at them. "No! Get back inside! Go away!" The children scattered away from her.

Her behavior seemed peculiar. Then suddenly Jerzy realized he had witnessed the scene before. This woman had not. "People will want to put down flowers," he explained. He was no longer repulsed. "I'm – I'm sorry you had to watch it." He was trying to explain the process to her. How, how could he do this?

The woman struggled to find a response for herself. "The Russians. They will stop this – yes?"

* * *

It was late in the evening, not long before curfew. Saint Casimir Catholic Church was crowded with people attending a special evening service for the Madonna of Czestochowa. Only several candles lit the entire church, casting flickering shadows on the rugged stone walls. The archways were decorated with red and white flowers. The air was filled with the sounds from the wheezy old organ. Father Marian led the congregation in singing a hymn. Karol and Eugene Pietraszewicz were standing at the end of a pew. But Bronek was not with them.

Bronek crept in alone. Wearing his father's jacket, he went up the worn stone steps, all the way up to the organ loft. He knocked on the door.

A teen-aged boy opened the door a crack.

"Let me in."

"I can't," the boy retorted testily. "The organist is playing."

Bronek opened his jacket, and pulled out his Walther PPK pistol. He rotated the barrel so that the metal would flash. "Let me in."

The door opened, and Bronek climbed up behind the organ. Now he was as high as the tops of the stained glass windows. The organist, a middle-aged woman in a faded house dress, glanced at Bronek briefly, but kept playing. Hiding behind the organ, Bronek again flashed his gun. "'God, Who Hath Poland Saved,'" he whispered, "Play it." He returned the gun to his pocket.

The woman did not stop playing, did not even look up at him. "I can't play that song. Please. I'll be arrested."

"You can. They want to hear it."

"I'll be executed. Father Marian will be executed. I can't do it."

Bronek bit his lip. He knew that she might not be willing. He squeezed his hand into a fist. Then he lunged forward. His fist glanced against her cheek, his knuckle scraping across her dry skin. Bronek retreated behind the organ, surprised at how difficult hitting her had been.

A drop of blood welled up on her cheek. The old woman stared at Bronek, shocked, wide-eyed.

Bronek studied the cut; it had to be sizable enough to convince the police that she had indeed been attacked. Satisfied, he again pulled out his Walther. "'God, Who Hath Poland Saved.' Play it!" His voice trembled with tension.

At last she stopped. For a second there was an awkward silence as people went silent, surprised. And then the woman played the first chords of the national hymn.

A loud murmur of shock and recognition erupted from the congregation. Bronek heard people shifting as they looked back at the organ loft. The organist continued playing.

Then it began, from the gallery first. Soon everyone joined

in. The whole church resounded with the forbidden lyrics:

"Before Your altars, we in supplication,
Kneeling, implore You, free our land and nation.
Bring back to Poland ancient mights and splendor,
And fruitful blessings bring to fields and meadows;
Be once again our Father, just, tender,
Deliver us from our dire shadows."

They were shouting the words with all the energy they could. Bronek inhaled deeply, inhaled the hope that suddenly filled the church. It was worth all the risk. People remembered. A tear spilled down the organist's pale cheek. Bronek felt a tear well up in his own eye, and he hastily wiped it away.

Bronek decided not to wait any longer. "Thank you!" he shouted over his shoulder. He bounded down the stone steps. Already people stood to leave. They crowded the entrance, pushing to get out. Bronek was caught in a mass of desperate humanity. He pushed himself forward until at last he was outside.

In minutes, not a soul remained in the church. The echoes of the forbidden hymn reverberated off the empty stone walls even as the worshipers rushed to their homes. Grinning irrepressibly, Bronek snuck back home alone.

* * *

Bronek kept to himself the afternoon of November 19. Discreetly, he traveled a circuitous route. He got on and off various streetcars, to make sure he was not followed. This was part of his skill. Bronek had an inner voice that told him when the police were near. He always obeyed this voice, when others ignored it and were arrested.

At last he made it to Kaliska Street. He walked into the bombed-out house. He walked down the dirt-crusted hallway, to the loose brick among thousands. He slid it from the wall. Inside was the message from Zebra. He never knew the rendezvous point in advance, to protect the others. The coded message would give him the date and time for the rendezvous. It would take place that night.

The sky was cloudy that evening, and darkened early. Bronek was just across the Vistula River, in the eastern suburb of Praga. He climbed aboard the streetcar heading toward the Warsaw East train station. Luckily, there were several Poles on board. He could blend in. He paid the conductor and went to the back, where the Poles were allowed to ride, and sat on a wooden bench. He tried to be quiet, inconspicuous, and bland.

The streetcar rolled on in the darkness. There was no moonlight. Bronek stared out, and shivered. Warsaw was traveling backward in time, he observed; there were more horse-drawn carriages than cars. He thought of Anna's warm, smiling face. Lately, when his thoughts wandered to nothing in particular, he thought about her. She was often frightened. He remembered the way she held onto him, and pressed her head against his chest. He missed her. He squinted his eyes and shook his head; he had to concentrate on his mission.

Bronek silently got off the streetcar, and walked down the block and around the corner. It was so close to curfew that the neighborhood was deserted. Behind him he heard a dog-like growl.

Bronek turned around. He grinned with relief. It was Wiktor and Jerzy.

"We're waiting for you," Wiktor whispered sternly. Even darkened by his coat, cap, and wide mustache, Wiktor's anger chilled the air. Wiktor hated waiting even one minute.

They started walking eastward. For a long time nothing was said.

Bronek spoke first. "Has anyone heard about Kiev?" he whispered. It was not a good idea to speak. But they were across the river, and they had seen no police.

"I have heard nothing," Wiktor replied.

"I heard the Panzer Corps counterattacked," Bronek commented. "I wondered what you had heard."

"Nothing," Wiktor repeated.

"I wonder when the Russians will liberate us. Maybe this year –"

"The Russians will never liberate anybody," Wiktor declared flatly.

"What do you mean? They're fighting for us. The Atlantic Charter guarantees it."

"Bah!" Wiktor actually raised his voice, scoffing at the term. "The Atlantic Charter is a scrap of paper. Worthless."

"But Granit, this war is about Poland. The Atlantic Charter guarantees it. It guarantees our freedom."

"If you want your freedom, young man," Wiktor declared with finality, "I suggest you fight for it yourself."

Bronek considered what Wiktor had said. "Is that what you think, Akrobat?"

Jerzy could only mumble.

"What's that, Akrobat?" Bronek asked. "I thought you had an opinion about everything."

"I don't know what to think," Jerzy muttered, and that was that.

They walked on in silence, huddling inside their ragged coats. Bronek blew on his hands, to keep them warm.

At last they reached the train tracks. "All right. Let's go."

The street was dark, and cold, and empty. Nobody was out. Wiktor nodded his head. "This way," he said determinedly. They walked together silently, past Warsaw East train station. It loomed over them, old, cavernous, forbidding. "Keep your ears open," Wiktor whispered. "You can hear the police before you see them."

When they reached the railroad tracks that crossed the street, Wiktor stopped. "Akrobat, stay here. Keep out of sight."

"I know, Granit."

"Remember, if you see the police, make a bird call. But make it twice, so I know it's you."

"We've gone over this, Granit."

"Especially look out for the *Bahnpolizei*."

"I know this already."

"Don't forget. Lot – let's go."

Bronek and Wiktor left Jerzy at the street. They followed the tracks around several buildings and vacant lots. They reached the edge of the city limits, to the express track. Finally they came upon a small wooded patch, about a kilometer across. "This is perfect, Granit," Bronek said admiringly.

There, the tracks plunged into a small patch of short trees. Within them, Bronek could see a small culvert where a creek – a drainage ditch, really – cut across. The tracks bridged the gap with a short wooden-trestle bridge, only a few meters long and a meter high. The tracks curved at that point, so the conductor would have no chance of spotting any problem. "An express train from the Russian front uses this track," Wiktor explained. "One is due here tonight. In – twenty minutes."

"Full of German soldiers? Perfect," Bronek remarked. "How will you measure the fuse, to cut it?"

"No ridiculous piece of string. Look." Wiktor pulled a glass tube, like a test tube, from his coat pocket.

Bronek stared quizzically at the little tube. "What is that?"

Wiktor held it up proudly. "It's an acid switch. The tube is full of acid. There's a small glass case inside. The wire is inside the glass case. When the train breaks the glass case, the acid disintegrates the wire. When the wire breaks, the switch is tripped."

"Terrific," Bronek said. "How long does it take?"

"It is immediate. Every time."

"But, why not just let the train do the work?"

"Too unreliable. The train may knock the wires aside. You must make sure. This was harder to get than the dynamite. It took a lot of bartering to get one of these."

"Where did you get it?"

"I know a man who deals in such things. The same man who sells me bread."

Bronek nodded, impressed. Wiktor was an amazing man. Apparently he could produce anything. He was so stoical, no one would suspect he was carrying dynamite, and wires, and a chemical fuse. "Where do you want me?"

"Follow the tracks. Go through this wooded section. If you see any police, signal me."

"How long do I wait?"

"Dynamite, battery, switches – ten minutes. I'll give you a signal."

Bronek nodded. "Yes, sir." He walked on the railroad ties, over the little bridge. When he reached the far curve in the tracks, he stopped. He could not see Wiktor from here.

Bronek checked his watch: just past eight o'clock p.m. Curfew had started. He was far from home. He nervously clenched and unclenched his fists. He thought he saw a black uniform emerging from the black trees behind him; but it was nothing, just some trees swaying. He blew on his hands, and jumped in place. He tried thinking of Anna, of that time when he watched her get dressed. That made him feel warm. He looked up at the cloudy sky, and waited.

Just then he saw something. A patrol – four police. They were walking along the tracks. Long overcoats, gray helmets, black rifles. Bronek held his breath. Panic shot through his body. He squinted his eyes. There were green eagles on their gray sleeves: Schupos. What were they doing out here? They were barely ten feet from him. Bronek forced down his fear. He slumped into the shadows. He could not run toward Wiktor; they would see him. He could signal Wiktor with a bird call, but they were so close they might find him. And the mission was still paramount. He had to wait.

The policemen stopped, just a few feet from Bronek's hunched form. They lit cigarettes, and talked to themselves in German. Bronek heard their boots shuffle on the road. He did not know German well, but he gathered that they were disparaging the war on the Russian front. Bronek froze and waited. Soon they put out their cigarettes and walked farther down the tracks. Right toward Wiktor. Bronek had to run for it. *Blessed Mother, grant us strength!*

Suddenly there was a clanging sound of a trash can tipping onto the street. The Schupos looked that way. *Was it Akrobat?* Bronek wondered. Whoever it was, the Schupos held onto their rifles and ran toward the sound. Bronek watched them until they were gone. It took minutes for him to risk walking back to Wiktor.

"Anything?" Wiktor asked.

"Schupos," Bronek said anxiously. "They went after that sound. Was it Akrobat?"

"That was not Akrobat. He is ahead. Let's get out of here."

"Perfect." Bronek really admired Wiktor, grumpiness and all. He could do anything.

The two men returned to the city alongside the tracks. "Lot," Wiktor asked, "What have you decided about that girl?"

"Oh – her." Bronek was surprised by the question, out here on a dangerous mission. "So far . . . nothing."

"What do you mean?"

"I mean, I can't decide anything. Every option is no good."

"I see."

"I guess I'll just – keep her as she is. Do you know what I mean?" Bronek could barely even see Wiktor. It was like having a conversation with the darkness.

"Yes."

"I'll wait until after we're liberated. I'll decide then."

"Hmm." Wiktor said nothing for a second.

"I don't know, Granit. I don't see any other way."

"So you will wait for your liberation. And then you'll see."

"Right. Doesn't that make sense?"

"I suppose. That's what she wants?"

"I don't know. I didn't explain it to her yet."

"You'll tell her this?"

"Oh, sure. I'll tell her. Sometime."

"That would be a good idea." They walked on until they reached Jerzy, hiding in an alley.

"Finally!" Jerzy exclaimed. "What took you so long? I had to dodge two police patrols."

They split up to go home, Bronek going south, Wiktor and Jerzy going west. Bronek stuck to corners and alleys. Despite the police patrols, he did not encounter a single soul, even crossing the Poniatowski bridge easily.

Sure enough, soon after he left, he heard a dull rumble in the east, from where he had come. Wiktor's chemical fuse had worked. Those soldiers from the Russian front were now welcomed to Warsaw. Bronek smiled. It was a fitting, for Warsaw to be more dangerous.

When he reached his home Bronek slipped inside. He hoped to not be caught sneaking around after curfew. That hope was quickly dashed. "Bronek!" his father shouted. "Bronek, Bronek!"

Bronek stood at the door. "Hello, Papa." The carbide lamp hurt his eyes.

His father rushed to him, and grabbed his shoulders. "Bronek! Where have you been?"

"I was just – I was –" He did not know what to say.

"Do you know that it's past curfew?"

"Yes, yes, I know."

"Well, thanks to God you're here!" Karol shook his son by his shoulders.

Bronek shrugged, until his father let go.

Karol pointed toward the kitchen counter. "This came for you while you were gone."

"For me?" There, on the counter, was a small beige-colored envelope. He reached nervously for it, fearing to read it. His fingers actually trembled as he opened the letter and squinted.

"Bronek," the letter began, "I need to see you. I must discuss something very important with you."

XIII

Bronek Pietraszewicz hurried into Under the Snout. He scanned the crowded room nervously. People were huddled inside their heavy coats this frigid afternoon, and he had to search for Anna. At last he walked to a table along the far wall.

"Anna," he said anxiously.

"Hello, Bronislaw."

He sat down across from her, not attempting to kiss her hand. "I received your message." He raked his fingers through his hair, pushing it back from his forehead. He tried to calm himself inside his jacket, but he could not relax. He shook his hands to relax his fingers, a trick he learned while playing the piano.

Anna wore the same drab trenchcoat as before, and her faded beige dress, so thin it was almost gauze. But her skin was still perfect alabaster, her eyes still round blue pools. "Would you like a coffee?" Anna asked.

Bronek shook his head. "I only have money for the street-car."

"Oh." She sat very still, her hands in her lap. "Bronek, who are you looking for?"

Bronek was eyeing everyone. "I don't like it here. How do you know it's safe?"

"I feel safe here. I've come here for years."

"I haven't been in here since the Gestapo raid." It was the day they had met.

"Bronek, can I discuss something with you?"

Bronek still glanced around. "Gestapos come back. We never use a place after Gestapos raid it."

"Bronek, look at me!" Anna raised her voice, and wrinkled her brow. "I asked you here to tell you, in person."

Now Bronek paid attention. His fingers suddenly felt very clumsy; he shook them again. He peered at her for a clue.

"Bronek, I –" She began to stammer. "I –" She looked down. She suddenly seemed nervous. "I've come to a – a decision. I think that you are a – a very sweet boy . . . a wonderful . . . wonderful. . . ." Her soft voice fell silent.

Bronek watched her, disbelieving. Around them the restaurant clattered with life. But between them there was just an anguished awkwardness. "Anna, what are you saying? Tell me."

She did not look at him as she spoke. "But, I've decided, that – the way things are, my family needs me so badly, I can't – I can't –" Her body shivered inside her coat.

At last her meaning tore through the dismay cloaking Bronek's mind. A horrible sensation suddenly hit him in the chest. He felt as if he were smacked with a club. It was impossible. And yet here she was, saying this thing.

"I cannot see you."

She raised her deep blue eyes, meeting his. Yes, it was Anna. She paused, seemingly to gain strength. "I can't spend my days in cafés, making conversation with every nice boy I meet. Not now. I hope you understand."

Bronek knew that he did not understand. He felt himself exhale, his shoulders sag, his lips droop. "Oh," he finally uttered. "Oh." He looked away from her.

"I can't spend my days in cafes. I can't," she repeated.

Bronek's mind swirled with confusing thoughts. He could not believe that Anna was saying these things. He reached for some response, grasping for some sense.

"Well . . ." Anna said, "How are your father and brother?"

Bronek did not respond. He sat still.

"They're safe, then?"

"Fine – fine." He made no effort to hide the displeasure in his voice.

"You are lucky. We think that my brother Aleksy has rickets."

Bronek still did not respond.

"He sits outside as much as he can now, to get sunshine. But it's so dangerous."

Bronek sat still, angrily.

"Good. . . . I wonder what's happening at the conference."

Bronek mumbled something.

"The conference in Teheran. Stalin, Churchill, and Roosevelt himself. They're planning the course of the whole war, right now."

"Oh."

"Have you heard anything? What are they planning?"

"I don't know, Anna," he replied. He could not think about the Teheran Conference.

"They will fight for our independence. They have to. It's in the Atlantic Charter. It's guaranteed –"

"– I don't know!" He waved his hand.

"Well, all right, then. Why don't we go?"

They left the restaurant.

Outside, the cold air attacked Bronek's face. "Well. . . ." He suddenly felt very thirsty, thirsty for a large bottle of cheap *bimber*, the kind that gave him a horrible stomachache. He wanted to drink until he got sick, until he did not know which direction was up. "You live that way."

"Can you walk me to the streetcar stop?" Anna asked abruptly.

Bronek looked into her large, deep eyes. Before, he had thought she was the most beautiful woman in all Warsaw. And he still did. "I can," he mumbled.

They walked up the block to the next streetcar stop. A sizable knot of people waited impatiently; old women in babushkas bulged unnaturally with smuggled food beneath their huge skirts. Bronek and Anna said nothing as they waited. Bronek shifted his weight from one foot to another, trying to keep warm. Even the sunshine today seemed to mock him.

They waited. Bronek wondered why she wanted him to escort her to the streetcar stop, or anywhere else, for that matter. She did not seem to want to say anything. He began to wish he were back with Granit, and Akrobat, and Nowak. People he understood. One thing was certain: he would never go to Under the Snout, ever again.

At last the westbound streetcar rolled up, and people pushed on board. "Help me aboard, please?"

He helped Anna up the steps and boarded. Bronek shrugged his shoulders apologetically to the conductor, who nodded and let them board for free. The conductor was eager to deprive the Germans of some revenue. His gesture also meant there were no inspectors on this tram.

The streetcar was severely crowded; or at least, the Polish section was. The streetcars were racially segregated. The front half was marked "*Nur für Deutschen*" (Only for Germans); it carried exactly two passengers, both German civil servants, bald and overweight. All the Poles were crammed into the back half. Bronek and Anna nudged themselves back as far as they could.

They had not moved ten meters before the German, the fatter one with a small mustache and little wire spectacles, stood in the aisle. He looked down his short nose at the crowd. He was the supreme bureaucrat, positively Wagnerian in his bureaucratic myopia. "*Die Vorderehalfte ist nur für das deutsche Volk!*" He waved his finger angrily, his pudgy cheeks turning red. "*Die Hinterhalfte ist für das polnische Volk!*" (The front half is only for the German race! The back half is for the Polish race!)

Bronek glanced down; he and Anna were standing too far

forward in the aisle. Bronek pushed them back, until they stood behind the rope dividing the two sections. Now all the Poles were jammed together, with no room to move. Satisfied, the stubby German bureaucrat returned to his spacious wooden bench.

Bronek and Anna stood with their hips rubbing together, surrounded by women bulging with black-market food. An unbearable discomfort filled Bronek. He glanced down nervously; then he looked away, and then out the window, and then back at her. They rocked back and forth against each other. Bronek tried to pull his body back away from her, but there was no room to even turn.

It mattered for nothing, but he decided to speak. "I – I don't want to leave you."

Anna looked into his eyes suddenly, sharply.

"It meant everything to see you, even just for a few minutes. You made me feel anything was possible."

"Bronek – I can't risk everything, just to drink coffee in cafes. Just to see a – a friend."

"I'm not just a friend. I love you. I want to marry you."

Anna glanced away for a brief moment. Her lower lip trembled, and not from the motion from the streetcar.

"But not now, not yet. I thought – when we're liberated, or later –"

"When we're liberated? Bronek, how – how can you say such a thing?"

She rocked against him. He felt her chest press against his, filling his body with a tense, unbearable energy. His arms hung awkwardly at his sides, and he yearned to hold her, to wrap his arms around her and somehow squeeze his tormented feelings into her.

Bronek glared angrily into her eyes. "I am not ignoring you. I have plans for us. After we're liberated."

"You want to push me aside, until we're free? Is that what you want to do, when you say you love me?"

Bronek bit his lip. "I am not just some friend you pass the

time with," he protested bitterly. The tension was unbearable. There was nowhere to move, nowhere else to look but into her wide, unblinking eyes. The streetcar stopped, and then moved again. "I love you!"

"You must make a decision, Bronek. I need more. More to risk my life for."

"There is more. I want to marry you."

Anna studied his face. "When, darling? When?"

"Right now!" The retort came not from Bronek but from a frail, wrinkled woman standing behind them. "Don't be a damned fool!"

"Thank you, but this is our –"

"Bah! All young people are fools!" Wrinkles cut deep crevasses across the old woman's face, and her cheeks jostled when she talked. "Do you want to marry her?"

"Yes, but –"

"Then do it today! Before time runs out!"

Bronek swallowed. Suddenly the words spilled out of his heart, unchecked. "Anna – will you marry me today?"

The smile that had started on her lips had now spread to her whole face, her whole being, like a sunrise. "Yes." She nodded frantically. "Yes!"

Bronek held Anna, pulling her tightly against him. He bent down and kissed her, and he felt nothing but joy.

"It's about time!" the old woman proclaimed.

Bronek looked down at Anna, her delicate face framed by her halo of blond hair. All that nervous tension was gone, drained from his body like dirty bath water. He felt relieved, and exhausted, and wholly bonded to her.

"I thought you wanted to leave me," he inquired.

"I thought I had to."

"You didn't want to leave me?"

"I thought you didn't love me."

"That's foolish!" He grabbed her shoulders, and held her. "You are the most amazing, wonderful – on the first day I saw you, I loved you. Wait . . . Anna, are you smiling or crying?"

Anna hastily wiped her eyes. "Both. I'm smiling and crying, I guess."

The streetcar screeched to a stop. "Come on," Bronek said, grabbing Anna's hand. "Let's get out of here."

"But Bronek, this isn't my stop," Anna protested, but he pulled her forward.

"Ah," the old woman sighed, "More room."

Bronek stopped beside the bald German bureaucrat, and thrust out his hand. *"Vielen Dank!"* Bronek said, shaking the man's hand vigorously. *"Vielen Dank!"* (Many thanks!) The stunned German stared at the couple as they bounced down the streetcar steps.

Outside, Bronek stopped to take in a deep breath. The sun felt warmer now. The city was the same, the people were the same. And yet they were all different. They were seen through the eyes of a new person. "Come on," Bronek said.

"Where are we going?"

"We're getting married, aren't we?" He looked down at Anna's bare hand. "We need to get you something for that hand."

They walked south to Ochota, Bronek holding Anna's hand. Bronek opened the door to a drug store. "In here."

The store seemed to be abandoned. The old man behind the counter seemed to be no more than a mannequin against the bare shelves. "Mister Znaniecki, it's me, Bronek."

"Eh!" The old man pulled himself from his chair. "I know who that is."

"Mister Znaniecki, I'll be right back. Can you make sure she's safe?"

Mister Znaniecki looked at Anna and nodded. "What are those bastards doing now?"

"Nothing." He turned to Anna. "You'll wait here?"

"Yes, yes."

"Okay. I'll be back in ten minutes." He kissed her cheek, and hurried out the door.

Mister Znaniecki wiped the dust from his hands onto his

shirt. "Can I interest you in anything? Clothespins, spoons? I have pencils with no leads."

Anna forced herself to be polite. "No thank you," she said. "I'll just wait."

Bronek half-walked, half-ran, to his apartment and slipped inside the door. No one was in the kitchen. When he rushed through the parlor, he was surprised to see Eugene, sitting on the sofa.

"Eugene! What's going on?"

Eugene sat up on the sofa. Before him, on the coffee table, was his old black typewriter. "Bronek! Next time, let me know it's you! I almost fainted."

"I'm sorry. Listen, Eugene. I have to tell you something. Where's Papa?"

"He's out shopping for dinner. We don't have anything but black bread and coffee."

"Listen: promise me that you won't tell him what you're about to see."

"What's that?"

"Promise."

"Sure, sure, I promise."

"Good." Bronek went into their father's bedroom and opened the dresser drawer. He pulled out the false drawer bottom that held the family heirlooms.

"Bronek, what are you doing?" Eugene called from the parlor. "You can't go in there!"

Bronek searched. He pulled out a diamond ring. "Ah, ha!" It was silver, with a round diamond surrounded by two swirls of smaller stones. He slipped the ring into his pocket and returned to the parlor.

"Listen, Eugene. I had to take Mama's wedding ring."

Eugene propped himself up with his cane. "Papa is going to be mad, Bronek."

"No, because you're not going to tell him. You promised."

"But Bronek –"

"You just tell him this: I won't be home tonight."

"Where are you going?"

"I can't say. Just tell him I'll be safe."

Eugene grinned. "Is it dangerous?"

Bronek considered that question for a second. "No, Eugene it isn't. If it's right, it's not scary. It's really – a lot of fun. It's wonderful."

"Have you heard any news?" Eugene asked.

"There's a newspaper boycott," Bronek said.

"When?"

"Friday. Don't buy a paper. Remember, tell Papa that I'm safe. Good-bye, Eugene!" On the way out, Bronek grabbed a small slab of black bread, and slid it inside his jacket. Then he left his home.

Bronek hurried back to the store. As soon as he entered, his arm was yanked. It was Anna. "Bronek, you're back!" she said appreciatively.

"What's wrong?"

"I've been explaining to her," Mister Znaniecki said, "What those bastards have done to me. Look at what I can sell!"

Bronek nodded. "Oh, I see. I should have warned you."

"I'm glad you're back."

"Are you ready?"

"I'm ready. Are you ready?"

"Completely. Let's go. Thank you, Mister Znaniecki!"

The young couple rushed from Mister Znaniecki's store. Holding her hand, Bronek led Anna down the street and around the corner, to Saint Casimir Catholic Church. They went to the small parish house behind the church, and Bronek knocked forcefully on the door. When Father Marian opened the big oak door, Bronek spoke enthusiastically, inevitably. "Father Marian, it's me, Bronek Pietraszewicz. We have something for you to do."

Father Marian found two altar boys to act as witnesses. Cold and hungry, uncertain of everything save their one certainty, they were married that afternoon in the cavernous stone church, the red and white stained glass coloring the rays of the sun.

* * *

Bronek was worried. He paced back and forth, alone, in abandoned Apartment 2. Already he cursed himself for agreeing. He knew it was dangerous, but Anna had pleaded and begged so emotionally that he had finally given in. Her final words echoed in his ears: "Please, darling, I must go home for one thing. . . . You don't need to come with me, I'll be extra careful. . . . I don't want you waiting outside for me. . . . Please, please!" So at last he had relented, and now he regretted it. *It can happen at any moment, it can happen at any moment.*

He walked over to the window, and set his black bread on the sill. He pulled off his coat, rolled it into a ball, and set it on the sill. Then, violating his own rule, he slipped his finger behind the shade and pulled it back. The street below was almost empty – just a couple children kicking a homemade soccer ball. No police, no SS.

Just then there was a knock at the door: twice, then once, then once again. Bronek sighed, and he even mumbled some thanks to the Virgin Mary.

"Is this the Honeymoon Suite?" Anna asked with a sly grin.

"Get in here, now!" Bronek closed the door behind her.

"I told you that I'd be careful."

"Thanks to God, you made it!"

"Were you worried about me?"

"You're going to cause me some headaches, aren't you."

"A few." She smiled at him, a mischievous, childish smirk. "Is that all right?"

"It's absolutely all right." He walked across room to her, his shoes shuffling across the wood floor. He wrapped his arms snugly around her, and he kissed her soft, full lips, and he felt a flash of lightning surge through him. "Does it . . . feel different?"

"Yes. I'm kissing my husband."

He admired her blue eyes, her strong jawline, her distinguished nose. Bronek repeated the word to himself: *husband,*

husband. He bent down and put his lips by her pink, cold ear. "I love you."

"I love you."

"You can take off your coat. It's just me here." Bronek reached for the lapel of her coat.

"No! That's my surprise! Wait here!" Anna dashed into the other room.

"What are you doing?" Bronek called after her.

"Don't look in here!" Her voice was shrill. "I'm not decent!"

Bronek thought better of the situation, and stopped. "Can you tell me?"

"No!" Anna called out from the other room. "Then it won't be a surprise!"

"Oh." Bronek put his hands in his pockets. "I'll wait here, then." This must be what women do when they get married, he decided. He waited in the living room, and thought about what she might be doing. Since she went into the dining room, she must have brought some food with her. Maybe pastry of some kind.

He strolled tensely around the big, drafty room. Plaster chunks lay on the floor, and a floor plank was missing. This grim place did not fit his frame of mind, he decided. He felt thrilled, relieved, excited, contented. Bronek repeated that word over and over, testing it, smoothing it like a stone in a streambed. Husband, husband, husband, husband. It felt good, he decided. He did indeed feel different. He was a new, different person.

But coupled with that realization were new concerns, new fears. *It can happen at any moment.* He feared for their future. Could she look after herself? Could she always avoid the police? When would they be liberated? And then there was the curiosity he felt about her, his wife. He had no idea how much he should know about a new wife, but he perceived that he did not know everything about her. What would she wear, if she could buy new clothes? Why did she seem more cultured than he? Did she admire him?

The shadows in the room were turning a deep gray. Bronek struck a match and lit the candle, casting a long, dim shadow across the room. He thought about the woman in the next room. He did not know he could feel so intensely for someone. She was –

"Benny? You can turn around now."

"Oh? What do you have for me –?" Bronek turned around and stopped. He stared at her, wondrously. His eyes gazed up, then down, then back up again. On her feet were black slipper-sandals. Her skirt was calf-length, black with a bright red plaid design, filled out with a petticoat. Her vest was black, snug against her chest, stitched with elaborate yellow and green flowers. Her big white blouse billowed from her arms, as if she were in clouds. A necklace of red beads lay around her neck. And in her blond hair were ribbons, red and white and pink, trailing down her back. It was a traditional Polish folk dress from the old days, when people danced in the streets to celebrate holidays, and there were no executions.

She stepped forward, into the amber light. When she was close she stopped, and looked down sheepishly. "I swore I would never wear it again until we were liberated. But this is special."

Bronek said nothing.

"I think you were hoping for kielbasa."

Bronek shook his head. "You are the most beautiful woman in all Warsaw."

She peered up at him, hopefully. "I need more petticoats, and my shoes are wrong, and my hair is wrong –"

"– Don't change a thing."

She smiled, one of her "just a little bit" smiles. "It's okay, then?"

Bronek approached her, and rested his arms on her shoulders. "Did you know, the day I first met you, I thought you were the most beautiful girl I had ever seen?"

"I have a secret for you," she said softly. "When I first met you, that night, I told my sister that I would marry you."

"And you did."

"Do you want to see my ring?"

Bronek's eyes alerted at that phrase: *my ring*. Anna held up her hand. "See?" She had the ring on her middle finger.

"Hm," Bronek sighed. "Does it look good?"

"Of course. I love it. It's on my middle finger because it's rather big."

"Oh. I'm sorry."

"Don't be. I can get it re-sized."

"You can? They can – shrink it?"

"No, silly. A jeweler cuts it and rejoins the ends. You do have a lot to learn, don't you."

"I guess."

"Silly boy." She stood up on her toes, and kissed him, sweetly. "I have so many things to teach you."

As she moved, Bronek's arms slipped down to her slim waist. He held her there, feeling the slender curves of her torso beneath her folk dress. Without effort, he pulled her close to him. His arms tingled, his fingers twitched. She was magical, an angel, in his arms. "Anna – I have a thousand questions I want to ask you. There are so many things I want to learn."

"Not now, darling."

Suddenly Bronek backed up a step, and held her waist in his hands; his fingers nearly touched across the small of her back. "To your love, oh, Jasiu, please return," he sang lightly.

Anna's eyes grew wide. "Oh, Benny," she gasped.

"Can you dance?"

"Can I dance!"

Bronek sang, not too loudly, the words to the song. He stepped up, and she stepped with him. Just like that they were spinning in a circle, like a polka but looser. Bronek was no great dancer, but he stepped on her toes only once. He spun her 'round and 'round, and she became lighter and lighter, skipping on her toes, her skirt lifting out, her blouse billowing from her arms in the breeze that they created, her ribbons in a twirl, her mouth open in glee, her eyes sparkling, her cheeks becoming flushed. Her voice was quieter, but she too sang the words, and they formed a perfect duet:

"Bloom the buds of all our roses white,
Far from battle where the fierce foes fight,
To your love, oh, Jasiu, please return,
'Tis for you and for your kiss I always yearn,
Oh, to your love, oh, Jasiu please return,
'Tis for you and for your kiss I always yearn!"

Bronek kept dancing, dancing, not willing to stop. He restarted the lyrics over again, and their shoes slid in little swooshes across the wood floor until Anna gasped, "Please!"

At last they stopped, and they sat against the wall. Bronek commented playfully, "I learned something. You like to dance."

"Wait – wait –" Anna panted.

Bronek slid his hands down, and held her little hands in his, and waited until her panting stopped.

Eventually, Anna beamed. "I love to dance, you silly fool." She squeezed his hand appreciatively.

"There's so much I want to know."

The room was nearly dark now. The only light in the room was cast by the candle. They sat in a dark shadow. "It must be late," Anna commented. "It's dark."

"Your smile lights up this room."

"I just remembered something," Anna said, grinning.

"What's that?"

"Tomorrow is the Eve of Saint Andrew."

"Yes, that's right." Saint Andrew's was a Polish tradition.

"It's the day for girls to predict who they will marry," Anna recalled fondly. One tradition was for the girls to write the names of eligible boys on a slip of paper, and mix them in a basket. The name the girl drew from the basket would be her future husband.

"I didn't know my name was in the basket." Traditions like

that seemed distant now, like memories from their discarded childhood.

"I already drew your name, darling." She curled up against his arm, and clung to him firmly.

Bronek felt how she needed him. She was so fragile, so frightened. She tried to be brave, but she relied on him, to make her feel safe. He yearned for her to be happy. As happy as he could possibly make her. "I'll take care of you, *Golebica*," he whispered to her.

Anna's round eyes froze. "Benny – dear – what did you call me?"

"*Golebica*. Because that's what you remind me of. A frightened dove."

"How did you guess?" Anna whispered into his ear, "That's my other name."

He knew what she meant. "Oh." Few people knew her code name.

"I must tell you about me. I am in an Underground school, to get my diploma. My code name is Golebica."

"I see. I have a code name, too. It's Lot."

"So . . . you are in the Underground."

"Yes, Anna. I am in a force called Agat. And I have killed. I killed a Pawiak guard."

"Oh, Benny!"

"My Underground name is Lot. Not even my own family knows that name."

"I understand." She nodded, comprehending this new man she was learning about. "And, did you try to help Jews in the Ghetto?"

"You knew?"

"I guessed."

"We tried to help. Several of us boys smuggled food in through basements. The wall was above, but we dug a path through the basements."

"You're so brave."

"It didn't work. We only got a tiny bit of food in. I think we did no good at all."

"You helped them. You let the Jews know you were with them."

"Anna, my dove, we cannot tell anyone about us. About our marriage, our new life."

"I understand."

"It's too dangerous. I must trust you now, with my life. But we need to protect our families."

"And I agree with you. But we can have nothing between us, darling. We must be one, now."

Bronek felt her fingertips lightly graze his neck. The touch sent a charge through his body. He felt her warm breath on his face. He was not sure if he should move. Then he felt her soft, full lips brush his. Her kiss was warm, and open, and complete. He heard her breath, coming in short pants.

"I have things to learn, too," she whispered.

He raised his hand and touched her cheek. "We both have a lot to learn," he sighed.

"Blow out the candle."

"Wait." He got up on his knees, and blew out the candle. Now total obscurity enveloped them. Bronek felt her arms squeeze his waist, her face press against his stomach.

His mouth went dry. He held her shoulders, and he breathed deeply. He reached down, and tilted her head up, and then he kissed her, passionately, as she had kissed him, and suddenly the nervous tension dissolved and there were no barriers between them, and they held each other tightly, and their kiss did not end, and they melted as one, and their breath was halting, and they touched, and they sunk to the floor, and they shared the exhilaration that leapt from them.

XIV

That Friday dawned quietly. German police turned in after their nightly patrols, and streetcars rolled out from the yards on steel rails. The streets were mostly empty.

But soon it became apparent that something was not normal. The German-owned shops remained empty, and had no business. The official newspaper, the *Nowy Kurier Warszawski,* remained in stacks at the newsstands, not bought and not read. A boycott had been called. Governor-General Hans Frank would be most unhappy. The people had passed a message. They still obeyed someone else's orders.

At the Kruczyk household, Wiktor sat silently at the kitchen table, as imposing and solid as a stone mountain. A bottle of *bimber* sat on the table in front of him. His thick fingers rested on a shot glass, nearly enveloping it. His narrow eyes did not move. Presently he checked his wristwatch. He said nothing.

Magdalena sensed his concern. "He's just five minutes late," she said matter-of-factly.

Wiktor grumbled something unintelligible; his wide mustache did not move. Young Zbigniew, too timid to approach his father, went into the parlor and stared out the front window.

Just then there was a loud, rapid knock. "Get the door!" Wiktor shouted militarily.

Magdalena opened the door. "Jerzy!" she said with her own sense of relief.

Jerzy entered the kitchen as Zbigniew came running in from the parlor. "I went down side streets," he explained.

Wiktor rose from his chair, and stared into his younger brother's eyes. His mustache seemed to bristle; his eyes narrowed to angry slits. "You are five minutes late," he announced, putting all his formidable authority into every word.

"Wiktor, leave me alone," Jerzy answered defensively. "It's terrible outside! Every street is dangerous!"

"Wiktor, Jerzy, stop that," Magdalena said scoldingly. "Jerzy, what do you have?"

"There." Jerzy opened his jacket and pulled up his shirt. "There you are." Wrapped around his chest were numerous red posters. "It was terrible trying to walk with these things. They kept slipping."

Zbigniew pointed at Jerzy's smuggled cargo. "I saw those! They were on the kiosks! He stole them!"

Wiktor stared. "How many do you have there?"

"Eight. I have more. They're at every hiding place I know of."

Magdalena looked closely at them. "They're Kutschera's announcements." Forty people executed, thirty people executed: the posters listed hundreds of names. "How did you get them?"

"Zbig was right. I stole them."

"Well, sit down, sit down. Wiktor, pour your brother a drink."

Wiktor sat on his chair, and slid the bottle over. "Have some," he said laconically.

Jerzy sat down, threw a shot of *bimber* to the back of his throat, and swallowed. "I have more." Jerzy pulled up his pants leg. There, strapped to his leg, were several sheets of note paper. He tossed them across the table.

"What's that?" Wiktor asked.

"Take it, Wiktor. Get these things off of me."

Magdalena studied the slips. "Look, Wiktor," she whispered, awestruck, "Dates, places, even the weather. He really did it."

Wiktor nodded his head, almost imperceptibly. "Did you find every execution?"

"There was one on Pius Street that I missed. Otherwise, I found every one. All my interviews are here."

"That's amazing," Magdalena commented. "Thanks to God, we have proof."

"Jerzy," Wiktor asked gruffly, "How is it outside?" Wiktor pulled out one of his wrinkled cigarettes and lit it.

"Quiet," Jerzy commented grimly. "Scary. Like curfew, but all day."

"As I expected."

Jerzy fidgeted with his shot glass. Suddenly he released what was pent up inside him. "Wiktor," he stammered, "I – I hate doing this. Asking these questions. People are so – shocked, and hurt. I feel – I'm attacking them. I have dreams about it all. They won't go away. Do you understand, Wiktor?"

"This is important, Jerzy. It must be done. Our children will owe you a debt." There was no wavering, no hesitancy, with Wiktor. He pulled his son onto his knee, and he poured himself another shot of *bimber*, expertly balancing his son with one hand and his cigarette and the bottle with the other. He gazed over the stack of posters and notes dumped onto his kitchen table. "Well, Magdalena, can we find places to hide all this? The police tend to frown on people stealing their posters."

His wife turned her attention to the new contraband she now needed to hide. "We have so much in our basement now," She complained. "Well, we'll find a hiding place for this, too."

Wiktor tipped up his drink, while bouncing Zbig on his knee. "Well," he finally said to his brother, ". . . Good work."

Jerzy did not smile. He reached for the bottle, and his fingers were trembling. "Take it," he said, pleadingly. "Please, take it all from me." He swallowed another shot of *bimber*. "Please."

* * *

At the Pietraszewicz home, Karol Pietraszewicz was putting away the dishes from their dinner of black bread, potato soup thickened with barley meal, and ersatz coffee. His two sons sat at the table and sipped the bitter coffee. They watched their father gingerly stack the porcelain dishes.

"The boycott worked," Eugene remarked. "Nobody bought the *Nowy Kurier Warszawski*."

"I saw that, Eugene," Karol replied coldly.

Bronek nodded, but did not respond. It had been a quiet, awkward, dinner, with almost no conversation. Now Bronek felt profoundly uncomfortable. *Why am I even here?* he wondered. He was getting messages from Zebra, his messenger girl, and meeting with Wiktor. Wiktor was planning a new operation soon. And he had a new person who knew his secrets, a person who brought him both joy and worry.

It was easier to be completely underground, he decided. Nowak could bring him food coupons, false identifications, and money. This was too difficult, leading a double life. Now when he looked at Eugene he saw a child, a boy who was a part of his old family. He did not belong here any more. He already spent most nights in his other abandoned rooms. He stared at the front door.

"I need to stand up," Eugene said abruptly. Reaching for his cane, he stood from his chair and stepped precariously into the parlor.

Without a word, Bronek followed his brother into the other room. Eugene was standing, stretching his knees. The only light came in through the front window. "Eugene?"

Eugene emitted an agonized grunt.

"How is your leg?"

"Oh, it's – not bad. Not too bad."

"Well, keep working it, can you?"

"I do, I do." Eugene carefully lowered himself onto the overstuffed sofa and, straightening his knee, began to rub his thigh.

Bronek looked at his younger brother in the gray, shadowy window light. "Tell me if there's anything I can do. Will you?"

"Sure."

"Keep busy, Eugene. Perhaps you can type some – messages tonight."

"Oh, that," Eugene sighed, "My typewriter."

"What about it?"

"Well," he said, wincing as he massaged his leg, "It's gone. I sold it this week."

"You did? Eugene – your typewriter?"

"I had to. Typewriters are illegal. And, we got 25 zlotys for it. That's something, isn't it?"

"Yes, that's pretty good."

"I don't mind losing the typewriter, really. But," he said, smiling mischievously, "Have you ever read an essay by someone named 'Z'?"

"Those essays by Z? In the *Biuletyn Informacyjny*?"

"Well, not any more."

Bronek's jaw dropped open. "You? You were Z?"

"Actually, several of us are Z. I was, too. But I'm not. Not any more."

"Those – some of those – were by you? That's what you did with your typewriter?" Bronek stared at his younger brother quizzically. "You? But you're just – a silly kid."

"I like to write, Bronek. You know that."

"Yes, but – Eugene!" Bronek was truly surprised. This boy had a child's face and walked with a cane. Even his smile seemed vulnerable. Bronek pitied him, because he was helpless. "How? How did you get essays to the paper?"

"I did, Bronek."

"No, don't answer that. I shouldn't know." Bronek stared at his little brother. He was both confused and heartened. The police were failing. The Underground truly was everywhere. Even with his younger brother. "You are amazing."

"Well, I like to think so."

"Bronislaw!" his father called from the kitchen. "Come in

here."

"In a minute," Bronek answered, not realizing that his father had used his full name.

"You come in here – now."

"Uh-oh," Eugene said.

Bronek was puzzled by the harsh tone. He left Eugene in the parlor and returned to his father.

The kitchen was immaculate. All the dishes were out of sight, and the coffee cups were off the table. Karol was sitting at his spot at the head of the table. "Sit down, Bronislaw," he said quietly.

Bronek, puzzled, dutifully sat down across from him.

"I want to know. Where were you this week?"

"Oh. I was – out."

"Where?"

"I can't say."

"Bronislaw, where is your mother's wedding ring?"

Bronek suddenly felt very uncomfortable. "Eugene! You promised!"

"Sit back down. Do you think I wouldn't notice that it was missing?

". . . Oh."

"Tell me, and tell me now. Where is the ring?"

"I – I – can't say," he repeated, unable to think of a better answer.

Karol bit his lip. Bronek perceived that something was happening inside. "Bronek, we need that ring to buy food this winter." His voice built, slowly, to a near-shout. "What we do with that ring is for me to decide, not you!"

Bronek leaned backward, surprised. He had never seen his father this angry before. Or at least, not in a very long time.

"Our lives are at stake!" Karol paused, and regained his composure. Bronek squirmed in his seat.

"Now, I want to know, where is the ring?"

"I – I didn't sell it."

"You gave it away? To some girl you happened to meet, I

suppose? Bronislaw . . . that is even worse. I decide what to do with our valuables. Not you."

"But I can, too."

"No, you cannot." Karol's cheeks and broad forehead were flushed. "Well, here we are. Your constant absences, I guess I must tolerate. But you steal a ring, and then you refuse to tell me what you did with it. There's only one thing for me to do. Bronislaw, you are grounded."

"Wh – what?" Bronek stammered, dismayed.

"You are grounded until you tell me what you did with that ring. You can go out in the day. But you must return to this home every night, for curfew."

"But – you can't do that."

"Yes, I can."

"But I'm twenty years old! I'm grown up!"

"I don't care how old you are. You still live in this home, and you will not harm this family."

Bronek wrinkled his brow in confusion. Here he was, deciding so many things, and changing in so many ways. Now he was being grounded. His father was treating him as if he were still a child. It was unfair. He did not know what to do, or what to say. He sat on his chair, and he sulked.

"Now," Karol concluded, his face relaxing, "We are going down to our prayer service. Why don't you help Eugene? He seems to be hurting today."

"Yes, sir," Bronek answered, almost in a whisper. He dejectedly pulled himself up from his chair and headed into the parlor. His mind raced with concerns. Something in his life had to change. It had to.

* * *

Later that evening, at the Krzykowski household, Anna at last found time to sit on the front windowsill and stare out at the street below. In her hand she held a cup of ersatz coffee; it tasted terrible, but it was all there was. It had been a gray day, with scattered rays of sunshine but no snow either. She looked both ways out the window. The street was nearly deserted. Only a few stray men or women appeared in public, and then hurried away. Being outside too long increased one's chance of being arrested.

Gazing at the street reminded her of what had happened the day before. She was still attending her classes, and she was getting better at sensing danger, sensing when she was being followed. The day before, she had felt the danger, and had "shaken" someone who was following her. It had to be a Gestapo. Bronek would be proud of her. Perhaps his confidence was affecting her.

Slowly, secretively, she felt for the ring in her skirt pocket. Yes, it was there, it was all still true. Anna yearned, ached, to be someplace else. She felt herself being pulled out of her home, away to a different place, to where she truly belonged. Anna Krzykowska. Anna Pietraszewicz. She turned the names over in her mind, imagining herself as a new person. Yes, they were united, they were one now. Yet she was still here, waiting, waiting. And she imagined their children, four of them. They would need her constant care and protection. She would not wait for the liberation. She was starting her family, and soon. This was God's wish. She would not let the General Government control her like that. But when, how –

Her thoughts were interrupted by noises from the kitchen. "Aleksy, we still have to go outside. You need your treatment." That was their mother's name for it: his treatment.

"Mama, I don't want to sit outside. It's too cold."

"Stop complaining, and come outside."

"Aleksy," Krystyna told him, more scoldingly, "Don't complain. You have to get your sun."

Anna considered briefly going to help her mother, but then thought better of it. Mama and Krystyna had Aleksy well under control. Besides, the sight of her brother made her heart ache. Aleksy had become such a pitiful figure His skin was sallow and cold, and his legs were as thin as table legs. Worst of all, they bowed outward. No wonder: dinner had been black bread, marmalade, and ersatz coffee. The previous dinner had been more black bread, potatoes, and millet grain. Before, Mama would have thrown out such moldy things. Now they were the entire meal. They were slowly starving. This could not go on. They had to find more food –

"Anna," a voice said weakly. "There you are."

"Oh," Anna exclaimed, shaking her own thoughts away. "Papa. I'm just finishing my coffee." A twinge of foreboding made the hair on her neck stand up.

He approached her, walking tentatively, as if he needed a cane. "Ah, Anna," he said, "What are you doing?" His hair was white, his eyes eerily blank.

"Nothing, Papa. Just – thinking."

"Well . . . then . . . it's time to go check."

"Oh, no, Papa –"

"Yes, yes! We must check for names!"

"Papa, we have to be very careful. Please – can we go check, and come straight home?"

Anna's father put on his coat, leaving Anna to shiver. With tension coursing through her body, she led him outside.

Being outside in Warsaw, with the dying sunlight and gray clouds, was a terrifying, unreal experience. Everything felt different, nothing was normal. Blue police, Gestapos, SDs, Schupos, SS – at any moment it could happen. Pulling her father, feeling him lean on her arm for support, she felt the fear.

They walked down to the corner and then over one block. There, on the opposite corner, loomed the kiosk. They walked slowly; her father no longer walked confidently. "Are you going to make it, Papa?" Anna asked.

"Yes, yes, we must keep going."

They stepped gingerly across the streetcar tracks and approached the kiosk. Abruptly, her father stopped. He stared at the round tower, as if he were inspecting it. "Is it there?" he asked weakly. "Is a new one there?"

Anna squinted her eyes. "There's a poster there . . . it's from yesterday, Papa."

He said nothing for a while. No sound or movement. At last, he said, "Read it, Anna."

Anna dreaded those words. "Come with me, Papa. I can help you get closer."

"No, no. Read it for me."

"Papa, please. I'll stay right with you."

Her father lowered his head and looked away. "Read the names."

Anna sighed. She knew that her father could read. He was not so blind, nor so feeble. But he behaved like a doddering old man. "Yes, Papa," she replied. Squinting her eyes to read the small print, she read from the poster. "'Announcement,'" she read. "'On November 26, 1943, security police vehicles were again treacherously attacked on Nowy Swiat Street in Warsaw. Two uniformed police members, one German SA serviceman, and one person working in German service were severely wounded by gunfire and explosives thrown by . . . criminals. In retaliation for this, I ordered the following 30 – criminals – condemned by the Security Police Summary Court but eligible for clemency, to be executed publicly on December 2, 1943.'" She swallowed. "And then – then it gives the names, Papa."

Her father looked away, into the distance. "The names, Anna," he said into the cold air, "The names."

"There are thirty names, Papa."

"Yes, yes."

"Papa – it hurts so much to read them." Anna took a deep breath, and wiped away the tear she already felt in her eye. "All right. 'Jedrzejczyk, Jan. Zoller, Janusz. Kwiatkowski, Jerzy. Smiechowski, Piotr. Swadkowski, Eugeniusz. Kwiatkowski, Jan –'"

Suddenly her father's head jerked. "Who was that?"

"Which one, Papa? Jan Kwiatkowski?"

He seemed to nod, but his entire body bowed.

"It says, 'August 19, 1896.' He was your age. You – you knew him?"

Her father groaned the name, plaintively. "Jan, Jan, Jan."

He nodded his head, but to Anna he seemed to drift even further away.

"Papa, let's stop now."

He closed his eyes, lost in his own memories. Finally, he said, "Go on."

"Papa, please!"

"Go on, Anna. Go on."

So she continued to read, shaking in the cold. She read the names of 30 executed prisoners. Only one other name elicited the same response in him.

At last Anna sighed. "That's all, Papa."

"What else? What else is there?"

"Just the same threats, Papa. Come, Papa. It's too cold out here. Let's go home."

"Yes, yes – wait."

"What is it?"

He pointed at the kiosk. "What does that say?"

"It's nothing Papa, really. It's just propaganda."

"Tell me what it says."

"No, Papa. I – it's terrible. I can't."

"Tell me what it says, Anna."

"No, Papa – please! Please don't make me!"

"I want to hear it, Anna."

Anna bit her lip. She could not refuse her father, not even this. On the kiosk, beside the official announcement, was a large black poster. It showed a *Wehrmacht* soldier, his rifle lying on the ground. In his arms he cradled a little Polish girl, in a traditional folk dress. The girl's head was tilted back, like a lifeless doll. Anna read, bitterly. "It says . . . 'This is your doing. Why do you provoke this?'" They stood together for what seemed like a painful eternity.

Finally, Anna tugged on her father's arm. "Let's go home now, Papa." They walked together in silence, Anna helping her father along. Suddenly she stopped. "Wait."

Off in the distance, she heard a rumbling sound. It was just a noise, but something about it drew her attention. "I feel it.

That feeling."

Then she saw them. Three black trucks turned the corner and barreled down the windswept street. "SS!" People turned and ran away from the big trucks. "Papa, we have to go!" She started for home, pulling on her father's arm.

Suddenly there were people, people dashing past them on both sides. "Wait, wait," her father protested.

The trucks drew closer, their low rumble growing to a mechanical roar. "Papa, please! Run! Now!" She tugged on his arm.

He took a step, unwillingly. "Anna, daughter –" he pleaded, "I need to know."

The trucks were now only a block away. They gained speed; the red swastikas were clearly visible. Anna saw the driver of the head truck, his gloved fingers gripping the steering wheel. "Home, Papa! Now!"

The street was chos; people ran in every direction. She yanked on her father's arm, as hard as she could. At last she pulled him, and he moved.

With Anna pulling, they staggered down an alley. Anna dared not look back; she whispered a prayer, her eyes shut tight. She heard the noise grow. "Mother Mary, save us!" She heard two more trucks.

And then they faded into the distance.

Not daring to stop, she nudged her father along. "Papa," she said, "Let's go home, Papa. Right away." It was dark, and Anna felt along the cold stone walls. She gently tugged him through the alley, until at last they were back home.

It was not their time yet; apparently the SS were heading someplace else that day. Nothing more was said about the incident, although it certainly did not aid her father's emotional state. But for Anna, it was too much to bear any longer. They were starving, and wasting away, and losing their minds. And in her soul there remained the vision of a new family, one that she belonged to. She needed her Bronek. She would be destroyed while she waited.

* * *

The next day, Saturday, was sunnier but colder. Ice covered the puddles between the paving stones, and clouds of frost hung in the air before people's faces. The boycott successfully concluded, the streets were back to their normal level of activity, which meant the busiest in all occupied Europe.

Adam stood in what had been a janitor's closet of a small, burned-out hotel on Leszno Street. The Germans would not live here because it was in the Jewish Ghetto, before the Ghetto was shrunk to its final 1943 boundary. A couple mops and steel buckets still cluttered the corners, and the musty smell of wash water filled the air. Nonetheless, it was large enough for three or four people to meet. Adam looked through the tiny circular attic window. Here he could see over the Ghetto wall, across the acres of burned-out buildings of the Ghetto. And there, deep in the Ghetto, he saw the white edifice. It was Pawiak prison. Too far removed from the city for the Underground to raid it, or even provide much assistance. At that moment, Polish people were being held, tortured, shot. Adam looked at the austere prison walls helplessly, and he noted with sad bemusement the parallel with his own life.

Adam's real name was Adam Przezdziecki. However, his identification papers were in the name Czeslaw Nowak. In 1920 he had fought against the Russians at the Battle of Warsaw, and had learned about fortifications. After that war, he had become a construction foreman. He knew which building inspectors to see to keep projects going. A follower of Polish premier Jozelf Pilsudski, he was not a committed socialist, and fit in with the new parliament when Pilsudski died in 1935.

When war broke out, he had helped to erect anti-tank fortifications in the city. He tried to join with General Wladyslaw Sikorski, but was trapped in Warsaw when the government collapsed. He was deeply shaken when, in July 1943, the Germans triumphantly announced Sikorski's death in a mysterious airplane crash near Gibraltar. Sikorski's death was a terrible blow to the Underground, and to the status of Poland in the Allied war effort. Sikorski was so esteemed that he was replaced by two men. Stanislaw Mikolajczyk became the Prime Minister, while Wladyslaw Sosnkowski became the commander-in-chief of the military. The two men together did not fill Sikorski's role, and Underground agents like Adam were plotting their own course.

And Adam had his own concerns. If the Russians came, he could not stay in Poland; he would certainly be imprisoned, because he had fought against them. But he had to stay. His wife, his beloved Zofia, was performing forced labor at the Ravensbrück concentration camp for women, north of Berlin. He expended considerable efforts receiving updates from informers about her condition. He would not flee without her.

Adam gazed through the small window, down to Leszno Street. On the street, several wagons carrying artillery shells and boxes of munitions rolled eastward. He saw a few VW cars, probably carrying SS officers, speeding toward the city center. However, not the man he was after, he thought with a silent chuckle.

On the tile floor, Adam noticed something. A mouse scurried across the slippery tile, heading for some paper towels in the corner. It was where he had built his nest. Adam bemusedly watched the gray mouse sniff and scurry, scurry and sniff. He did not chase the little creature. Even a mouse needs his chance to survive.

Just then he heard a knock on the door, then three more knocks. Adam stepped over the mouse and cracked open the door.

He was relieved to see Wiktor in the hallway. "Herr Becker's office, please." This was his message that he was not followed. Adam's own false identity was that of an electrician, which let him plausibly search buildings for fuse boxes.

"Why do you need to see it?"

"I'm here to paint it. I need to take measurements first."

"Yes. Come in." He opened the door.

Wiktor came in and locked the door behind him. He glanced around at the dingy closet. "Nice room, Nowak," he commented dryly. "We're becoming more important, I see."

"Ah, Granit, it's – refreshing – to see you again. Zebra found you all right?"

"She found me, but I wasn't all right. I was having a *bimber*. No one else here today?"

"No, Granit, this is just between you and me for now." Adam tapped his fingers nervously. "The boycott was successful?"

"As far as I can tell."

"Fine, fine. Any arrests?"

"A street arrest. SS. But I don't think it was because of the boycott."

"Thanks to the Blessed Virgin for that."

"But did you see the police poster for December 1?"

"I'm aware of the problem, Granit." The recent poster was the first to identify the Polish Underground as the PZP (*Polski Zwiazek Powstanczy*), or Polish Insurrection League.

"They have identified the code name for the Underground, Nowak. I say that is a problem indeed."

"It is not so bad, Granit. The Gestapo must have tortured an agent, who revealed a code word he did not think would damage us."

"But how does that look to people, seeing code words on official posters?"

"People will understand. The General Government is trying to prove it has broken the Underground. It will not make people afraid of us."

"You are an optimistic man, Nowak."

"I must be, Granit."

"Well, Nowak, why did you call me into your fine office?"

"Of course, of course. You know, Granit, your comment was right on target. We are becoming more important."

"What do you mean?"

Adam leaned forward. His voice was now barely a whisper.

From inside the janitor's closet, he said the words. "The *Agat* unit has received new orders. Top priority." Adam did not explain that the order had come from a man named Dyrektor. Adam in turn did not know that Dyrektor was the code name for Adam Borys, a parachutist captain. The Underground functioned by revealing as little information to each agent as possible. Messengers carried most information between agents.

"What is that? Another train? A Pawiak guard?"

"No, Granit." Adam shook his head slowly. "We have a new assignment . . . to assassinate SS *Brigadeführer* Franz Kutschera."

Wiktor took a deep breath, and waited for the news to sink into his large frame. At last he nodded, as the army wagons passed on the street below.

ANNOUNCEMENT

On December 2, 1943 again a treacherous attack was carried out on a police van traveling down Pulawska Avenue in Warsaw. On this occasion 5 Security Police officers and 1 member of the Waffen-SS were killed, and further a Security Police officer was injured. Through evidence obtained from one of the participating assailants in the raid, the Pole WOJCIECH LESAKOWSKI, born February 1, 1923 in Dublin, of 26/9 Zurawia Street, Warsaw, it has been proven indisputably that the attack was carried out by a terror group of the secret resistance organization "PZP," which is in the pay of England.

In retaliation for this, I have ordered the following 100 criminals listed here, who were condemned to death by the Security Police Summary Court on November 16 and December 2, 1943 for being in possession of weapons and belonging to forbidden organizations under Sections 1 and 2 of the Decree for the Prevention of Attacks against the German Work of Reconstruction in the General Government of October 2, 1943, to be publicly executed on December 3, 1943:

1. Gajderowicz, Tadeusz — b. 10/01/1911
2. Szymanski, Jozef — b. 02/01/1908
3. Pruszkiewicz, Jan — b. 03/05/1910
4. Klos, Zygmunt — b. 12/23/1916
5. Pawlow, Eugeniusz — b. 05/17/1912
6. Zlotkowski, Zbigniew — b. 05/24/1924
7. Koza, Stanislaw — b. 12/15/1919
8. Koscielski, Franciszek — b. 10/04/1922
9. Koscielski, Tadeusz — b. 09/10/1924
10. Laskowski, Wladyslaw — b. 05/01/1921
11. Pachulski, Marian — b. 02/04/1923
12. Paldyna, Mieczyslaw — b. 07/28/1924
13. Prksler, Wladyslaw — b. 09/03/1912
14. Rogala, Romuald — b. 07/22/1921
15. Rudzinski, Henryk — b. 02/01/1916
16. Symonowicz, Plotr — b. 05/28/1912
17. Trojan, Zenon — b. 01/02/1912
18. Wierzbicki, Jozef — b. 03/19/1919
19. Zielonka, Zygmunt — b. 11/11/1920
20. Zimny, Jan — b. 12/17/1911
21. Froelich, Stanislaw — b. 02/08/1904
22. Fickie, Tadeusz — b. 03/08/1925
23. Krolikowski, Leonard — b. 11/06/1921
24. Paradowski, Mieczyslaw Feliks — b. 10/10/1919
25. Kowalski, Jan — b. 04/28/1922
26. Sliwinski, Henryk — b. 10/29/1912
27. Owoc, Jan — b. 04/21/1883
28. Trzonek, henryk — b. 10/29/1912
29. Bryla, Stefan — b. 08/17/1886
30. Talarek, Stefan — b. 12/25/1918
31. Nowacki, Teodor — b. 08/13/1902
32. Kaminski, Kazimierz — b. 03/04/1922
33. Nowacki, Stefan — b. 09/21/1900
34. Kowalski, Stanislaw — b. 11/23/1907
35. Tybora, Kazimierz — b. 01/11/1914
36. Czajkowski, Mieczyslaw — b. 05/19/1898
37. Stankiewicz, Leszek — b. 11/25/1923
38. Czyzewski, Jan — b. 06/26/1899
39. Stypulkowski, Witalis — b.09/23/1923
40. Wojcik, Tadeusz — b. 10/03/1921
41. Fickie, Julian — b. 01/18/1879
42. Bebarski, Stanislaw — b. 01/16/1919
43. Debniak, Wladyslaw — b. 06/09/1920
44. Zurek, Ludwik — b. 08/30/1907
45. Sloczynski, Kaazimierz — b. 11/25/1921
46. Gawski, Stanislaw — b. 04/22/1922
47. Zaborowski, Jerzy — b. 11/17/1901
48. Lisiecki, Konstantyn — b. 07/14/1913
49. Czechowski, Stanislaw — b. 09/17/1919
50. Hauzenplas, Zdzislaw — b. 10/08/1921
51. Bieliec, Jan Antoni — b. 06/20/1921

52. Wegrowski, Stanisaw — b. 09/01/1917
53. Prokurat, Wladyslaw — b. 05/17/1914
54. Pawelczyk, Tadeusz — b. 09/05/1920
55. Dominiak, Henryk — b. 10/19/1919
56. Kropczynski, Leonard — b. 07/16/1922
57. Pracki, Jan Wociech — b. 12/28/1915
58. Chorzela, Wiktor — b. 12/28/1899
59. Zielenkiewicz, Aleksander — b. 02/26/1890
60. Buyno, Tadeusz Ludwik — b. 10/29/1904
61. Karski, Jan Wladyslaw — b. 06/27/1894
62. Dlutek, Stanislaw — b. 12/29/1912
63. Rozbicki, Stanislaw — b. 11/07/1902
64. Koltun, Xczeslaw — b. 02/05/1920
65. Kuczynski, Boleslaw — b. 02/14/1915
66. Stankiewicz, Jan — b. 03/20/1903
67. Kaminski, Jerzy — b. 11/20/1920
68. Sulkolski, Waclaw — b. 02/25/1916
69. Bowszys, Nikodem — b. 04/21/1909
70. Kozlak, Stanislaw — b. 08/24/1922
71. Lewandowski, Witold — b. 02/26/1901
72. Balazinski, Maksymilian — b. 12/20/1914
73. Dutkiewicz, Zdzislaw — b. 03/22/1887
74. Moroz, Jerzy — b. 08/21/1917
75. Kaminski, Jozef — b. 08/27/1895
76. Kaminski, Krzysztof Antoni — b. 02/16/1925
77. Szurmak, Aleksander — b. 09/22/1899
78. Walczak, Kazimierz — b. 05/12/1901
79. Dluzniewski, Marian — b. 04/28/1909
80. Siedzieniewski, Stanislaw — b. 12/21/1903
81. Pietruszynski, Wojciech Wladyslaw — b. 11/15/1922
82. Tomaszewski, Jozef — b. 02/26/1904
83. Tumidajski, Leszek — b. 07/26/1921
84. Sulikowski, Ignacy Jozef — b. 09/13/1922
85. Pytlakowski, Jozef Stanislaw — b. 03/02/1895
86. Bojucki, Kazimierz — b. 06/16/1916
87. Debek, Szczepan — b. 12/02/1896
88. Szumillo, Mieczyslaw — b. 01/12/1900
89. Haberko, Zdzislaw — b. 01/01/1918
90. Grudzinski, Stanislaw — b. 04/30/1906
91. Turkowski, Jan — b. 05/14/1919
92. Balecki, Witold — b. 01/15/1925
93. Nalecki, Czeslaw — b. 03/21/1918
94. Dyminski, Roman — b. 05/03/1908
95. Kozlowski, Boleslaw — b. 07/09/1921
96. Swynecki, Zygmunt — b. 04/15/1910
97. Szymulski, Jozef — b. 06/30/1905
98. Gilski, Waldemar — b. 02/26/1923
99. Gurlaga, Ryszard — b. 03/20/1911
100. Bogacki, Kazimierz — b. 02/08/1911

The executed men belonged to resistance organizations in the pay of England and predominantly to "PZP," and were partially eligible for clemency.

Warsaw, December 3, 1943

**SS AND POLICE LEADER
FOR WARSAW DISTRICT**

XV

"Hurry, Anna, we must keep walking," Izabela Krzykowska ordered scoldingly.

"I am, Mama, I am." Fear went with Anna whenever she went outside, but she still disliked being told what to do, even by her mother. The fact that on this Saturday, December 11, they were shopping for her did not brighten her spirits one bit. Perhaps that was because she was not optimistic about the outcome.

"Look at me," Aleksy said cheerfully, "Even I can keep up."

Anna watched her brother as he walked. In truth, he appeared to waddle. His legs were so weak that his feet pointed outward. He could walk, but only in a sauntering, waddling gait. "Oh, Aleksy!" Anna bit her lower lip. Her brother looked so pathetic, she suddenly felt ashamed of complaining at all. "You're doing fine, Aleksy. Mama, can't we try for Aleksy first? I don't need shoes that badly."

"Nonsense. You certainly do need shoes. Just look at what you're wearing."

Anna looked down. Her shoes were completely worn through in the soles. She had tried to tack wooden soles onto them, but the tacks had worn through the leather uppers, and now the things were held together by some strips of cloth.

"Well, perhaps I could work on them."

"Your shoes are done for," Izabela declared.

"I'm sorry, Mama."

Izabela, followed by her two children, entered a small store a safe two blocks from their home. The store certainly did not inspire confidence. The shop window displayed shoe boxes, but large tags warned, "*Leere Schachteln*" (Empty Boxes). The dark, unlit store appeared to be empty. "Mister Dziewiontkoski?"

A middle-aged man with greasy hair, a large bald spot, and an unruly mustache appeared from the back room. "Who's there?" he asked suspiciously. "Ah, Misses Krzykowska," he answered himself, nodding. "What do you need today?"

As her mother haggled with the shopkeeper, Anna glanced around the store. This had once been a men's clothing store. A three-way mirror still stood along the wall, and signs pointed to areas marked "Ties," "Suits," and "Handkerchiefs." But there were no ties, no suits, and no handkerchiefs. There were just bare racks and bare shelves, with a few hangers dangling here and there. But closing was considered sabotage by the General Government. So he had to stay open, or risk arrest and forced labor. Now all of Mister Dziewiontkoski's business was done from the back room.

"Do you have a coupon?" the shopkeeper asked.

"No, I don't. No coupons."

"That makes things more difficult, Misses Krzykowska." Shopkeepers did try to hoard coupons for Polish customers, at substantial personal risk. But the coupons used to purchase items were increasingly rare. Even coupons had to be paid for. And Izabela did not have enough money to get past Mister Dziewiontkoski's first denial.

"Well, let me see what is available," Izabela told the clothier.

Mister Dziewiontkoski walked, shoulders hunched, into the storage room.

"I think he may have something," Anna's mother whispered.

In a minute Mister Dziewiontkoski returned. "You are in luck," he said. He placed the merchandise on the counter.

Anna stared at them. "They're wood, Mama."

"I thought we could get leather shoes," Izabela commented.

"Eh, well, you cannot get leather shoes, even with a coupon. If you were a German, well, perhaps. But," he continued, waving his arms for emphasis, "I have had no leather shoes for weeks, so all I can get for you are these. If you don't want them, well, many other people will take them. So, it is up to you. What would you like to do?" Finished, Mister Dziewiontkoski folded his arms across his chest.

"Well . . . can I buy a coupon?"

"I'm sorry, Misses Krzykowska. I have none."

"Well, what do you think, Anna?"

"These are good shoes," Mister Dziewiontkoski said, rather defensively. "These will last."

Anna picked up a shoe and inspected it. It was not as chunky as a Dutch clog. It was smooth and lightweight, with small blue flowers painted across the top. "They're wood, Mama."

"Well, if you wear heavy socks to keep your feet warm . . ." Izabela suggested.

"Mama, let Aleksy have them."

"Nonsense, Anna. You must take these."

"No, please. Give them to Aleksy. I'll do without."

"I'll take them!" Aleksy blurted out.

"See, there's a smart young man," Mister Dziewiontkoski said. "These are good shoes. So, what would you like to do?"

"She'll take these," her mother said.

"No, Mama, help Aleksy first!" Anna protested. Then she corrected herself. "Yes, Mama."

"Good. Now I need to see about the price."

* * *

The air was chilly that afternoon, but the wind was weak;

puffy clouds blocked the sun. Bronek was on Kaliska Street. He was in work clothes, assuming his false identity. He disappeared behind a collapsed brick wall and walked down a hallway of what had been a house.

Bronek went to a brick in a corner and pulled it out of the wall. A feeling of relief eased his hunger pangs; a slip of paper was hidden inside the hollowed-out brick. He no longer met with his messenger girl, Zebra; personal meetings were too dangerous, due to the increased street patrols. So seeing the message was a lifeline for him. Zebra was still delivering messages. Wiktor was still planning the next mission.

He slid the paper into his underwear. He would decode it later. He had another mission first. He returned the brick and left the bombed-out house.

Bronek walked cautiously eastward. Police patrols were all over. He especially maneuvered around SS soldiers. He negotiated his way through the city center, until he reached Jerozolimskie Avenue. Then he turned east. Soon he was out on the bridge.

Poniatowski Bridge, the great old stone arch bridge, connected two cities. On the west was Warsaw, on the east the suburb of Praga. Beneath him the Vistula River flowed lazily north, past the monumental Royal Castle, to the Baltic Sea. According to the old legend, a mermaid lived in the river. Warsaw's symbol, in fact, was a mermaid wielding a shield and sword. The city's motto was *contemnit procellas*: defying the storms. Ha! Bronek laughed inside. He imagined a long-haired mermaid, defying the Nazi empire. The image fit Warsaw perfectly.

Bronek leaned against the stone rail. When he was young, he and the other boys held swimming races across it. Then they ran away, so the police would not report them to their parents. Bronek wanted to jump into the water now, and let it carry him away. The icy water would cleanse him, washing all the memories and the fear from his soul. Just downstream, north of Warsaw, lay the Kampinos Forest. In the forest there were no police patrols, no SS arrests, no street executions. Just an army of gendarmes to avoid. He could leap right now, and be in the river. But he did not leap. Instead, he leaned against the rail and felt the chilly north breeze bite into his cheeks. And he thought.

That was as long as he dared stay. He could not risk being stopped and searched. He had to complete his missions. He went to Apartment Two, and he waited.

At last he heard a knock at the door. Anna came in, bundled in a babushka and her long trenchcoat. "Anna, thanks to God –" She grabbed him, and held on tightly.

"Anna, Dove," he whispered, "You're sobbing."

She held on to him for long moments.

"You're here now, you're safe," he told her soothingly.

At long last she looked up at him with tears in her deep blue eyes. "Benny, darling. It's terrible outside. The police are everywhere."

"I know, I know." He gently wiped a tear from her red cheek. "You're wearing wooden shoes." He just wanted to take her mind off her fear.

"Mama bought me new shoes. I got them from the finest store in Warsaw," she added with a weak sniffle.

Bronek smiled. "How are they?"

"They're cold. Even with socks on."

He knew Anna. She was intensely emotional, but she was able to recover her balance well. "Are you recovered now?"

"Only with you, darling. Without you, I'm so frightened. You did not write for three whole days. I was shaking, I didn't know what to think. I thought they took you – Lord, no!"

"You know they won't catch me, Dove. I can't write you a letter every day. I write you three or four a week."

"I know. And I save every one."

"You do?"

"Of course I do. So don't sign your name!"

"I guess I won't, then. It's not easy to get letters to you. Did you know I'm still grounded?"

"Benny, why don't you tell your father everything?"

"I can't. He wants to know where the ring is. And I can't tell him. We agreed."

"I know, but –"

Bronek slid her babushka back from her head. "It's cold in here. Do you want to leave your coat on?"

Anna nodded. "Thank you, Benny," she said appreciatively. Bronek led her over to the windowsill. They sat on the ledge in their coats and dangled one leg. Anna's foot swung in mid-air. She took some calming breaths, to regain her composure.

So she wore a man's overcoat, wooden shoes, and no make-up. Her blond hair was thin, and she did not tie ribbons or yarn in it any more. But she still parted it on the side, like a boy. She was both petite and strong, girlish and fascinating. She was the most adorable person in all the world. He wanted to make her the happiest person as well. "I hate this, Anna. I hate every-thing."

"We all do, Benny. Our priest tells us – to keep faith."

"We can't go on this way. I'm your husband. I want to see you every morning, and be with you every day."

"But we still live with our families."

"We can change that, Anna."

Anna studied his face, as if it could reveal a clue. "What do you mean?"

"We have a home. This apartment. My commander doesn't use it any more."

"It's just an empty room. It has no heat."

"So what? No one has heat. There's no difference."

"But how can we –?"

Bronek gripped her hand tightly, as excitement coursed through his fingers. "We can live together, Anna. I know we can. No one will know where we are. Even our families won't know, to protect them. We can live by bartering for food."

"But . . . what will we do? What about our future?"

"In the spring we can escape to the Kampinos Forest, and live in the woods. But we must stay in Warsaw through the win-ter. We just need to survive until spring. Then we can escape – to the forest."

He felt her grip his hand in return.

"December 3. Did you hear?"

"Yes, yes. I – heard the announcement on the loudspeakers."

"On Pulawska Street. Another street execution. One hundred people killed. And more at Pawiak prison, nearly every day. Those aren't even announced."

"I know, I – I know."

He repeated the number angrily. "One hundred." Bronek tried to keep his composure, but sometimes bitterness escaped in his words. "This is what Kutschera has planned for us. He'll kill you and me, when he has the chance." Bronek stood, and held her in his arms. He stared into her deep blue eyes, and suddenly the pain and longing that he felt poured out of him. "Anna, I don't know what may happen to us. I just know that I love you. I don't want to live without you any more. I would gladly give my life to be married, really married to you. Can you understand?"

She nodded, hesitantly.

"You're frightened, aren't you."

She nodded again.

"You must trust me, Anna. We can do it, I know we can."

For a long time, Anna did not speak, or even move. Finally her voice came, quietly, tentatively. "Darling . . . all I can do is give you my life."

"We can both carry out our work until the spring. Then we can leave this place. The Russians are stopped now, for the winter. They won't reach Poland until the spring. We'll meet the Russians as fellow soldiers."

"We can live on our own? We can make it – yes?"

"Don't worry, Dove. I will never leave you."

They stood together for a long moment, and Anna seemed to absorb his strength into herself.

"We have to tell our families," she said at last, "So that they know not to look for us."

"We'll each write a letter. But first we need to pack what we can. Candles, blankets. It may take a few trips – we'll have to smuggle it all under our clothes. Perhaps by the beginning of the year."

"Then we'll have our home?"

"We'll have our home."

"This is it?"

"This is it."

She leaned up in her wooden shoes and kissed him, a warm, firm kiss, meant to reassure her soul. "I'll go home and pack."

* * *

Wiktor and Bronek were in the city center. The afternoon was sunny, and the air noticeably colder, but Wiktor wore his same clothes: a plain shirt and the pants and vest from an old wool suit. He was the sort who could get along without a coat.

Bronek walked several paces behind Wiktor, wearing his worker's pants and short, oil-stained coat. No one would guess that they were together. Nazi police patrols were on nearly every corner. Even some truckloads of *Wehrmacht* soldiers headed east along Jerozolimskie Avenue – toward the fighting. But they were all in trucks or marching in groups. That was no good for the mission.

On the sidewalk, walking south, Wiktor stopped. Farther up the block was a German *Wehrmacht Unteroffizier* (sergeant) in full combat uniform: boots, helmet, long gray overcoat. Over his shoulder was slung a German MP 40, blowback-operated, 9mm machine pistol. It was small and light, with a folding stock and a 32-round magazine – an attractive prize. Carrying it so publicly was an incredible mistake – instead of warding off thieves, he was attracting them. And, most importantly, he was alone; even German soldiers were so afraid of Poles that they usually went in groups. This sergeant was probably a Russian front veteran, on leave in Warsaw. Wiktor made no signal, but he began to follow the German. Bronek trailed behind him. At the next block the sergeant, not comprehending the danger in this civilian battle zone, actually boarded a streetcar.

Wiktor climbed aboard, but Bronek was still outside, pushing past some pedestrians. Quickly, Wiktor turned to the conductor, a middle-aged Pole. "Sir," Wiktor said, "Does this car go to Zoliborz?" Wiktor rested his thick fingers on the throttle.

The conductor looked at Wiktor, incredulously. Then he looked at the throttle, enveloped by Wiktor's hand, and he understood. "Why, of course it does." It did not. This was a westbound streetcar, and Zoliborz was north of the city center.

"I'm going to Potocka, in Marymont." Marymont was a suburban neighborhood north of Zoliborz. "How about there?"

"Well," the conductor said, "You can stop in Zoliborz, and then go up on Mickiewicza."

"I see." At last Bronek leapt on board – too fast, Wiktor thought, like some circus acrobat. "I'll do that, then. Thank you, sir." Wiktor lifted his fingers from the throttle and walked sullenly to the back of the streetcar. Bronek sat down away from Wiktor, as the streetcar lurched forward.

After just three stops the *Wehrmacht* sergeant left the streetcar. Wiktor left behind him, and Bronek followed Wiktor. They followed the soldier as he turned a corner, down Lindleya Street. They were lucky; the street was deserted. The German walked silently, casually, his arms resting on his gun. Wiktor closed in behind him.

Then Wiktor reached inside his belt and pulled out his Radom 9mm. He jumped in front and raised his gun. *"Halt! Hände hoch!"* Wiktor whispered loudly. He pressed his gun barrel against the German's chin.

The German sergeant stopped.

Bronek was behind him. *"Hände hoch!"* Bronek hissed. He pressed his Walther PPK 7.65mm to the German's neck, to make sure he could feel the snub-nosed barrel. Polish civilians walked by, a short distance away, and did nothing.

The German did not raise his hands. He froze, his arms at his sides. His eyes were flat, like a combat veteran's. He did not wish to surrender his weapon. *"Hände hoch,"* Wiktor said again, leaning closer. The machine pistol dangled enticingly.

There was no time to wait for him to obey. Bronek reached out and slipped the gun off the German's shoulder.

Suddenly the German's right arm snapped upward. Wiktor's hand clenched. The bullet from the Radom hit the German's mouth, and his head flew back. It was so loud, Bronek thought the entire city could hear it. The German covered his face with his hands and crumpled down; Bronek saw blood spurt through.

"Take it!" Wiktor shouted. "Come on!"

Just then Bronek heard a sharp voice behind him. *"Halt!"* Two policemen, Schupos, were at the end of the block. Bronek yanked on the machine pistol; but he could not lift the sergeant's arm. Bronek dropped the gun and ran. The crack of a gunshot ripped through the air. Civilians scrambled in every direction.

Bronek turned the far corner, and kept running. He heard another gunshot, and another; he heard a bullet whiz off the brick wall. "Split up!" Wiktor shouted. At the next street Wiktor disappeared around a corner.

Bronek was alone in the city. He dashed eastward on Jerozolimskie Avenue, his gun still in his hand. He darted down a narrow alley. His heart was pounding up in his ears. All he heard was thumping. But he knew Schupos were there, he felt them.

They alley was wet and winding, a canyon barely an arm-length wide. Bronek kept running. Suddenly he stopped. It was a wall. There was nowhere to go. He looked around him desperately. He saw a door. He grabbed the knob and shook; it was locked. He jerked his head about frantically: no ladders, nowhere to hide. Then he looked down: a sewer cover. He dove at it. With furious strength, he slid the iron lid aside; a hole opened beneath him. Behind him he heard footsteps. He heard, *"Halt!"* He jumped.

Bronek went straight down. Then his foot hit something, and he heard a brittle, "Snap!" Immediately, something was different. He looked down at the sewer water. All he could see was blackness. But from his right foot a horrible pain arose, intense, excruciating.

He had to move. Above him he heard police. He limped away from the shaft of light, into the blackness. Just in time. Three bullets whizzed down, and splashed in the black water beside him. Bronek stumbled away with a half-limping gait.

Now he realized where he was. Built sixty years before, the sewer formed a labyrinth under the city. The tube was tall enough, but the floor was curved and slick, full of boards and broken glass. And then the stench hit his nose: the smell of Warsaw's raw sewage. As he sloshed through it, knee-deep, things floated by him. He heard the frenetic squeaks of rats. There was no light; he could not see. He could only hear, and smell, and feel.

He came to a crossing; gurgling sewage echoes went in different directions. He felt his hands along the curved walls. All the time the pain throbbed in his foot. It was unbearable now, he could not put any weight on it; his shoe was about to burst open. He limped farther. He heard nothing from behind; the police did not follow him. He went deeper and deeper into the blackness.

His foot was swelling up; he could not breathe. He saw a pinprick of light. He reached it and looked up. It was a sewer cover above him. A little sliver of sunlight slipped around it. Using his one good leg, he pulled himself up the slippery rungs. He pushed on the iron plate. It was too heavy; he couldn't lift it. He pushed and pushed. Nothing.

At that moment the feeling hit his belly like a punch. He doubled over, and he retched and he retched. The sewer water splashed beneath him.

Bronek dangled on the topmost rung, sucking clean air through the little hole. The pinprick of light was precious. Soon, he fell down again. His chest slapped against the foul, soupy sewer water. And then everything went black.

XVI

Jerzy Kruczyk was at the markets that morning of December 18. He was staring at food he could not afford, and thinking of older days, of peaceful days. He thought back to times with his older brother, Wiktor. They had fought often, back then. It was silly, of course, considering their age difference. But Jerzy was a fighter. He wanted to fight his older brother. Perhaps that was why Wiktor had allowed him to join the Underground, even with the added risk it entailed. That was a long time ago. He felt old.

Then he had heard the rumor – rumors spread quickly in Warsaw – and he had to confirm it. He could not wait for the loudspeaker announcement; the evidence, and the witnesses, would be gone by then. But he could not hurry to his destination. Once, he could dash through the city streets like an athlete, like an acrobat. But now the paving stones were uneven, and slick with snow. He had to watch his every step.

When he reached 77 Wolska Street, in the heart of Wola, he stopped. It was a working-class neighborhood, with crumbling brick buildings and weeds growing alongside the sidewalk. This was the spot. All the signs were here. Children stood around, staring uncertainly at the irrational scene. Knots of people, shivering in the cold, converged uneasily. A crowd could somehow express feelings collectively that individuals could not. This crowd expressed not anger, but shame and bitterness.

Jerzy approached and slipped through to the front. Kneeling on the sidewalk were several women in tattered coats and babushkas. They were swaying back and forth, wailing prayers; their rosary beads swung from ice-blue fingers. Before them were heaps of flowers, and candles, and simple crosses, and figurines of the Virgin Mary. The brick wall had substantial damage; chunks of brick littered the ground. On the wall were lines of bullet holes, and splashes of water meant to wash away the blood.

Jerzy knew he should warn the people to leave. Even though the evidence was washed away, the Germans often returned, to scatter people away. But, the old women would not listen to him. The SS had to beat these women with their rifle butts to get them to move. It was all too much. He could not worry about protecting mourners any more.

For a moment Jerzy forgot his mission, and he stared. From behind, a little girl nudged around him. She was perhaps five years old. A few snowflakes floated down, and rested on her tiny babushka. She walked to the wall and gingerly placed a red rose atop the pile of flowers. Then she dutifully crossed herself and hurried away, her pudgy arms swinging at her sides.

Jerzy watched the little girl until she disappeared into the crowd. He had already accepted that the government was going to carry out street executions. He had conformed himself to that reality. But now he felt something new and alien inside. It was something like despair. The Russians would never reach Warsaw. He would go on tallying numbers forever.

Jerzy spotted a young man standing near him. He seemed to have his senses about him, so Jerzy approached. "Did you see what happened?" Jerzy asked innocently.

The young man had a haunted look to his deep-set eyes. "Who are you to ask?" he said sullenly.

"I'm recording this," Jerzy said sadly.

The young man stared away, at nothing.

"London will know about it. Even Churchill himself."

The young smirked. "Then what?" he asked.

"Well, it will be recorded," Jerzy commented defensively. "For history."

For a long time, the young man said nothing. They both watched the old women kneeling on the sidewalk, moaning in prayer. Every so often, someone would help a woman away. Then someone new would kneel, and moan new prayers. "It won't matter. We'll be wiped out before then."

"That's not so –"

"– Yes, it is," the sad young man interrupted. "The Jews were first. We'll be next."

There it was, again: *We will be next.* Jerzy studied the man's tense, haunted face. "Well," Jerzy asked, "Can you tell me how many there were?"

The young man stared at the wall. "Ten, twenty," he said vaguely.

"What was it, exactly?"

"They cleared the street. I was a block away."

"Which was it, exactly?"

"I don't know, you fool. I couldn't see. I could only hear."

"Oh." Jerzy studied the brick wall again. The bodies had been removed in trucks, so it was never easy to get the correct number. For some executions, he could only record an approximation. He sighed; he would have to talk to more people. "I'm sorry. I'm sorry I asked you any questions at all."

A light snow, as light as dust, began to fall. They all let the snow settle onto them, as if it did not matter.

"Something will happen. We will fight back. This will stop."

The young man shook his head. "No," he replied. "No, it won't."

* * *

The feeling was in Karol's heart. He sensed it before he knew it formally. He was out shopping at Hale Mirowski, when clouds were blanketing the sky and keeping the temperature somewhat moderate. He was haggling with a woman over the price of her bread. The government-issued black bread was so foul, so clay-like, that he had resolved to make bread a goal of his shopping missions.

He had just worked a deal with the woman for two loaves of bread, and was waiting for her to pull the product from her wooden box, when he felt something – a gust of cold air, a voice in the breeze. "Did you hear something?" he had asked her.

The woman had said no, there was no sound.

But Karol knew. He felt.

Now he was back home, in the security of his kitchen. Misses Rogala was sitting with him. The worried expression on her tired face told Karol what to think of his own suspicion. "This is unusual, isn't it," he said.

"Let's think about this first," Misses Rogala offered. She sipped her coffee. "Oh – pretty bad coffee today." The ersatz coffee was just brown water with a bitter aftertaste. But it was hot. She forced her face to smile, exposing deep wrinkles for a young woman.

Karol did not move. His coffee went cold in the cup in front of him. "This is not like Bronek. Not like him at all."

"Please, don't jump to conclusions, Karol," Misses Rogala said. She pushed her thinning brown hair away from her eyes. "We don't know anything yet."

"I don't have to know. I feel it."

"Well, when did you see him last?"

"The eleventh," Karol answered. "He asked permission to go out. I let him."

"He asked permission to go outside?"

"Yes, he – we've had a disagreement recently, that's a different story," Karol explained. He chuckled bitterly at the thought. "I was – punishing him."

"And that's the last you heard from him?"

"Yes."

"So you don't know anything else?"

"Nothing."

"Have you checked the posters?" Suddenly Misses Rogala froze. "Karol – I'm so sorry. I hope to God he's not there – I just meant –"

"– Yes, I checked today. Nothing." Karol slowly, numbly, fingered his coffee cup. It was cold; his hands no longer felt warm touching it. "The fire's going out in the stove. I need to look after it."

"I'm fine. I'm not too cold."

"Well, then, it's getting dark. I need to light a candle." Karol got up and lit a small candle on the counter. He set it at the center of the table and sat down again. Karol Pietraszewicz felt the shadows closing in around him. At last he spoke again. "He's been gone before, Halina. That's – how he is. But never this long. Never this long."

"Perhaps he just forgot. You know how forgetful boys his age are. He's really just a boy."

"He's not a boy any more. He's out of my control."

Just then there was a knock at the door. "Let me get that for you." Misses Rogala got up and went to the door.

Karol heard Mister Stachowiak at the door. "Halina, I heard a rumor outside. Something about Bronek."

"Come in, Mister Stachowiak, come in."

Stanislaw Stachowiak strode purposively into the kitchen. "Karol, what's going on?"

"It's Bronek, his son," Misses Rogala explained. "He's missing."

"What? Missing? For how long?"

"Since yesterday."

"Hm. Has anyone checked the posters?"

"Hush, Stanislaw! Karol did. Nothing has turned up yet."

Mister Stachowiak was tall, and he naturally tilted his head when he spoke. "Karol? Is that true?"

"Yes. I just feel it. I know it –" Karol tried to say more, but the words stopped.

"Do you know anything else?"

"No, nothing more. Please, have some coffee. It may not be hot, but there's some left."

"No, thank you. How about Pawiak prison? Have you heard anything from Pawiak?"

"No."

"I see. Listen," Mister Stachowiak offered, casually touching his narrow mustache, "I know some friends who have connections. They have bribed a guard at Pawiak. The guards will talk, for enough money. I can find out who's being held there, and who's been executed. It may not happen today, of course, but I can find out. Just give me some time."

"Thank you, Stanislaw, thank you. That would be good."

"I'll find out for you. Don't worry about that."

"We'll stay with you, Karol." Misses Rogala sat down at the table, and she squeezed Karol's hand. "We've all been here before."

Karol clenched his teeth; he did not want his emotions to show. "Thank you both," he quietly replied.

Karol heard the reassuring sound of a cane tapping against the tile floor. He looked up and saw Eugene enter the kitchen. Eugene looked at his neighbors. "Misses Rogala, Mister Stachowiak. Hello," he said, quizzically.

"Eugene, thanks to God you are here," Misses Rogala said.

"Sure I am," Eugene answered. He stooped a bit, even as he stood straight. His cane trembled slightly, but he smiled brightly. "I was just sleeping, on the sofa."

"I know you and Eugene need to talk." Misses Rogala stood up. "I need to get dinner ready. Come on, Stanislaw." They both headed for the door. "Remember, we're all with you, Karol."

"Don't worry, I'll find out what I can," Mister Stachowiak repeated.

"Thank you so much, thank you both."

Eugene turned and stared at his father. "What's happening? Why were they here?" His face looked even more boyish, more cherubic, in the flickering candlelight.

Karol stared at his youngest son. Then he sighed, with all

the sadness in the world bearing down on him. "Eugene, let's sit in the parlor. There's something I have to explain to you."

* * *

"Granit, Akrobat," Adam said with relief, "Thank the Blessed Virgin, you made it."

It was mid-afternoon. Adam was in another anonymous apartment. Everything of value, the stove and furniture and even the wallpaper and wood flooring, had been looted. Even the pipes were broken from the wall, for their copper. Like most Warsaw apartments, it was unheated. Adam sat on a wooden crate at a dilapidated wooden table. From behind his craggy face and unkempt silver-and-black bangs, his blue eyes twinkled as he smiled.

Wiktor and Jerzy sat side-by-side on milk crates, uncomfortably. "Move, Akrobat," Wiktor said.

"I can't," Jerzy retorted. "There's no room for my legs."

Wiktor squirmed on the bench. "There's plenty of room, if you sit properly," he muttered.

"Gentlemen, please," Adam interrupted, "Have you heard about the Russian offensive?" Rumors circulated that the Russians had launched a winter offensive, but information about it was difficult to come by.

"They're just outside Vitebsk," Wiktor said matter-of-factly. "Not much of an offense."

"Hm. Not promising. Well, we have pressing business to discuss." He rested his large forearms on the table, and eyed Wiktor purposefully. "Does he know our mission?"

"Of course not," Wiktor said. "I told him nothing."

Adam continued. "Akrobat, we at first weren't going to tell you this. We thought you might be too young."

"He is too young," Wiktor commented. "It just can't be helped."

"But," Adam continued, his voice barely a whisper to account for the quiet in the room, "Things have changed. And you've shown great bravery in documenting the street executions. We think you can assist us in our next mission."

"What is it?" Jerzy asked hesitantly.

"To follow General Kutschera." Adam's whisper was so quiet that it was barely even audible.

Jerzy glanced at Wiktor, and then back at Adam. "Really?" This was clearly an important matter.

"As you know, this is a secret that you must guard with your life."

"Of course," Jerzy said.

"You know what that means, Akrobat," Adam continued. "We must watch police headquarters. Day and night. Everywhere he goes, everyone who guards him."

"It will not be easy," Wiktor observed. "He is not a public person."

Adam smiled at his friend's ability to find sarcastic humor in any situation. "Quite true, Granit. But, Akrobat, the situation has grown intolerable. The executions are up to three hundred victims per week in Warsaw alone. We must make a statement. Do you see?"

"Yes, yes," Jerzy said.

"You and I must start surveillance," Wiktor said. "Watch Kutschera, find out when he's vulnerable."

"But we don't know anything about him," Jerzy protested. "We don't even know what he looks like."

Adam and Wiktor glanced tensely at each other, and Jerzy knew a treasure was about to be divulged. Sure enough, Adam produced a glossy black-and-white photo, and handed it over. "Here is General Kutschera."

Jerzy held the photo by the corners. It showed a cluster of men approaching a Mercedes, all in plain black caps and black trenchcoats. Jerzy squinted his eyes. In the middle was a tight-lipped man with an angular face, dark sideburns, and a narrow, piercing stare. But his trenchcoat was open, and revealed lapel patches of three oak leaves. *"Brigadeführer!* It's him!"

"An Underground agent happened to see the group on a warm day," Adam explained. "This photo means we can distinguish him from his bodyguards."

Jerzy stared at the man who had started the street executions, and he noticed his fingers were trembling. The photo slipped from his cold fingers, and fluttered to the floor.

"Be careful, fool!" Wiktor ordered. "This is the most valuable photo in all Warsaw." Wiktor leaned over and retrieved the glossy. "I'll protect this."

Suddenly a thought occurred to Jerzy. "What about Lot? Won't he be helping, too?"

Wiktor flashed a worried glance at Adam. Adam answered the question. "Akrobat, Lot is – missing."

"Missing?"

"Yes. For a couple days. That was my other business. What do you know, Granit? Anything?"

Wiktor shook his head decisively. "Nothing."

"Are you sure? Did you retrace his steps?"

"I don't know which way he went. I never saw him again after we split up. As you know."

"Has Zebra heard anything?"

Wiktor shook his head.

"Any news from Pawiak?"

"I've checked my source there. No one mentioned anyone like him."

"No news at all?"

"That's what I said." Wiktor's stern, resolute face told Adam everything.

"This is bad news. Very bad news."

"We need to take our precautions, Nowak."

"Yes, yes. Until we find out more, we cannot meet anywhere that Lot knows of. Did he learn anything about you, Granit? Your name, where you live, your relatives?"

"Of course not," Wiktor replied firmly, with no trace of recognition toward his brother.

"You, Akrobat?"

"No."

Adam rubbed his square chin thoughtfully. "Of course, this

changes the planning for our mission."

"I would say it does."

"Well, I would like to tell you to be careful, but we have our mission. We have to continue, no matter what the risk."

"Agreed," Wiktor said.

"Akrobat –"

"Can I stop? Please?"

"You must also continue to document the executions. It is important. If not for us, for our children."

"But, sir . . . those faces . . . yes, sir." And Jerzy felt a bit less alive inside.

"You know, once Lot told me about a girl he had met. He was really in love with her." Adam shook his head sadly. "May God help his poor soul." Adam sighed mournfully. "Now, we must get back to work."

* * *

It was all wrong; everything was wrong; it felt wrong. He always wrote to her, at least every four days. He would not leave without telling her. They were planning for their future together. But Anna could not do anything, or think anything, that made sense.

"Golebica?"

Nothing.

"Golebica?"

At last Anna returned. She was sitting in a small, cold apartment with garish Victorian wallpaper. The other students were staring at her. Their instructor, Ryzy, was watching her with aged, but hopeful, eyes.

"Yes, sir?" she asked.

"Perhaps you can enlighten us?"

Anna looked around. She did not even know which subject they were studying. She looked at her mimeographed sheets. It was English. "Oh."

"And the present participle and past participle for the verbs?" Ryzy did not raise his voice at her. He probably could not raise his voice. But Anna did not know which verbs he meant.

"I'm – I'm sorry, Professor Ryzy. I – I must go." She pulled on her coat and wrapped her babushka around her head, and she wandered toward the door.

"Golebica!" Ryzy snapped, but Anna walked out, leaving her English text on the dining room table.

She went outside, her coat still open and cold wintry air blowing against her. She did not check for any police. Panic flooded her mind and her heart. *He can't be gone, he can't be, he can't be.* But it was all she could think. He was gone, he was missing.

Trembling with fear, she leaned against the wall, huddled inside her coat, and rested. Her hair fell out of her babushka. A tear trickled down her red cheek. She was exhausted, and cold, and alone. She wanted to sit on the ground and have someone hold her, so she could cry and cry.

She had to keep control of herself. With frigid, shaking fingers, Anna felt in her secret pocket inside her skirt, for his ring. It was still there.

Suddenly there was a man there. Anna shrieked; her hands flew up. She turned, recoiled, shrank against the cold wall. She hid her face behind her arm.

The man shook her, and Anna peered over her sleeve. The man was wearing wooden shoes, much like her own. She looked up. He was middle-aged, nearly bald, with a cultured, aristocratic – Polish – face. The man smiled reservedly. "You'd better run, girl," he said in a smooth voice. "SS patrols are out!"

Anna felt her heart pounding inside her chest. "Th – thank you – thank you," she said hoarsely.

"Go home! Good luck!" the gentleman whispered.

Anna walked. Her heart was still racing; her lungs felt exhausted. It was too much for her. She needed her husband. She wandered, staggering, through the narrow canyons of the city. Up above her, the buildings swirled around. Light snow as delicate as dust began to fall, settling on her head and her shoulders. Her shoes slipped on the wet sidewalks. She walked without knowing where.

Presently, Anna turned a corner onto Wolska Street. Ahead of her, at 77 Wolska Street, there was a commotion. People were milling about with no purpose. The snow was falling on them, turning them into white, sluggish statues. She did not know that Jerzy Kruczyk, having documented the execution, was just leaving the scene.

Anna bumped her way into the crowd. "What's happening?" she asked a young boy.

"It was an execution," the boy said sheepishly. "But my father said it was a massacre."

Anna looked at the flowers heaped against the brick wall, at the bloodstains smeared in the fresh snow. "How many?"

"Twenty, I heard. Four were women."

"Who? Who were the victims?"

"I don't know."

"Who were they? Tell me! Was he – was his name Benny?"

"I don't know!" Frightened, the boy turned around and ran off.

Anna stumbled against the wall. Her cheek struck the cold, slick bricks, and she slowly slid down, down to the snowy sidewalk.

XVII

Wiktor pushed his little paint cart ahead of him. As he gripped the handle, his knuckles turned purple in the cold morning air. The incessant noise of the wheels, which squeaked at the same point in their rotation, drove him to distraction. He walked slowly on the sidewalk, silently cursing those damnable squeaking wheels.

Ahead of him, four SS soldiers approached him. Instinctively, Wiktor adopted the submissive position. He slid his wooden cart out of their path, which was the law, and he lowered his head. The soldiers glanced at him and his meager wooden cart, but they ignored him. Wiktor listened keenly as they walked by. He perceived that they were bitter; they complained about Hans Frank, and the failures in Russia. Wiktor waited. When they were a safe distance down the street, he continued on his journey.

His mission this morning was a simple one. When he got to the corner of Rose and Ujazdowskie Avenues, he waited. A streetcar was ahead of him, and he waited for it to go past. Then he waited some more. He checked his wristwatch: 6:52. He looked up at the intersection. There they were.

By themselves, they were not noteworthy: two black Mercedes-Benz sedans. They had no markings, nothing distinguishing at all. Only Wiktor knew: inside one of those cars was General Kutschera. He waited for the cars to come closer.

When they were about to turn onto Ujazdowskie, Wiktor pushed his cart full of paint cans onto the street. He pretended to be oblivious to the traffic. But in truth, he was listening, feeling for the lead car. When he felt them get closer, Wiktor suddenly pushed his cart forward. He looked the other way, as if he were distracted by something to his right.

Now his creaky cart was directly in front of the lead car, but he was just to the side. The car had almost no time to slow. It did not. It even accelerated. The Mercedes smacked Wiktor's cart squarely, sending it skidding across the street. Wiktor leapt back to the sidewalk. Both cars sped past him, and continued down the street.

Wiktor watched the cars. There, in the back seat, on the passenger side: Kutschera. The SS *Brigadeführer* looked back through the window, and for a moment Wiktor saw him. Plain face, narrow eyes. But that didn't matter. The car careened around the next corner, out of sight.

Wiktor's cart skidded to a stop several meters away from him. White paint and red paint flowed slowly out from the ruptured cans. A couple Blue Policemen stood across the street, and pedestrians nudged around him. No one stopped to assist him. As Wiktor knelt to right his little cart, he noted in his memory all that he had learned.

* * *

The first thing he felt when he awoke was a sense of quiet, of serenity. Then immediately came the pain. It started in the arch of his right foot, sharp and throbbing. Then it shot up his leg, into his calf, to his knee. The pain filled his mind. The pain was merciless.

Rolling over, Bronek lay on his back and groaned. He looked up at the wooden floor beams above him. And then he remembered. He was lying in a cellar, damp but not cold. He was on a bed, or a cot; he felt the metal springs against his back.

He had a blanket over him. Gray light filtered through a tiny cellar window. And he smelled the sickening stench of raw sewage. Then he remembered that he was the source of that smell.

Just then he heard a commotion above him. Bronek raised his head and saw a boy crouching on the cellar steps. He had short, straw-colored hair and blue-gray eyes. The boy looked at him, and then dashed upstairs. Bronek heard some muffled voices. "Mama, Mama!" he heard the boy say excitedly. "He's awake! Let's go see him!"

Bronek lay back and waited. He had seen these people once before. He remembered something: he had been dragged in here and deposited on the bed. He had awoken, once or twice. But everything else was still fuzzy in his mind. He felt on his chest for his lucky locket; it was still around his neck. He breathed deeply, and rested.

He heard the door open. Bronek watched as a woman came down the stairs. Her house skirt flowed around her legs, and she seemed to float downward. The boy followed close behind, jumping down the steps eagerly.

Bronek raised himself up on one elbow. "Hello," he said. Immediately he felt dizzy. The cellar swirled around him. He rolled onto his back.

The woman came over to him, holding something in her hand. "Don't get up," she warned. "Just lie still." She was medium-height, with brown hair and brown eyes. It was her eyes that Bronek noticed. They were deep, and dark, and haunting. Her skin was nearly ghost-white, and weathered. She looked as if she had aged twenty years in the last two. But she was beautiful to him. Bronek watched her as she folded a wet cloth. "You've been through an ordeal." She wiped the cloth across his face.

Bronek felt the cool water trickle down his cheeks. "Where am I?" he asked, surprised by the frailty he heard in his own voice.

"Don't you mind where you are." She placed her soft white

fingers on his forehead. "Fever," she commented softly. "You probably have dysentery."

"My name is –"

"– We don't need to know your name," the woman interrupted. "You can call me Irena. This is my son. You can call him Henryk."

The boy, Bronek now saw, was a teen-ager, and as tall as his mother. "Hello," Bronek said. "You can call me – Lot."

"That's fine." Irena turned to her son. "Henryk, get Lot some food."

"No, I don't need to take your food –"

"– Nonsense," Irena answered. "Friend in the home, God in the home. Henryk, go get him some bread and water."

"Yes, ma'am!" Henryk bounded up the stairs in four huge steps.

Bronek glanced around the cellar. The stone walls were decorated with little pictures and wall hangings. There were also a dresser, an armoire, and a couple of tables down here. Bronek guessed that this had been turned into a bedroom, for a family member whose home had been requisitioned by the Germans.

Irena turned the towel over. "How do you feel?"

"Better," Bronek said. "But my foot is on fire."

"Ah, your foot. Let me look at it." She pulled the blanket off the bed. Immediately, she wrinkled her nose. "Ukh!"

"I'm sorry," Bronek said. "I remember I was in a sewer."

"Yes, you were. We heard some noises from the sewer beneath the street. We pulled off the lid, and found you inside. We couldn't very well let you float away, so we dragged you in here."

"Who? I want to thank them."

"No, that is not possible. There are many relatives living here. But only my son and I will see you. That is for our safety."

"I understand."

"You are not the first person we have found in the sewer, you see. We happen to live near the opening."

"Then – you have saved others."

"Well, what else can we do?"

Bronek heard Henryk run back down the steps. He tried to lift up his head, but he dropped back down again. "I can't believe how terrible I feel," he groaned.

Henryk handed Irena a small loaf of black bread. "Henryk, go light a candle for our guest." Henryk went over and lit a candle on a little table, eyeing Bronek all the time. "You're very lucky you didn't suffocate down in the sewer."

"How long was I down there?" he wondered aloud.

"Only God knows," Irena said. "But you've been here seven days. Today is the twentieth."

Bronek gasped. "Nine days? Ten days?" He tried to think. "I have to go." He tried to roll himself out of the bed. But intense churning sensations hit him in the stomach, and the dizziness hit him again. He managed to get his arm over the side; then he flopped back down.

"Stop that!" Irena said sharply. She leaned down and pushed him onto his back. "You must stay here for a while. Until you regain your strength, and recover."

"Recover." As soon as the dizziness subsided, Bronek felt that stabbing pain again. "What's wrong?"

Irena pulled the blanket completely off Bronek's feet. "Let's take a look at this again," she suggested. There was a reassuring, motherly quality to everything she said, even as she gave orders, and Bronek felt he could trust her. He peered down at his feet, as his toes shivered in the bare cold.

What Bronek saw unnerved him. "What's that?"

His left foot was pale and bony. But his right foot was bright red, and black and blue. And it was swollen up to a grotesque shape. It looked like an overripe tomato. And with every heartbeat, a new pain stabbed up into his leg. "Irena – what happened?"

"Well, it looks as though you've broken a bone in your foot. Perhaps even two. That's quite a bit of swelling."

"No," he said beneath his breath. Bronek tried to think. He

had to do something. "Listen – Irena, Henryk – I need my shoes back."

"Oh, no. Your shoe won't fit on your foot."

"But I have important work to do!"

"Is he an Underground soldier?" Henryk suddenly asked, wide-eyed.

"Henryk, no. No questions!"

"But I can't stay here. If anyone finds out, you'll be in danger."

"You let us worry about that. Now, here – Henryk, hand me the bread – you try to eat something." Irena tore off a small bit of black bread. She slid her arm behind Bronek's head. Cradling Bronek's head up in the crook of her elbow, she fed him a nibble.

Bronek sighed unhappily. "Thank you." He chewed on the bread. Angrily, he realized that it took all his energy to swallow. "I'm so thirsty."

"Is it good?" Irena asked.

"Sawdust," Bronek admitted. "But thank you."

Irena smiled. "I'm sorry we can't do better. It's all we have."

"You've done too much already." It felt amazingly good to eat some food. Irena fed him another bite, with the candlelight casting a faint yellow light on her face. Then she opened a small brown bottle, and poured out a large spoon of reddish liquid.

"What's that?" Bronek asked.

"Iodine and bicarbonate of soda." She pushed the spoon into his mouth as he gasped. "It's for the dysentery. Now some water." She took the cup, and tilted his head up higher. Bronek drank a sip of water. Somehow, it was delicious. Even the little bit that dripped down his chin cooled him.

Soon Bronek looked up. Irena suddenly appeared fuzzy to him; he could not focus on her. "Why do I keep getting dizzy?" he asked her.

"That is your dysentery. You also probably have a concussion from your fall."

Bronek groaned. "When I try to look up, everything goes upside-down."

"You must relax, Lot." Irena stood up. She pulled the blanket back across him, and tucked it under his chin. Bronek sighed frustratedly. But as soon as he closed his eyes, his mind fell into the deepest pit of blackness. From somewhere far above him, he heard the soothing words, "We'll take care of you."

* * *

Karol and Eugene Pietraszewicz finished their dinner in silence. Karol set the dishes in the sink with a little clinking sound, and he began scrubbing. He had no soap tonight, so he had to scrub the dishes under water as diligently and as thoroughly as he could. Eugene sat at the kitchen table and said nothing.

Presently Eugene stirred. "Would you like me to wipe the table?"

"Thank you. That would be fine."

Eugene stood, walked over to the counter, and retrieved a dishcloth. Leaning on his cane with one hand, he wiped the tabletop clean. Then he set the cloth back on the counter, and he sat down. Again, he said nothing.

Karol remained hunched over the sink, and continued to scrub the dinner dishes. Eugene stared at his father's back for a while. Then he stared at the old iron stove.

Soon there was a knock at the door. "I'll get that," Eugene offered.

"You don't need to, Eugene. I can get it."

"No! I can do it." Eugene stood up, grabbed his cane, and went to the front door. "Oh, hello, Misses Rogala," he said.

"Hello there, Eugene." Misses Rogala walked into the kitchen. "Hello, Karol," she said sympathetically.

Karol looked up from the sink. "Hello, Halina," he said, as he wiped his hands on the dishcloth. "Thank you so much for coming. Please sit down." Karol pulled a chair out from the table.

"Thank you, thank you." She sat down, and set a package wrapped in newspaper on the table. They all sat around the kitchen table. For a second she stared at them, and no one said anything.

"This is for you two," she began, "We had some leftover bread and onions after dinner, and I was afraid it would go bad on us, so I thought I would bring it over for you. Can you use it?"

"Yes, thank you, Halina," Karol said courteously. "God bless. Look, Eugene, we have some onions for dinner tomorrow."

"We've been getting all kinds of food lately," Eugene replied.

"Was anyone else here today?" Misses Rogala asked.

Karol nodded politely. "Yes, Mister Stachowiak was here for a while, and then Mister Zukowski was here. But he left before dinner. It's been quite busy around here."

"So," Misses Rogala offered, in a delicate way, "No . . . news?"

"No, nothing."

"We don't need news," Eugene proclaimed. "We know he's coming back."

"Eugene," his father said, "Don't talk that way. You'll take away our luck."

"There's no luck about it, Father. He's coming back."

"Eugene, we need to wait and see. Don't upset things, please. We've prayed for luck, and we might still get it, if we don't upset things."

Eugene paused. "He's coming back," he mumbled sulkingly.

"I understand, Eugene," Misses Rogala offered. "I really do. And we're all going to help any way we can."

"You have, Misses Rogala," Karol commented. "Thank you."

Misses Rogala observed a candle on the kitchen table. It sat on a teacup dish, burning a low flame. "I think your candle is almost out. Do you need some more?"

"That's a candle for Bronek," Eugene said.

"Eugene wanted to start that, Halina."

"It's to light the way. It will stay lit until Bronek comes back." Eugene crossed his arms stubbornly, defiantly.

"I see. That's a good idea, Eugene. You know, we're all praying that he's safe. We all want to hope for the best." Something caught in her throat. Suddenly she spoke more brightly and confidently. "I just wanted to tell you gentlemen that it's time for our prayer service in the courtyard. I know we're all going to pray for Bronek. Do you want to come down now?"

"Thank you," Karol said. He sighed, and he nodded his head. "I think that would be good for us."

* * *

The stone wall felt cool on her cold cheek. It consoled her, reassured her. The brick and stone walls, cold and gray, undeniably existed. Nothing to fear about them.

Now she left the comforting wall and headed away. Where was she going? She was headed . . . west. After all, she had spent the entire day in the city center, and had learned nothing at all. Now she determinedly headed west, toward the sun hanging low in the December sky; it shined in her eyes, and made her eyes squint, and that felt fine. Her wooden shoes slid against the stones as she walked. Damnable shoes, miserable things. They made her feet sweaty and cold. She might as well wear nothing on her feet at all. How could she do anything, with these shoes hindering her?

Ahead of her, Anna heard voices. She saw three women approach her. They looked so regal in their clean coats, and their felt hats, and their glowing skin, and their leather shoes. They were so cheerful and gay, gossiping about shopping and silliness – in German. There she stood in wooden shoes, no socks, her last dress, her father's trenchcoat. Well, she would not give them any cause to suspect her. Anna stepped aside, pressed her back against the wall, and bowed, letting the German women pass in front of her. She was safe so long as she stayed against the wall. The women passed by, and never even noticed her.

She continued westward, toward the setting sun. The air bit at her cheeks, and burned her bare ears. She stayed against the buildings. There she would be protected from the cold.

Something was on the wall ahead of her. Cautiously, she stopped. There it was: a poster. She bowed her head before it. Slowly, meekly, she raised her hand and touched the red parchment with her fingertips. Inwardly, she implored it: *Please, please, spare me.* Her fingers trembled as she studied the text:

"ANNOUNCEMENT

The Security Police Summary Court has sentenced the following persons to death under Section 1 or 2 of the Decree of October 2, 1943 on many charges, including belonging to illegal organizations, aiding criminals, hiding Jews, possessing weapons, not informing about others in possession of weapons, and distributing leaflets."

Then came the names. The names. Perycz, Jan, and Perycz, Zbigniew, down to Solka, Franciszek, and Paplinski, Jerzy. Then came the standard exhortation to turn in Underground agents. By the SS and Police Leader for the Warsaw District. December 17, 1943. Today was the twenty-first.

That was all. Just ten names. Her quivering fingers moved down. He wasn't there. He wasn't there. No Pietraszewicz, Bronislaw, born April 4, 1923, on the list. Yes, she was grateful. This poster had saved her. She wanted to cry up to Heaven, to proclaim her joy; but no words came from her lips. Her eyes were transfixed on the poster. It loomed over her: huge, awesome, mystical.

At last she pulled herself away and stumbled to the corner.

She looked up. The sun was barely over the tops of the build-ings now. It did not burn her eyes, even when she stared direct-ly at it.

She was at a corner. She looked this way and that, down each narrow street. Why did she waste her day in the city cen-ter? She had learned nothing there. She felt something, some force that was pulling her to the right. She went that way. It had to be that way. She saw a commotion, like an approaching rapids upriver. She neared, closer and closer, still keeping her distance. But then suddenly she was in it, and it was swirling all around her.

All around her was chaos. People were everywhere, run-ning, dashing into each other as if they were boulders. She could not tell which way was forward. She jumped up, but she was too short, she couldn't see, she was pushed about. She thrust ahead, unsure of where she was or what was happening. And then she came to a placid area.

Up ahead was the source of the rapids. SS soldiers were spread across the street, their rifles pointed out like spikes, pushing everyone backward. Behind the line, there were more police, Gestapos and Schupos, their rifles raised, scanning the windows above them for eyewitnesses. And behind them, the trucks, black, ominous. Over the loudspeakers, a voice crackled brutally: "Keep away from the windows. Anyone who shows his face will be shot."

Before her, people stood their ground. They stood in the street and cursed, shouted, waved their arms. It was all noise and commotion. The gray line grew closer. Anna now saw the face of one soldier. His freckled face looked small inside his huge steel helmet. His arms sagged while carrying his rifle. This boy appeared no older than herself.

He came toward her, and Anna stepped back. "This," some-one shouted, "This is what you've brought us!"

The boy-soldier glanced over his shoulder, causing a gap in the rifle line. When the boy turned back, lifeless tears dropped from his innocent blue eyes. "I am sorry," he shouted, in poor

Polish. "I am sorry. I am sorry."

The older soldier beside him shouted louder. *"Erich! Halt die Klappe! Halt die Klappe! Befehl ist Befehl."* (Pipe down! Orders are orders.)

The boy with the rifle wiped his cheeks. Then he raised his arms. "I am sorry," he whispered hoarsely, "I am sorry. I am sorry." He pushed Anna ahead of him.

Now the gray line reached the end of the block. Poles scattered down the side streets, or wherever the current carried them. Anna tried to keep her position. At the far end of the street, the trucks' gates swung open, and several soldiers jumped out. They pulled out the prisoners, in prison clothes, blindfolds, and gags. Anna saw someone climb down from the truck. Her heart leapt. He was the right height – it had to be him – she could call out his name – "Benny!"

Just then someone grabbed her from behind. A man, a tall man, pushed her away. He pushed her around the corner, into a small alley, and held her against the wall.

With all her strength she struggled and fought him. "No, no!" she cried out, "I must see! I must see!"

"Stop!" the man said. "They'll shoot you for trying! Don't go near them!"

They tumbled to the stones. Anna struggled to free herself. "No, let me go! Please! I saw him! He's there, he's there! I saw him!"

But the man held the sleeves of her coat. She struggled and struggled. She heard a commotion, a few angry orders shouted in German. Anna froze. She heard a pause. And then the command: *"Schiessen!"* It was a machine-gun volley, loud and final. She listened helplessly as the noise struck her ears.

Anna cowered and held her face in her hands. *Dear God,* she asked, *Make it go away. Make it go away.* She tried to vanish into the wall. But she could not escape it. Then came several fated shots from a handgun.

Soon enough, there was a revving of powerful truck engines. The long arms that were pinning her in place loosened.

She stood again, and looked around her. Everywhere, people slowly stood up and checked their things, as if a storm had passed through. Tentatively, the river returned to its normal course. Anna followed behind.

The street surrounded her, enveloped her. The sight was too big for a small young woman. Yet it was all before her eyes, and as she took it in she felt herself become even smaller.

Several old women wrapped in tattered blankets knelt before the wall, praying and wailing, their rosary beads hanging from their fingers. Already the sidewalk was littered with flowers of every description. And there was the wall. Drips and puddles of blood. Steam rose from the warm blood as it dried on the cold stones. Anna staggered and stumbled closer, closer, until she was against the hard stones. Her mind was still viewing the scene from before, the young man in prison clothes. She leaned against the wall, and she stared at the man she had cried out for. His vision was before her; but just as suddenly he was gone. She trembled. "Do you see him? Do you see him?" she asked to the cold blue sky. "He's a sweet boy. . . . He's a sweet boy."

Her wooden shoes slipped beneath her, and she slid down, her cheek scraping against the pale gray stone as she went.

XVIII

On December 14, 1943, the Red Army launched a winter offensive. The Soviets captured Cherkassy and reached the outskirts of Vitebsk, while the Germans tactically retreated and recaptured Radomyshl. But these cities were on the great Eastern plain, more than 250 miles from Polish territory. Despite the boasts of the Soviet commanders (received via radio by the Underground) that the Red Army soldiers enjoyed the cold, their tanks did not; and the realization settled over Warsaw that the Red Army was still months away. This would be another Christmas under occupation.

In Warsaw, the same battle continued. Underground agents continued to attack policemen on the street, killing them and stealing their guns. Police and SS staged more street sweeps to arrest more civilians. Underground newspapers printed more calls for resistance. Police trucks rumbled through the city. Trains continued to be sabotaged, and derailed. And the executions went on. Each street execution was followed by a terse loudspeaker announcement of the action. Only communists and resistance fighters were being targeted, the announcements explained. Then the next group of hostages to be executed was read. The government's hope was to turn people against the resistance movement. So it was hoped.

On the morning of December 23, Jerzy Kruczyk rode a streetcar west from the city center. He could not wait for the official announcement. He had to check out a rumor, verify it, and add it to his list.

He reached 14 Gorczewska Street just past 9:30. Men and women were standing in the street, staring at the wall of an apartment building and at each other. Again, heaps of flowers were strewn about. Again, puddles of blood were freezing on the sidewalk.

Jerzy noticed one young woman among the crowd who stayed very still. She stared at the parallel lines of bullet holes, unblinking. Jerzy approached the young woman. He noticed that she was blond and attractive, only a bit older than himself. Her hair was pulled back from her face, and went down to her shoulders in back. She looked like an aristocratic, like old Poland. "Did you see what happened?" he asked matter-of-fact-ly. He did not know this was Misia Myzwinska, a friend of Anna.

The young woman did not answer him. Her whole body, inside her old patched coat, shook. "Beasts," Misia Myzwinska finally said through clenched teeth. She spat the words onto the sidewalk, sneering all the while. "Filthy. . . filthy. . . vicious. . . beasts!"

"Anybody," Jerzy said more loudly, "Did anybody see it?"

The young woman turned her face to Jerzy. Her face was tight, and rigid. When she spoke, it was with a rage, a barely controlled fury. "Give them . . . their time!"

Jerzy backed up a step, intimidated. "I'm – I'm sorry."

She did not respond. For a long time the woman stood still. Something was changing behind her pale blue eyes, something profound and mysterious.

"Did you see how many?"

Again she did not address him.

Jerzy suddenly did not know what to say. He stood beside her, and did not move.

Misia wiped her cheek. "I know why they did this. Oh, I

know why."

Jerzy did not say anything. She seemed to need her own time.

"Because it's Christmas."

"I know," he said sympathetically. "They had to remind us who is in charge. That's why we have to tell this. To the world."

Misia glanced up at Jerzy, with an icy fire in her eyes.

"I can tell London."

Misia took a deep breath. For a moment she said nothing; she just bit her lip and waited. Then she told her story. As she spoke, her breath froze in the air. "It was nine o'clock. My mother heard a noise. I came to the window and saw three trucks. Big, black trucks. A dozen policemen blocked off the street, and chased everyone away. Then came the loudspeaker. A man told us if we showed our faces, we would be shot. My mother pleaded with me to get away from the window, and hide with her. But I couldn't. I – had to watch. Even when a police-man shot at me."

Jerzy looked across the street. There, on the second floor, the window of an apartment was shot out. This girl had a per-fect view, he noted.

Misia continued, never looking at Jerzy. "I hid behind the curtain, so they couldn't see me. I watched. They brought the prisoners out of the trucks. They were handcuffed together, in pairs. They had cloth sacks over their heads. They walked – stu-pidly, as if they were drunk."

"They were drugged, probably with opium," Jerzy offered. "They had rags stuffed into their mouths, to keep them quiet."

"I watched. They lined them up. Right here. Against the wall. The police were over here. And then they fired."

"How many?"

The girl did not respond.

"How many groups of prisoners?"

"Three," she finally said.

"Did you count? How many, in total?"

Again the girl said nothing. Jerzy knew what she was feeling: hateful, humiliated. Jerzy waited for her.

Misia spoke. "Forty-three," she answered, looking down at the sidewalk.

Jerzy's jaw dropped in surprise. "Forty-three?"

"Yes."

"Then they took the bodies away? Back in the trucks?"

"An officer walked over them. With a pistol. Someone moved, and he, he. . . ." She said nothing more about the officer.

Jerzy looked at the young woman pensively. She really was beautiful, with delicate lips and a high, graceful forehead. He realized he was feeling – not so old. He felt something for her, something like empathy. This was no exciting mission, with police to elude and information to collect. He felt ashamed for her. "I'm sorry. I'm sorry you had to watch it."

The girl did not say anything. She just stared away.

"Listen," Jerzy said, "The police will come back, to wash away the evidence. You have to go. You all have to leave! Right now!"

Misia suddenly raised her voice. "Leave?" she asked bitterly. "This is our home."

"I'm – I'm trying to help," Jerzy stammered. "I mean – I wish there were something I could do."

Misia raised her face. Glaring at him, she spoke in a low, moaning whisper. "Kill them," she said. "Kill them all." She helped an old woman to her feet, and walked back across the street to her home.

And later that cold day, Michalina Myzwinska stood at her window, staring, staring at the wall across from her home. She did not move, not even when her mother begged her to sit down and rest. Instead, she watched as various neighbors set flowers and said hasty prayers at the site. It was clean now, they had washed it down. But Misia would remember. They would not clean away her memory. She grabbed for a pen when the loudspeakers crackled, and the announcer read the usual dry statement:

"On December 18, a Polish Police corporal was attacked while on duty by three armed criminals on Zawisza Street in Warsaw. On December 20, a police patrol was fired on by four armed criminals on Gorczewska Street. One police officer was shot, and another seriously wounded. On December 21, 1943 several criminals assaulted a *Volksdeutsche* on Dluga Street, mortally wounding him. In retaliation for this, I ordered the following criminals sentenced to death by the Security Police Summary Court but conditionally eligible for clemency to be publicly executed on December 23, 1944."

With a fountain pen, she wrote each name on a small sheet of paper. She wrote so furiously that she tore the page several times. Then she slipped the paper inside her skirt. Now she had proof, proof for the hatred that burned in her heart. She would not let her hatred die. Never.

And across town, Anna Krzykowska huddled in the corner of her parlor, and she trembled. She covered her ears, and prayed for the names to stop; but they would not stop. The voice spread the names everywhere, and she could not escape. She cowered like a frightened bird, helpless in her cage, as the names settled all around her.

* * *

"Is everything ready, Mama?" Krystyna asked.

"Well," her mother thought aloud, "Bread, potatoes, carrot soup –" Izabela dipped a wooden spoon into one of the pots on the wood-burning stove. "– No, the potatoes need another minute. What a shame we have no *oplatek*." The *oplatek* was the traditional Christmas wafer, stamped with Nativity symbols. And of course there was no Christmas tree; instead, the cramped home was decorated with paper cutouts of angels, dolls, and their old ornaments. Izabela looked around the kitchen, dark except for a candle on the counter. "Doesn't the table look nice, with the good china, and the hay, and the candles?" She sighed appreciatively. "I love Christmas Eve dinner."

"I'll light the candles," Krystyna offered.

Izabela watched as her daughter lit the candles on the table. Krystyna was tall and broad-shouldered. Wearing a yellow blouse and wool skirt did not hide her rather masculine carriage when she walked. "Krystyna, you're so lucky to have good clothes to wear."

"These are old, Mama. This skirt must have twenty patches in it."

"But you look so nice for dinner tonight. Maybe it's because you're still healthy."

"I'm the last one, then. Lord knows, no one else is," she added beneath her breath.

Izabela decided to ignore that comment. Instead she said, "Krystyna, when you're done, why don't you help everyone to the table?"

"Of course. They all need my help."

"Krystyna –"

They were interrupted by a gleeful voice from the parlor. "I see it! I see it!"

Izabela sighed. "Aleksy saw the first star. Let's help them in now."

"All right, Mama," Krystyna sighed. "Papa, Aleksy, Anna, it's time for dinner." Krystyna circled around the kitchen table and went into the parlor.

As she waited, Izabela leaned against the counter, and she rested. Wearily, she remembered to thank the Lord for preserving her family, and she quickly crossed herself. But secretly, even to herself, she dreaded what she was about to see – what the members of her family had become.

"Come on, Papa," Krystyna said coaxingly. "Dinner is this way."

Jan stepped slowly into the kitchen. His shoulders were slightly stooped, and he looked as if he were about to lose his balance. Krystyna was at his right arm, and Aleksy, weak though he was, held up his left arm.

"Come on, Papa," Aleksy offered. "Even I can walk this far."

"See, Papa?" Krystyna said. "We have Christmas dinner, ready for you."

Their father looked at the table, set with good china, white tablecloth, candles, and hay. "The potatoes?" he asked. "Where are the potatoes?"

"They're coming, Papa," Krystyna told him. "They're still cooking."

Izabela pulled out his chair for him. "Right over here, Papa, that's it." Working together, they eased Jan into his chair, and Izabela scooted him forward. "Now, Aleksy, let me help you." Taking Aleksy's arm, she helped her son over to his chair.

"What's for dinner?" he asked.

"You just wait and see. It's going to be wonderful." Izabela glanced up at Krystyna. "How's Anna?"

Krystyna shrugged her shoulders. "I couldn't get her to even to stand up. I don't know what to do."

"She said she doesn't want anything," Aleksy remarked.

Izabela sighed exhaustedly. "Oh, no." She shook her head despondently. Then she gave Krystyna an order. "Go in there, and tell her that she has to eat. No one can eat until she comes out here. You carry her in here, if you have to."

"Yes, Mama." Krystyna went back into the parlor. Izabela grimaced nervously as she waited for her daughters. From the other room, she heard Krystyna plead.

Finally, Krystyna reappeared. "This way, Anna, this way. I'll help you."

Even after steeling herself, Izabela was taken aback. Krystyna inched into the room, followed by Anna. Or rather, it was a mere wispy shadow of her. The real Anna had been live-ly and energetic; this shadow was gaunt and trembling. She seemed as weak as an old woman. Her fingers shook as they clutched a small blue shawl that hung around her shoulders. Her skin was pasty-white, her once-beautiful blond hair tangled and oily. Worst of all were her eyes. Once stunningly blue, now they were sunken and lifeless. Dark circles made her eyelids appear to droop. Izabela glanced down and saw that there were no shoes or socks on this shadow's bare feet.

"There you go," Krystyna said coaxingly. The shadow eased into her seat. Her eyes darted fearfully at the people around her.

"Now we can all have dinner," Izabela said, relieved. "You sit down, Krystyna. Let me serve everyone." Izabela excitedly poured the food from the pots into big china serving bowls, and put ladles and spoons into each. Then she began setting the bowls on the table.

Already she saw that her daughter was eyeing strangely the hay that had been spread across the table. "What – what is that?"

"That's hay," Krystyna explained slowly. "For the manger."

"Anna," her mother said, "You know that. We always set out hay for Christmas dinner."

Anna did not respond. But her head shook, as if she were terrified of something. Izabela could not guess what.

"Mama, she's not going to eat," Krystyna said.

"Nonsense. She has to eat. She's lost so much weight." She set the last bowl, the plain carrot soup, on the table. "See, Anna, this is our best dinner in a long time. You have to eat something." Warily, Izabela sat at the table.

Suddenly Anna spoke, with a voice hoarse yet strong. "Can't you see Saint Stephen the martyr? He is so sad. Why will no one help him?"

Izabela glanced at Krystyna. "Why, I don't know, Anna."

"There was a little boy. He tried to sell me a carrot. I told him no, no, I cannot buy one from you. Where is he now?"

"Anna," Krystyna responded, "What boy?"

"He is gone. Torn away. Can't you feel his absence? Can't you feel the coldness?"

"Anna, we don't understand," Krystyna said. "You are not making sense."

"It's cold now. Colder than ever before. A million times

colder than ever before."

"She's talking nonsense, Mama," Krystyna complained.

Suddenly Anna pointed at the end of the table. There an empty plate and glass had been set, for a possible guest. No one was sitting there. Anna's mouth opened, but no words came out.

"What? What is it, Anna?" Krystyna asked.

"It's the place setting," Aleksy observed. "She's afraid of –"

Anna's eyes grew wide. "No – no –" She put up her hands, as if to protect herself.

"Anna, it's okay," her mother pleaded. "It's the other plate. For a guest."

Anna recoiled at the sight. Her shawl fell from her shoulders.

"What's she doing?" their father asked, confused at the scene.

"She's afraid of it, Mama!" Krystyna said angrily, as she stood up.

Anna let out a shrieking, howling sound. She clutched desperately at Krystyna's blouse. It ripped at the shoulder.

"Anna, no!"

She buried her face against her sister's chest, and she made a terrible noise, a sob that would not end.

"Anna, child, we've always done that. Please! We always set out a plate for a guest!"

"Anna –" her sister tried, "– Look again! There's no one there!"

"Oh!" Izabela muttered beneath her breath. "Anna! Make sense!"

Anna grabbed Krystyna and held on tight, with no intention of letting go. She looked up into her sister's eyes. "Did you see him?" she asked finally. "Is he here?"

XIX

Sponge-washed, and his clothes cleaned, Bronek was eager to walk again. He lay on his bed and waited for the front door to open and shut several times, until he did not hear any more sounds. At last the house emptied. He hastily swung his feet over the side of the bed. He inched himself forward, and carefully pressed his bare feet against the cement floor. So far, his foot worked. Feeling encouraged, he stood up. Immediately the pain shot back into his foot, up his leg, and through his throat. He shouted, and he fell onto his back. That experiment did not go so well.

Just then he heard the lock click, and the basement door open. He saw some shoes, and then Henryk leaned down and peered at him. Bronek waved weakly. "Still here," he offered.

Henryk came all the way downstairs. He stood over Bronek and stared at him inquisitively. "Are you hurt?" he asked.

"No, no. I just – tried too much."

"Oh." Henryk watched him for a while. Finally, he spoke again. "Merry Christmas."

Bronek's eyes grew wide. "Today is –?" He counted to himself. "Yes, it is. My days are so mixed up, I didn't remember. Well, Merry Christmas, Henryk."

"My Mother is making a breakfast for you. She sent me

down to see what was the matter."

"Oh – thank you. I just – tried to walk a little too soon." Bronek sighed, disheartened.

"Are you – an Underground soldier?"

Bronek was startled, but kept his face a blank. "I know nothing about the Underground," he said automatically. He realized that such a story was not going to fool this boy, so he pulled himself up and sat on the edge of the mattress, making sure to keep his feet off the floor. "Henryk," he began, "I'm very grateful for all that you've done. You probably saved my life when you pulled me out of the sewer. But do you understand why I can't tell you more? I can't know who you are, and you can't know who I am. I'm just – a fellow named Lot. That's all."

Henryk leaned forward. Bronek could tell that something was burning inside of him. "I – I –" he stammered. Then he said it, in a rush. "I am, too!"

"You are?" This boy was probably not even fourteen – too young to be in the Underground. "You?" Worst of all, he was full of youthful exuberance, a dangerous trait for this work. Still, people were being lost every day. More were needed. "Well, Henryk . . . welcome."

"We're going out tonight on a training exercise. Out in the Kampinos Forest."

"After curfew?"

"Oh, yes. All night."

"Does your mother know about this?"

"Oh, no. I'm supposed to never tell her."

"Really. Listen, Henryk, I shouldn't know any more, either. You'd better keep that your secret, all right?" Bronek liked this boy, burning to tell someone his great secret. He was too young and enthusiastic, with his wide brown eyes, but he was full of zeal. "Henryk, I can hear the loudspeakers, even down here. They are still announcing executions. On December 18, December 20, December 23. What Warsaw needs is a whole army of soldiers like you."

"There are. There are a hundred of us training."

"Good news. Remember, Henryk, always tell yourself: I will survive, I will survive. God has chosen you to survive. You have to believe it, completely."

Henryk nodded. "I believe it."

"Good. Say, Henryk, can you find my shoes? I want to try to walk."

"But Mother says you can't walk yet."

"Well, your mother doesn't know how fast I recover. It's amazing, isn't it? Come here."

Bronek put his arm around Henryk's shoulder. "Help me, now, Henryk."

"But Mother says –"

"I don't care what your mother says. Let me walk!" Bronek stood up on his good foot. "See? I can do it. I can –" The instant he placed any weight on his right foot, he cried out. "Oh, no!" He sat back down.

Bronek stared at his foot, discouraged. "Damn!" he muttered. "I can't stay here! I have to get home." He shook his head angrily.

"Are you on a secret mission?"

Bronek looked at this boy, so eager to win the war by himself. "No, Henryk, that isn't it. You see, I have to get home. People – depend on me."

"Really?"

"Really. One, especially. She needs me. That's the most important mission you can ever have. You will understand that some day."

"Yes, sir."

Bronek grinned. "Say, Henryk, when you go tonight, can you do something for me?" Bronek lowered his voice to a whisper. "Something that will help my mission."

Henryk's boyish blue eyes grew wide. "Yes, sir!"

"Good. I'm going to write a message. But I can't write the address on it. If I tell you the address for you to deliver this message, can you remember that?"

"I think so."

"Can you deliver it tonight?"

"Yes, sir."

"Wonderful. Maybe I can survive a little longer in this cellar then. Tomorrow I'll write another message to send."

* * *

She had to be cautious. She could not make a sound.

Anna sat in her kitchen, pensively. She was clever. She had feigned an upset stomach, and they had left her alone in the kitchen. Now she had her shawl wrapped around her shoulders, and she listened to her family in the other room. They were playing a game that everyone in Warsaw played, to pass the time. "On the first day that we're liberated," she heard Aleksy say, "I'm going to take all our money, and I'm going to buy a whole pig. And then we'll barbecue it on a huge spit, for eight hours. And we'll have all the neighbors over, and we'll eat all night, until we eat the whole pig. Even his brain!"

"On the first day we're liberated," she heard their mother say, "I think we should go down to the church, and make the organist stay all day, and sing every hymn we know, and light candles when it gets dark, and sing all night."

Anna stared at the front door. It loomed like a monolith, dark, forbidding. Outside that door, they were increasing the arrests. Rounding up people by the hundreds. Huge street sweeps. Beyond that door, there was no safety.

This was her chance. First was to stand. She cautiously edged her chair away from the table. It made no sound. She straightened her knees. There: she was up. Not a sound.

"Come on, Papa," she heard Krystyna ask, "What will you do?"

Now she had to walk to the door. Her wooden shoes: they were going to make noise. She crept toward the door, as gingerly as a cat. Still no sound.

Their father stammered, grasping for an answer. "Well, I don't – I don't know what to do," he began.

Anna did not dare slide her coat off the hook – too noisy. There was still the door. It was heavy, solid oak, with an old steel knob. She just had to turn the knob, carefully, quietly. She pressed her body against the steel knob. It worked: no sound. The door opened for her. Anna hurried down the front steps. She was outside.

Anna bit her lip and lowered her head in determination. She had endured enough of her nightmares; she was going to learn the truth. She walked east to the city center, and then south on Nowy Swiat as the sun shined in her eyes. Her feet slid inside her wooden shoes. She was not wearing socks, and her bare toes caught against the wood. The wind blew at her back, sending a chill up her ankles and down her neck; she now wished she had remembered her babushka. Anna huddled inside her thin wool shawl. But she refused to stop, even when the wind whipped her hair around her face, and her shoulders shook uncontrollably.

At last, after a grueling, painful walk, she turned onto a crooked, angled street called Szucha Avenue, renamed *Strasse der Polizei* by the Germans. Yes, it was there, looming before her: 25 Szucha Avenue, Gestapo headquarters, Security Police (SIPO) and Security Service (SD) high command. It had been the Polish Ministry of Religion and Public Education. But now this building meant something utterly, profoundly different. It was one of the few buildings secure enough to fly a red swastika flag. Rows of barbed wire stretched out in both directions. And on the street was a gate and guards, guards with rifles. Just outside the gate were two pillboxes of cinder blocks and sandbags. Inside the pillboxes, other guards manned machine guns mounted on tripods. The building overwhelmed Anna, and she unknowingly cowered before it. No defenseless Polish girl dared approach it.

But somewhere deep in her heart, she knew she had to approach Gestapo headquarters. This was what she had snuck out for. Facing the power of the German empire, she would approach this building. And she would learn. She silently whispered a prayer for the Virgin Mary to hear. And then she stepped forward, across the paving-stone street, onto the far sidewalk.

Immediately, two guards in gray helmets and overcoats were on her. *"Halt! Halt! Hände hoch! Hände hoch!"* They ran up to her, blocking her advance, and jabbed their rifles in her face. Anna stopped. Then she looked at the pillboxes; the machine guns were pointed directly at her, their long, shiny-black muzzle glistening in the Christmas sun. *It's the end*, she thought. *Mary, save me!*

Just when she feared the worst, she heard someone else mutter, *"Oh, Scheisse!"* Then another guard walked forward, lethargically. *"Klaus, Friedrich, halt es."*

They lowered their rifles and backed away. One of them complained, *"Was ist los mit Ihnen? Polnisches Schwein."* (What is wrong with her? Polish pig.)

This guard, older and heavier than the two younger men, approached Anna. His rifle remained slung on his shoulder. Anna stared, terrified, at this guard, an SS *Scharführer* (Staff Sergeant). Slowly, she began to feel she would not be shot. And that emboldened her. She stood as tall as she could, and she held her hands straight at her sides, and she thrust her chin forward.

The older guard sighed. "So, what is up with you?" he said.

Anna took a deep breath. *This is it*, she told herself. She stared directly into the guard's steely gray eyes, even darker than his gray uniform. Her hands were trembling; she held on to her legs to still her fingers. "I want –" she began, surprised by her own timidity. She started again. "I – demand, to know . . . . Where is . . . my husband?"

The old guard did not move. He did not even blink. "You – demand?"

Anna felt stronger. "I refuse to read – your posters," she proclaimed, boldly. She made a feeble fist, and waved it in the cold Warsaw air. "I demand the truth!"

The guard paused. Then he chuckled. And his chuckle grew to a full, enthusiastic laugh. He turned to the other guards. *"Klaus! Friedrich!"* he said between guffaws. *"Sie will wissen, wo ihr Mann ist."* (She wants to know, where her husband is.)

The guard made a fist and shook it, mimicking an angry house-wife. He returned to the guardhouse and slapped his friends on the shoulder. *"Klaus. Sie will!"* They all had a hearty laugh. Even the machine guns swung harmlessly away, as the gunners sniggered.

Anna stood alone on the sidewalk, and she listened to the men. She wanted to run home. But she was frozen to this spot, too frightened to turn and run. She suddenly realized that she must look pathetic, in her wooden shoes and old patched dress. So she stood, and she let them laugh at her, and she recognized that she was a miserable shadow of the person she once was.

"So denn!" the older guard continued. *"Wo ist ihr Mann?"* (So then! Where is her husband?) He checked around the tiny guardhouse. *"Ist er hier? Finden Sie ihn jetzt!"* (Is he here? Find him now!)

One of the guards pointed at Anna. *"Ein polnisches Mädchen! Ich werde sie ficken, und sie auf die Strasse werfen!"* he suggested. (A polish girl! I'll f__k her, and toss her into the street!)

"Ich biete mich für die Mission!" (I volunteer for that mission!)

Anna looked away, ashamed.

The Staff Sergeant returned to Anna. He carried his rifle loosely, and he grinned at her. "I am sorry. Your husband is not here. But I will notify General Kutschera right away! We will search until we find him!"

Anna glared into his cold gray eyes.

"Klaus! Call General Kutschera right away! We must find her husband!" He spoke Polish, so she could understand him.

Anna glared at this man. In her mind she saw images of the little boy who had vanished, and her father whose mind was destroyed, and her own nightmares. At last, she could not control herself. *"Ich weiss, was Sie sagten,"* she said through clenched teeth. *"Ich spreche Deutsch."* (I know what you said. I speak German.)

The grin vanished from the guard's face. Suddenly he

sneered at her, with an anger that surprised her. "Good!" he snapped. He lowered his voice to a spitting whisper that only the two of them could hear. "Listen to me, Polish – pig. Every day we are killed by your – Underground. Four of my friends – friends I trained with – have died this year. In no other city in the entire Reich do we have these problems. Stupid – criminal – Underground. We cannot even walk outside without fear, thanks to you – Slavs."

And then Anna saw this guard for what he was. Arrogant, sadistic, brutish – he was the same as all the others. And her awareness freed her. She was freed from her fear. He might arrest her, or he might not. What she said made no difference. Anna felt her trembling fingers relax. She took a deep breath, and then she said it. "Then there is only one way you can feel safe. You must kill every one of us," she told him, with all the anger and defiance her frail body could muster. "*Fröhliche Weinachten!*" (Merry Christmas!)

Anna turned and walked away. She did not dare look back. With large blisters swelling on her toes and her bare ankles shivering, she strode away purposefully. This humiliation was only the start for her. Now she would stop at nothing.

* * *

The winter sun was setting over Warsaw. Another Christmas under Nazi rule was ending. The final church service was finishing, and the people hurried to get home before curfew. Police checked in to begin their nightly rounds.

Behind the looping brick wall, inside the old Jewish Ghetto, silence reigned. The buildings were burned out from the Ghetto Uprising of the previous April. Now the Jews were gone, and the Ghetto was empty, lifeless. Almost lifeless.

Deep inside the Jewish Ghetto, an imposing white building still stood at 24 and 26 Dzielna Street. Its guard towers and high white walls enclosed a large courtyard. The building had once been a Tsarist prison, when the Russians had controlled Poland. Now it was the principal political prison of the

Reichssicherheitshaupamt (National Department of Security), specifically its Department IV, the Gestapo. The Germans used it for interrogations and executions. Its name was Pawiak.

Somewhere inside Pawiak, inside a small, sterile room, was Henryk the boy soldier. His wrists were handcuffed to a plain wooden bench with no backrest. He could not raise his arms; he could not lean back. Before him was an office desk with a green table lamp, a typewriter, and stacks of folders. A small window had frosted glass, so he could not distinguish day from night. Henryk glanced curiously at the tools on the bookcase: hand-cuffs, chains, bludgeons, thumbscrews, shiny knives, a Walther pistol, and a larger machine pistol. Behind him stood two SS guards; they were holding iron bludgeons. Henryk bent his neck and peered at the bare light bulb over his head; it was harsh, but not unpleasant. This seemed more like a small office than a tor-ture chamber. He wondered what would happen next.

Before him was the interrogator, a Gestapo man. He was well-dressed in a starched white shirt, black suit and tie, and black gloves; he wore no Nazi armband or emblem at all. His clean trenchcoat hung from a coat stand in the corner. In his gloved hand he held a rumpled white handkerchief. He had blue-gray eyes and blond hair, oiled back on his small head. He was so thin that his skin stretched across his skull. He looked quite a bit like Reinhard Heydrich, the security police chief whose picture Henryk had seen once; he wondered if they were related.

The Gestapo interrogator strolled across the herringbone wood floor before Henryk. "You understand, of course," he said with a polite grin, "That you are a dead person. So sad for such a young boy. This cannot be helped. You must understand, boy, that all this suffering, all your beatings, will be because of these – criminals in the Underground. These are known criminals, employed by London." He circled around to the small desk. "These people, who are safe and protected – they are the cause of your death."

Henryk did not know what to say. He was sorry he was here.

He wanted to go home.

"So, boy," he asked calmly, "What is your name?"

"Adam," Henryk said politely. He noticed that the Gestapo man wore black leather boots, polished to a high shine. From head to foot, he was almost all black. "Adam Szypowscy."

"Please, boy, do not insult my intelligence. This is merely preliminary. When you were stopped, you had no identification on you. You know that you must carry valid papers on you at all times. This alone is a crime. Tell us your name, and perhaps we will treat you better."

But Henryk knew better. If they learned his real name, they would go back to his mother, and uncle, and cousins. "My name is Adam Szypowscy," he said. "I'm a Cadet in the Fire Brigade." In the Fire Brigade, he could be out after curfew, going to the fire station to report for duty.

"And your uniform?"

"There's a shortage. I'm waiting for one." This was a reasonable excuse. After all, there was a shortage of everything in Warsaw. "There are my *Kennkarte* and work permit."

"Ah, yes," the man sighed, tapping the identity papers that lay on his desk. "These – obvious forgeries. The seals are smeared, the signatures are childish, the paper is rough. Truly a crude effort." He dropped the papers, and wiped his black gloves with his handkerchief, as if he had somehow dirtied himself.

"My name is Adam Szypowscy," he repeated. "I'm a Cadet in the Fire Brigade." This story would surely work.

The Gestapo man shook his head, and tapped his toe on the wood floor. He held his handkerchief up to his face. Suddenly he leapt at Henryk. "Who is this Anna!" He screamed at Henryk through this protection.

Henryk rocked back. "I don't – I don't know."

"Who is this Bronek!"

"I don't know."

"That is a lie! These are all lies! Lies! Lies! We have the proof! It is right here, taken from your own pocket!" With his

free hand he pushed a note into Henryk's face, scratching his
cheek. "Here is all the proof we need! Proof that you are a messenger for the Underground! Filthy Slavic swine! Who are
they!"

Henryk felt the two uniformed SS men become excited.
They tapped the iron clubs in their hands. "I told you. Please –
I don't know."

"Why are you passing messages for them! Why! Why!" he
shouted through his handkerchief.

"He asked me to. As a favor." That was the wrong thing to
say.

"Who is he! Where is he! Tell me! I may spare you a beating!"

Henryk did not know what to say at an interrogation. His
prepared story suddenly evaporated. "I – I don't know. I just
want to go home."

The interrogator stood up straight and nodded; he seemed to
consider the request for a moment. Henryk thought he saw a
grin. "You want to go home. Just so. Well, let me tell you something, boy. I am Gestapo now, but I am truly just a soldier. They
tell me to go somewhere, I say '*Jawohl*' and I go. So I come to
Warsaw." He pushed his face so close that his handkerchief
grazed Henryk's cheek. "And I discover everywhere are – Slavs
and Jews. Those – round-headed beasts, spreading – typhus and
cholera! It is known that they live in their own sewage, like ani-
mals." He swallowed, dryly. "We have exterminated the vermin
Jew, and still he is everywhere in Warsaw! He is in my toast
every morning, he is in my sheets with me at night, he infests
the air in my lungs. His disease crawls inside my very skin. It
is more than a civilized person can bear! And now we must deal
with you Slavs! You brutes, killing us at every turn! And you
wish to go home! Well, boy, you are not going home! I will die
in Warsaw, and so will you! Spare yourself a senseless beating!
Tell me! You swine, you diseased, filthy Slavic beast! Who is
this Anna! Who is this Bronek!"

"I don't know. Please let me go –"

"That . . . is . . . a lie!" The interrogator turned around, and fell silent.

The SS men raised their clubs. The men laughed and joked to each other as they started their work. One of them touched a spot on Henryk's back: *"Schlag da!"* (Hit there!) Then they struck him on that precise spot. They joked about their accuracy. Henryk felt the iron bludgeons slam against his back and shoulders. He strained at his handcuffs, trying to fend off the strikes, but it was no use. He felt his energy drain away. After a while, he could not raise his hands. He slouched over, defeated, and absorbed the bludgeon strikes. The clubs hit again, again, again.

The Gestapo interrogator opened the small window to the night air. He slumped against the windowsill, feeling polluted, sucking the air of the Ghetto through his handkerchief. He rested as the SS men joked and laughed.

After several minutes, he turned around. "Now, Polish pig, we will try again." On the desk he set a note, a note that began, "Dearest Anna, I am alive." Then the interrogator returned to young Henryk.

XX

A cold sleety snow fell across the city like a soaked blanket. The morning sun glanced off the rooftops, still too shallow to warm the streets below. On Ujazdowski Avenue two unmarked Mercedes-Benz sedans rolled, their tires rumbling steadily as they bounced on the paving stones. A few clumps of snow collected on the cars' roofs as they turned down a narrow side street.

Just then a young man leapt from the sidewalk, a clear glass bottle in his hand. He cocked his arm and shouted: "Now!" He lit the fuse and threw the gasoline-filled bottle: "In the name of the Polish Republic!"

In an instant, the street erupted. Two other young men opened their coats. They each raised a handgun and started firing. The windshield of the rear car shattered. In a huge wave, the pedestrians fell against the stone walls and covered their heads, as if they were practicing a fire drill.

The first man watched anxiously as the bottle flew through the air. It sailed between the two cars. It glanced off the rear car's grill, skipped along the slush-covered paving stones, and bounced harmlessly into the far gutter. The fuse went out. Gasoline trickled out the top.

The front Mercedes roared its engine and sped away. The

rear car abruptly slid to a stop. The three men stood still, lost in a fog of confusion. They looked at each other, puzzled. And then they ran. Their pistols fell from their hands, rattling on the sidewalk.

Four Gestapo guards jumped from the car. They quickly raised their rifles and fired, as the pedestrians stretched out flat on the wet sidewalk. Two of the attackers tumbled to the street, wounded. The other man kept running.

Two guards shouted: *"Halt! Halt!"* Then they ran after him. The other guards stood over the wounded Underground agents, raised their rifles, and fired.

The narrow street was good for an ambush attack, but no good for an escape. The youth careened around a corner, and darted down an alley. But the alley went nowhere. He scrambled against the walls, frantically searching for a window. There was nothing.

The guards stopped running when they saw him. They had time, so they caught their breath for a second. The young man turned around and held up his hands. *"Nicht schiessen!"* he pleaded. *"Bitte! Nicht schiessen!"*

The guards stood still. They glanced at each other, and nodded. They raised their rifles, aimed, and fired.

In the street, the civilians slowly got up off the sidewalk, brushed off their clothes, and hurried away. A few of them paused over the lifeless bodies, whispered a quick prayer, and crossed themselves. And a safe distance down the street, Franz Kutschera lay across the back seat of the first Mercedes as it sped toward Gestapo headquarters.

* * *

"Did you hear what happened?" Jerzy asked.

"Yes." Wiktor was lying on his stomach, atop a roof two blocks south of Szucha Avenue. Well north of them, across the street, was Gestapo headquarters.

"I heard it happened yesterday." Jerzy was lying on his back, staring up at the gray morning sky. "There was an attack on Kutschera. They attacked his car."

"I know." The wind blew in Wiktor's face as he peered over the edge of the building. A few light snowflakes landed on his mustache. His cheeks turned bright red, like a cheery saint.

"They threw a Molotov cocktail at his car, but it didn't explode for some reason. Just like that."

"Bad luck."

"Who do you think did it? Was it the Communists?"

"Not likely. They don't have the skill."

"Was it one of us?"

"I presume so."

"But isn't that good news? It shows that he's vulnerable. They followed him, learned his routes, a hundred other details."

"Did it work?"

"No. The Molotov cocktail didn't explode."

"So Kutschera's still alive, isn't he."

"Yes."

"Then where's the good news?"

Jerzy did not respond. Jerzy rolled over onto his stomach and peered over the top of the building façade. Szucha Avenue was a massively guarded Nazi stronghold. Gestapo, SS, and German police headquarters were all here. On the sidewalk were two circular pillboxes, with machine guns and guards.

The wind was making his face cold, so Jerzy rolled over onto his back again. "Do you remember what tomorrow is?" he finally asked.

"Saturday."

"It will be January 1. Nineteen forty-four."

"Yes."

"Maybe we'll be liberated next year."

"Maybe."

"Wiktor, I – I don't want to document executions any more."

"Shh!" Wiktor hissed determinedly.

"What's up?" Jerzy rolled back over onto his stomach, and cursed the biting wind.

There, on the street, the two black Mercedes' stopped at the gate. After clearing the gate, the cars rolled past the barbed wire, up to the building. A guard got out of one car and opened the rear door. A man in a plain uniform leapt from the car, closely followed by the four guards from the other car. As quickly as they appeared, the soldiers disappeared inside the building.

"Damn," Wiktor grumbled.

"What's wrong?"

Wiktor checked his wristwatch. "Not even four seconds. Kutschera is only outside for three and a half seconds. And he wears a plain uniform, no general's markings. Even if we had the best sniper in all Warsaw, he can't get any closer than we are. So our man would have to shoot everybody."

"That would be tough."

"A bit. A sniper is no good. It won't work." Wiktor rolled over onto his back. For a while, the two brothers stared up at the sky together. "There's no easy way to get to him."

"So, what do we do now?"

"We think some more."

"Wiktor, did you hear what I said before?"

"Yes. What do you mean?"

"I'm sick of researching these executions. They're horrible. They're happening almost every day."

"Don't you see that it is important?"

"I suppose so. But people are – destroyed by them."

"Jerzy, resistance work is not easy. It's the hardest thing in the world. Would you rather we practiced – nonviolent resistance?" Somehow Wiktor made the concept sound wretched and unpatriotic.

"Of course not. Never. But this has to stop. Won't there be an uprising someday, or something?"

"I suspect there might be."

"I sure hope so. Have we heard from Lot?"

"Nothing."

"He's gone, too." Jerzy shook his head. "Wiktor, I can't do this any more."

"All right, little brother. Just calm down. We'll keep working on a plan."

"Wiktor?"

"Yes?"

"Happy New Year."

"Oh, yes. That, too."

* * *

Bronek knew there was a commotion going on upstairs. He heard snippets of conversation through the cellar door, but he could not discern what they were talking about. For the moment, he ignored the conversation and sat up on his bed. Leaning forward, he wiggled his toes in the air. His foot was still black and blue, but the swelling had lessened considerably. Best of all, his dysentery was nearly cured, and his headaches had gone away. He could only think about going home, about finding Anna. He had not seen Henryk in a couple days, and did not know whether his message had been delivered. He looked around until he spotted his shoes, lying in the corner.

Just then the lock clicked, the door opened, and Irena marched downstairs. She was carrying a small half-loaf of black bread. "Here is your breakfast," she said curtly.

Bronek nodded. "Thank you, Irena. Set it there, on the table."

"You need to eat it."

"I know. I want to try to walk first."

"You must eat now . . . because you must leave today."

"What?" Bronek responded, surprised. "Today?"

Irena trembled noticeably, as if she were very nervous. "We have discussed it – and there is no other way. We have decided, you cannot stay."

Bronek eyed her, puzzled. She was being much less polite than she had been before. Then he noticed her red eyes, and realized that she had been crying.

"Well – I see," Bronek stammered. "You know, Irena, it's an amazing thing. I was able to try my foot this morning. I think I can walk out of here today."

"That is fine. Because you must go."

Irena retrieved Bronek's shoes, and placed them on the floor by his feet. Bronek felt uncomfortable as she stood over him, her arms twitching. She rested her chin in her hand, but her fingers still quivered. Bronek pulled his shoe over his swollen foot, as Irena watched and then looked away.

"Well," Irena at last blurted out, "Henryk is lost. We have not heard from him in . . . over four days."

"He's – lost?" Bronek felt his jaw drop open.

"No one knows where he is. Our priest has connections at Pawiak, but – nothing."

Bronek knew what that meant. "Henryk? No . . . not him. That can't be."

"We went out checking posters today, but there is . . . nothing. . . ." Irena's voice faded into silence.

Bronek wanted to help her, somehow. "Irena, I'm – I'm very sorry."

She hastily wiped her weathered cheek. "Yes, you can be sorry. That is fine. But you cannot stay here. You must leave."

"Yes. I understand, Irena. How can I leave?"

"You cannot come upstairs. There is a hatch leading to the next basement, behind the dresser. There is a cellar door in my neighbor's basement," she commanded, pointing with a tear glistening on her fingertip. "Use that door."

Bronek had inspected Irena's basement, and had not found a hidden passageway. It must have been well disguised. "Yes, I'm sure I can make it." Bronek tested his foot. Again, he shouted. The pain shot through his foot like a long needle. "It's better," he lied. "I can put some weight on it, I think."

"Then you can go now." She handed him his coat.

"Yes, yes. Let me pull on my other shoe, and I'll be gone." Bronek laced up his left shoe, but he had to leave his right shoe untied. "Thank you," he muttered, as he put on his coat. "I'll take this?" he asked, holding up the slab of black bread. When Irena said nothing, Bronek tucked it inside his coat. He stood up, resting all his weight on his left foot. He stood before the beautiful woman with the gaunt, tired face. "Irena," he said,

"Thank you. I owe you my life. The people I know are – grateful to you. We will all pray for Henryk."

Irena did not look at him. She cast her eyes down at the floor, and then up at the ceiling. "Yes, well . . . go now." She turned and headed up the cellar steps.

"Irena!" Bronek called out.

She stopped halfway up the stairs.

"Irena, I know Henryk was out after curfew. But I know where he was going. There's hope for Henryk. I – I can't tell you why. I can't tell you what he asked me to keep secret. But I know – he might still be safe."

Irena watched him for a second. Then she went upstairs. Bronek heard the door lock behind her.

* * *

Anna had just exchanged code words with the woman guard, and was in the apartment. Ryzy, the aged professor, noticed her. "Golebica," he said, nodding, "Well, you are alive, after all."

"Professor Ryzy, I am late. I apologize. But don't begin class. I must tell you something."

They were standing in the anteroom of someone's apartment. Anna knew immediately by the warmth and the lack of dust that this apartment was inhabited. But she could not see, did not want to see, the other students.

Ryzy stopped and peered at his returning student. His wrinkled brow shifted from relief to sad concern. "Just what do you mean?"

"I mean that I – I came to a decision."

"What is that? What do you mean, Golebica?"

From somewhere deep in her heart, Anna found the strength to look directly into Ryzy's eyes. He had tired eyes, eyes that made her pity him. But still, she looked at him and spoke, softly but clearly. "I decided I must leave school."

"What? Why?"

"Because I have something else that I must do. Something that is more important to me."

Ryzy squinted his eyes. "Golebica, you cannot – quit."

"Ryzy, I must. I cannot live two lives, one here and one there. I have another mission now."

"Well – well –" he began, and then stopped.

"What I must do will take all my energy, and all my courage. And I only have a little bit."

"This is a sad development, Golebica."

"Ryzy, I think you're very brave. I hope you think I'm somewhat brave." Anna heard the other students whispering nervously.

Ryzy's hunched shoulders seemed to sag even more, as he stood in the anteroom. He glared at her. "You know who we are," he said unhappily.

"Ryzy, I'll never reveal what I know. I've destroyed all my textbooks. God be with you."

For a long moment Anna watched him, hoping he might say more. "Final examinations begin soon, you know."

"I know. This is something I must do."

Ryzy waited, and pondered. "Well," he wheezed at last, "God be with you, Dove."

Anna walked carefully on the wet streets. The air was warmer now, and the light snow was melting into a few mounds in the streets. Anna was thankful that she had remembered to wear a coat and babushka today. Everything about the morning was gray: the sky, the snow, the people, were all gray. Her wooden shoes were slick on these stones; she frequently slid when she took a step. But that would not stop her. She clenched her teeth, more determined than ever. She was going to take action. She raised her arms for balance, and went on.

She walked past a sheet of wood attached to a wrought iron fence. Every centimeter of the board was filled with signs and posters. Anna stopped. She had to check every poster, every board, every kiosk, in the city. She would no longer hastily walk by, hoping not to see anything disturbing. Now she approached the board, fully cognizant of the anguish that might await.

There, at the center of the board, was a red poster. Anna whispered a prayer for strength. She closed her eyes. She could not escape the image she had seen so often, the image from her nightmares: in her mind she saw the name, and she, like so many others, staggered away, sobbing with grief.

Slowly, she felt a calm wash over her. The prayer was working; the Lord was helping her. She opened her eyes and read:

"ANNOUNCEMENT

On December 18, a the Polish Police corporal was attacked while on duty by three armed criminals on Zawisza Street in Warsaw. On December 20, a police patrol was fired on by four armed criminals on Gorczewska Street. One police officer was shot, and another seriously wounded. On December 21, 1943 several criminals assaulted a *Volksdeutsche* on Dluga Street, mortally wounding him. In retaliation for this, I ordered the following criminals sentenced to death by the Security Police Summary Court but conditionally eligible for clemency to be publicly executed on December 23, 1944."

Next came the horrible task. Anna slowly, delicately, read the entire list of names. Because four people had been attacked, she knew there would be 40 chances. She read from the first name, Stanislaw Kowalczyk, all the way to the fortieth name, Jozef Krakowiak. Bronek's name was not there. She took a deep breath before she continued, through the list of newly condemned – the next group scheduled for execution. She scanned all 63 names of condemned men, from Stefan Stefanski to Wladyslaw Bakowski. Again – she was spared. Today would not be the day that destroyed her. She checked the date at the bottom: December 27, 1943. Today was the thirty-first, so this poster was already four days old. A thousand things might have happened since then. Still, Anna whispered a prayer of thanks.

Before she turned away, she noticed an emblem painted across another poster. It was a "P" attached to an anchor:

Below that was scribbled the slogan, "Poland fights!" Anna nodded appreciatively; someone had taken a great risk to remind her of that. Then she resumed her search.

What was her goal? Now that she had a moment to think, she considered the vastness of her mission. Warsaw was a big city. Her family could not help her; the bureaucrats would not help her. And the posters only listed a fraction of all the names of people who had been executed. What did she hope to find? Her mission was a risky gamble. The odds of success were slim. And if she were successful – that was too horrible to contemplate. It was an image that filled her nightmares, that kept her awake night after night. But still, something inside of her compelled her, forced her to go forward, to find the truth. She had already been in the depths of despair. Now she was working, progressing, searching. She could not think of quitting. She had no plan, no strategy. All she had was a need, a driving need, to know.

She soon found herself in Hale Mirowski, the black market. It was as busy as most market areas in peacetime, full of wooden stalls, stores, vendors on the sidewalks. Anna felt a small rush of optimism. People were producing a noisy ruckus: "Cigarettes for sale!" "Newspapers for sale!" "Flour for sale!" "Pork for sale!" At Hale Mirowski everything was for sale: kielbasa, liquor, bread, guns, radios, information. Information. Surely someone here knew something. And if she had to buy the news, well, she would buy it.

On one corner a fortune teller was kneeling on the sidewalk, wailing, "The Russians have broken through! I see the vision! They're reaching our border!" On another corner she spotted a boy shouting, *"Nowy Kurier Warszawski! Nowy Kurier Warszawski!"* That was it; a paperboy would know everything. She walked over to him, leaning down to be at his height.

"Hello," Anna said. Her voice wavered, not from fear but from weakness. "What do you know?" she asked hoarsely.

"*Nowy Kurier Warszawski* for sale! *Nowy Kurier Warszawski!*" The boy practically pushed the paper into Anna's unwilling hands.

"Say, young man, do you know any news?" Anna felt dizzy. She shut her eyes momentarily, until the feeling passed.

The boy shrugged his shoulders. "The Russians cut all the rail lines out of Vitebsk. It's right here, in the paper. Russians cut rail lines out of Vitebsk! Russians cut rail lines!"

"Doesn't this have any special news inside? Like *Biuletyn Informacyjny*? Or *Rzeczpospolita Polska*? *Wolna Polska*?"

The paperboy eyed Anna suspiciously. "I don't know anything about them," he said angrily. He turned his back on Anna and waved his paper over his head. "*Nowy Kurier Warszawski!*"

"No, wait, please," Anna pleaded, "I want to talk to you."

"I do not know anything." He tried to turn away from Anna, but she circled faster.

"Do you have some news?"

"Well, I heard something."

"What did you hear?" Anna asked eagerly.

"Something on Towarowa Street."

"What address? Please – what address?"

"I don't know anything. I just heard a rumor. Now, go away."

"Thank you. Thank you," Anna said quickly, as she turned and left.

Anna walked as quickly as she could toward Towarowa Street. The sidewalks were still slick, and her wooden shoes slipped so often, she was certain she would fall. But she compelled herself to go forward. She knew what awaited her. It would be a heartbreaking sight. But perhaps she would learn something. She forced herself through the streets of Warsaw, slush chilling her ankles, the gray sky casting a gloom over her. But nothing would stop her.

She reached 4 Towarowa Street. She was not too late. Dozens of women were there, kneeling on the wet sidewalk, praying and crying. Bunches of flowers were strewn about, a sad gesture toward the victims. Several candles were standing on the sidewalk, faintly casting light on the tragedy. Dozens of people stood around, chatting amongst each other, cursing the names Frank and Kutschera.

Anna approached the stone wall. She swallowed nervously. It was there again. Scattered bullet holes were chipped into the stone. Puddles of wash water, from where workers had scrubbed away the blood, blended in with the melting snow. She bit her lip, overcome by nausea and revulsion. She gasped and fell against the wall. But this time she waited; after several seconds the feeling passed, and she forced herself to continue.

She approached a woman kneeling in the slush. "Did you see this? Did you see?" The woman's face was hidden by her babushka. Anna leaned forward and saw that she was elderly and feeble. "Did you see a young man? With dark hair, combed back?" Anna asked again. But the old woman closed her eyes, lost in her own world, a world of European culture and civility where massacres did not happen.

Anna looked around at other people. Clusters of men stood apart, smoking stubby, home-rolled cigarettes and swearing intensely. They projected a masculine anger that made Anna feel intimidated. Then she saw a boy nearly her own age, standing several meters from her. He seemed to be watching people in the same manner that she was. She trained her gaze directly on him, so he would not get lost in the crowd. Anna stared at him until she was beside him. "Did you see what happened?" she asked.

The boy, Jerzy Kruczyk, shook his head sadly. "Forty-three," he said. "Forty-three. I don't know how to feel any more."

"Were you here? Did you see their faces?"

The youth eyed her curiously. He seemed to be uncomfortable being asked questions. "I saw nothing, ma'am –"

"– Perhaps you saw him. He's taller than you, with dark hair. He often has it in a pompadour. He has a dimple on his chin, but it's off center."

Jerzy shook his head. "I didn't see anyone. Really."

"Please. Please help me. His name is Bronek. Bronek Pietraszewicz."

"Believe me, I don't know any Bronek."

"He goes by another name. Lot."

Something in Jerzy's eyes perked up. He stared at her. Then he looked away. "I don't know any Lot."

Anna gasped. "You do! You know him!"

"No, I don't. Now, I have to go."

"Wait! You know! Where is he!"

Jerzy turned away. "I don't know any Lot. I have to go." He threaded his way through the throng.

Anna felt a rush of energy shoot through her. "Stop! Please!" She frantically pushed through the people, chasing after that boy. But her shoes slipped on the snow, and she tumbled to the sidewalk, tearing her skirt. When she recovered, he suddenly was gone.

Just then, someone shouted, "Police!" Anna looked back. Farther down the block, two large patrols of policemen turned the corner and approached. They held their rifles in front of them. They were coming to clear the crowd. People started pushing to get away. The street became chaotic.

Anna ran as fast as she could to the end of the block, and looked in every direction. The boy was nowhere to be seen. And right then, something inside of Anna was lifted. All the tension she had felt, all her uncertainty and panic, ceased. She had to find that boy. He knew her husband. Weaving through pedestrians, she picked a street and she began walking. She took little steps, to keep from slipping. She looked at every person she met. Already she felt different. Everything inside her, every ounce of energy she had left, was focused on that one goal. She would not stop now, not ever.

Frantically, Anna searched. Her babushka fell back to her

shoulders, and her tangled blond hair blew around her face. She hurried everywhere she could, and did not even step aside when an SS soldier walked past. All she could do was study each face on each person she saw. Her numb fingers, her hunger pangs, her lack of sleep, all meant nothing now. She would not rest until she found him.

Anna spotted a couple of youngsters walking away from her. She could not see their faces. She hurried, until she caught up with them. She grabbed one and spun him around; the boy Jerzy was not one of them. Anna turned a different direction, and headed that way.

Just then she looked farther down the street. She stopped, and was still. She was stunned by the vision, as if she had been slapped in the face. Her heart at first refused to believe what she saw. And then, a feeling of exaltation leapt up inside her. Her heart swelled as she watched Bronek walk toward her. Yes, there he was! He was limping, but there he was! Even from this distance, he stared into her eyes. Anna could not contain herself. Her face beaming with joy, she started to run. She had to hold him, touch his arms and his face, assure herself that he was real.

When she was a couple meters from him, his face suddenly changed. He anxiously shook his head and mouthed some words to her, but she could not hear what. Then she glanced beside him; two Blue Policemen happened to be next to them. She felt tears of relief tumble down her red cheeks, tears she had longed to feel, and she raised her arms to him; but Bronek would not speak, would not acknowledge her. He walked beside her, his eyes wide, his head shaking ever so slightly. He was about to walk past her. It was too much; her head spun dizzily; and suddenly she fell to the sidewalk.

Seconds later, she opened her eyes. Bronek was there, holding her. She blinked and looked again, just to see his face. She felt his arms supporting her, propping up her head. She could not control her jumbled emotions, and she sobbed, joyfully, gratefully. "It's you, it's you," she uttered.

"Shh!" Bronek warned. "You don't know me. You don't know me!"

The two policemen pushed their way through the pedestrians and pulled Bronek up. Then they pulled Anna up to her feet. *Not now*, she thought, *Not the police now.*

True to their vicious habits, they both pulled their pistols. "What's going on here?" the older one asked. They were obviously not Polish, possibly Ukrainians brought in by the Germans. They pushed Bronek and Anna over against the building behind them.

Anna let Bronek speak; she could not even think of words to say. She heard her sobs turn into giggles. "She fainted," she heard Bronek explain. "I was just helping her."

"Is that true?" the other one asked Anna.

Anna glanced at Bronek and smiled through her tears. "Yes," she finally said, nodding. She wiped the frozen tears from her cheeks. "I'm so – weak and hungry. I – I – must have fainted." *Say nothing. Pretend to know nothing. Be ignorant.*

"See? She's just a weak, wonderful," he added, grinning at her, "Wonderful woman."

Anna opened her mouth to laugh. She had to be careful to not actually make a sound.

"Your *Kennkarten*, then," the older policeman said with a trace of tedium in his voice.

The policemen perfunctorily checked their identification papers, and frisked them. "See?" Bronek said reassuringly. "My name is Stanislaw Kwiatkowski. I work for the power company. Would we try to pass messages right in front of you?"

Anna listened. He was reminding her of his false identity.

The policeman seemed disinterested in arresting anyone, if it could be avoided. "You two go on – to wherever you're going." He waved them on with his pistol.

Anna watched Bronek desperately. For several seconds, they stared at each other. She burned to talk to him, but the policemen stood there, and Bronek slowly walked away. He was careful not to look back at her. Soon she lost him in the crowd. Anna glanced nervously at the policemen, and walked the other direction. Now, at last, she knew where she was going. She was going home. Anna hurried as quickly as her wooden shoes would take her, giggling and whispering prayers every slippery step of the way.

XXI

"It's a miracle."

Karol Pietraszewicz was sitting at the head of the table, leaning forward on his elbows. Bronek was sitting at the kitchen table, Eugene beside him. "Thank the Blessed Virgin, it's a miracle."

Bronek fingered his cup of ersatz coffee nervously. "It really wasn't, Papa. It was – just luck."

"Just luck!" Eugene exclaimed. "You escaped the police, and you jumped into the sewer, and you broke your foot, and then you were rescued by a beautiful woman –"

"I never said she was beautiful."

"Well, I bet she was."

"Eugene . . ." Bronek began, and then he chuckled. "Well, all right. She was beautiful."

Karol chimed in. "And on New Year's Eve, even. You were lost, and now you're found. How better to begin the year! Here – do you need something? Are you still hungry?"

"No, let Eugene have it –"

"Here, you need some more breakfast." He slid a brown patty from the frying pan onto Bronek's plate. "Have another pancake."

"Oh." Bronek stared at the object. "I thought we were finished." His father had ground up potato peelings into a paste, and fried them like pancakes. The only way to force them down was by softening them with butter, or coffee, or anything else handy. Bronek spread some ersatz coffee over the potato-peeling pancake, and tried to digest a bite. It had a gritty, sandy texture; he felt as though he were eating dirt. He chewed and chewed, grinding the pancake with his teeth, finally forcing it down with more coffee. The breakfast did not help his hunger pangs. "Thank you, Papa."

"Do you need more? I'll make you another one."

"No! I mean, no thank you." He chewed, laboriously. "Eugene can have the next one."

"It's a sign," Karol continued ebulliently. "It's a sign, it must be."

"A sign?"

"Sure it is," Eugene agreed.

"Yes, it's a sign from Heaven. Praise God, I think 1944 will be the year the German occupation ends!"

"What?" Bronek studied his father. He was never a very emotional person. There was always a layer of politeness between them. But now, his father's face was red, and his smile radiated a supreme joy. Bronek had never seen his father so unabashedly happy. "Believe me, Papa, I didn't plan to come back on the new year. It just –"

There was a knock on the door. Karol practically jumped from his chair. "I'll get that. Do you boys need more coffee?"

"No, I'm fine," Bronek said firmly, and then he mumbled, "For the twelfth time."

Karol opened the door. "Is he here?" Bronek heard a woman ask.

"Yes, yes, he's here, Halina. Come get a look at him."

Misses Rogala swept into the small kitchen, her arms spread wide. "Bronek, you beautiful boy! You're safe, you're safe!" She grabbed him around the shoulders and squeezed hard.

Bronek coughed from the pressure. "Hello, Misses Rogala," he said politely.

"I just heard from Mister Stachowiak that you came back yesterday." She kissed him on the cheek. "I thought I'd never see you again!"

Bronek raised his hand to wipe off his cheek, but then thought better of it. "Thank you, Misses Rogala."

"He told me the most amazing story, Halina," Karol said.

"He escaped from the Nazis!" Eugene blurted out, pride beaming in his voice.

"Really!" Misses Rogala exclaimed.

"That's not all," Karol added, sitting back down in his chair. "He escaped through the sewer."

"Bless the Virgin!" She rested her arms around Bronek's shoulders. "And I heard you broke both your arms."

"What? That part's not true." Bronek said quietly. He fidgeted inside Misses Rogala's thin arms.

"This must be a sign," Karol speculated. "He came back to us on the thirty-first."

"Yes, yes," Misses Rogala assented. "Only Providence could ordain it."

"I don't feel like a messenger from God," Bronek remarked. He wished Misses Rogala would let him go.

"We'll have to do something special," Bronek's father commented. "Something to celebrate. Our son has come home."

"Yes, something marvelous. How about a special meal? We'll all bring our best food."

"Yes, yes," Karol agreed.

"And *bimber*!" Eugene added.

Bronek looked at them sheepishly. "Thank you, all of you. But really, I'm happy to sit here in the kitchen, and have coffee. This fake coffee tastes – wonderful today."

"Don't listen to him, Karol. The whole neighborhood will do something. Everyone will all be so thankful. I have to go tell everyone!" She finally let go of Bronek, and scurried to the front door. Karol got up to let her out. "We have something to pray about tonight!"

As soon as their father got up to unlock the door, Eugene

turned to Bronek. "Quick, tell me. What was it like?" he asked eagerly.

Bronek shook his head ruefully. "Eugene, it wasn't exciting. I feel – disappointed. I'm only here because of luck. Just luck. And I missed everyone. Even you," he added with a grin.

* * *

Bronek took a streetcar east and stepped off on Nowy Swiat. He walked north along the Royal Way, where the great families of Warsaw built their palaces. Across the street was the gate of the Radziwill Palace. Built by the Radziwill family, it was now used by the General Government. The palace was white and formal, with rows of windows and decorative Greek columns. The sun shone brilliantly in the winter sky, making the white palace even more vivid. In front was a pedestal for the statue of Prince Jozef Poniatowski. But the statue was destroyed, and now the pedestal was empty. Several soldiers and a mounted machine gun guarded the palace.

He saw her there, tapping her wooden shoe nervously. Bronek breathed a sigh of relief; she had gotten his note. She went half a block from the palace, past a small bend where the guards could not see her, and went down an alley. Bronek waited, and then followed her. But he had to avoid limping, and attracting attention to himself.

The alley he had chosen was short, but had a pile of rubble they could hide behind. If found, they would pretend to be sneaking away for a kiss. He went around a mound of bricks and mortar. She was there. Suddenly Bronek felt uneasy; he wasn't sure what he was supposed to say. He approached her hesitantly.

"Thanks to God," Anna said softly.

"I'm not so sure." He watched as Anna wiped a small tear from her cheek. She was wearing her shabby coat, patched dress, wooden shoes, and a babushka tied under her chin. She looked cold. But her smile was heartfelt.

The bombed-out wall made a good hiding place. Now

Bronek studied Anna's face inquisitively. "Anna, what happened to you?"

"I – I had a bad time."

He wrinkled his brow. "Did you lose weight?"

"Yes. I – I couldn't eat."

"Take that off," he said, pointing to her babushka.

Anna slowly reached up, and Bronek noticed her bony fingers and split fingernails. She pulled back on her babushka. "I lost some hair, too," she admitted, smiling nervously.

Bronek gasped. "Dear God!" Her appearance hit him, deep in his stomach. Anna's hair was frizzled and oily. Her scalp showed through in several spots. She looked like a discarded doll, bony and broken. "Are you . . . my wife?"

Anna looked up at him. Her blue eyes were even more striking, larger because of her gaunt face. She slid her hands inside his; he felt a chill from her bare fingers, as cold as icicles. "Yes, it's me. Like you always say – I will survive."

Bronek stared at her, at her ghostly white skin and her fluttery blue eyes. Suddenly he was overcome. *How she must have suffered,* he thought. His absence had devastated her. He had to stay with her, make her whole again. "We should keep moving. Can you walk?"

"Well, a short distance."

"I'll help you." He gingerly pulled her babushka back over her head and they set off, walking south from the palace. Bronek felt her lean against his arm as they walked, so he held his arm out stiffly, to support her. This also helped to disguise his limp. He held her hand inside his and rubbed her fingers gently. Bronek thought of a hundred things he should say to her, but at the moment he was not feeling talkative. Feeling her holding his arm, leaning on him for support, was all he needed to know.

Ahead of them he saw a patrol of four Blue Policemen. Bronek kept his eye on them, trying to sense where they were looking. *Never look them in the eye.* The police passed by without noticing them.

"I was . . . so worried about you," Anna said gratefully. "I prayed and prayed to see you again."

Bronek was surprised that she had any energy in her voice. "I prayed for you, too."

"Where were you? What happened to you?"

"Well, I was – on a –"

"On a mission? What happened? Were you arrested?"

"No, I was –"

"Were you injured?"

"Yes, I fell and –"

"Oh, I knew it. I felt it. I just knew you had been injured. Where?"

"My foot, I broke a bone –"

"Oh, my Lord, you broke your foot? Is that why you're limping? How can you even walk?"

"Well, it's getting better –"

"Did you go to a doctor? Did you get a cast for it?"

"No, I –"

"Oh, Benny, I was so worried for you!" Anna stopped walking. "Why are you smiling?"

Bronek felt his cheeks tighten into a wide smile. "I don't know for certain," he said. He heard himself chuckle. "I guess I'm just very lucky. I'm lucky to be walking with you right now. I don't know if it's the blessing of God or just luck. But every breath I take feels like one I'm not entitled to."

"You can imagine how I feel," Anna confided. "I was so worried about you. I had no idea what had happened to you."

They turned the corner, and Bronek helped Anna keep her balance. "I sent a letter to you," he said. "Please tell me you got it."

"I never got any letter, Benny. I searched and searched for you, but I never found out anything."

Bronek looked down at her. "No. Please, no."

"I even went to police headquarters at Szucha Avenue. That's how frantic I was. I was nearly arrested."

Bronek thought back to the eager young boy who had wanted to be a soldier.

"I studied all the posters for your name. The posters – they destroy you inside. But I never saw your name."

"Then – it's true."

"Benny, darling – what's true?"

Bronek turned away from her, his head reeling. He reached out and grabbed onto a streetlight pole. For a long time he could not say anything.

"Benny?" he heard Anna ask cautiously, "What's the matter?"

Bronek felt the frigid air burn his throat. For a moment he could not raise his head. "There was a boy," he said, down to the sidewalk. "He helped me. He and his mother. They fed me and protected me. He said he would deliver a message for me."

"I never received any message."

"I had hoped. But now . . . I know."

"He was –?"

"Arrested. I'm sure of it."

"Who was he?"

"I don't know. He said his name was Henryk. He and his mother saved my life. That's all I know of them."

"Oh, dear."

"But I know he didn't reveal any information. They never learned his true identity. Or else the Gestapo would have raided the house."

"May God have mercy." Anna quickly crossed herself. She touched his hand. Others passed by them, not noticing them. Even a police patrol went by on the opposite sidewalk. For a moment the world ignored them. "Benny," Anna continued, "We have both suffered so much. There's only one way to escape this."

"Escape . . . how?"

"Do you remember what we had said before?"

"About the forest?"

"That's the only way. Benny, I can't live like this. I can't live through – that ordeal again. I'm almost too weak to go on.

Let's make our escape. Not later. Now!"

Bronek looked into her eyes, and he saw the yearning in her soul. He realized how deeply she needed him. Without him, she would collapse from the fear and the strain. She was correct; he knew it. "But I – I don't know if I can leave," he whispered, almost imperceptibly.

"Benny, that can be our victory. Our survival, our children. That will be our achievement."

He did not respond. He looked at her, and then up at the pale blue sky, and then at the streetcar that lumbered down the street. Finally he looked back into her eyes. "I have to keep my mission, my Dove. I have to fight."

"I know you do, Benny. We can join with the saboteurs in the woods."

Bronek nodded. "We can do it, then."

"We'll plan for it, then. We need to find clothes, and coats, and food. If we try our sources in the black market, we can find what we need." Anna smiled, a hopeful, relieved kind of smile. "We're on our way."

For some reason he could not quite identify, Bronek felt hesitant. But he nodded anyway.

* * *

"Stand right here," Wiktor ordered, pointing at a spot on the bare wood floor. "This should be quite a sight."

Bronek and Wiktor were in a little room upstairs from what had once been a corner drug store. It was cluttered with wooden crates, notebooks, and a couple rickety office chairs; all the useful things had been pillaged long ago. Now the floor was covered with hunks of plaster and chips of paint. In several spots, Bronek could see through holes in the floor, past the wooden beams, to the abandoned store below. One small window provided the only light in the room. Bronek rubbed his hands together to keep them warm. "Is this the new meeting room?" he asked.

"Just the latest one," Wiktor told him. "The janitor's closet was a nice little place. Couldn't afford the rent, I suppose."

Bronek smiled. "Granit, I truly missed your sense of humor."

Wiktor shrugged. "What sense of humor?"

"That's what I mean."

Just then Wiktor raised his hand. "Shh!"

There was a single knock at the door, then three quick knocks. Bronek watched as Wiktor approached the door, raising a little cloud of dust behind him. He opened it a crack. "Yes?"

"Power company," Bronek heard a familiar voice say. "I need to see the meter for this building."

"Yes, it's here," Wiktor responded, "If you can hurry."

"I'll be just a second," the other voice said.

The man entered, and Wiktor locked the door behind him. "Granit, what's so important?"

Wiktor pointed, and the man in the faded coat turned around.

Bronek recognized the sloppy salt-and-pepper hair, the prominent jaw, the faded coat, the gently hunched shoulders. "Hello, Nowak," he said.

Adam's eyes popped open; his wide jaw dropped. His arms flew up, as if lightning had jolted through him. "Lot!"

Bronek felt his smile grow. "Reporting for service."

Adam practically leapt at him. He held Bronek's arms, and gasped for air. Finally, he spoke. "Lot!" he whispered incredulously. "Lot!" Bronek felt himself being hugged yet again. This time, at least, there was no embarrassing kiss on the cheek.

Finally, Adam let go. "Thank the Blessed Virgin!"

"Go ahead. Everyone else has."

"But why did I not learn you were safe? Your messenger girl could have sent a message to mine."

"We decided on this approach," Wiktor said without further explanation.

"Well, come over here, Lot, sit down. You must tell me all about what happened."

Adam pulled Bronek across the room, and they sat on the

creaky chairs. Wiktor leaned glumly against the wall as Bronek detailed everything that had happened to him. Adam rubbed his chin and listened intently to every word.

When Bronek finished his story, Adam fell back in his chair, is if he were exhausted. "Well, Granit, isn't that a story!" He leaned forward and rested his roughened fingers on Bronek's shoulder. "God was with you, my boy. He truly was."

"I was just lucky," Bronek shrugged.

"Lucky is walking home without being arrested. Only God could save you in that way. Thanks to Him now!" Adam quickly crossed himself. "Well," Adam continued, raising his voice, "This changes our plan, doesn't it, Granit."

"I suppose," Wiktor said with a sigh, "Such as our plan is."

"Yes, we need to analyze our mission."

Slowly Bronek felt himself change inside. As they talked, somehow his mind pulled away from Adam and Wiktor. He felt as if he were in the far corner, watching them from a great distance. Adam and Wiktor spoke, but they seemed exceedingly quiet. Bronek remained silent so he could hear, as if he were straining to hear a conversation across the Vistula River.

"We have been given a new mission," he heard Adam say from the opposite riverbank. "Our mission is . . . to assassinate General Kutschera."

"It's one tough assignment," he heard Wiktor remark, and Bronek had to watch him carefully to hear what he had said.

"Let's not get discouraged, Granit," Adam told him. "We knew this would be difficult."

"No one is having much luck at it," Bronek heard Wiktor comment dryly. In his mind, Bronek imagined he and his wife, living in the forest, free of Warsaw and its misery. They were both happy and smiling and protected by the woods.

"Yes, yes, I heard about that. What do we know, Granit? You've been following him long enough."

Bronek watched Wiktor scratch his shiny dark hair unhappily. "This is a terrible deal, Nowak. Kutschera is not your typical Pawiak guard." Bronek listened appreciatively to the discussion. He felt truly lucky to be alive at all.

"Well, how? He's just one man. There must be a way. We've got to think this through, that's all."

Wiktor's chest moved up and down, in a heavy sigh. "Franz Kutschera travels to and from his post in two heavily armed cars. There are no markings on them. The cars are for his body-guards. They go with him everywhere he goes. He also changes his route every day. And his drivers don't mind running over civilians to get away."

"Well, what about a bomb attack?"

Wiktor shook his head. "That's what was tried." Bronek watched Wiktor as he paced about the room, pulling detailed bits of information from his memory. He looked like a large for-est troll, with his slouching shoulders, dark mustache, and dark vest and pants. "Those brave souls were 'floaters.' They just waited and waited, every day, until they saw Kutschera's car."

"Well, couldn't that work?"

"Nowak, it is not so easy to stop a car. A machine-gun attack may not do it. A bomb may not do it. That is what we saw. Those men tried to attack from the side. I'm afraid that is not sufficient. Their sacrifice was – not complete."

"Well, there's a chance, isn't there?"

"Well, what do you want to do, Nowak?" Wiktor asked, raising his voice. "Do you want to kill him, or just perhaps kill him?"

Adam bit his lip tensely. "Granit, Granit . . . there must be a way. What about a sniper shot? One shot from a rifle, that is all it would take. We have fine marksmen we could enlist."

Wiktor shook his head. "No good. For one thing, Kutschera doesn't wear any general's markings, nothing to distinguish him at all. And he's only exposed long enough to enter Gestapo headquarters, or his home. Even then he's surrounded by his bodyguards. Sometimes they're in uniform, sometimes in plain clothes. A marksman would have to shoot everyone, just to be sure. And the rooftops are patrolled at both locations. No, a sniper attack just won't work."

"Damn it!" Bronek was surprised to hear Adam raise his voice. Bronek had never seen him so angry. He rose from his chair and shouted anxiously at Wiktor. "Damn it, Granit, there has to be a way! Should we just – stand by and let him carry out his – executions?"

"I didn't say that, Nowak."

"Well, we must think about this! What about his body-guards? We've bribed guards at Pawiak. What about his body-guards?"

"No good. His bodyguards came with him. They were hand-chosen from Berlin. They're dedicated to him."

"Well – well – what about that woman I've heard about? He has a lover, does he not? A woman he is to marry? Can we get to her?"

Wiktor snorted dismissively. "You mean his fiancee? Ha! Kutschera's fiancee is Heinrich Himmler's sister."

"Himmler's sister?"

"The very same. I'm afraid she is quite loyal."

"Well, doesn't he go outside? Somewhere where we can get close to him?"

"Nowak, he doesn't go swimming in the Vistula River! He lives like a mole! He never goes outside!"

Bronek watched the conversation. He saw desperation spread over Adam's reddened face. "Well, – there must be a way! Think about it, Granit!"

Wiktor turned and faced Adam. "I tell you, there is only one way to kill the beast!" he shouted, slowly and demonstratively, hitting his hands together for emphasis. "Walk up to him," he explained, pointing his finger at Adam, "Place your pistol directly against his forehead," he continued, "And whisper in his ear, 'In the name of the Polish Republic.'" Wiktor was now leaning against Adam's ear. "That," he concluded firmly, "Is the only way."

When he turned and walked away, Adam had a pensive, troubled expression; his brow showed deep wrinkles of worry. "That is the only way?"

"It is the only way to be sure."

"Granit, what you are describing here is – is –"

"I know. A point-blank attack." He stared at Adam from across the room, stone-faced. Bronek stared at the scene, almost incredulously. He could hear them, could sense their distraught emotions, but yet nothing penetrated the layers of his mind. Their conversation seemed surreal, alien, to him. He watched them from his far-off vantage point.

Adam returned to his chair and sat down. He appeared to be exhausted, somehow. "Can you carry out this mission?"

Wiktor paused before he answered. "I've made three kills."

Adam nodded. "That's correct, that's correct. That is the rule. Only three assassinations." Adam glanced over at Bronek. "No hardened assassins, that is our iron rule. We cannot have people who learn to love killing. Granit cannot do the deed, and neither can I. Besides, we may too old for what this mission requires." Adam turned back to Wiktor. "What about Akrobat?"

Wiktor shook his head. "He's too young. I don't trust his nerve. To kill Kutschera, a man needs – a special quality."

Suddenly a cold feeling swept through Bronek; he stared at the two men wide-eyed, unable to speak. An icy feeling jabbed into the pit of his stomach.

"Well, then, who do you recommend, Granit?"

Adam paused. "I've only seen one man show that quality."

Bronek gazed at Adam as he spoke wearily. "There are 165 soldiers in the *Agat* unit," Bronek vaguely heard him explain. "But there is really just one person we can trust to do the job. We thought he was lost, but now he has returned to us." He placed his hands on his knees and pushed himself up from his chair.

Bronek stared up at Adam, studying his blue eyes, eyes that no longer twinkled. His commander looked sad, even defeated. Bronek felt his mouth drop open, his eyes go blank. "Lot," he heard his commanding officer say.

XXII

Bronek Pietraszewicz circled the Old Town square on January 5, a solitary figure amid the throngs of food smugglers. Snow was falling across the city, a heavy, wet snow that clung to the bricks and the streetcar wires, covering everything in a blanket of white. Food smugglers, their coats bulging with bread and potatoes, whispered deals with shoppers. Fortune-tellers knelt on the sidewalks, snow still on their necks and shoulders, and predicted the imminent breakthrough of the Red Army.

He walked around the Old Town Square in wide, aimless circles. The homes in Old Town dated from the fifteenth century, built by merchants and burghers. Painted in bright contrasting colors, they jostled against each other, cutting off the plaza from the city. Bronek searched for something, some proof that told him this was the Warsaw of his boyhood, Warsaw before the occupation. But he could no longer even imagine that place. Everyone wore the same expression. It was grim kind of face, sad, bitter, hungry. It was an appearance that would be impossible to mimic in peacetime. It was a look not only of defeat, but of despair. After four years, people bought and sold their foul food without much concern for the police; if they were arrested, they were arrested, and that was that.

A bicycle bounced by him, and Bronek watched. It was a bicycle converted into a three-wheeled rickshaw, with a wooden seat mounted across the rear axle. The boy pedaling the contraption was about the same age as Eugene; he was so weak that he struggled to keep the thing moving. Bronek noted the German in the suit who had paid for the ride. He was proud, superior, lordly. How different he seemed to be! Even the snow melted when it touched his black overcoat.

It was inexplicable. Poles and Germans hated each other. Close to ten Germans were killed in Warsaw every day. Germans lived in guarded neighborhoods, and rarely traveled alone. To deliver payroll and guns to police stations, the Germans used *Wehrmacht* tanks. Police, Gestapo, and SS were never out of sight. And yet the black markets still flourished, boys still carried Germans in rickshaw bikes, fortune-tellers made loud predictions, people drank in cafes. And probably all of them could produce a false identification clearing them to work in the German service. In its way, life in the city was overwhelming. Bronek walked with his head down.

Presently Bronek noticed people move toward a tall kiosk in one corner of the square. A little girl beside him interrupted his thoughts. "Pick me up, Mama. I want to see."

"No, Zofia," the girl's mother said. "Mama can't hold you any more."

Bronek glanced down at the little girl. She wore an olive-green army blanket, sewn into a simple body-length covering, and wooden shoes. She wore no hat, no gloves, no socks. "What's there, Mama?"

"I can't see the names, Zofia. I need to get closer."

"Pick me up, Mama. I want to see!" She was no older than five; a woman with normal strength could easily have picked her up.

"No, Zofia. I can't."

"I can see it," Bronek volunteered. He felt lilt in his voice, for a change. Perhaps he could help this woman.

The woman looked up at him with tired, hollow eyes. Her

shoulders were permanently stooped, and she could not stand up straight. With one hand she clutched a knitted shawl around her. She could have been twenty, or twice that age. "Please?"

Bronek moved to the back of the knot of people and stood up on his toes. There was a new poster on the kiosk. People cautiously examined the red parchment, with hushed awe. This, too, did not offend the police. "It says January third," Bronek said. "Today is the fifth, but I haven't seen this poster before. It was just posted."

"Please?"

Bronek read: "'On 27 and 28 December 1943, there were four more incidents of Germans and Poles acting in German service being cravenly assaulted and in some cases robbed. One German soldier was killed and another wounded. At the same time one Polish policeman was killed and another wounded. In view of this I ordered the following 40 persons to be publicly executed on 31 December 1943.' There are forty names," Bronek warned. "Do you understand?"

Her pleading expression let him know that she wanted his help.

Bronek arched his neck and read through the snowfall. "'Stanislaw Waledziewski.'" No reaction. "'Tadeusz Fiedorowicz. Mieczyslaw Asienkiewicz.'" Still no reaction, so he continued. "'Antoni Kuchta. Wladyslaw Pyzel.'"

Suddenly the woman's eyes opened wide. Her entire body seemed to stiffen in its stooped position. "Dear God – please, no."

"'Born, September 23, 1922.'"

"What is it, Mama?" The little girl tugged on her mother's shawl.

"It is not your father," she explained wearily. "It had the same name as your father. But the birthdate is not right."

Zofia looked bashfully at the people who surrounded her. "Where is he?" she asked, expecting her father to appear in the crowd.

"My husband has been missing for four months," the

woman offered. "Zofia, she does not understand."

"I'm – I'm sorry," Bronek said, lifelessly. His words sounded wretched, even to him. He had tried to help them, and it became something ghastly.

The woman seemed to shrink before Bronek's eyes. "I think," she said, "That I will die soon. I will just – not go on." Snow piled on her dirty shawl, and in her daughter's hair.

* * *

Bronek rode the streetcar down to his meeting location, just south of the city center. He was receiving messages from Zebra every day; plans for the mission were proceeding on several fronts. Bronek went inside an abandoned office supply store, and upstairs to the last room on the right. He checked his wristwatch; wandering through Old Town had made him a few minutes late. He knocked twice, then three times. To calm his nerves, he tried whistling a snippet from a Chopin waltz he remembered, the "Grande Valse." But its cheerfulness repulsed him. He went silent.

Wiktor answered the door. "Lot," he muttered.

Bronek went inside as Wiktor locked the door behind him. The space had been a big storage room for the store downstairs; it smelled of dust and old papers. There was no furniture in the room at all, just a few old pails and tin buckets. "You're four minutes late," Wiktor told him.

"I apologize," Bronek replied.

"You made us wait."

"I know. I tried not to."

Wiktor stared for a long moment, then decided to drop the matter. "It must still be snowing," he commented.

Bronek saw that snow still clung to his oil-stained coat; he brushed it off with his fingers. The snow dropped to the wood floor and formed clear puddles.

There were three new people standing across from him. Bronek glanced at them nervously. Wiktor quickly took control. "Lot," he said, "This is your command."

Bronek nodded hesitantly as Wiktor introduced them. "This is Sokol, Juno, and Cichy."

Bronek looked over the soldiers. Marian Senger (code-named "Cichy") had dark wavy hair and a narrow face, with a narrow nose and slightly droopy eyes. Zbigniew Gesicki (code-named "Juno") had striking blond hair and round, child-like eyes; he reminded Bronek of his cherubic brother Eugene. Kazimierz Sott (code-named "Sokol") had dark hair, like Bronek; his flat, pale face made his dark eyes seem especially piercing and intelligent. Their true names were never mentioned. They were all young, as young as Bronek. They were dressed in the usual dirty, patched coats, to blend in with the crowds. But there was something immediately different and striking about them. They looked enthusiastic. There was a dynamic strength to them. Their youthful faces shined. *That had better change when they leave the room,* Bronek thought.

Wiktor, nearly overfilling his blue vest, paced back and forth. Without his usual cap and cigarette, he appeared even more serious than ever. "Gentlemen," Wiktor began, "You have been selected for a vital mission. We have never seen such a police chief as General Kutschera. He is killing up to 300 people every week."

Marian spoke up first. "How is that, Granit? We see the posters, we hear the reports. We are not hearing so many."

"Cichy, the posters only include a fraction of all the victims. There is much more going on at Pawiak prison. These executions in the streets, they are aimed to make people afraid. Pawiak is where Kutschera is doing his real work. We must send the message to Berlin. We will not stand by. Kutschera must be stopped – by any means."

Bronek felt the implication that Wiktor did not mention.

"You have been chosen from the entire *Agat* organization," Wiktor went on. "You are young, brave, fast. Perhaps, I am . . . too old for such work. But you, you are the best qualified men in all Warsaw."

Marian spoke up again. "When do we carry out this mission?" He had a certain air of incredulity in his voice.

"No date yet. We will set one."

"Will it be soon?" Kazimierz asked eagerly.

Wiktor ignored Kazimierz' question. "As is customary in *Agat* actions, there will be four groups: a cover group, a reconnaissance group, a group of drivers, and an attack group. You, my friends, are the attack group. We will also have doctors who are friendly to us, on duty at the hospital."

Again, the three missed the import of that last precaution.

Wiktor continued. "Lot is in command of this mission. He will plan the location and details of the action."

The other three turned and looked at Bronek admiringly. Bronek felt himself blush for some reason.

"Lot, what about Kutschera?" Kazimierz asked. "When do we go after him?"

Bronek felt their eyes focus on him. Even Wiktor stopped pacing. He lit a wrinkled cigarette, and folded his arms.

Bronek swallowed nervously. "Granit has informed me of what we are facing," he said. He fought to control the waver in his voice. "You know what this mission is – what it requires. There is only one way to kill Kutschera. What we will do will be – more than dangerous."

"What is the plan?" Marian asked.

"There is only one plan," Bronek replied. "A direct attack. Point-blank range. Stop Kutschera's car. Pull him out. Put a gun to his forehead."

"Just like that?" Zbigniew asked.

"It's the only way to be sure."

"But what about the bodyguards?" Marian inquired. "What will happen to them?"

"We have to take them all out. It's that simple."

The three soldiers paused. "Where, exactly?"

"At Gestapo headquarters. On Szucha Avenue."

"Right in the middle of the street?" Zbigniew asked.

"It's the only place we can get to him," Bronek replied.

"What about the pillboxes?"

"I know, Juno. The pillboxes."

"They have two machine guns, Lot."

"Yes, yes."

"The police patrols?"

"I know, Juno. I know." He stared as firmly as he could.

"Lot," Marian finally said, "Will we be able to do this?"

"Cichy, I know you can," Bronek reassured him. "You are the bravest – the finest soldiers in Warsaw. . . ." For a second he thought of his friend Henryk, training in the forest, eagerly patrolling the forest trails. But Henryk was not in the forest. "Everyone will be proud of you. . . ." Bronek's words stopped. Images of Anna, of dancing with her and caressing her waist and kissing her eyelids, crowded his mind. He struggled to continue. "They need you. They suffer through so much. I know you can – help them –" He went silent again and looked down at the floor.

The other three looked at each other. Uncertainty showed on their faces.

Wiktor quickly spoke up. "You'll know more when we know more. Stay in contact with your messenger girls." The meeting broke up, rather awkwardly.

Wiktor watched coldly as Marian, Zbigniew, and Kazimierz left the room in two-minute intervals. As soon as Kazimierz left, Wiktor dropped his cigarette to the floor and stepped on it. Sternly, he approached Bronek. "Listen, my friend." He gripped Bronek firmly by the arm.

Bronek looked down, surprised. Wiktor's grip was vise-like, nearly cutting off the circulation in his arm. He felt Wiktor's hard stare, and he finally met it, nervously.

Wiktor spoke quietly, barely more than a whisper. "Lot, you have been given an order. You cannot have – any fears or distractions."

"I know, Granit."

"Have you heard the rumors? 'This police chief is – satanic, he cannot be killed.' People believe they are powerless. That is fatal to us."

Bronek tried to look away; but Wiktor's stare was as inescapable as his grip on Bronek's arm.

"Your mission requires bravery, Lot. You must put aside – all else."

"I understand, Granit."

"Your thoughts must be on that objective. Nothing can distract your mind. Nothing."

"I'll be ready, Granit." Bronek yanked himself away from Wiktor's grip and left him alone in the apartment.

Outside, Bronek wanted to hurry back to his home on Mianowskie Street. He wanted a dinner at home, even a bad one. He wanted to hear his younger brother yell at the dinner table, and toss food around. He wanted to hear his father get upset. It was always funny. He reminisced on those old memories. But, now, he spent most nights at his cover address, so it would appear he still lived there. He visited his family briefly. And he could not go from a meeting to see them; he might be followed. He would spend this cold, lonely night separated from everyone.

* * *

"Krystyna, please, I don't want to go!"

"We're going, and that's that," Anna's sister said resolutely.

Anna followed her sister onto Gorczewska Street. "But it's dangerous here. We need to go home." The street was full of children and parents. Anna's wooden shoes slipped on the snowy sidewalk. "Slow down!"

"It's too late now." Krystyna headed into the apartment building and rapped firmly on the door.

"Stop it! Don't knock the door down."

"Anna, I am going to find out what is going on with you. If you won't tell me, then you'll tell her."

Anna tapped her foot impatiently as they waited. "Krystyna, whatever you do, don't tell Mama!"

Misia Myzwinska appeared in the doorway. "Krystyna – Anna? Yes?"

"Misia, thanks to God, you're safe. You have to help me."

"Help you? Help you how?"

"It's Anna. She gets letters."

Anna made a fist and stamped her foot. "Oh! Krystyna!"

"And she packs her things in a potato sack, and then she unpacks them, and rearranges it all, to make everything look like a bunch of potatoes."

"Krystyna, that is none of your business!"

Misia stared at the squabbling sisters. Her expression was severe, and frozen.

Anna detected the silence from their friend. She tugged on Krystyna's coat sleeve. "Krystyna, I think this is a bad time."

Krystyna turned to Misia. "Misia, what's wrong?"

"Krystyna, I – I can't be bothered with such things."

"I thought you could talk to Anna. Don't you want to know?"

"Krystyna. . . ." Slowly, a change came over Misia. Her blue eyes grew narrow and smoldering. Her jaw sharpened, her face tightened. She pointed down the hallway, out toward the street. "Look out there. Look!"

Anna and Krystyna saw across the street. Rows of bullet holes marked the stone wall. A few aged flowers, now stiff and brittle in the winter cold, lay at the base.

Misia glared savagely. "The police did that. Right before my eyes. They did that! The beasts!" She sneered as she said the words.

Krystyna stammered awkwardly. "Oh, Misia. I – see. When did – that happen?"

"Two weeks ago. December 23. Two days before Christmas. Of course." She clenched her teeth. "Beasts," she muttered again.

Anna stepped forward from behind her sister. "Misia," she asked their long friend, "Did you see it?"

"They tried to shoot me. But I still watched. They couldn't stop me."

Anna reached out and held Misia's hand. She spoke quietly,

soothingly. "Misia, over Christmas I thought I had lost someone very important to me. It made me horribly sick."

"It's them," Misia said bitterly. "The police. They are destroying us."

"I thought I hated them, too, Misia. But I learned. I don't know what will happen to me. But I don't hate them. I don't hate."

Misia stood, quietly. She glanced into Anna's eyes, then at the cracked hallway wall.

"Misia, a long time ago, you gave me some advice. You told me to never give up my own life. You said that would be my victory."

"Yes. I remember."

"Then, Misia, you understand what I want to do."

"What is that?" Misia asked. But she thought for a moment, and then she knew. "Yes, I understand, Anna."

"Anna," Krystyna interrupted, "What are you talking about?"

"Misia, I may need to leave Warsaw. Very soon. Can you help me?"

Misia nodded wisely. "Anna, I used to spend my summers in the Kampinos Forest. With my father."

"Yes?"

"There is a good shelter I know of. Very few people ever go there. I doubt the gendarmes go back there."

"Oh, Misia, thank you."

"It's not much. It's a heavy roof, and bare walls, and a stone fireplace. It has a dirt floor, so it's probably not used in the winter. But it's near a small lake. My father and I fished it."

"God bless you, Misia."

"Perhaps that will be your victory. God be with you, Anna." With that, she slipped back inside her apartment and locked the door.

Anna and Krystyna glanced at each other. As they slowly walked outside, Krystyna asked, "What do you mean, you might leave?"

"Just wait and see, Krystyna."

* * *

The next day, the gray sky broke at last, and spots of deep blue appeared overhead. The snow hung on the streetcar wires and the streetlights. Bronek sat at the streetcar stop, and he gazed across the plaza at the Royal Castle. The castle's tall dome was shot off, its roof partially collapsed. Snow clung to the exposed roof beams. In front of the castle, old King Zygmunt III still stood, high atop his column. King Zygmunt was lucky, Bronek thought. He should stay above the streets.

He had walked by here with Anna, once. Images of her filled his mind, making his longing all the more painful. He recalled every one of her expressions. He could read her face, her emotions, everything she felt. Her heart was an open artwork to him. Now he slouched inside his cloth worker's coat, and jammed his hands into his pockets.

At last he heard a fragile voice.

"Benny? Are you safe?"

He did not dare look at her. Being outside was not safe. She sat beside him on the iron bench. "I am so glad to see you –"

"– Don't look at me." Meeting like this was dangerous, but Bronek often changed his meeting locations. His habit was to avoid having habits. Other people milled about them, waiting for the streetcar. They had to appear to be strangers.

He glanced down at her bare hand. They were softer now. "Your fingernails – they're healing."

"They feel better." With a sweep of her arm that seemed dramatic, she pulled her babushka onto her shoulders. "My hair is growing back, too." Her flaxen hair framed her face again, the way it had when he first met her.

"Don't!" he said between clenched teeth. "Put it back on."

Pretending to sweep her hair from her face, Anna slid her babushka back onto her head. "I'm going to get better," she declared. "I'm going to be the most beautiful girl in the world."

Bronek watched as a smile slowly spread across her face.

Bronek looked both ways. Seeing no streetcar, he stood up. "I cannot wait any longer," he said unemotionally, for others to hear. He crossed the plaza and walked north, alongside the ruins of the Royal Castle.

After another minute, Anna also stood up and walked north. She followed Bronek beneath the narrow arched gate that was the entrance to the walled Old Town.

Old Town was a tangle of short, narrow streets, with people coming and going that served as cover. Bronek was confident no one else had followed them through the Old Town gate. He still had to watch for police at every corner, and for anyone who paid any interest in him; they were Gestapo.

Soon she was beside him. They walked slowly on the ancient stone street. "Do you remember," he asked her, "How we were the day we met?" That day, she had clung to him for support. Now he glanced sideways at her, and he knew that she was not so frightened today.

"Of course I do. I was afraid. Why do you bring that up, darling?"

He did not say anything.

Anna edged near him. "What do you have planned?" There was a bright, girlish tone in her voice. In other times, Bronek would have felt flattered.

"Anna, take this." Bronek slipped something into her hand, smoothly.

"What is it?"

"It's a key. To our room."

She squirmed slightly. "My own key?"

"It took a lot of work. I gave up a lot. But there it is."

"It's our room now?" Anna dropped her hand and slipped the key into her palm. Then she shivered, and put her hands into her pockets. "That's wonderful."

"You may need somewhere safe to stay. Somewhere not even your own family knows about." He watched her as her face beamed. She was smiling now, that complete, warm-hearted smile that made everything else seem trivial. "You can go to that room, if you need to," he said at last.

"I have some good news, too, Benny," Anna announced eagerly. She held on to his arm. Bronek recoiled, and she let go of him. "My mother knows a shopkeeper. I went to see him, and he thinks he can get me some heavy boots. Isn't that amazing?"

"Yes."

"I can't hike in these wooden shoes, after all. I'm going to need some good, sturdy boots. They'll be terribly expensive – maybe even a piece of furniture – but we'll have to manage. And – I have more news, darling."

With all the effort he could manage, Bronek looked into her blue eyes, those stunning eyes that had captivated him months before. He saw the hope, the eagerness, the renewed joy, rise up inside her. In his mind they were already resting in the woods, and the dark Vistula River flowed leisurely past.

"I talked to my friend, Misia," she gushed. "She used to go out in the woods every summer, when she was younger. She told me there's a shelter at the north end of the Kampinos Forest. Just a roof and a dirt floor, really. But it's something. And there's a lake there, with plenty of fish. Doesn't that sound perfect?"

Bronek felt his pain well up in his throat. "But Anna –"

"Benny, we don't need to wait till spring! We can leave now! We'll leave Warsaw, and escape together. Isn't that what we want?"

"Anna, can you," he began haltingly, "Can you promise me something?"

"What? What is it?"

He was not sure what he was saying. He just spoke. "No matter what may happen to us – can you remember that I love you – and I always will? Can you – carry that inside, and keep it with you, even when you're liberated?"

"What are you talking about?" she asked, searching his face. "You're going with me, aren't you?"

He could not find words for all the thoughts and feelings

that were spinning in his mind. He was only capable of an anguished nod. "Anna, Dove . . . All I want is to be with you forever. Even if you can't see me or touch me – in some way – I'll stay with you."

"Benny, we can escape! Now!" She stared into his face.

His words, his neat little speech he had worked on that morning, vanished from his mind. "Anna, you are so precious to me. I love you – more than I can explain. . . ." He slumped down, and did not move.

Anna waited. "Benny?" she asked timidly. "We will – be able to go?"

He wanted desperately to comfort her, to tell her anything that would make her happy. But he felt his throat go dry. He looked away, at the ruins of the Royal Castle above them.

"Tell me!" Anna gripped her fingers around his arm. As the sun set over the western edge of the city, they stood in silence, and in their small way they were together, isolated, away from Warsaw.

XXIII

The morning was unusually cold. The puddles in the street were circles of ice that cracked underfoot. Pedestrians shivered and blew into their hands as they hurried about their business. No one looked at the blue sky.

The only vehicles out were a few horse-drawn wagons and a couple military cars. On Ujazdowskie Avenue, two plain black Mercedes-Benz sedans sped south, toward police headquarters on Szucha Avenue. One of these cars carried SS Brigadier General Franz Kutschera to his work. Unnoticed, another car pulled up behind the two big sedans.

Suddenly the rear car revved its engine and raced forward. The car windows came down, and two men inside thrust out their arms. They were holding pistols, a Radom and a Walther. The two men fired at the speeding Mercedes-Benzes. In an instant, all three cars were careening crazily.

The bullets ricocheted off the heavy cars, but one shattered the window by Kutschera's head. His car swerved sharply, bumping the attacking car. It jumped the curb; pedestrians leapt away until the car dropped back onto the street.

The two attackers kept firing their pistols, but the bullets bounced off the Mercedes-Benzes. The attack car swerved into Kutschera's car, but only dented the fender. Then Kutschera's car slammed into the attacking car, sending it skidding sideways. The disguised car crashed into a streetlight; the sheet metal crunched around the pole. The two black sedans sped toward Szucha Avenue.

The three men inside the crumpled car kicked and pushed furiously on the doors, but the doors would not open. A patrol of four SS men, who had crouched for safety against a building, now casually arose. The soldiers strolled over slowly, silently.

The failed assassins inside the car panicked; one of them fired the last bullet from his Radom. The SS men merely ducked and continued walking. They looked inside to make sure there would be no more danger. Then they raised their rifles, and they aimed.

Frantically, one of the trapped Poles pulled his shoulders through the open car window, but became stuck. He waved his hands and screamed, "Surrender! Surrender! *Nicht schiessen!*" (Don't shoot!)

The soldiers fired, and the glass shattered. Then the SS soldiers rested. Their gray helmets shone in the bright morning sun, as pedestrians rose from the sidewalk and hurried away from the scene.

* * *

The next morning, Adam received an urgent communication from his messenger girl. The note instructed him to go to a certain apartment at 10:35, with no weapon or documents. He was not to tell anyone else about the meeting.

Promptly at 10:30, Adam entered the aging, dark apartment building and went up to the third floor. He was early, so he did not have to rush. In the hallway, he passed a teen-aged boy sitting at a small window. He had a view of the street, and had seen Adam approach. Adam said nothing, but knocked four times at apartment 8.

A serious young woman opened the door. After exchanging the code phrases from the note, she let him inside and locked the door. "Wait out here. You will be called in," the woman said coldly.

Adam waited patiently, smelling the musty air and eyeing the pale flowery wallpaper. Soon the woman called him into a small study, and she returned to the front door.

Inside, four men in plain coats and civilian clothes sat at a small dining table. One man was tall, with a craggy square face and serious, squinting eyes. This was General Taduesz Pelczynski (code-named "Grzegorz"), chief-of-staff of the Home Army. The second man was unknown to Adam; seeing a stranger made him hesitate nervously. Adam figured the new man must be a representative of the government-in-exile, who reported to London. At the end sat a man Adam recognized. It was the commander of the *Agat* group, Adam Borys, code-named "Dyrektor." He had thinning hair, and his round ears stuck out, and he looked like an accountant.

In the middle sat a slight man with a round, balding head and a short mustache. He looked like the refined aristocrat he was. But the most endearing thing about him was his eyes: they were large, gentle, sad, wise. This man seemed to understand all the pain in Poland. "General Bor," Adam said.

General Tadeusz Komorowski (code-named "Bor") came from low Polish nobility. He had fought on the Eastern and Italian fronts during the First World War. A fine horseman, he was on the Polish equestrian team in the 1924 and the 1936 Olympics. Before the invasion he had commanded the Polish Cavalry Center. His cavalry background made General Bor an anachronism; he did not fit the modern times. But Adam knew Bor was a superb conspirator, smart and cautious. The most wanted man in Warsaw, an entire section of Gestapo agents was devoted to finding him; yet he still eluded them. This, Adam knew, was why Bor was named commander of the Polish Home Army. The hope for freeing Warsaw and establishing an independent Poland rested with him.

General Komorowski motioned for Adam to come forward. "Come, Nowak, sit, sit," the General said.

Adam sat in the wooden folding chair, still watching the

unknown man uneasily.

Despite Komorowski's military background, the meeting was friendly and informal. They did not use ranks or titles. "To begin with," Komorowski said, "I want to inform you that a second attempt was made on Kutschera's life. The mission was unsuccessful."

"I see," Adam remarked calmly. He already knew this information.

"Therefore, you still have your mission. The first two have failed. Nowak, can *Agat* succeed?"

"Bor, *Agat* has the finest soldiers in all Poland. I am certain we can succeed."

The three officers looked at each other, and nodded. "That is good. Tell us, how are you proceeding?"

"We have assigned our best four soldiers as our attack group. They are young, but they are very brave."

"Good, good. And who is leading them?"

"We have assigned Lot. He is just twenty, but he took part in the attack on Franz Bürckl in September."

"And you trust him to lead this mission?"

"I trust him completely." Actually, he recently had doubts about Lot. Granit had reported Lot's unusual, timid behavior at the last planning meeting. But Adam had chosen him. Lot was the leader, unless he absolutely had to be replaced.

"Then we must move to the next step, and set a date. We must move, quickly."

Adam nodded.

It was Dyrektor (Adam Borys) who spoke next. "February first," he said firmly.

It seemed unusual for him to speak in Komorowski's place, Adam noted. However, Komorowski nodded his assent. "The first. Nowak, have you set the time?"

"Nine o'clock," Adam said. "Outside police headquarters, when Kutschera is in his car. According to our intelligence, the morning is when there are few patrols out, when he is most vulnerable."

"Yes, Nowak," Komorowski responded. "Dyrektor, we have less than two weeks to finish our preparations."

Adam's commander, Dyrektor, nodded. "We will be prepared," he said simply.

"Nowak, two attempts on Kutschera have already failed. This is highly destructive to morale." Komorowski looked at Adam with his sad eyes, eyes that seemed to understand the whole four years of occupation. "The people feel helpless. This is poisonous to us."

"I'm well aware of that, sir."

"I know the price we must pay. I estimate that 200 Poles will be executed. But we must succeed this time. Your brave young soldiers must be willing, too."

Adam nodded. He and Komorowski were about the same age. They were both of the old generation, a land of peasant farmers and soldiers on horseback. Younger people would be the nation's future. "Yes, sir."

The meeting ended with a toast to their success. The woman at the door let Adam leave. Adam saw her tap on the plaster wall; that must be how she communicated to the boy down the hall. He left still hiding his doubts. He would have to see Lot for himself.

* * *

Bronek knocked four quick times on the door. He remained motionless in the hallway until Wiktor let him in.

The upstairs storage room had not changed. It looked as hollow as before. But all the faces were there: Wiktor, Zbigniew, Marian, Kazimierz, and even Adam. "Do we all have to be here?" Bronek asked hastily. The more people in one place, the greater the risk.

"I'm afraid so this time, Lot." Adam smiled reassuringly through his heavy, square face. "We have a great deal to discuss."

Bronek shifted his weight uneasily, but he said nothing.

As usual, Wiktor took the initiative. He attracted everyone's attention just by the power of his hard stare. "You probably have heard there was another attempt on Kutschera. Three days ago. It failed. Therefore, our orders stand."

Adam continued the story. "We have sent General Kutschera a final warning letter." Adam reached into his pocket and unfolded a soiled scrap of paper. He read slowly, squinting his eyes to focus. "'General Kutschera,'" he read, "'The Directorate for Civil Resistance has documented more than 2,000 civilians executed since you became police chief of Warsaw. We have confirmed that you directly ordered each of these killings. These victims were civilians, executed without trial or findings of guilt. The people of Warsaw hold you personally responsible. The executions are as follows: October 16, 1943, Niepodleglosci Avenue, 20 persons. October 17, Pius Street, 20 persons.'" Adam scanned down the list. "We catalogue all the executions we know of," he explained. "The people who compiled these lists performed a heroic service for us."

Then he continued. "'You escaped the Underground in Belgium and in Czechoslovakia. General Kutschera, your luck has ended. You will never leave Warsaw alive. We have already ordered the date of your execution. If you do not order an immediate end to the killing of civilians without trial, we will proceed as scheduled.' Signed, Commander-in-Chief of the Home Army." Adam pulled out a match and swiped it against the brick wall. As he lit the sheet, he muttered, "As we know, nothing has changed." He dropped the burning paper to the floor.

Wiktor nodded sternly. "So it falls to us."

Marian spoke up. "What is the date, Nowak?" He was young, but Marian carried himself like an older person. A level of maturity tempered his enthusiasm.

Adam looked them all over. "February first," he said.

"Will you be there?" Zbigniew asked, rather loudly.

Wiktor shook his head. "Lot is leading this mission," he said.

Zbigniew, Kazimierz and Marian glanced at Bronek.

Bronek took a quick measure of what he saw in their youthful eyes. Their hesitation was obvious in their faces.

"Can you be there, Granit?" Marian asked.

"Listen to me. Lot is your commander." Bronek felt their eyes turn back to him. "Lot?"

Bronek waited, motionless, for several seconds. When he at last spoke, he was stern, emotionless – the way Wiktor commanded his men. "We know," Bronek began, "What does not work. Tossing a bomb is no good. Firing a pistol is no good. We must do both."

He stared at Zbigniew until his eyes were trained on him again. He was shorter than anyone else, with full cheeks and energetic eyes. This boy, Bronek knew, needed control. "Granit is right," Bronek continued. "We can't just 'perhaps' kill him. We must be sure." Bronek walked over to the corner of the room, where a layer of dust covered the bare wood floor. The others, including Wiktor and Adam, circled around him.

Bronek knelt on the floor and dragged his finger in the dust. "The first thing we have to know is where to attack."

"He changes his route, Lot," Marian observed.

"Yes, but we know where he lives. At 2 Rose Avenue. He has to go to the police headquarters on Szucha Avenue. That part never changes." He drew a square into the dust with his finger.

"But there are two machine guns there," Zbigniew said nervously. "They have two pillboxes, right on the street."

"Of course," Bronek replied reassuringly. "We all know that." He drew two lines into the dust, in front of the square. "But he always turns from Rose onto Ujazdowskie. If we stop him right there, it takes away the machine guns."

"That works," Wiktor observed.

"Exactly. But we must stop his car, here." Bronek tapped his finger at the intersection. "So we don't face the machine guns."

Marian grimaced, an anguished expression showing on his face. "But Lot, he has excellent drivers. How do we stop them?"

"We will have a tough time convincing them to stop where we say," Wiktor conceded. "I lost a paint cart to the cause."

Bronek noted Marian's anxiety, and he knew Wiktor's sarcasm always hid a serious concern. "I know about the two other attempts. Those men were brave. But they failed because they couldn't stop the car."

"So what do you hope to do?" Marian asked.

"Use all our resources. First, we cut him off with another car. Then, we throw a hand grenade. Can we get a grenade, Nowak?"

Adam thought for a second. "It will be inside the car. Right, Granit?" he added with a smile.

Wiktor merely grunted.

"Good. We must disable both of those cars. So there's no escape."

Bronek looked around at the men's faces. They were all considering what he had said. "It's all we can do. When Kutschera turns at Ujazdowskie," he explained, drawing a line with his finger, "A car will pull in front of him and cut him off, here. We will throw a hand grenade, to wreck his car. Then you, Juno, and you, Sokol, will walk up from behind, with guns drawn. There will be nowhere for them to escape to. We kill everyone in both cars. The bodyguards right along with Kutschera." Bronek looked firmly at every person in the room, including Adam. Especially at Adam.

Wiktor rubbed his wide mustache. "It does what we have to do," he admitted. "Pistols?"

"Pistols are no good. Machine pistols. For all of us."

"Four? Why not just one?" Wiktor asked.

Bronek glared. "Granit, do you want to kill him, or perhaps kill him?"

"Well . . . I can find them," Wiktor replied. "STEN guns may have to do. We'll have Parabellums as back-up."

"But we have to make sure we get Kutschera," Adam commented. "He wears no General's markings."

"I am leader of this mission. I will get Kutschera."

"How? They all dress alike, sometimes they wear civilian clothes –"

"That's why we must kill them all. I know which one we believe is Kutschera. I'll take his identity papers with me, as proof. Then there will be no doubt."

Wiktor considered the plan. "That makes sense," he declared to Adam. "Four men with STEN guns, and Kutschera trapped between."

"It's our best chance," Adam replied.

"Of course, there are still the police and SS patrols to contend with," Wiktor added, almost as an afterthought.

Zbigniew interrupted the older men. "What about our escape?"

Adam and Wiktor suddenly fell silent. Bronek was aware of an awkwardness in the room.

"Yes, I've thought of that, Juno," Bronek answered, nodding. He stared firmly into the three soldiers' eyes. They had to believe that there was an escape. "After I get Kutschera's identity papers, we all get back into the car. Then – God willing – we get across the river, into Praga, right away, before the police can block off the streets. If we keep our heads down, we will pass for a Nazi staff car. That way, we can stop at the hospital in Praga. What's it called, Nowak?"

"The Hospital of Our Lord's Transfiguration," Adam answered. "We have doctors there friendly to the Underground."

"Look: we know the risk. We're willing to take that risk, to do our job." Bronek waited for a response from the other three.

"We know that, Lot," Marian said sheepishly.

"We leave our wounded at the hospital. Then we drive the car west. A military car driving back into Warsaw shouldn't be noticed. Granit will tell us where to hide the car, and then we blend in with the people. It's that simple."

There were nods, slight but unmistakable. Bronek felt a wave of assent in the room. He tapped his fingers on the dusty wood floor. "The date is February first."

"The plague will be lifted," Adam commented.

Bronek swept the dust aside with his hand. Wiktor stood like a statue, his arms crossed in front of him, and said nothing. The meeting ended with no more dissent. Bronek did not ask whether his plan was accepted; he felt it.

Marian was the first to leave, and then Zbigniew and Kazimierz. Adam checked his wristwatch. "One more minute, Granit. Then you can go."

Wiktor walked to the door, his heavy boots scratching against the wood floor. "I have many things to track down. A car, a hand grenade, STEN guns."

"Four STEN guns."

"Yes, four."

When he was beside Bronek, Wiktor stopped. "Best of luck, my friend." Wiktor reached out his large, powerful hand.

Bronek shook Wiktor's hand, vigorously. Wiktor was an amazing man. Nothing cracked his stone will; nothing seemed beyond his capability. "God be with you, Granit."

"Godspeed, young man." Then Wiktor left.

For a few seconds Adam and Bronek stood awkwardly in the room, waiting for the time to pass. Adam shifted on his feet. He glanced at the wall and then at Bronek before he finally spoke. "This is it, Lot."

Bronek looked at Adam. His blue eyes twinkled inside his red, craggy face. His salt-and-pepper bangs fell sloppily across his high forehead. "Many people are depending on you, Lot," Adam sighed. "God willing, you will do well."

"Yes, Nowak. God willing."

"Lot, the people my age, we are gone, we are all dead. Our hope lies with the young people. With you."

"Nowak, I used to believe I would survive anything. But I know what we are facing. I just don't want to be arrested, and tortured, at their mercy. I want to remain free. As I lived. Can you help us?"

"With the grace of God, Lot, we will provide for you."

A sudden feeling of loss pierced Bronek's heart. He recognized the many risks that Adam had taken to help him. He had forwarded him money, and donated the apartment he often used. Bronek already missed him. "*Pawiak pomscimy*" (Pawiak will be avenged), Bronek said quietly.

"Yes. Yes, indeed. God be with you, Lot."

He opened the door. Bronek slipped outside, leaving Adam alone in his darkened meeting room. It was sunny and cold outside. Bronek decided to go by the train yards, to collect some discarded wood or coal for his father. Bronek walked over a block to Nowy Swiat, the busy north-south thoroughfare. He merged into a small crowd waiting for a streetcar. He got on the northbound streetcar. Even though there were no Germans aboard, he sat in the back with other Poles.

They had gone only a block when the conductor sighed. "Well," he said dryly, "We are stopping."

Suddenly Bronek's arms tensed, his teeth clenched. His eyes locked on the silver-haired conductor.

"Yes, we are stopping." He reached for the brake, and pulled on it with his whole body.

"Oh, dear Lord!" a woman beside him wailed.

Bronek glared behind him. It was a black Volkswagen military car, open-air, with the spare tire on the hood. A patrol of four SS soldiers rode high up on the seats, ready to leap out. The conductor was warning his riders, to give them a chance to flee.

He had to act – now. Bronek ran to the front of the streetcar and leapt to the street. He landed on a patch of ice, and he hit the paving stones.

"*Halt! Halt! Hände hoch!*"

Bronek scrambled to the sidewalk. He knew what to do: *Don't run, don't run.* But he ran. West, where he knew the maze of angled streets. Into the nearest alley.

He heard a rifle shot. More shouts. "*Halt! Halt!*"

He ran to the left, then to the right. Down another alley, across a street, into an alley. The trick was to keep turning. *Keep turning. Always head west. Don't go in a circle.*

He could not hear their boots. But he felt their presence. They were still after him.

A streetcar. Luck! Bronek coasted to the other side of a north-bound streetcar. He kept on the sidewalk. He was panting, dizzy. He was too weak to run, he was not strong any more. He half-walked, half-ran alongside the streetcar. If he kept the streetcar between himself and the SS, they might not see him.

He walked north for a few blocks, fighting the urge to glance behind him. Then he turned off onto Jerozolimskie (Jerusalem) Avenue. It had police, but it was busy. He could merge into the crowds. He saw an old brick warehouse, bombed out and never cleared away. He ducked behind a brick wall, and he rested.

He felt so dizzy, he nearly fainted. He panted until his mind came back. He had a few moments; his thoughts raced. *How many were there?* Apparently just the patrol of four. Not Gestapo. It was a random identification check. He was not followed from his meeting. *Worst of all, what does it mean?* That was the worst part. He had just come from a meeting. He might be compromised. The Gestapo and police could be after him now. Some police official might see his picture, and connect him to his false identity and cover address. His cover identity was compromised, Bronek decided. He would have to stay at his safe location, abandoned apartment two. Bronek shook his head morosely. This was a terrible development. He was intensely involved with the planning for his mission. He often met with fellow conspirators. If the Gestapo followed him, they would all be arrested. But he had to carry out his mission.

For a time Bronek rested his head against the wall, and he touched his locket around his neck. He stared at the open sky, and let the winter sun burn his eyes. He would have to prepare a message for his messenger girl, Zebra, to deliver. He would have to explain this to Nowak. Nowak would know what to do. Bronek took a deep breath. Then he got up and returned to the street.

* * *

Bronek and Anna met in a corner café called the Nectar. Anna ordered a small coffee in a large cup. Bronek ordered nothing.

"I've been planning for us to leave, Benny," Anna said eagerly. "Can we use our apartment? Can we store supplies there?"

"Yes. You can." He glanced this way and that, for the Gestapo. "I should not have come here."

"What do you mean?"

"I can't explain. But I can't stay. It's not safe. I must go now."

"Benny, what day should we set for our escape?"

"I don't know, Anna," was his reply. "Perhaps in a few weeks."

"But Benny –"

"Anna, I must go now."

"But we just arrived –"

"You cannot leave with me. It's too dangerous. I'm sorry."

He left her alone in the café. Anna stared at her coffee until it went cold.

* * *

Over the middle of January, Warsaw experienced a lull in street executions. But the arrests increased. On January 5, German police forces raided a sociology class of the underground Western Territories University, held in a house at 35 Slowacki Street. The police arrested the students, the professor, and everyone in the house – 15 people in all. For their crime, most of them were killed in new rounds of executions.

The shootings at Pawiak prison increased. On January 13 and 14, approximately 300 men and several women were shot in the prison courtyard. Rumors permeated the city that thousands were being executed there.

On Monday January 24, Jerzy Kruczyk approached the intersection at 2 Kilinski Street and Dluga Street. An execution had taken place. As retaliation for several attacks in which three policemen were killed and two others wounded, fifty victims were shot. All men, their ages ranged from 18 to 65.

The crowd pressed in toward the wall, craning to see more. Young Jerzy Kruczyk stood around the perimeter. He sighed; he had a wheeziness in his lungs, and he felt constantly tired. He found a somewhat elderly man who stepped away from the wall. "Excuse me!" Jerzy said.

The man raised his head and stared at Jerzy. He wore an old black raincoat that went nearly to his ankles, too thin for winter weather. In his hand he clutched a handkerchief, soaked in dark red. He stood in place, a profoundly confused expression on his face.

"You saw what happened?" Jerzy said.

The old man took a long time to respond. At last he said, "Who are you?"

Jerzy did not respond. He waited for the man to answer.

The man looked down at his handkerchief. It was freezing into its folds. He sobbed, "I am – I'm sorry –" He took a deep breath to say more.

Jerzy tried to pity the old man. He truly did. But he did not feel pity. The bloody handkerchief did not affect him. Jerzy could not feel anything any longer. Instead, he asked, "Did you see? How many?"

People pushed between them, holding flowers, candles, or little crosses. "I want to help," the man offered. He clutched his blood-soaked handkerchief tightly. "It will end. It will end, yes?" The old man stared at Jerzy, the young man, hoping for the reassurance he so desperately needed.

"I don't know," was Jerzy's reply. "I don't know if it will ever end."

The police truck did indeed return, and people scattered in a hundred directions. The police collected up the flowers and candles and crosses, and they began to scrub the wall clean.

Jerzy wandered south, along the Medieval wall that encircled Old Town. He felt tired. On the wall, he saw a symbol. It was a capital letter "P" atop an anchor. Beneath it was the phrase, "Poland fights!" He vaguely remembered a long time ago, when he too painted slogans. He painted with a boy named Lot, someone he had not seen in a long time. But lately, he did not help Lot or his brother. He just followed executions. Slogans painted on walls did not encourage Jerzy.

Someone suddenly caught Jerzy's eye. It was a girl wearing a trenchcoat and wooden shoes, walking the other way. Jerzy knew her, he recalled her face from somewhere in his foggy memory – those big blue eyes, that strong face. But where, where? Then he remembered: she had asked about the boy he knew. She knew him from somewhere. Jerzy turned around and followed her. He stayed several paces behind the girl, so he would not be detected.

The girl calmly walked by four SS soldiers, who had two civilians pressed against the wall. One SS man had a rifle pointed at the detainees; the other three were studying their identity papers. The civilians were frantically explaining themselves over their shoulders to the SS soldiers, who ignored them as they studied the *Kennkarten*. The girl glanced in their direction, then passed by. Jerzy observed her cross herself.

The girl ducked down a side alley; Jerzy followed her. Where was she headed? How did she know Lot? She turned down another alley, and Jerzy turned the corner.

Suddenly his left arm was yanked. It twisted behind him, and pain tore into his shoulder. Before he could react, he was pushed against the wall. "Who are you?" he heard.

Jerzy's arm felt ready to pop out of its socket. "Ow . . . please!" He twisted the other way. As he spun, she kicked his knee, and he went down. He hit the sidewalk with his hip.

"Why are you following me?"

"Stop it!" Jerzy said, anguished. "I'm just curious!"

Anna patted his arms and waist for a gun. At last, she got up. Jerzy shook his arm. "I think you broke my arm," he complained.

"If I wanted to break your arm, I would have. Now, get up."

Jerzy slowly rose to his feet. He glanced around; luckily,

there was no one else in sight. He squeezed his hand into a fist; it still worked. Then he looked at her. She was the one he had seen in December. "I remember you. I want to talk to you."

Anna said nothing as he shook his hand. "About what?"

"Can you at least tell me your name?"

"Well . . . Anna. What's yours?"

"Jerzy." Too late, he remembered he should have used his code name.

"What are you doing out here, Jerzy?"

"My – job is to document the executions. We're compiling a record: places, dates, people."

Anna nodded. "That's important work."

"No. I can't do it any more. How do you know Lot?"

"So, you do know Lot?"

"Yes. He's – well, I know him."

"Then tell me." Her tone changed. "Tell me, Jerzy. What is he doing? What has happened to him?"

Jerzy eyed her suspiciously. These were dangerous questions. "Why? Who are you to ask?"

"Because, you see, I am his wife."

Jerzy blinked; he felt his jaw drop open. "You're his – wife?"

Anna reached into her skirt pocket. She held something in her fingers. "See?"

Jerzy leaned closer. It was a silver diamond ring. "A diamond!" he said. "I never knew he was married." Lot would never mention anything like that, of course.

"Jerzy, what has happened to him? Why does he – stare at nothing, and not talk to me? I try to ask what is troubling him, but he won't tell me, he's – walled up inside himself."

"Anna – I know secrets. I should not tell you."

"Jerzy, tell me. Tell me what you know."

"Anna, don't – don't ask any more –"

"Please, Jerzy. I beg you. Tell me what is happening to my husband."

XXIV

Bronek awoke as if he had been startled. He lay on his blankets and stared, wide-eyed, at the ceiling. He blinked several times and did not move. It was Monday, January 31. January 31, January 31, January 31.

The last several days had been a hectic blur of activity, fear, and anxiety. He had informed his commander of his encounter with the SS soldiers. Nowak agreed that an informer might have tipped the SS to stop the streetcar; if so, the Gestapo would be looking for him. But there was no time to create a new identity. Bronek was leader of the attack. He was vital to this mission. He would have to remain hidden until February 1. So the attack group had changed its meeting locations. Bronek had stayed in Nowak's Apartment two. Every moment since then, he wondered if he were being followed. And he had not seen his family, or Anna, in several days.

Finally he got up on his knees, and pulled on his plain white shirt, patched wool pants, and coat. He rode the streetcar to his home on Mianowskie Street, changing his streetcar twice. Risk or no risk, there were things he had to do.

Bronek went into the kitchen of his family's apartment. He wanted to see his brother sitting at the table and his father at the counter, making coffee. But they were gone, already at work.

The place was empty and cold. Bronek hung his coat over a kitchen chair and sat down without speaking.

He thought of his father, all he had done and all he had endured. "Thank you, Papa," Bronek said gratefully into the coldness.

The coffee pot on the stove was barely warm from breakfast, but Bronek poured himself a cup of tasteless *ersatz* coffee anyway. He slid his fingers over the big iron stove, where so many miserable meals had been cooked. He leaned against the kitchen table, the old wooden table with the fancy inlay his father had designed. Here he had fought with his brother, and thrown food at him. They had informed each other of every important development, and prayed a thousand times for their liberation. Now that time was over. Even as those memories washed back over him, Bronek felt a stranger here. This place was no longer his.

Bronek found some fancy stationary paper in the kitchen, and a fountain pen. He sat down at the kitchen table. Bronek realized how much his father had lost. Nowak was right. The people that age had lost not just their freedom. They had lost everything they knew, how they understood the world to be. He felt the same way. He was not sure what to think, but he did not feel like a 20-year-old any more. In the unlit kitchen, Bronek started with "Dear Father" at the top of the page.

Bronek thought and wrote carefully. He explained what he was doing, and why. He mentioned that he loved him, and appreciated everything his father had done. When he finished, Bronek started with a fresh page. He wrote "Dear Eugene" at the top of this one. This letter was tougher to write. He tried to tell his brother how sorry he was, but then decided that was no good. He tore up that sheet and started over. Finally, he had two completed letters. He folded them in half and left them on the table. Then it was time for the last letter. He took a new sheet. On it he wrote, "Dearest Anna." Morning turned to afternoon.

When he was done, he set down his pen. It was time to go. He slid on his coat. He went into his father's bedroom, pulled a flask of *bimber* from the trunk, and slipped it into his coat pocket; he knew Karol distilled illicit *bimber*, even though they never discussed it. In the parlor he bent down and slid out the mopboard, and took out his Walther PPK. It was illegal to be caught with one, but he might need it for this mission.

Bronek walked into the white tile bathroom at the end of his hallway, and he filled the sink with water. The water was ice-cold. He washed, leaving some soap on his face. Then he got the straight razor and shaved. The long blade slid smoothly across his neck; his father must have sharpened it. The steel blade made a tinking sound when he tapped it against the sink. When he was done he rubbed his chin with an old towel. He wanted to feel clean. And then Bronek departed this borrowed apartment for the last time.

For a moment he considered visiting his neighbors, Mister Stachowiak and Misses Rogala and everyone else. But no one was outside. His street was nearly empty.

Bronek snuck into Saint Casimir Catholic Church. The church was cold, empty, cavernous. He sat where he had sat next to his father and brother, through three Masses every Sunday. He used to watch his neighbors in the other pews, as they sung hymns in the bombed-out, ransacked church. He wanted to say good-bye, somehow. But no one was there. He hunched forward, and rested his arms on his knees.

"Hello, Bronek." Father Marian's voice echoed gently from the altar.

"Oh – Father Marian. I'm sorry to interrupt anything."

"I always have time for you, Bronek Pietraszewicz." He approached Bronek, and leaned against the pew where Bronek sat. "What can you tell me?" Because they held so many secrets, priests faced great risks. Police still rounded them up, and tortured them for information.

Father Marian had perfect Polish features. He was a gentle soul. He seemed too gentle for these times. Bronek had known him for many years. Seeing him now just unsettled him. "I think you should replace the stained glass windows, Father," he finally remarked.

"Oh, we will. We will, when the fighting is over. If we are liberated."

Bronek noted his wording. "Some things we cannot understand, Father." His voice echoed in the stone church.

"True. True enough. Can you tell me, how is your wife?"

"She's safe. With God's help, she'll remain safe. She is my greatest wish. My hope."

"I know, Bronek."

"Father, I – I need to confess something," he told Father Marian.

"Bronek, if you need to confess a sin, we should go –"

"I am about to commit the sin, Father."

"About to sin? What are you talking about?" Father Marian asked uncertainly.

Bronek knew he could not divulge his mission. "I killed once before, Father. I didn't confess that time. Somehow I knew I would survive. I was so confident, back then. But this time – this is different. I hope – am I still with God?"

There was only a timid reply. "What – what are you doing, Bronek?"

Father Marian could not absolve him for an act he had not committed. Bronek felt out of place in his old church. And he could not stay in one place. "It is the sin of murder, Father. God be with you." He got up and left the church.

Bronek walked north. The sky was dark and gray and cast a dismal pall over the city. Bronek blew into his hands and hurried his pace. His walk seemed to last all day. Perhaps it was because he did not want to say what he had to say.

Finally he reached the apartment building. He went inside and knocked on the door. A splinter in the door scraped the skin on his knuckles.

A young boy answered. "Yes?" he asked suspiciously. He had sickly pale skin, as white as a ghost.

"Is – is Anna here?"

"Who are you?"

"It's important. Is she here?"

"No. She left this morning. She said she was shopping for food." His eyes widened. "Are you –" he asked, "Are you –"

"I can't say."

"You're her boyfriend!" the boy exclaimed. "You write all those letters!"

"Can you tell me? Where is she?"

"She's not here. I'll get my sister. Krystyna!"

"No, don't tell anyone." He handed the boy his letter for Anna. "Can you give her this?"

Aleksy took it from his hand. "Are you going to marry her?"

"Yes. I hope to. Thank you." Bronek left the apartment building and went outside.

The cold air attacked his nostrils, startling him from his gloom. He hiked until he felt sores on his soles. He did not ride any streetcars, even though several rolled past him. He looked north amid the gloom and despair, at the ruins of the Royal Castle, and the massive, medieval wall around Old Town. He could not escape it. February first. Fewer than twenty-four hours. It would be a fine achievement. A great day for Poland. February first: everything would change. Bronek had never cried before, not during the entire war; but at that moment he wanted to cry. Walking slowly, he finally reached the abandoned apartment. The clouds were so low that the narrow streets were dusky. Bronek walked into the old building. The hallway was so dark that he felt for the lock before inserting the key. Slowly, the door opened.

Something was not right; a candle glowed inside. Bronek held the doorknob and hunched behind the solid door. There was no sound. Cautiously, Bronek peered inside.

On a windowsill was a short candle, casting a feeble orange light around the room. And there beside the light the woman turned around. She had creamy skin, and a strong Slavic jaw, and blond hair parted nicely on one side, and captivating blue eyes.

When she turned her body froze, like a frightened bird. She was wearing a white dress he never saw before. She made a step toward him, then halted. Bronek stood there awkwardly, clutching the doorknob. Then he reached out his arms. In an instant, they met and embraced. He wrapped his arms around her shoulders, and he kissed her, kissed her more forcefully than he ever had. For a moment the outside world vanished, and only these two existed, united as one.

At long last she rested back on her heels. "I decided to come here," she explained, "I guessed – I hope I did the right thing."

"Anna, Anna, darling. Thanks to God I can see you. I went to your home. You weren't there."

"I've been here all day. Since this morning." She smiled, and Bronek noticed there was something forced about it.

"I tried to see you," he explained, "To say good-bye." He saw her smile tremble and weaken. Quickly he changed the subject. "What are you wearing?" he asked in a friendly voice.

She stepped away from him and raised her arms. "My sister and I made it," Anna said. "Is it all right?"

"What is it?"

"It's just a dress. We made it from two tablecloths. Mama is going to be furious when she finds out!"

"White tablecloths?" Bronek heard himself chuckle. "Ingenious."

"This is a special occasion." Anna placed a hand on her hip, and spun like a fashion model. The dress had short sleeves, and it went just past her knees, showing her calves and ankles. She was a vision of delicate white in a drab, dreadful world. When she spun, there was enough material that it lifted away from her legs. "How's that?" she asked, giggling.

Bronek said nothing. He nodded appreciatively.

"It was hard to sew. A tablecloth is heavier than normal material."

"What's the lace?" It had a circle of white lace around the neckline.

"Oh, that. It's a doily, from our chairs."

Bronek laughed. "A doily? Of course."

The flickering candlelight gave the dress a faint orange hue, like the morning sun. "I wish I had some silk stockings, and real shoes to wear – not these wooden things. But this will do."

"You have a ribbon in your hair again."

"I wanted to have some color. It matches my earrings." She lifted her hair, and wiggled her blue clip-on earrings.

"My Dove, you look more beautiful than ever."

He stepped toward her and held her delicate fingers, letting them rest in his. Then he saw that his mother's ring – Anna's ring now – was on her middle finger. "You have your ring on, too."

"Yes, well, as for the ring – I decided I will wear it forever. I'll never take it off again."

Bronek met her eyes. "You are my wife now."

"Forever," she said softly. Suddenly she jerked her hands away. "I have something else for you!" she blurted. She dashed over to the windowsill. She picked up her coat. When she turned again, she was holding a loaf of black bread.

Bronek gasped. "A whole loaf?"

"Just for us!" She led him into the dining room, where they had eaten once before. "I'm on a mission, too!" she proclaimed.

"What?"

"My mission is to take care of you, and see that you're safe. And then, I'm staying here with you. For good."

"But the danger, for you –"

"And I accept that danger. Benny, my life is your life. Your risk is my risk. No more letters, no more nights apart. Never again." She sat at the carved walnut table. "I'm sorry I couldn't get any marmalade. The bread will be dry. Sit down and eat. And that is an order!"

"Well, yes, ma'am." As he tossed his coat into the corner, Bronek pulled his flask from his coat pocket and unscrewed the metal cap. "I have something that will help."

Anna giggled. "More champagne? Like at our first dinner?"

"This is pure vodka. Trust me." Bronek sat down. "Thank

you. For seeing me today."

Anna tore the bread in half. "We need to find plates some-where in here, and glasses –"

"Don't get up, Dove. Stay with me."

"Well, all right." She handed him half the loaf of bread.

Bronek studied it admiringly. "Real bread," he commented. "No sawdust."

"It's the best we had. Mama is going to be so mad at me!"

"Tell her it's for a good cause." The only light came from the candle, and a narrow shaft of gray light that spilled in from around the window shade. It was just enough to see her face.

"Wait!" Abruptly, Anna reached for the bottle between them. "A toast!" She smiled as she raised the bottle toward him. "To our long and happy life together," she announced proudly.

Bronek was still. He did not say anything. He glanced down at his piece of bread and swallowed.

"Someone told me once that if you make a toast to yourself, then it will not come true. But no one else is here, so we must make allowances. Now your turn!"

Bronek stared at the bottle before he belatedly took it from her. He looked deeply into Anna's eyes as he quietly told her, "I will love you forever."

"Well, that's not a toast, but – thank you."

Bronek raised the bottle to his lips. He took a long, relaxing swallow of the clear liquid. It burned reassuringly the entire way down his throat and into his stomach.

"Now let me try." She took the vessel from his hand and, eyes closed, quickly swallowed. Her series of anguished expressions reflected the progress as the burning liquor went down. She stifled a cough. At last she looked at Bronek tri-umphantly. "I did better that time," she said in a hoarse whis-per.

"Good job."

Anna fidgeted in her seat. "Reach across." She leaned for-ward and held his hands. She shut her eyes tightly. "Dear Lord, Please bless this food we are about to receive. Please guide us in our daily lives. We ask that You please, with Your mercy, bless us with liberation, and – protect us in our missions, so that we may live our lives and grow old in Your image. In the name of the Father, the Son, and the Holy Spirit, Amen." They both crossed themselves.

"Sort of a picnic, isn't it?" Anna asked as they tore pieces off their bread. "Except that we're not outside."

"Sort of. Thank you for the bread." In the Warsaw custom, they ate very slowly, to taste every morsel.

"It's nothing, really. A wife should provide better than this for her husband."

"This is perfect."

"I tried to find some kielbasa or some pork chops, but – there was no luck there."

"Not even from Mister Jablonski?"

"I tried and tried. I'm so sorry, darling."

"Anna – I didn't expect any food. Just seeing you is everything to me."

"It's wonderful to see you, too. You forgive me for coming?"

"Forgive you? How did you know?"

"I found someone who knows you. He found me, actually."

"You did? Who? Who told?"

"Bronek, please don't be upset. It's a long story. I – I met a young man who knows you. He wouldn't tell me your mission. All I got from him was the date. He told me, 'See him by the thirty-first, that is your last chance.' That's why I'm here. I hadn't heard from you, I was frightened again. Honestly!"

"But I wrote you notes. Twice. I told you not to come here. I can't let you risk yourself!"

"Yes, I know, but I – I just thought –"

"I was followed by the SS. My identity is compromised. Do you see that I am endangered?"

"I thought you were glad to see me, dear."

"I am. I am." Bronek drank some more *bimber*. Clearly there was a slip in secrecy. Normally, he would be very upset.

But not tonight. "That's all right," he finally said.

Anna's fingered her bread tensely. "I would never tell your secret. Please believe me."

"No, Anna. I trust you. I trust you completely. Anna, I –" He ached to explain it all to her: what he had to do, and why, and how important it was. Suddenly his torn emotions filled the cold, dark room. "I need to stand." Bronek pushed back his chair and rose from the table.

"Benny, please!"

The young man paced back and forth across the room. "It's not your fault, it's not you." He ran his fingers through his hair.

"Benny –" Anna spoke calmly, soothingly. She turned her chair away from the table, facing him directly. She leaned forward and rested her elbows on her knees. "I don't mean to upset you. That's not why I came here. Come sit down. We can talk."

"Anna, I'm sorry, I'm sorry." Bronek stopped pacing, and he faced her. She was beautiful. But her face was revealing her fear again. "I – I don't have to tell you my mission . . . how important it is."

"I never learned your mission. I swear."

"Good."

"I've been making plans, too. For us. I talked again to my friend, Misia. She practically grew up in the forest; she knows all the roads and trails. She told me exactly where to go. She's – she's changed now. She's not the same as she was, poor girl. But I never told her about you."

When she spoke, a smile warmed her face. Bronek did not want to see her. But he could not turn away from her. He looked into her eyes, deep and passionate in the candlelight.

"And I've made all the plans. I'll stay here tomorrow. I'll wait for you."

"Anna – what –"

She was searching his face for a clue. "After tomorrow, you will have no more orders. You'll be free to leave. Isn't that right?" There was desperation in her voice. "And then we can – escape, escape to the forest, and we will be together, just as we had promised. . . ."

Bronek could not pull away from her eyes. He knew she wanted to hear his promises, his reassurance. He wanted to tell her exactly that. He waited a second, and tried to speak. He shook his head and tried to tell her, "Anna, Dove –"

Her face froze. And he knew that she knew.

She stared and stared at him, and she stared into the dark spaces all around them. He saw something inside of her shatter. Slowly, she bowed her head. Her shoulders trembled. A tear rolled from her eye, down her cheek. Then her hand clenched into a delicate little fist, and she pounded her knee, pounding out her dreams and her plans until they were all out of her. She mouthed anguished words that did not leave her lips. Without looking up, she hurried over to the corner, and she buried her face in her hands, and she silently sobbed.

Anna stood, hunched over, her body quaking. Bronek approached behind her. He yearned to say something, to comfort her, but he knew there could be no way. Cautiously, he reached out and rested his hand on her shoulder.

She lifted her face from her hands. "I can't," she whispered, "I can't bear to live without you!" She collapsed into his arms, and she cried against him. He held her, desperately, and felt her chest heave and fall, and smelled her hair, and he thought about how it would have felt to spend his life with her, and he felt a tear trickle down his own cheek. With his fingertips he gingerly lifted up her chin, and then he kissed her, and he tasted the salt of her tears, and she tasted his. Her body sagged limply, and he held her, supporting her, keeping her close to him in the cavernous old room.

XXV

They embraced for countless minutes, and he listened to her cry. Her anguish made him ache inside, and he stroked her hair and whispered to her, anything to help her. They rocked back and forth, until her heaving sobs calmed to long, exhausted breaths.

At last she turned her face toward his, and with her fingers lightly touched his cheek. "Is there – is there any way?" she asked with feeble hopefulness.

"Anna, this is the most dangerous mission the Underground has attempted. I cannot think about the future. I can only give everything to tomorrow."

"But I suffered for you, I dedicated my life to finding you. I can't lose you!"

"You know my mission, Anna. I don't have to tell you."

He felt her fingers clutch his shoulders. "Don't . . . don't say his name." There was an overwhelming sadness, a loss of vitality, of life, in her voice that made Bronek feel helpless.

"Anna, there is a way you can help me. I want to tell you everything, and to learn everything: silly things, important things, anything. We have this moment, tonight. We have to pack a whole lifetime of learning into this moment. Can you – come sit down?"

Anna nodded weakly.

Bronek spotted the blankets in the far corner, still spread out from the morning. "Let's sit on the floor. This way." He grabbed the bottle of *bimber* from the table, and he guided her across the ornate sitting room. "You can take little steps," he told her comfortingly. At that instant he remembered elderly couples he had seen, the way they helped each other take little steps from tables at cafes.

Bronek helped Anna down to the blanket, and she tucked her knees under her new dress. He sat beside her. The room was almost dark now; the candle cast a flickering, faint orange light on Anna's face. Her eyes were still red and misty, and she sniffled.

"I'll find you a handkerchief."

"No, this will do." She pulled up a corner of the olive-green blanket, and she dabbed her eyes and patted her cheek. "It's scratchy." She forced herself to chuckle.

Bronek slipped his arm around her, and he lightly touched her arm. He felt exactly how deeply this pained her. "Anna, I wish I could say something to help you. Anything."

She spread her skirt in a circle around her, fussing with each fold in the fabric. "My sister and I made my new dress for a – special occasion," she commented mockingly, "And this is the occasion."

"I know what you're feeling, Anna. Part of you is angry, but part of you is not. I know, deep inside, you accept."

"Accept? Why should I accept anything?"

"Because you do. Anna, I can't be at peace until I know that you're at peace."

Anna fell silent for a moment. "How? How can I accept?"
He reached out and held her trembling fingers, so they would be warm. "I still need you. There are a million things I want to tell you."

She looked up at him with mournful eyes. "What do you mean?"

"Well, do you remember when I was injured? I never told

you all that happened. I jumped into the sewer because I was running away from the police."

"You were?"

"Yes. I was stealing a gun from a German. A police patrol came by right then. Only by the will of God did I escape."

"Dear God." Anna whispered a prayer, and crossed herself.

"I was rescued by a wonderful woman. I broke a bone in my foot, and she helped me get better. Her son, Henryk – he risked everything to help me. He tried to deliver a letter for me. But I know that he was arrested. He never made it to you."

"Oh, Benny."

"After that, after what he did – I know I can't be concerned about myself."

"That was when I got sick, searching for you. I couldn't eat, or sleep."

"Is that why you looked that way, when I found you again?" Anna nodded. "I dedicated my life to finding you. I went to police headquarters, to try to get information. I even quit my schooling."

"But you told me you were going to be a teacher."

"Benny, I made a decision in my life. I used all my days searching posters, and – street executions."

"Searching for me?"

"I dreamed of us, together. That vision, it's all that kept me going."

"That's enough, Dove. I understand what you went through." He thought of her, wrapped in rags, examining posters for his name, and he understood. "You never should have suffered so, just for me."

"Benny, may I tell you a secret?" Anna asked.

"Yes."

"Do you remember the day we met, at Under the Snout?"

"Of course I do."

"Well, that night, I told my sister that I wanted to marry you." Anna giggled slightly. "I told her that if you asked me, I would say yes. And then it happened."

"That is amazing," Bronek remarked. "I'm glad you're smiling again. You know, when you smile, it starts slowly, but then it spreads across your whole face."

"Oh."

"Don't be embarrassed. I treasure how you smile."

Anna leaned forward, and she stroked the back of his hand. "Tell me another secret. Something you would never tell anyone else." Anna scooted over beside him. Now their bodies were casually touching. "Tell me."

Bronek smiled. He lifted the bottle from the floor, and downed a healthy swig of *bimber*. "Well – well, I was a Boy Scoutmaster."

"You were? Really?"

"I was. Before the boys – well, most of them were taken. For forced labor."

"Yes, I can see it in you now. I bet you were a terrific Scoutmaster." Quickly she leaned forward and kissed him.

"My – what was that for?"

"For helping all those boys."

"I played piano, too." He smiled expectantly. "Do I get another kiss?"

"I knew that, silly."

"You tell me a secret."

"Let me see." She picked up the flask and, building up her resolve, had a delicate sip. "Well, I will go back to school. When we're safe, I'll go back."

"Being educated is important to you, I think."

"My parents always said that their children were going to be educated."

Bronek chuckled. "You're more educated than I am. I stopped, after the schools were shut down in 1939." He reached out his hand. "Hand me that, please."

Anna handed over the *bimber*. "Hm, half empty."

"Half full."

Anna grinned. "Did you know that I went to Berlin once?"

"You did?"

"Just after the Olympics. I went to London, too."

"You've been all over." He waved the flask for emphasis. "I've never left Poland in my whole life."

"Not once?"

"Not once. I went hiking in the Tatry Mountains a couple times, but I stayed on the Polish side."

"There's a whole world out there to explore."

"I know, Anna." He held her hand for comfort. "Would you like to know something else?"

"Of course." She smiled again.

"Do you remember those essays in the *Biuletyn Informacyjny*? The ones written by someone named Z?"

"Hm . . . yes."

"That was my brother. Eugene."

"Your brother?"

"It sure was. Several of them."

"Oh, my." She lightly kissed him again. "Another secret, another kiss."

"My brother is a great kid." Bronek picked up the bottle again. "He's a pest, but he's great, too. . . . He really is."

"The two of you are close. I can tell."

"I mean that he – he really tries to do good things. Even when we get into fights. He's a great kid." He leaned forward near her face, and he whispered in a secretive voice. "I feel sorry for him now. I feel sorry for my father, too. I feel sorry for everybody."

"Don't blame yourself, Benny. We're lucky our families are together."

Bronek watched her silently.

"My family, we are in a bad way. My brother, Aleksy, is getting sicker every day. We try to help him, but he just gets weaker."

"He's that boy. I saw him." Bronek nodded.

"And my father is – not well. Every day I worry he will be arrested for not doing his job."

"I know. Every day there is danger." Workers who were

weak from hunger risked arrest for not doing their jobs efficiently. It was called economic sabotage. "I bet you're closer to your mother, and your sister."

"Oh, my sister Krystyna – she always thinks she knows everything."

"But you listen to her. You do as she says."

"Who told you that?"

"No one. I can just tell."

"You know . . . that *bimber* tastes pretty good, finally."

"Have some more."

"I think I will."

He began to hand her the bottle, then stopped. Her eyes were turned away; he hurriedly kissed her lips. They were cold, but they were soft. "It's my turn to steal a kiss."

"Silly boy."

"You told me a secret."

"Oh."

The candlelight, in its last moments, flickered shadows across her face. Bronek watched her lips press against the mouth of the bottle, watched her throat tighten, watched her swallow. "Thank you, Dove."

"For what?"

"For making a dress, just to see me."

"I wanted to do something special for you." She lightly stroked his arm, up toward his elbow.

Her closeness made him feel tense inside. "There are still a million things I want to tell you."

"There are a million things I want to know about you."

"I – don't talk about myself much."

"Don't apologize, darling."

"There is a reason for that." The candle wavered, and nearly went out. "Can I tell you more – the worst secret about me?"

"There is no worst secret. Just tell me."

Bronek felt a hand gently touch his cheek, silently coaxing him. "But this secret is why I go to the Ghetto."

"I know why. You tried to help Jews in the Ghetto. Before

the Uprising."

"No. No, Anna. There is more. It happened – four years ago. On September twenty-fifth. During the Invasion." He stopped.

"Darling – there is just me here. Share it with me."

"The German Army was at the edge of the city. There was an air raid again, and we were all hiding in the basement, with our neighbors. A – a squadron of Stuka dive-bombers attacked our street. You know when a certain bomb is for you; you can hear it. The bomb hit our building, and – and the floor above us caved in. The explosion killed twelve people. And Eugene . . . the beams broke his hip, and his pelvis. His bones couldn't be set properly. That's why he's injured. He can walk a little, with a cane, but . . . not really."

He heard a sigh. "Oh, precious," she murmured, and he felt her kiss his hand.

"And that was when my Mother died. She died right away. On the twenty-fifth."

"Benny, darling. . . ."

"Two days later, Warsaw surrendered. Soon the Nazis came with trucks and wagons everywhere. They moved the Jews in. They said that the Jews carried typhus. We knew it was a lie, but they moved us out anyway. Our home was taken over for the Jewish Ghetto. Eugene and I, we – lived our entire lives there. Now it's – behind that wall."

". . . Is that why you go to the Ghetto wall?"

"The person I went to see – is her. She is still in the Ghetto." He pulled his locket from inside his shirt, and held it in his hand. "This was hers."

It was a small, heart-shaped locket. The silver was worn dull. "See?" Bronek clicked it open. Inside were tiny photos of two smiling people with shiny faces.

Anna squinted in the dim light. "Are they your parents?"

"When they were married. I always carry it with me. For luck, I guess. When I wore it, I felt I couldn't be defeated. That's what I told myself, at least."

The candle flickered, and then it was only a red ember, and

the room was cast in darkness.

For a long time they sat together in the dark, holding hands and saying nothing. "Now, darling, I do understand." She shifted on the blanket, and the dark shape of his wife leaned over close to him. "Why did I decide to love such a sweet, brave man?"

He felt her warm presence near his face. "Why did I decide to love the most thoughtful woman in the world?"

Bronek slid his hands up her smooth arms, gently touching her cheek. He could just make out the outline of her face, the fullness of her lips. He stared at her, wondrously. With his fingertips he stroked her soft cheeks, her eyelids, the edge of her lips. "I want to remember you," he whispered.

He slid his hands down and touched her chin, her graceful neck, her delicate chest. He tried to memorize every curve, every sensation he received from her. Then he felt her cool hands press against his shirt. For a second he paused, uncertainly.

Slowly, Anna leaned forward and kissed him. Her kiss was slow, and tender, and loving. As he held her he reached around, behind her back, and gingerly undid each button of her dress. She sat up straight, smiling. Her dress came forward, sliding off her arms and bunching uselessly at her waist. Bronek stroked Anna's sternum, and then her creamy torso. He concentrated, trying to remember every bit of her. And he felt Anna's hands on his shoulders, his neck, unbuttoning his shirt. He touched her wrists, her arms, up to her neck. Every sensation of her made him dizzy. He wondered if it were really happening.

Bronek felt sensations, explored her soft slopes and curves completely, without words or lights. He felt her hands touching his face and shoulders, exploring him. He sought every tiny feature of her, and he knew she was seeking the same knowledge. He felt the effects of her illness. Her hair still had thin patches, her fingernails were rough, and her shoulders and arms were bony. But then he discovered the airiness of her hair, and the mole on her stomach, and the scattering of freckles across her chest, and the way she wanted her neck kissed, and the thrilling way she caught her breath, and a thousand other particulars about her. He explored her, so finely that he could have drawn a perfectly detailed picture of her. He was both with her and swept away, in the moment and in a timeless moment, and he desired complete knowledge of her, knowledge to survive life itself.

And then, with a sheer release of tension, images and sensations blended in Bronek's mind in a dizzying jumble. Without questioning, Anna fell against him, and she melted into him, and he encircled her in his arms. In the dark, he saw the outline of her face as it neared him, silently, and then he felt her lips, and they kissed as if they were sharing an eternity. They moved awkwardly, stroking and holding, but they did not separate from their close contact. And at some moment in the night, he joyously learned that there was knowledge and awareness that will transcend this petty world, and that he could carry in his soul and treasure forever.

His mind became overwhelmed, and they collapsed on the blanket, and immediately a deep sleep dropped around him. But somewhere, perhaps from a vague dream, Bronek was aware of a beautiful blond woman, with endless blue eyes and a profound need to feel protected. He felt her lean over him, and he felt a delicate kiss against his cheek, and he heard the whispered words, "You will never leave me."

Bronek was awake. Abruptly he reached out his arm, but he felt only the scratchy blanket. He looked around the room; there was no sign of her. Only the candle in the other room, burned down to a hard puddle of wax, remained.

He was lying between two blankets. His clothes were scattered around him. Bronek felt around for the tiny ticking sound he heard, and he grabbed his wristwatch. It was 6:25 on February first.

XXVI

The city was gray that morning. Dark clouds hung gloomily; the air did not move. A faint layer of snow covered the city like a silk shroud.

In her home on Twarda Street, Anna sat on the parlor floor in her big nightshirt. Her arms were wrapped tightly around her legs, her knees under her chin. She determinedly rocked forward and back, forward and back. She did not notice when her sister came in to check on her.

"Anna?" her sister asked, leaning over her, "Won't you come to the kitchen for breakfast? What's wrong?"

At last Anna stopped rocking. When she looked up at her sister, it was with desolate, tear-filled eyes. "Something beautiful will happen today," she pleaded. "It will be beautiful, yes?"

On the south side, police headquarters on Szucha Avenue was quiet. The street bristled with barbed wire, armed guards, and machine-gun pillboxes. It appeared to be one of the few safe places for German military men. So it appeared.

At the streetcar stop nearby on Ujazdowskie Avenue, five young men in dirty coats stood silently; a young girl innocently picked up twigs and put them into her coat pocket. A passing SS man noticed them, but did not pay them much attention.

At 9:05, two black Mercedes-Benz cars turned from Rose

onto Ujazdowskie Avenue. They coasted south toward the intersection with Szucha Avenue. The girl stood upright and peered
at the approaching cars, noting who was sitting in each seat.
Then she reached into her coat pocket, pulled out a white handkerchief, and wiped her right cheek.

Down the street, parked in an alley, was another car. It too
resembled a German military car. The two young men inside
wore long overcoats, the same type German soldiers wore.
Between them lay an MP-40 German machine pistol, and a
STEN gun. Wiktor had done his work.

Marian sat in the passenger's seat. He studied the girl with
the handkerchief. "He's in the front car. Front seat. Passenger
side. Are you ready, Lot?"

Bronislaw Pietraszewicz raised his youthful face. All the
emotion, all the tension, all the fear were drained away. He felt
only the power of unrelenting determination. "Yes," he said
firmly. He shifted the car into first gear. The car lurched forward.

Bronek drove the car onto Ujazdowskie. He coasted. "God
be with us," Marian muttered. He rolled down his window.

The disguise worked; the Nazi cars continued to coast down
Ujazdowskie Avenue. They were almost at Szucha, which
angled to the west. In seconds, it would be too late.

Bronek's car approached. He gauged the distance. Then
suddenly he said, "Now."

Everything happened at once. Bronek jerked the steering
wheel left, and the car swerved. The other car almost hit him,
but jerked to a stop just short. The rear car stopped, pinning the
middle car.

In one movement, Bronek reached inside his coat and
pulled out a German "egg grenade." He pulled the pin and
tossed it out. It exploded with a hard boom. Bronek felt his car
shake; the grenade was so powerful that Marian's door was
smashed in, the frame bent. He and Marian frantically pounded
their shoulders against the doors.

Kazimierz and Zbigniew dashed across the street. They

unbuttoned their coats and grabbed the STEN guns strapped to their torsos. They had to get to the rear car. In barely a second, they were there. The four SS guards had rifles in their hands, raising them to fire. But Kazimierz and Zbigniew were first. They each fired from their STEN guns, whipping the barrels at the front seat and then the back. The windows shattered into razor-sharp shards. That quickly, the military escort was killed.

"Go!" Bronek and Marian leapt from the damaged car. Marian ran past the car's mangled front end, his gun raised. Bronek looked up. Gun barrels protruded from the nearby windows; SS guards were coming from the south. Getting to Kutschera would leave him exposed. At that moment he heard guns firing from every direction. Bullets pierced the fender in front of him. The glass windows shattered. It was now. "Cichy! Juno! Cover me!"

They crouched behind the car and fired at the high stone buildings. Underground soldiers from the cover group leaned around stone walls, firing at any gray uniform they could see.

Bronek stood up and fired a quick burst. He ran around the front of the car, to the front passenger door. Now he was exposed to the guns. He shot at the door lock and yanked the door open. Then he reached inside and pulled on the coat. It was Kutschera.

The general tumbled out of the car and lay at Bronek's feet. He had a long face, dark hair, sideburns. Human. But now Kutschera's eyes strained with terror. Blood trickled from a cut on his forehead. The general flailed his arms, opened his small mouth, and screamed: "No! Please! Please!"

Bronek held the general by his coat lapel. He pressed his MP-40 to Kutschera's forehead. He felt no fear, heard no guns, was aware of nothing but the small space between himself and the *Brigadeführer*. "In the name of the Polish Republic," Bronek muttered coolly, so that only the general could hear.

He pulled the trigger. The general's head opened. The body fell limply to the ground.

Instantly, Bronek became aware of his world again. In front

of him, two cars of SS soldiers lay dead. The blood of Franz
Kutschera mixed with snow and made a sticky pool at his feet.
And at least eight Underground agents were crouched down,
firing. "Down!" Marian shouted.

And then Bronek heard the gunfire. It was everywhere.
Soldiers at windows across the street firing down at them. Four
police across the street kneeling and shooting. His cover group,
shooting from alleys. Machine guns. Bullets whistling past. The
fender popping from bullets.

"Down! Keep firing! Keep firing!" Bronek dropped to the
street. He threw open Kutschera's black coat, soaked with
blood. No papers. Gone.

"Lot! Go! Go!" Marian waved him back to the car. Bullets
whistled everywhere. The fenders creaked.

"His papers!"

"Lot! Move!" Marian repeated.

"His papers!" Bronek dropped flat on his stomach. He
reached beneath the car and felt around. At last! He clutched the
white SS identity card. Kutschera's photo and signature were at
the bottom. It was him! Bronek stood again.

"Lot! The car!"

Bronek stuffed the papers into his coat. He fired his
machine pistol at the windows. The 32-round cartridge emptied; he threw it down. The STEN guns were all empty, and they
were using their backup pistols. "Go! The car! Now!" There
were two getaway cars, just a few meters away.

Suddenly Bronek was slapped across his back. He stumbled
against Kutschera's car. He looked down. This was bad. Dark
blood oozed from his shirt. It hurt to breathe, hurt worse than
anything. His rib was shattered. He managed to wave his arm,
for the car to come by him.

The attack group soldiers were running, firing up at the windows. Bronek leaned back, pointed his pistol up, and fired. He
tried to run; instead he staggered. A car door opened. The
reserve car, to transport wounded. It seemed a kilometer away.
Bronek stumbled in and lay on the passenger's seat. Someone

closed the door. The pain. Oh, God, the pain. No breath.

Bronek felt the car move. He opened his eyes. Kazimierz thrust the car into gear and sped forward. "East! East!" Bronek yelled as he felt the car spin.

"We're going east," Kazimierz replied.

"Praga. Get to Praga." He was exhausted. He wanted to sleep. But each bump seemed to push a knife into his chest.

"Don't go out on us, Lot! Stay awake!"

"The . . . hospital."

"We're going there, Lot."

"Praga. Hospital of . . . Transfiguration. The doctors know . . . ."

"I know that – ho!" A bullet pierced the rear window. Kazimierz wiped his temple. "I was just hit!"

"What – what happ –?"

"Someone fired at me. It grazed my ear, I'm all right. I'm still driving."

"Who is – who is –"

"Juno and I are fine. But you and Cichy are hit. We're taking you to the hospital. Right away!"

Bronek's eyes were half open. "Are we clear?"

"Yes, we're clear. But we have to get you to the hospital. Stay awake, Lot!"

"We did it?"

"Yes, Lot. We did it!"

Bronek pressed his hand against his chest. But he was powerless. He craved morphine, please, end the pain. His eyes closed, and he fell unconscious as the city passed by his window. The mission had taken less than two minutes.

* * *

Kazimierz drove along the prearranged route. He crossed over the Vistula River into Praga, until he reached the Hospital of Our Lord's Transfiguration. Then he dashed inside.

A doctor and two nurses in surgical smocks were waiting for them. The doctor looked at Kazimierz. "Who needs help?"

"Two people," Kazimierz answered. "In the military car."

The doctor was young, not even thirty. He nodded. "All right."

Soon Bronek and Marian were up on stretchers. Nurses wheeled them into the emergency room. As they were being whisked away, Kazimierz gripped Bronek's limp hand. "Come through this," he said optimistically.

Then Kazimierz turned to Zbigniew. "We can't stay. The police will check all the hospitals. And the car will draw attention."

"Where do we go?" Zbigniew asked.

"We follow the plan."

Kazimierz climbed behind the driver's seat, and Zbigniew sat beside him. The two young soldiers headed west, back to Warsaw.

"This feels funny, going back to Warsaw," Zbigniew remarked.

"That's the plan," Kazimierz reminded him. "The police won't be looking for a car going west."

Just then they heard an isolated police siren, soft and distant. "I hope that's not for us," Zbigniew remarked.

They drove on, speeding down narrow streets. Soon they were on the iron, box-girder Kierbedz Bridge. The huge, beautiful city of Warsaw loomed in front of them. "That siren is getting —"

Zbigniew fell silent. There, ahead of them, stood a line of men in gray uniforms. They formed a barrier across the street.

Kazimierz gripped the steering wheel. "Hold on!" He veered sharply. "Praga!" He spun the car, but it slid on the wet pavement. The car skidded at an angle and struck a bridge railing.

The young soldiers bounced forward off their seats. Kazimierz yanked the gear shift into reverse, but the car did not complete the U-turn. "They're coming for us!"

"What do we do?"

"Run for it!"

Kazimierz and Zbigniew leapt from the disabled car. Kazimierz ran east, back into Praga. Then he stopped. "No," he gasped.

At the east end of the bridge appeared two German motorcyclists with rifles slung across their backs. They sped onto the bridge.

From the Warsaw side, the uniformed police ran forward. "Sokol! Where do we go?"

Kazimierz ran to the rail of the bridge. "The river!" He stripped off his coat and climbed over the iron balustrade. "Jump!" One of the policemen aimed his rifle and fired.

Kazimierz and Zbigniew spread their arms wide. In a smooth, graceful arc, they dove thirty meters into the icy Vistula River. Four hundred kilometers away lay the endless Baltic Sea. "Swim! Swim like crazy!"

Zbigniew threw his arms forward, forcing himself to move in this frigid water. Behind him he saw the bridge fill with police, rifle barrels pointed at him, firing. Beside him, Kazimierz gasped and tried desperately to swim. Zbigniew saw, on the riverbank, clusters of Poles watching him with pleading eyes. Seeing them energized him. With extra-human strength he kept swimming, but his arms were heavy in his street clothes. His chest muscles clamped his lungs shut; he could barely force his lungs to open for air. Bullets bounced off the river, pinging the water all around him.

"Sokol! Sokol!" Zbigniew shouted over the gunfire. "See them? See the people? They see us!"

Kazimierz did not answer. Zbigniew splashed his way over to his friend. "Sokol!" He gripped Kazimierz' coat, his knuckles white.

Kazimierz rotated face up, and then Zbigniew saw. "Lord!" Kazimierz' eyes were closed; his face looked peaceful and bloodless in the icy water. "God have mercy on your soul." Zbigniew released Kazimierz to the river

Zbigniew paddled furiously downstream. He was a good swimmer, but he was gasping for breath. He found that if he forced air through his windpipe, his lungs would not lock. The gunfire had a vague, distant sound. The gunners were no longer accurate at that distance. Perhaps he had cleared their range.

Then, ahead of him, Zbigniew heard a new sound. He stopped paddling and held his head above water. The sound was a small engine. Then he saw the outline of a speedboat. Zbigniew paddled as frantically as he could toward the far bank, the Praga side. From the corner of his eye he saw the boat growing larger, like a black apparition. Now he could make out two gendarmes holding rifles. He continued to stroke, stroke, stroke.

Zbigniew dove underwater, into the icy black calm of the river. For several seconds he stayed under, in silence, safe from the rifles. Then he surfaced. He gasped for oxygen, and he heard rifle shots.

The speedboat circled around him. The two soldiers fired several shots. Then the boat idled and waited. Soon, the body of Zbigniew Gesicki floated up. The gendarmes dragged the body aboard. The people on shore turned away and whispered bitter prayers. Then the boat spun around to retrieve the body of Kazimierz Sott.

* * *

Through the afternoon, Bronek perceived indistinct thoughts and impressions surfacing in his mind. Someone touched his forehead. He opened his eyes enough to see a nurse all in white leaning over him, patting his head with a wet cloth. He wanted to thank her; but no words came out. His eyes closed again. He saw a forest, and Anna was there, and everything was green and lush, and somewhere was the sound of rushing water.

At some point he heard a commotion. He opened his eyes again. He strained to see what was happening. He heard male voices: "This is a hospital!" in a Polish voice. Then, "They are now prisoners of the Gestapo!" in a German voice. Bronek saw two young men in Gestapo clothes: black boots, leather over-coats, shirts and ties, and Hamburg hats. In their hands they held metal identity tags, called warrant discs. Their suits looked baggy on their boyish frames.

The Polish doctor and two nurses stood in their way. "These men are seriously wounded. They have just come from surgery," the doctor objected. "They cannot be moved."

"You will get out of our way!" The Gestapo men raised their fists. Bronek saw their arms swing forward. Suddenly the doctor and the nurses were wiping blood from their cheeks; Bronek spotted the death's-head rings on the Gestapo men's hands. Before anyone could react, the Gestapo agents waved their pistols, Walther 38's, in the air. "Move away! Now!"

The doctor glared at them as if he might just fight back. Then he stared at the guns pointed at him. At last the doctor lowered his hand. He relented: "Let them go."

Bronek felt one of the Gestapo agents grab hold of his stretcher. He did not want to be arrested; he struggled to raise his arm, to resist. "No," he protested hoarsely, "Let me – let me go." But he felt himself rolling away.

With each bounce of the wheels over the tile floor, sickening pains ripped through his stomach. A nurse rushed toward him. She kissed him on his cheek. "Thank you, thank you!" she whispered. A tear trickled down her face. "God bless you!"

All Bronek could manage was to close his eyes again.

* * *

Anna still sat in her parlor, staring grimly out her front window. She had changed into her blue blouse and black skirt, but she would not go outside today. She would wait, because it was her duty to wait. She sat in her parlor and watched the street. She counted all the police patrols and SS soldiers dashing this way and that. It was obvious that something important had happened. The police forces were in disarray.

Late in the afternoon Anna saw someone else. A young man, barely eighteen, walked toward her home. Anna perceived that he was watching his own movements and eyeing the police patrols. When a policeman turned the corner, he disappeared into her apartment building.

Without waiting, Anna leapt from her seat. She was already in the kitchen when there was a knock at the door. She took a deep breath to control her fears, and she opened the door. "Yes?"

The messenger was even younger than he had appeared at a distance, barely ten. "Are you Golebica?"

"Yes," Anna answered tensely.

"Come with me."

* * *

Twenty minutes after Bronek and Marian were taken away, another black car drove up to the hospital entrance. Two Gestapo officers and two SS men holding rifles strode purposefully from the car into the lobby. Ignoring the attendants, they marched in military fashion through the lobby. They knew exactly where to go; someone at the hospital had notified them. They entered the recovery room, where the doctor and the nurses remained, consoling each other in their grief.

The head Gestapo officer marched up to the doctor. He stared down his nose, in typical German condescending fashion. "We are here for the prisoners."

The doctor eyed the police detail suspiciously. "What prisoners?" he asked.

"The Underground criminals. The craven criminals who attacked police chief Kutschera."

"What are you talking about?"

"They have gunshot wounds. We know they were taken here. To this hospital. You will show us where they are."

The doctor shook his head disbelievingly. "They're not here."

"Doctor, you can tell us, or we can arrest you, and make you tell us. So – where are the prisoners?"

"They are not here. Two Gestapo men already came –" The doctor paused. Suddenly, he remembered. And he started to smile. He fought it, but he smiled just the same. "Two men in

Gestapo clothes came for them. They punched us – we have bruises, see? – and waved their guns at us." He stared at the nurses, who looked back joyously.

The Gestapo officer said nothing. His condescending demeanor drained away, along with the color in his face. "No." Just that quickly, his face turned white. "Where are they! Tell me, Polish pigs! Where are they!"

The doctor shook his head, triumphantly this time. "Your prisoners are gone."

Furiously, as if every moment were still important, he turned to his policemen. *"Suchen Sie nach ihnen! Jede Ecke!"* ("Search for them! Every corner!") The other Gestapo man and the two policemen ran out of the room. Soon the sounds of screaming nurses, smashing bottles, and crashing trays filled every floor of the hospital.

The lead officer looked around him. The room was nearly empty – just one sick old man on the bed in the corner. A young nurse was delicately sponging his head. Angrily, the officer pulled out his pistol and grabbed her shoulder. "Tell me! What did you see?"

The nurse tried to pull away, but the Gestapo pushed her against the wall. She cowered in fear, staring at the gun. "I – saw – two Gestapo men. They said they were here for the prisoners. They punched the doctor, and they pointed their guns."

The officer placed the gun barrel against her neck. "And you said nothing? You did not question their authority?"

The nurse shook, her eyes wide with panic. "No . . . never."

For a long moment, the officer's finger rubbed the trigger on his Walther. At last he angrily slapped the gun against his leg. "Stupid!" he shouted. "Stupid!"

The doctor and the nurses huddled together, drawing strength from each other. They watched the Gestapo officer as he marched out of the room. At the doorway, he stopped. Beside the door, atop a simple pedestal, was a small ceramic figure of the Virgin Mary. She stared out at the recovery room with serene eyes. The Gestapo man grabbed the figure and smashed it to the tile floor. With his shiny leather boots he stomped on the ceramic shards, breaking them into smaller pieces. Then, with an acrid glance back at the doctor, he marched away.

* * *

That evening, when the sun was nearly down and the curfew was fast approaching, the boy led Anna into a small church in the neighborhood of Zoliborz. They went down stone steps to the cellar, cold, dank, and quiet. On a table two candles flickered. A blanket lay on the stone floor, covering the motionless form of Bronek Pietraszewicz. "He asked for you," the boy said simply. "I cannot protect you any longer." The boy darted back up the stairs.

All the terrible thoughts that had tormented her melted away; now she saw only him. "Benny!" She rushed to his side and fell to her knees beside him. "Benny, Benny!" She held his hand tightly inside hers and kissed his fingertips gratefully. His hand was so cold it made her shiver.

Bronek just barely smiled, and then Anna saw. His eyes were blank; his face was nearing peace. "Anna. . . ." he whispered, his lips not moving.

"Darling!" She tucked the blanket up under his chin. "You're so cold. You need to stay warm, so you'll get better!"

"Anna, Anna . . . Dove. . . ." He stared up for several seconds. "We did . . . good. It was. . . ."

"Yes, yes. It was. Save your strength. You'll need to be strong when we – make our escape."

Bronek forced enough energy to make one more utterance. His lips trembled. "I – promised – I would never leave you."

Anna stroked his cheek soothingly. "And you never will." She choked back her tears, trying to stay calm before him. She raised her left hand, and showed him her wedding ring. "You never will."

"I take – a part of you – with –" For several seconds Bronek relaxed. His eyes opened, but he stared beyond her, at the blackness above her head.

"Benny, darling. Stay calm." She gently pressed her hand against his forehead. Desperately she hummed one of his favorite songs, "Ave Maria."

Bronek's eyes were pleading for relief. "It – hurts," he whispered. "It hurts."

His pain tore into her heart, and she ached to hold him, to take his pain away. "Darling, there's a farm house . . . in the forest. We will – be free there. We will be surrounded by trees, and everything will be green and beautiful. We will dance together, and you can sing me songs. Every night I will lie in your arms, and we will be safe – to love each other."

Bronek managed to feebly speak. "When you – when you go. You feel it. Feel it leaving. It leaves. . . . Calm."

"Benny! Please, stay!" She fell onto him, and hugged him passionately.

His body stiffened. He looked up at something. "Lights! Lights!" Then Bronek's body relaxed. His head slipped back on the blanket.

Anna looked lovingly at the face of her husband. A tear fell from her cheek, onto his forehead. Delicately she touched his eyelids, and slid them closed. "You never will," she whispered into his ear. And she kissed his cheek.

ANNOUNCEMENT

In spite of repeated public appeals, on February 1, 1944, criminal elements from the secret organization P.Z.P., which is in the pay of England, again committed a treacherous, under-handed attempt in which two Germans have lost their lives. Therefore, 100 members of the P.Z.P., who were condemned to death for political offenses by the Security Police and SD Summary Court but were eligible for clemency, were publicly executed in Warsaw on February 2, 1944.

Warsaw, February 2, 1944.

**SECURITY POLICE AND SD COMMANDER
FOR WARSAW DISTRICT**

XXVII

The funeral procession was huge. Numerous SS dignitaries, including Heinrich Himmler himself, attended the funeral beneath a cold blue sky. The coffin of SS *Brigadeführer* Franz Kutschera lay on a high wagon, surrounded by flowers and draped by a red swastika flag. A team of show horses pulled the wagon through Warsaw, the city Kutschera had tried to make safe. SS soldiers marched in slow goose-step alongside. The Germans turned thousands of Poles from their homes along the procession route.

On the morning of February 2, Ujazdowskie Avenue was cleared, and one hundred prisoners were taken out of Pawiak prison in nine large trucks. They were civilians, not guilty of any crimes at all. They were killed at 21 Ujazdowskie Avenue – the spot where Kutschera had been slain. Announcements were read every half hour over the loudspeakers. Never was there any official mention of the assassination of Franz Kutschera.

Kutschera's body was taken by train to Berlin. A rumor went through the city: Himmler's sister was so grief-stricken, she "married" Kutschera's corpse in a gruesome ceremony.

* * *

On February 9, the week after the attack, Adam Przezdziecki walked tentatively among the black market vendors at Hale Mirowski. He watched, detached, as people whispered and traded, bought and sold, for food and for soap. It was a cold day, and Adam kept his hands in his coat pockets. His steps were cautious. He felt a heavy exhaustion, as if he had just run a great distance.

Ahead of him, a woman stood on the sidewalk shouting, "Barley! Barley for sale!" She was not holding anything; the barley must have been in bags beneath her billowing skirt.

Adam stopped. "You're selling barley?"

"Good barley grain! No sawdust. All grain, ready to use!"

"You don't fear the police?"

The woman shrugged. "I have to eat. Perhaps they should fear us, eh?"

Adam smiled. "Yes. Perhaps they should." He walked on. Seeing the people all around enlivened him. They did not know the whole truth, but they all knew what had happened. They carried their heads up, and spoke with life in their voices. They had agreed to bear the price.

Confident that he was not followed, Adam went into the burned-out hotel on the south side of Leszno Street. He still would not go to any room that Lot knew of. He entered the janitor's closet; mops and steel buckets still cluttered the corners. Now that he had a moment, his concerns returned to his wife, Zofia. The last news he had heard was distressing. Things were very bad at Ravensbrück. Dozens of women had died over the winter, of pneumonia. His informant could not confirm that Zofia was among them. He had to learn more, Adam decided. He would approach a civil servant, and attempt to bribe him. No, better yet, he would risk traveling to Danzig, and crossing the border into Germany.

At precisely 2:10, there were three knocks on the door. After exchanging the codes, Wiktor entered. We was wearing his usual white shirt, blue trousers and vest, and cap.

"Don't need a coat, Granit?"

Wiktor shook his head silently.

"I wish we could sit down somewhere, but the cafes are closed. I don't even have any *bimber* to offer you." He waited for Wiktor to light one of his customary cigarettes, but his comrade merely folded his arms, so Adam continued. "Did you hear of the penalties?" Adam commented ruefully. "All Polish restaurants are closed until further notice. The curfew was extended. And the General Government placed a fine on the city."

Wiktor nodded. "I heard."

"One hundred million zlotys. I would like to know how they expect that to be paid. But, I suppose that is not the point."

Wiktor did not answer. His sour expression did not change.

"Granit, it was a great day. It wasn't just Kutschera. On the same day, Willi Lubert was killed – one of the men who organized the street roundups. And Albrecht Eitner – a trustee of stolen Jewish property. It was the Underground's greatest day."

"I know," Wiktor admitted.

"Yes, we lost four fine soldiers. And one of them was Lot. I had such – hopes for him."

"He did his job," Wiktor concluded with his usual finality.

"Granit, you don't appreciate. . . ." Adam stopped, and watched his old comrade. "Granit, look at the people. Look at everyone out there. They are different. They're proud today."

The stern man did not respond.

"Granit, I know what happened on February second. I know about the 100 people killed at Ujazdowskie Avenue. I know 300 more were killed at Pawiak, may God have mercy."

"I think that will not be the end," Wiktor commented, dryly. "Why?"

"I have a feeling. A bad feeling. The police, they have more in mind. I heard that they raided Wola, and Zoliborz. Hundreds of homes. These new arrests – I just have a feeling."

"Yes, yes, that was what we feared. It is not over."

"No. It is not over, Nowak. That is why I called you to meet me."

"Why? What's the matter, Granit?"

Wiktor paused, and Adam knew it was a serious matter. "It's Akrobat."

Adam stopped. "What about him?"

"He's missing. He's been gone for two days."

"What do you know?" Adam asked quietly.

"Nothing. He's just . . . missing."

"I'll send a messenger girl out. We'll check our informers at Pawiak. We'll try to find where he is. If he is missing, we must change our meetings –"

"– Please do that," Wiktor said. "Good-bye, Nowak." Wiktor walked out of the room, leaving Adam alone.

* * *

The two sisters walked hurriedly north from their home. "Anna, hurry!"

"Krystyna, please slow down. I'm not as big as you."

Anna's trenchcoat was unbuttoned, and Krystyna was wearing an old shawl. Anna had been lying on the sofa, nursing a stomach cramp when her sister had rushed into the parlor.

"I heard something horrible is happening," Krystyna informed her. "We have to hurry." She did not slow her pace.

To keep up, Anna ran several steps, then walked, and then ran a few more steps. "Krystyna, please!" Her toes were pushing into the ends of her wooden shoes, and rubbing against her loose socks. She could already feel blisters forming. "Where are we going?"

"To Leszno Street." It was the afternoon of February 11.

Anna groaned and did her best to keep up. People were hurrying home from their jobs, and Anna kept being bumped.

At last the two sisters turned the corner onto Leszno Street. Abruptly, they stopped. Beneath a dismal gray sky, the sight opened before them.

"Oh, Dear God –" Krystyna gasped.

A feeling of disbelief, that this could not be happening,

swept over Anna. Her eyes surely must be deceiving her. She waited, just to see if the scene would disappear and reality would return. She blinked her eyes; but the scene would not go away.

Leszno Street was covered in a layer of slushy snow that showed every footprint. On the south side of the street, a long line of people, dozens of people, shuffled past. They looked up across the street, and whispered oaths, and crossed themselves. SS soldiers and policemen were nudging people along their cordon. To them they were as guards at a museum, guiding visitors past the most popular painting. They seemed to be proud of the large turnout.

Along the north side of the Leszno Street was the three-meter wall of red brick that still looped around northwest Warsaw. Behind that wall had been the Jewish Ghetto. The buildings were still burned out and abandoned from the Ghetto Uprising the year before.

Krystyna looked up over the wall and pointed. "How?" she asked aloud. "How could they?"

There was an eerie quiet; Anna heard the shuffling of feet but no voices. "Is it real? Is it true?" she asked weakly.

The people looked up beyond the Ghetto wall. There, along the wall, was a charred apartment building. All its windows were gone, and burn marks blackened the stone facade. A ragged curtain blew through an open window. But the building still had its wide balconies with fancy iron railings. And from the wrought iron spindles of the balcony 27 ropes were tied, in a precise, even row. At the end of every rope, a body hung in the frigid February air.

Krystyna covered her mouth with her hand. "Oh, Dear Mary, why?" A tear trickled down her red cheek. "Why?" Krystyna and Anna held on to each other for support.

Just then an SS soldier shouted at them. "No stopping!" He grabbed Krystyna's arm and shoved her forward. "Keep moving! Keep moving!"

The two sisters joined the line of viewers. They walked

slowly. The SS and police paced in front of them, between the civilians and the wall.

Tears rolled down Krystyna's cheeks. "I can't. I can't –"

Anna held her sister's shaking hand. She worked up enough courage to view the sight. The victims hovered in the air, just beneath the balcony. They were blindfolded, but their heads were not covered; their hands were tied in front of them. They were motionless. It remained a surreal sight, something across the wall. "Is it real?" Anna whispered.

"Anna –" Krystyna suddenly panicked, her arms trembling. "I can't look any more – I can't!" She glanced frantically at the SS soldiers, at all the shocked pedestrians beside her – anywhere to avoid looking up.

Anna turned away. In her mind she understood, but she did not accept. She remained a person surrounded by her own thoughts and feelings. She rejected this vision they presented to her. She had her personal victory, her liberation. And she was going to cherish her own victory forever.

Pedestrians continued filing past, glancing, whispering, praying, moving on. Thousands had come to Leszno Street because they had heard the rumors; now they were being pushed along so that they all could be horrified. They were meant to be humiliated, and they were humiliated. To them it was like an attendance line at a wake. And in their acknowledgment, a resolution formed. They resolved a purpose, a collective memory that the Nazis could not repress. That February afternoon, something hardened in their collective heart. The Russians were getting closer. Liberation was approaching, and the Poles would have their chance to repay. And they would remember.

The wake line moved forward, and Anna and Krystyna reached the end. "Just go now," Anna said. She helped her sister around the corner. Krystyna leaned against the old Law Court building, and wiped her eyes. Still sniffling, she reached into her coat pocket and pulled out the rag that served as her handkerchief. "I just – can't believe it," she said between sniffles.

"I know, Krystyna."

Her sister took several deep breaths. "Damn them," she whispered. She wiped her eyes again; Anna saw that they were red and sore. For a long time Krystyna gazed at the sky. "I will always remember – what I saw."

Anna grabbed her sister's arms. "Krystyna, don't. Don't feel what they want you to feel. Remember where your victory is." Anna held her older sister as she cried quietly. At long last, they departed from Leszno Street, and Anna helped her south toward their home.

They did not notice their friend, just a couple meters away in the throng. Misia Myzwinska faced Leszno Street, alone. She stared at the SS men in their gray helmets and black boots. The number filled her mind, blocking out all else. Twenty-seven. Twenty-seven. Twenty-seven. "They did this," she said aloud, her words barely escaping past her tight, curled lips. She felt the rage like an acid, poisoning her heart.

A *Wehrmacht* soldier, a mere teen-ager, noticed her. "Move, move, girl," he told her resignedly.

Misia suddenly glared at the young German. "You!" she sneered, so savagely that the soldier recoiled in surprise, "You – will never leave Warsaw alive."

They also did not notice the burly man beside them. At the corner, Wiktor Kruczyk stood, just away from the crowds, far enough away that the police ignored him. He stood motionless, stern, as people walked by him, swearing oaths and leaning on each other for support.

Wiktor did not acknowledge the other people. He stood like a stone statue, unblinking, unable to move. He stared, trans-fixed, at the boy hanging below the balcony. And he knew that the boy was familiar to him. Wiktor had played soccer with him, and listened to his youthful dreams, and fed him when he was hungry. Wiktor stared at his brother, Jerzy Kruczyk, and suddenly he did not know what to do.

* * *

Komorowski's estimate of 200 deaths as revenge for killing Kutschera proved sadly optimistic. On the morning of February 15, 190 men and 18 women were killed at Pawiak prison, and 40 more men were shot on Senatorska Street. On this day alone, nearly 250 Poles were killed. This final action marked an ending. Although secret executions were still carried out at Pawiak prison, the era of street executions was over.

* * *

In a little chapel at the Powazki Cemetery, a funeral was being held. The plain box coffin sat at the back of the chapel; a few simple flower arrangements lay around it. A handful of people huddled in the cold and listened to the priest. Occasionally they sniffled and wiped their noses with rags.

Without warning, the chapel door suddenly swung open. The funeral stopped; the priest stood still. A soul-chilling wind blew through the chapel.

Black leather boots scraped against the stone floor; the sounds echoed off the walls. The Gestapo officer glanced at the mourners, to assure they did not look at him. He wore a black leather overcoat, and a round cap cocked arrogantly on his head. Black gloves hid his hands. Behind him marched two SS soldiers, their rifles slung over their gray overcoats.

The Gestapo officer strode down to the coffin. The priest stepped back, and he stammered, "Why are you –?"

The officer raised a black glove at the priest. "Here was an agent of your Underground," the officer stated definitively, "He was a criminal, employed by London. His body belongs to the General Government."

He walked in front of the priest, and stood over the coffin. The SS soldiers stood facing the mourners. For a moment the officer touched the plain wooden lid proudly. *"Hier ist er. Hier ist der Mörder von General Kutschera."* (Here he is. Here is the murderer of General Kutschera.) Then, with a dramatic flourish, he flung aside the coffin lid. It clattered to the stone floor, raising a cloud of dust. The mourners gasped and held hands.

The Gestapo officer looked down. Slowly, his face relaxed. Then it frowned. There in the coffin lay an old woman, deep wrinkles covering her face and neck.

The SS soldiers glanced over their shoulders to see the murderer's face. Then they looked up the Gestapo officer, confused.

The officer jumped toward the priest furiously. "Where is the murderer!" he shouted. "Where is he!" Suddenly he was possessed of a black rage. He reached inside his coat, yanked out his service pistol, and pointed it directly at the priest's nose. "Polish swine! Tell me! Tell me now! Where is the Underground assassin!"

The priest cowered inside his vestments. His fingers trembled with fear. "I – I don't know. This is Waleria Lysakowska. She is – all there is."

The Gestapo officer stared down at the wrinkled old woman. He bit his lip angrily. His empty hand formed into a fist. Vainly, he slammed his fist against the side of the coffin.

The commotion frightened a white dove in the rafters above. His wings fluttering, the dove flew through the open chapel door, away into the bright Warsaw sky.

ANNOUNCEMENT

Twenty-seven Polish murderers, who belonged to the organizations P.Z.P. and P.P.R., have been sentenced to death by the Security Police Summary Court. These criminals were guilty of treacherous and under-handed attacks on Germans or persons in the German service, or were found in possession of guns and other murderous tools. Because of their treacherous and despicable behavior, these criminals were today publicly executed by hanging.

Warsaw, February 11, 1944

**SECURITY POLICE AND SD COMMANDER
FOR WARSAW DISTRICT**

Epilogue

"Mama, wait!" the boy pleaded. "I can't keep up."

Anna reached out to him. "Bronek, don't get separated from me. Take my hand."

"No! I can walk on my own. I'll be eleven years old in two months." Refusing his mother's hand, he walked as fast as his legs could take him.

Bronek and Anna Pietraszewicz walked north along Marszalkowska Street. She wore a pink cotton dress and a white hat pinned to her pale hair; he wore a plaid shirt and brown corduroy shorts with suspenders. As they walked, young Bronek watched his mother's feet. Her shoes today were pink. She probably had a hundred different shoes: red, and pink, and blue, and white shoes. She never wore plain brown ones. She had tried to buy him blue shoes once, but Bronek didn't want fancy shoes. He wanted hiking boots. Hiking boots were big, and made him taller.

Soon young Bronek looked up. He was surrounded by a crowd. All he could see were tall people. It was July, and they smelled funny, like the men on his block who smoked cigars and never showered. Now he squeezed his mother's hand, and he did not let go. *Everyone in Warsaw must be standing here,* he thought. "Mama, I can't see the building. I can't see!"

"All right, all right." She picked him up, and held him in her slender arms. "There's the building."

Bronek clutched her pink summer dress, and he craned his neck. "It's huge!" It was the biggest building he had ever seen. He counted the floors: one, two, three, four, five, six, seven, eight. "How tall is it, Mama? Is it twenty-eight floors?"

"It's thirty floors, Bronek."

"Oh. I counted twenty-eight."

"That's close."

"What is it for?"

"It's called the Palace of Culture and Science."

Bronek stared at the amazing building. It had lots of fancy trim around the edges. It looked like a huge square wedding cake. It zoomed up to a big point at the top. Bronek wanted to climb to the very top, and stand on the antenna. Up there he could stand on one toe, and see all of Poland. "I bet it's the biggest building in Poland."

"Yes, Bronek. It is." Anna's voice was not happy again.

Bronek did not see why the building made his mother unhappy. It must have something bad hidden inside.

Way far away, on a big platform, were several men in gray suits and gray hats. One man stood at a microphone. "Today," he said, "We dedicate this Palace of Culture and Science, this gift from the Soviet people, our Slavic brothers in the struggle to free the world."

"He echoes, Mama," Bronek said.

"That's the microphone, Bronek."

"Oh."

The gray man kept on talking. "Warsaw is our bulwark against Western imperialism. This building is a monument to our common pledge to create the communist workers' paradise. Not just for the Polish worker, but for all workers around the world."

"Come on," Anna said, all of a sudden. "Let's go." She lowered him back to the street.

"Where to?"

"To Powazki."

"But that's too far," Bronek said grumpily.

"We can't listen to any more of this." She forcefully took his hand and pulled him out of the crowd. They walked north from the wedding cake building.

They turned west on Leszno Street. Bronek hurried to keep up. In her pink shoes, his mother was a fast walker. If Bronek had his hiking boots, then he could walk fast, too. But in his plain leather shoes he had to practically run.

On one street corner Anna saw another woman and stopped. She paid her some zlotys and took some flowers with her.

After what seemed like forever, they finally reached Powazki Cemetery. It was a quiet place, with lots of trees. "We're almost there now, Bronek."

They walked back to the military section. Everywhere were rows and rows of white crosses, made from logs with white bark. "That's called birch," Bronek said.

"That's right, Bronek."

The crosses were almost as tall as he was. There must have been over a million crosses there. They were for people who had fought the Nazis. A few other people were walking between the crosses. People stopped at a cross, pointed, said a prayer, and then walked to another one.

But his mother always went to one cross. She pulled his hand. Then she stopped. "Here he is."

Bronek looked down. There, on the plain birch cross, was a little round sign like a badge. There was the name: "Bronislaw Pietraszewicz." Below that was the other name, "Lot." At the bottom the sign read, "Commanded action against Kutschera, 2/1/1944. Parasol Battalion."

Bronek did not say anything. He stared and stared at the sign. He knew it was his father's grave. But it was also his name on the sign.

"Look at these weeds. They must take better care of this place."

Bronek stared at the white wooden cross. He was not sure

how he should feel.

"Do you see the date? That was when your father left us. Before you were even born. You came during the Uprising. I was hiding in a basement, and there was a battle there, and you were born all of a sudden. On September 27, 1944."

Uprising, Uprising, Uprising. He knew about the Uprising. It sounded scary.

Anna knelt down on her knees. Her skirt hem rubbed the grass. "Bronek, don't pay attention to that – hideous thing downtown. And don't listen to the communist theory in your school. Just ignore all that."

"I know, Mama, you tell me all the time."

"They teach that to my third-graders. It's horrible. I want to jump at that man who lectures my children, and make him stop."

"You don't teach communism. That other man does."

"It's still wrong, what they do. This city is yours. Do you see?" His mother scooped a handful of dirt in her white hands. She poured the dirt over his hands, and it slid back onto the ground. "You can touch it. Your father made it so."

Bronek looked at her hands. They were pale and fragile, like they belonged to an older woman. On one finger she wore an old silver ring, with a swirl of small diamonds. It never left her, even when she got it dirty.

"We made so many plans, your father and I. He would teach you how to play the piano. He knew all kinds of music. . . ." She started to hum a song again. She had a soft voice. "That's Chopin. He loved Chopin, and 'Ave Maria,' and jazz music...." She smiled. "Sing along with me. It's called 'Moonlight Serenade.'" She hummed a few notes: "Dee, la, la, la."

Bronek liked it when she sang. She was happier when she had a song. He watched her mouth, and he tried to mimic her.

She laughed warmly. "That's very good. Perhaps you'll be a musician someday." She waited a minute, saying nothing. She closed her eyes, and swayed back and forth, and hummed songs for herself.

Bronek knew that she was back there, back where she was happiest. She was a million kilometers away. He wanted to make her that happy, too.

After a long time, she blinked her blue eyes, and she looked at him – for real. "Let's plant our flowers."

Bronek dutifully dug a little hole with his fingers.

"You got your hands all dirty, Bronek."

"Oh."

Anna placed the flowers into the hole, and pushed back the dirt. Now red flowers stood before the white cross. "There! Doesn't that look nice?"

"I guess so."

"Look, my hands got dirty, too." Anna looked up at the sky. "My, it's getting late. Let's go home now. I'll teach you a song on the way." She took his hand, and they walked toward the trees, with the earth of Warsaw still soiling their hands.

Appendix

The following table lists the street executions and Ghetto executions in Warsaw during Kutschera's campaign of terror. More victims were killed in undocumented executions. Many victims were never listed on posters.

Date	Place	Number Killed
October 16, 1943	141 Niepodleglosci Ave. at corner of Madalinski Street	20
October 16, 1943	Ghetto	14
October 17, 1943	17 Pius St.	20
October 17, 1943	Ghetto	22
October 19, 1943	Ghetto	20
October 20, 1943	Near Gdansk Station	20
October 22, 1943	2 Mlynarska St.	10
October 23, 1943	Ghetto (?)	300 (approx.)
October 23, 1943	Miedzeszyn Embankment	20
October 25, 1943	Ghetto	20
October 26, 1943	Leszno St.	30(approx.)
October 30, 1943	Towarowa St.	10
October 30, 1943	Ghetto	2
November 9, 1943	Grojecka Street at Wawelska Street and 2 Plocka Street	40(approx.)
November 12, 1943	49 Nowy Swiat and Kepna Street at corner of Jagiellonska Street	60
November 12, 1943	Ghetto	240(approx.)
November 13, 1943	Ghetto	120(approx.)
November 17, 1943	Western Station and Bialolecka Street	43
November 17, 1943	Ghetto	40(approx.)
November 18, 1943	Grodzisk	20
November 18, 1943	Zyrardow	20
November 20, 1943	Otwock-Lugi	20
November 24, 1943	18 Nabielak Street and Radzyminska Street	over 27

Date	Place	Number Killed
November 30, 1943	63 Solec Street	34
November 30, 1943	Ghetto	25(approx.)
December 1, 1943	Ghetto (?)	30(approx.)
December 2, 1943	64 Nowy Swiat	34
December 2, 1943	Ghetto	10-20
December 3, 1943	13 and 21/23 Pulawska St.	100
December 3, 1943	Ghetto	12
December 7, 1943	Ghetto	50(approx.)
December 9, 1943	Ghetto	146
December 10, 1943	Ghetto	47
December 11, 1943	Ghetto	50(approx.)
December 11, 1943	5 Leszno Street	30(approx.)
December 14, 1943	9/11 Wierzbowa Street and Ghetto	over 300
December 16, 1943	Ghetto	100(approx.)
December 17, 1943	Ghetto	39
December 18, 1943	77 Wolska Street and Ghetto	57
December 19, 1943	Ghetto	64
December 20, 1943	Skierniewice, 1 Rawska Street	40
December 20, 1943	Ghetto	50(approx.)
December 21, 1943	Details unknown	
December 23, 1943	14 Gorczewska Street	43
December 23, 1943	Ghetto	10-20
December 27, 1943	Ghetto	42
December 30, 1943	Ghetto	45
December 31, 1943	4 Towarowa Street	43
December 31, 1943	172 Krakowska Avenue	10
January 6, 1944	Ghetto	24
January 7, 1944	Ghetto	22
January 13, 1944	14 Gorczewska Street	40(approx.)
January 13, 1944	Ghetto	260(approx.)
January 14, 1944	Ghetto	over 60
January 15, 1944	Ghetto	20
January 17, 1944	Ghetto	10-20 (?)
January 19, 1944	Ghetto	33
January 21, 1944	Ghetto	40(approx.)
January 24, 1944	2 Kilinski Street and Ghetto	77
January 25, 1944	Ghetto	38
January 26, 1944	Ghetto	several

Date	Place	Number Killed
January 27, 1944	Ghetto	32
January 28, 1944	31 Jerozolimskie Avenue and Ghetto	200(approx.)
January 31, 1944	Ghetto	47
February 1, 1944	Ghetto	57
February 2, 1944	21 Ujazdowskie Avenue	100
February 2, 1944	Ghetto	200(approx.)
February 3, 1944	Ghetto	160
February 4, 1944	Ghetto	3
February 5, 1944	Ghetto	16
February 10, 1944	4 Barska Street and 79/81 Wolska Street	140
February 10-11, 1944	Ghetto	330
February 11, 1944	Leszno Street	27
February 12, 1944	Ghetto	4
February 15, 1944	6 Senatorska Street	40(approx.)
February 15, 1944	Ghetto	210(approx.)